MW01173606

Finding 50

The Saga

Finding 50

The Saga

by MiMi Foxx

Copyright © 2022 MiMi Foxx
All rights reserved.
ISBN: 9798833722572

For those who are still in search of society's illusive idea of happiness and personal fulfillment; those living their lives according to the expectations of others. It's never too late to be true to oneself and take steps necessary to make yourself happy and *Find your own 50.*

TABLE OF CONTENTS

PROLOGUE

She could see the wheels in their heads turning and knew more questions were coming. Questions that she didn't want to answer. Realizing she hadn't thought this through, she had to make her escape asap. Any minute now she could potentially be past the point of no return.

"I can see the looks on all of your faces and yes, it's a bit much even for you bitches. All I can suggest is that you look at it as a celebration, marking the end of our intimate relationship and the start of something more. But we'll have to discuss it later, right now I gotta go. Again, I'm sorry I forgot about meeting up and everything, but I know y'all asses will get over it...at some point, anyway."

"Uhm, the life and times of Zsasha Stewart. Ain't nothing like it!" Vonne chimed in.

"Well from where I sit, you all seem to have it going on just as good as I do." Zsasha remarked.

"Are you kidding me?" J'Nae piped in. "Girlfriend, I envy you, you and Simon. You two actually found a way to make that insane lifestyle work!"

"Don't envy me, J'Nae. Join me, or us, not literally but hell, aren't you ready to stir things up a bit?" Zsasha spoke firmly, trying to get the focus off herself. The look on J'Nae's face was priceless.

"Ah, not really." J'Nae confirmed.

Truth be told, J'Nae did join Zsasha for a one on one, girl on girl event several years back.... for a second time, not long after

A

Julian passed. Heartfelt emotions about her husband's passing, a half-gallon of Gin.... throw in a half ounce of weed and some blow.... made for a night of girl-on-girl sex that was so mind blowing J'Nae has refused to talk about it ever since, even with Zsasha. Hell, she still won't admit to or discuss the first time they hooked up back in college during their freshman year living as roommates. Yep, it was the best kept secret within the bunch. At least that's what J'Nae believed.

"Girl, you've been sitting on that shit of yours so long there's probably a mold of your pussy embedded in your couch cushion!" Zsasha added.

"Not probably", laughs Rona. "It is, it really is...Hell, I've seen it! You know how leather looks when it's old and dry...got cracks in it and shit."

"Y'all need to quit." Vonne joins in. "Some people can only handle one real love in their lifetime and when it's gone, it's gone."

"Now who exactly are you talking about, Vonne?" Zsasha asked. "Your situation or hers? Because ain't nobody trying to talk about love. This heffa needs to fuck. She needs to get laid out, all the way out, from top to bottom, front to back and inside and out. Laid the fuck out like nobody's business!"

"You might as well hang it up, Zsasha. She ain't doing nothing with that. Maybe she's saving it for the wax museum or something...have it preserved and mounted on a plaque." Rona said. "That's about all she's doing with that shit."

"Y'all know what, y'all can all kiss my booty butt!" J'Nae shouted. "Y'all know I ain't with all that. I don't just give it away for the asking!"

B

"Why is that?" Zsasha asked. "So nothing will ever enter your coochie corral again? Please girl, you're supposed to share your gifts every now and then, not let it dry up and grow cobwebs."

"Yes, I suppose so." J'Nae fired back. "But not with just anybody......not with someone you just met and don't really know. It needs to be special and have real meaning behind it, something other than lust."

J'Nae did not intend to throw shade on Zsasha's swinger lifestyle with her comments. She'd made peace with that long ago and had always been supportive of any related issues Zsasha may have shared. A moment late, Rona took this opportunity to share something she'd been wanting to say for some time.

"Well, J'Nae, there's something to be said about anonymity in all its forms. Sometimes you fuck just because you want to fuck, right then and right at that moment.... with that mother fucker that just caught your eye, no strings, complications, or pretenses. You know men and women initially put on a facade when they first start dating. You only see what they want you to see at first. It takes time for some people to reveal their true self. When you do it anonymously you do it without the drama of who's who and who wants what, when, where, and how and without expectations, plus not knowing is part of the illusion of seduction. The forbidden fruit that we're all taught is poison can be passionate and pleasurable and extremely erotic. You see, the problem with traditional dating is that there is always an expectation of something meaningful and long lasting down the line. At least from a woman's perspective because that's what we were taught.

Traditional and monogamous dating is where we're supposed to start in order to end up where we're taught, we're supposed

C

to be. For me, that's some bullshit. Nobody fucking knows what it is they really want until they come face to face with it and are willing to do uncomfortable things to keep it. In search of this or that, to me, is a colossal waste of time. People get so caught up in the so-called destination that they miss the journey......its unforeseen twists and turns, happy accidents, and the bumps and bruises along the way. It's what makes the final destination special and meaningful when in fact you reach it."

"Yeah, but what about finding your soul mate, your mister right?" J'Nae spoke softly.

"Mr. Right? That perfect guy women relentlessly search for? Who in the hell can live up to that expectation? Maybe for a moment but long term, come on, Just keep it simple. Remove the expectations society dictates one should have as the norm or how things should be and automatically the pressure is gone. Without it, oftentimes, people tend to be more open and freer with one another, embracing the natural spontaneity of their acquaintance, and who knows, it just might lead to an unencumbered and satisfying intimate entanglement or even a fulfilling relationship. Sometimes a person may say they're not looking for a mate and then unexpectedly the right person comes along under the right set of circumstances and before you know it, they're all in. You've found everything you didn't know you wanted. But when your destination is predetermined, orchestrated by societal norms and old school views of what happiness is supposed to look like, then so is your path. And when your path is predetermined your mind and your heart aren't receptive to the unambiguous nature of self-discovery on your journey of love. And when that happens, you've likely missed out

D

on the best parts simply because you're preoccupied with making sure all the boxes are checked. Don't live for society, or what society says you want, live for self. **Find your own unique happiness!"**

Chapter 1

The smell of freshly brewed coffee filled the house as J'Nae lay in bed. It was Crescendo, her favorite blend of Segafredo's Italian coffee. What for breakfast, she thought? I think I will make some of my famous fried potatoes with onions and peppers, some scrambled eggs, honey butter biscuits…. but for who? Who am I cooking for? It's just me. In that moment, she was filled with sadness thinking of her family and the noise that once filled her home. She knew she should feel a bit more excited with the realization of her new solo status, but she did not. Again, a wave of sadness came over her as the reality hit home. There wasn't anyone in the house to care for or clean up after. It was just her.

Four or five years ago, her son Aiden made his first attempt to leave the nest and branch out on his own. After an unfortunate event made it necessary for him to return, J'Nae was more than happy to welcome him and his young family back into the nest.

Several months later, his sister Taizja encountered a similar struggle. Husband Dante lost his job while she was seven months pregnant. Their first child was born two months later, and things hadn't really improved for the young couple. Being a caring mother, J'Nae insisted they all move in with her until they could get on their feet. This resulted in a full nest with both of her adult children at home with their new and growing families.

At first the house was full of love, happiness, laughter, and joy. What followed behind was chaos, clutter, sticky walls, and dirty dishes and never enough of anything in the house. But she loved it. J'Nae loved having her family around her.

A year or so later, Dante secured an excellent job with a great salary which took him, Taizja and baby Arianna to Atlanta Georgia, where they purchased their first home. Aiden remained at home a while longer before he decided to join the armed forces and left for basic training soon after. His growing family joined him immediately following basic training. #proudmama! That was three months ago, not long before J'Nae's forty-eighth birthday.

The recent change in her living situation should have opened a new and exciting chapter in her life, well deserved and long overdue. She should be ecstatic. No toys to trip over, no sink full of unwashed dishes and no youngsters running around breaking crystal and value what nots. All that is officially over. And even better yet, there is food in the fridge. Real food, not fast food stored in a heap of containers. Real food. The kind that takes longer than 10 minutes to prepare. And no empty pizza boxes in the oven or on next to the trash waiting to be taken out. The house is finally hers and hers alone. It should be time to break into her happy dance, but she just wasn't motivated to do it. She needed help. She needed music to stimulate her mind, body and soul and thought Pharrell could do it. Come on Pharrell, let's get happy.

J'Nae grabs her remote control and plays Pharrell's Happy. She gets up and begins to undress, while singing and dancing her way to the shower. As the water ran over her face, the music seemed to echo louder in her ears and her shoulders moved with every beat. She exhaled a sigh of relief feeling exuberated and free. Tell me Lord, is it going to be like this from now on…. please!

The shower ended and so did the song. Along with it went the feelings and motivation that temporarily ignited her soul. Everything she felt before came rushing back. She settled back in bed to find disturbing news on TV. Another attack involving gunfire, this time in California. 9 people killed and 13 injured at the hands of 2 assailants. When is this madness going to end, she thought to herself?

One of the downsides of living in bed watching endless television and news reports all day and night is that you hear practically all the negative news going on all over the world. This latest report was one of the worst ones yet and only served to reinforce her mood. She began clicking through the channels in search of something entertaining when there was a knock on the

2

front door. Looking out her front facing bedroom window she could see L.B. her friendly neighborhood landscaper at the front door. After grabbing a robe, J'Nae made her way downstairs and opened the door.

"Good morning Ms. J'Nae. How are you doing today?"

"I'm fine, L.B. How are you?"

"Doing well, doing quite well today. Just wanted to do some work on your shrubs today. Had a few minutes before I needed to be on the other side of town, so I wanted to run over and finish up what I started the other day. A real man never leaves a job undone! Oh, and I picked you up a cup of coffee….it was on my way."

"Thank you, L.B." J'Nae said. "That was awfully sweet of you."

L.B. nodded with a big grin. The whole time J'Nae could hardly keep a straight face. It was on my way, he said. Huh! From where? You live across the street and a few doors down. So, what did you do, go out the backdoor of your house, cut across the neighbor's yard, walk 3 blocks to the left, turn on Grassland Road and waited on the main strip for the #6 bus to pick you up and take you to the local convenience store? Right, she said to herself.

It was so obvious he was into her. He'd been flirting with her for a few years now but J'Nae always kept it neighborly and professional. No matter how many long passionate looks he gave her. She ignored every advance he ever made. But he never gave up. Not in all the years he'd been living in the neighborhood.

"Do you think you'll be done today, or will you have to come back another time to finish up?" She asked.

"Oh, I'm sure I'll be finished early this afternoon, then I'll be back on my regular schedule."

"Okay, great. Well, have a good rest of the day, L.B."

"You too, Ms. J'Nae. Great seeing you this morning."

J'Nae smiled and nodded. As he turned and walked away, she noticed he kept looking back at her as she stood in the doorway. L.B. was a genuinely nice man. Attractive, polite, and made a decent living. Can't imagine why no one has gotten his attention all this time. Oh well.

On her way back upstairs, J'Nae stopped at her desk to open her laptop. Sipping on what was now luke-warm coffee, she looked through her calendar to view her upcoming items for the week. There really wasn't much there of any real interest or importance to her, so she pushed those items into the upcoming weeks. The only thing of real interest was a job she had interviewed for three weeks prior but hadn't heard anything since. It was a position as a Software Developer with a well-known reputable company. She knew she was perfect for the position but being out of the workforce for so long may pose an issue, making it harder for her to rejoin the working class.

Luckily, Julian had been a financial genius and provided exceptionally well for his family. Being able to be at home for the kids when they returned home from school allowed her to be more hands on as a single parent. His investments and financial planning afforded her the opportunity to focus on completing her educational goals, once the kids had graduated and entered adulthood. Even if they all ended up under her roof for an extended period, money was something she never had to worry about again.

To J'Nae, Julian was so much more than a financial wiz at wealth management, he was her life partner and best friend and after all these years, she still missed him so. From the moment they met in college, they both knew they were meant to be. But those feelings were not shared by either his parents or hers.

At that time, obedience was crucial and taking a defiant stand against your parents was practically unheard of in the environment and or social circles they were accustomed to. But they were committed. They did everything they could to hide their love from their respective families, even going as far as branding themselves with matching wrist tattoos depicting a double strand multi-linked bracelet with tiny hearts connecting each link to the next. Each link was intended to represent the obstacles they would have to overcome in order to take the next step in embracing their love. The focal point of the bracelet being

4

two larger hearts, one from each direction, linked together representing their unbreakable and timeless connection and their love saga coming to fruition. He was and would always be the love of her life.

That love, his love for his family stretched beyond words igniting the foresight to plan for their futures. It enabled J'Nae and their children the opportunity to live their best lives, years after his passing. And while working part-time she was not only actively involved in her kids' lives; she was able to keep her software skills somewhat up to date by periodically taking classes in her field. In spite of her efforts, the growth in the IT field including new technologies, factoring in her incomplete college degree became an issue. That too was short lived. Once her kids moved back home, she let go of the part time work and focused on her unfulfilled educational goals. She not only completed her bachelor's degree in computer science, but she also completed a top-notch software development bootcamp that thrust her to the top of the list of those with the most desirable skills, making everyone in her life extremely proud.

Dropping out of college in her senior year to get married was not something she'd planned to do. Her parents weren't happy with her decision, but soon after Julian and J'Nae's first child was born, it seemed like it was no longer an issue for them. Taizja was a beautiful and healthy baby girl and their second child, Aiden, came two years later. It didn't take long for Julian's career to take off leading to the purchase of their first home. The big, beautiful house with the picket fence and two car garage was a nice start for the young couple. But Julian's success grew at record speed. A custom-built home twice the square footage of the first, three cars, countless family vacations and anything else they wanted was a real-life fairytale most only dream about.

Now, a widow of thirteen years, both kids off in their respective directions, J'Nae asked herself the million-dollar question.... Am I prepared for this? This stage of my life, this new chapter as I'm getting a bit closer to 50. An empty nester, bravely returning to corporate America. No baggage or parental commitments, only an abundance of feelings and emotions about what should be a happy and exciting chapter in my life. This time, this new time, should be all about me. Am I ready for this? I mean, what am I supposed to do? If marriage and children are behind me, what's next? What is the next stage in my life? What is it and will it be exciting? That's the million-dollar question. What's next for me now?

J'Nae found herself pondering that very question several hours later as she lay in her bed in front of the tv. Doing what she pretty much had been doing day in and day out.

* * * * *

Another day or two had passed and nothing much had changed. It was like playing the same record over and over. Not even the fresh aroma of coffee from the automatic coffee maker was enough to interrupt the warm embrace her body formed snuggled between her memory foam mattress, her plush mink blanket, and her worn out body pillow. She hadn't noticed the lights on the clock were flashing, signifying a loss of power had occurred and was completely oblivious to what had happened and was currently going on around her. She didn't want to move from her warm and comfortable spot she'd been in since L.B. stopped by a few days prior. No, J'Nae felt she was in the perfect resting place, devoid of any real responsibility or sense of necessity. Ain't nothing to do and no one's in need of her services. Moreover, the longer she lay there, the more comfortable she became.

The only thing on her agenda was figuring out her next move and she had plenty of time to do that. She turned over to her left and fluffed her pillow trying to get a bit more comfortable in the spot that had long ago taken on the shape and weight of her body. Her room was dark and without sound except for the slight hum of the ceiling fan which also provided a much-needed cool breeze from time to time. Damn those hot flashes! She didn't even bother to turn her TV back on. She grunted and pulled the covers up over her head just as she heard a loud knock at her front door. She chose to ignore it in hopes whoever it was would go away. But it continued and was eventually followed by the loud and familiar voice of her dear friend Rona.

"Girl, you'd better open this door. I know you're in there. Get up and answer this door right now!" Rona shouted.

Still lying-in bed motionless, J'Nae didn't stir a bit. She knew Rona was not about to leave and she also knew Rona knew where the spare key was kept. Any moment now she would let herself in and be on her way to her room. And Rona didn't disappoint. She entered the bedroom with an armful of mail and dropped it on the bed.

Rona stood about 5 feet 11 inches tall, athletic build at around 140 lbs. She kept her hair cut short, sides cropped with slightly longer curls at the top of her head in a sophisticated style that exacerbated elegance and confidence and all the power and glory that was Rona. On any given day, she was a force to be reckoned with.

Everything about her reflected strength and confidence that set her apart from most others. Her walk, talk, attitude, and presence took center stage anytime she entered a room. This time was no exception.

"J'Nae, get your butt up out of that bed. Enough is enough. What the hell is going on with you anyway?" Rona asked.

"Girl please, can you keep it down? I'm right here. There's no need for you to yell." J'Nae fired back.

"You've been posted up in the house for a few months now and from the look and smell of things around here, most of that time you've been laying up in the bed. We've barely seen or heard from you since we celebrated you and Zsasha's birthday. You haven't been answering your phone or email and you've missed coffee and wine so many times now, we almost gave your seat away. What's going on with you, girlfriend?"

J'Nae slowly sat upright on the bed, gazing over at a laundry basket full of magazines and junk mail she managed to file in chronological order. She caught a glimpse of a not so recent issue of Ebony magazine featuring Cam Newton and his mother on the cover which considering current events, she knew was more than a year old. It didn't matter as she was not in a hurry

7

to move past it. She was content, and enjoyed admiring his face, not noticing the subtitle in the lower left corner right away but eventually caught her eye. 'Sex and the Aging Single Mom...Is there a future?'. No need to be reading that article, she thought, then turned her attention to her friend who appeared to be annoyed.

"Look sista girl, you've been cooped up in this house long enough. Besides, the girls miss you. I miss you. Come on, get up and get dressed. We are meeting Zsasha and Vonne at Ahsasz for a wine tasting and I have strict instructions not to take no for an answer. Get up already!"

"A wine tasting?" J'Nae said. "Is that what y'all calling it now? Because we've been meeting there for some time now and all we do is taste wine...among other things."

"Well, yeah, pretty much, but this is something different. Zsasha is trying out some new wines she's thinking of adding to her repertoire to add more flare to her exhibits and the four of us are going to sample them!"

"Girl, you know y'all crazy right? Just sitting around thinking of reasons to drink wine in the morning. It's not normal."

"Yes, dear sister, I know we're crazy. We know we're crazy, we're all crazy, all day every day, but right now, you're the one looking cuckoo; hair all over your head looking like a bird's nest and you've been in those pajamas for a week!"

"Nah ah, you tripping!"

As Rona leaned in to touch her hair, J'Nae pulled back but not quickly enough.

"Girlfriend, your body's talking, and my fingers can't do no walking in that mess on top of your head and yes, those are last weeks' pajamas for sure. I can tell, I mean smell."

"Girl it ain't that bad!" J'Nae uttered.

"Respectfully I disagree, and by the way, it's not morning, it's afternoon, late afternoon. Now get up and get your funky behind in the shower and get dressed. We need to get moving."

J'Nae did just as she was instructed, grunting, and mumbling under her breath all the way to the bathroom. A short time later she emerged washed, dressed, and feeling refreshed as she did her best tucking her hair neatly under a stocking cap. Looking at herself in the mirror, she inventoried her appearance from head to toe. Most days she's a bit more put together, rarely transparent revealing her inner and outer disconnect even to those closest to her, but today was an exception. And despite her personal conflict she didn't look half bad. She was pleasantly surprised to see she was in pretty good shape. Even the few pounds she's put on during her period of isolation seemed to fall into all the right places. Still at a size 10, she looked good, and everything was on point, except for the hair which she usually kept shoulder length with medium spiral curls all the way around. But no matter what your level of pretty, black hair is still black hair and last-minute black hair is always a hassle.

"Thank goodness for wigs."

"Who you telling? But you know you're gonna have to wash that shit at some point, right?"

"You got jokes."

"Yeah whatever, let's just go."

The two ladies gathered their purses and headed out. A short time later, Rona and J'Nae arrive to find the gallery doors locked unexpectedly, but quickly noticed Vonne seated next door at The Coffee House waving them down. Looking a little puzzled they walk next door to join their friend.

Vonne stood 5' 7" with long flowing blonde hair, perfect make-up and petite in stature. Her small frame displayed muscular legs, a narrow waist and an upper body that looked as if she was barely able to carry the breast implants her husband gave her as a gift.

"Hey Vonne", J'Nae says as she approaches.

"Hey sweetie, look at you!" Vonne replied.

"Hey, what's up?" says Rona to Vonne. "How are you doing, girlfriend? You're certainly looking well today."

"Thanks baby. You always make me feel so good about myself...such a good girlfriend." Vonne said, now smiling like she won the Miss America pageant. "And J'Nae, girl, where have you been hiding and why? It's been a while, a long while, too long, what gives?"

"Yeah, it has been a while. I've just been at home in my own world, not doing much of anything."

"It's all good girl, we all go through stuff from time to time, I get it. It's just really good to see you and looking well." Vonne went in for a hug. "I'm just glad you came out. But have either of you heard from Zsasha? She's usually already in the gallery getting things setup for us. And I checked around back where she likes to park and there's no sign of her car or Simon's."

Just as Rona was about to respond, in walks Zsasha, beaming and smiling from ear to ear.

Zsasha was a tall voluptuous brown skinned African American woman that stood about 5', 9". She was more than petite yet less than full figured with a tiny waist, natural D size breast and ass for days. She turned heads everywhere she went and from all races of people.

"Wassup bitches!" Zsasha had a way of emphasizing the last word of her sentence for effect, especially when she had dirt to spill or some otherwise juicy information to share.

"Had a bit of difficulty getting out of bed, did ya?" asks Rona.

"Uhm, well…."

Before Zsasha could answer the question, Vonne Interjected. "We're fine. I'm fine, Rona's fine and look who's here, J'Nae's fine as well. Now what about you? How are you?"

They could read her from the moment she walked through the door of The Coffee House. It was obvious she had a story to tell and was eager to tell it.

"My bad, I'm a bit preoccupied at the moment. J'Nae, it's good to see you, glad you showed your face, luv."

"So, what's got you so upbeat today, Zsasha?" Rona asked.

"I don't know whatchu talking bout. Today's just like any other day."

"Yeah, right. We all know better than that."

"Come one girl, dish!" Vonne said, sharing Zsasha's eagerness and excitement.

"Hold that thought, ladies." Rona interrupted. "Let's move this next door and crack open some of that wine you wanted us to sample. That was the plan right...a light lunch accompanied with a bit of wine tasting?"

"Yeah Z, from the look of whatever you got going on this seems more like a wine and cheese conversation and less like coffee and croissants." Vonne added.

"Let's do it." Zsasha agreed.

J'Nae didn't say much of anything as the ladies gathered their belongings and went next door to Ahsasz.

Ahsasz, the art gallery named for Zsasha spelled backwards, which she owns along with her husband Simon. It is centrally located in the downtown area of DC and well known for showcasing up and coming artists with varying degrees of talent, style and modes of expression.

Simon, an extremely attractive and charming man five years her senior, is tall, handsome and seductively slender effortlessly capable of drawing the attention of anyone he desires with his charm, good looks or European accent. He was solely responsible for introducing Zsasha to the swinger lifestyle which they jointly incorporated into their marriage. The girls have always been aware of their lifestyle, but Zsasha made every effort to keep the details, events, and other developments private including the existence of *Ahsasz Down Under*.

Once inside, Rona headed to the kitchen area to gather some wine glasses while Zsasha retrieved a few bottles from the wine cooler in her office. Rona didn't seem the least bit phased by the excitement beaming for her friend. The truth of the matter was, she knew a lot more than she let on when it came to Zsasha and her affairs, both personal and professional. Even the parts of her life Zsasha never shared and tried to keep private had a way of getting out.

Rona owned and operated a very successful real estate company known as Rona Wright Realty marketed towards the rich and famous. As a result of her business acumen, buying and selling high end real estate to the wealthy and sometimes politically connected meant she and Zsasha frequently shared clientele. It was one of those things Rona and Zsasha didn't discuss, although both were fully aware of the overlap. In any event they both behaved like mature professionals, respecting each other's boundaries and knew better than to ever discuss, divulge or acknowledge the specifics. It's how Rona became aware of *Ahsasz Down Under*.

Soon the ladies were all gathered in a seating area located towards the far end of the gallery where several pieces of artwork hung from the moveable partitions surrounding them. The wine was poured, and the conversation picked up where they had left off next door.

"Well, I don't kiss and tell….at least not usually." Zsasha uttered while pouring wine for everybody. "Y'all know how it is."

"Oh, we know alright, that's why we're so eager to hear whatever tidbit you are willing to share." Rona exclaimed.

"So, let me guess," said Vonne, "You and Simon went to a party last night, didn't you?"

"Well, not exactly." She replied. "We just had a few friends over last night, catching up, you know. We hadn't connected in a while and they punk asses just came out of hiding."

"Oh, so like a private party or something?" J'Nae asked.

"Or something."

"Do tell, do tell." said Vonne.

"A blast from the past." Zsasha confessed.

"That must have been interesting." Rona implied.

"To say the least. You ladies remember Magda and Milo, don't you?"

Rona remembered right away. J'Nae and Vonne, not so much. Magda and her husband Milo, both of Italian heritage, were not part of the lifestyle when they wandered into Ahsasz to view artwork several years ago. While Zsasha was with another couple engaged in what she thought was a private conversation, Magda surreptitiously overheard portions of that conversation including what was supposed to be a private invite to a private affair. Both she and her mate Milo showed up.

Not having any experience or knowledge of the 'lifestyle' the two were quickly drawn in and allowed Zsasha and Simon to be their mentors. This encounter predated *Ahsasz Down Under*, the adult entertainment club Simon and Zsasha owns, operates, and manages in the basement level of the art gallery. For Magda and Milo, Zsasha and Simon's job was simple and straightforward. They were tasked with teaching them how to successfully live life as a married couple while engaging in the lifestyle.

In doing so, Zsasha and Simon established rules, regulations and guidelines they later referred to as 'Code of Conduct for Married Partners' and eventually their swinging circle grew.

Both had dynamic personalities and shared the ability to attract, organize, manage, and persuade others to follow their principles and best practices which later led them to establishing *Ahsasz Down Under*. But not before engaging in an affair with Magda and Milo lasting several months. Coupled with mixed emotions, unrealistic expectations only to be severed by a broken heart which led to Magda and Milo exploring their own open journey while traveling around the world.

"Well let me refresh your memory. Simon and I met Magda and Milo about several years ago. The gallery hadn't been opened yet, but we were active. At some point we shared details about our lifestyle, and they wanted in. We brought them in and showed them what's what. Vonne, you remember Magda, she was sweet on me for a minute, kind of early on."

"Oh yeah girl, I remember."

"Me too." Rona commented. "Go ahead."

"Well, we didn't really have it together back then. And by the time we figured out there was a problem, it was too late. After our experience with them, we decided not to swing with the same couple more than a specified number of times before cutting them loose and establishing rules of engagement, for those living the lifestyle. That way everybody stays friends and we're all cool and we preserve the primary relationship."

"Yeah, so what?"

"Well, we always saw ourselves as 'that couple', you know, the ones to show you the ropes, help establish the playbook, sort of speak. We were the ones to tell you what's what, how things work, we had it going on like that."

"So, what exactly are you saying, you guys picked back up with Magda and Milo again?" Vonne asked.

"Reluctantly yes, but it's more of a celebratory occasion. They want to invest in a joint business venture with us, so we figured one last rendezvous before ending that relationship and starting a new one of a professional nature."

"But isn't that against your own rule?" J'Nae asked.

"Only if we mix the two and we won't, not ever. That's part of the reason why we wanted to get that out of the way. But this time, OMG, Magda and Milo, well, what can I say…. the students have surpassed the teachers!"

"Really?" Rona asked with sarcasm.

"Hell yeah. In fact, I forgot all about our wine sampling this afternoon. To be truthful, I only came out to grab some coffee and refuel and catch my breath. Y'all know how it is."

"Oh my Gosh. Are you for real?" said Vonne.

"Hell yeah. Magda and Milo are still at the house right now. Ms. Honey was just setting out fruit and shit when I left for coffee and water."

"Don't y'all have all that at the house?" Vonne asked.

"Of course, we do but y'all know I gotta have my specialty blend. I don't feel right without it and since I was out, I wanted to stop and pick up some of that alkaline water I've been hearing about. It's supposed to replenish electrolytes and such when your energy level is down and you're feeling depleted, know what I mean…" Zsasha snickered.

She could see the wheels in their heads turning and knew more questions were coming. Questions that she didn't want to answer. Realizing she hadn't thought this through, she had to make her escape asap. Any minute now she could potentially be past the point of no return.

"I can see the looks on all of your faces and yes, it's a bit much even for you bitches. All I can suggest is that you look at it as a celebration, marking the end of our intimate relationship and the start of something more. But we'll have to discuss it later, right now I gotta go. Again, I'm sorry I forgot about meeting up and everything, but I know y'all asses will get over it…at some point, anyway."

"Uhm, the life and times of Zsasha Stewart. Ain't nothing like it!" Vonne chimed in.

"Well from where I sit, you all seem to have it going on just as good as I do." Zsasha remarked.

"Are you kidding me?" J'Nae piped in. "Girlfriend, I envy you, you and Simon. You two actually found a way to make that insane lifestyle work!"

"Don't envy me, J'Nae. Join me, or us, not literally but hell, aren't you ready to stir things up a bit?" Zsasha spoke firmly, trying to get the focus off herself. The look on J'Nae's face was priceless.

"Ah, not really." J'Nae confirmed.

Truth be told, J'Nae did join Zsasha for a one on one, girl on girl event several years back.... for a second time, not long after Julian passed. Heartfelt emotions about her husband's passing, a half-gallon of Gin.... throw in a half ounce of weed and some blow.... made for a night of girl-on-girl sex that was so mind blowing J'Nae has refused to talk about it ever since, even with Zsasha. Hell, she still won't admit to or discuss the first time they hooked up back in college during their freshman year living as roommates. Yep, it was the best kept secret within the bunch. At least that's what J'Nae believed.

"Girl, you've been sitting on that shit of yours so long there's probably a mold of your pussy embedded in your couch cushion!" Zsasha added.

"Not probably", laughs Rona. "It is, it really is...Hell, I've seen it! You know how leather looks when it's old and dry...got cracks in it and shit."

"Y'all need to quit." Vonne joins in. "Some people can only handle one real love in their lifetime and when it's gone, it's gone."

"Now who exactly are you talking about, Vonne?" Zsasha asked. "Your situation or hers? Because ain't nobody trying to talk about love. This heffa needs to fuck. She needs to get laid out, all the way out, from top to bottom, front to back and inside and out. Laid the fuck out like nobody's business!"

"You might as well hang it up, Zsasha. She ain't doing nothing with that. Maybe she's saving it for the wax museum or something...have it preserved and mounted on a pussy plaque." Rona said. "That's about all she's doing with that shit."

"Y'all know what, y'all can all kiss my booty butt!" J'Nae shouted. "Y'all know I ain't with all that. I don't just give it away for the asking!"

"Why is that?" Zsasha asked. "So nothing will ever enter your coochie corral again? Please girl, you're supposed to share your gifts every now and then, not let it grow cobwebs and dust mites."

"Yes, I suppose so." J'Nae fired back. "But not with just anybody......not with someone you just met and don't really know. It needs to be special and have real meaning behind it, something other than lust."

J'Nae did not intend to throw shade on Zsasha's swinger lifestyle with her comments. She'd made peace with that long ago and had always been supportive of any related issues Zsasha may have shared. Nonetheless, Rona took this opportunity to share something she'd been wanting to say for some time.

"Well, J'Nae, there's something to be said about anonymity in all its forms. Sometimes you fuck just because you want to fuck, right then and right at that moment.... with that mother fucker that just caught your eye, no strings, complications, or pretenses. You know men and women initially put on a facade when they first start dating. You only see what they want you to see at first. It takes time for some people to reveal their true self. When you do it anonymously you do it without the drama of who's who and who wants what, when, where, and how and without expectations, plus not knowing is part of the illusion of seduction. The forbidden fruit that we're all taught is poison can be passionate and pleasurable and extremely erotic. You see, the problem with traditional dating is that there is always an expectation of something meaningful and long lasting down the line. At least from a woman's perspective because that's what we were taught.

16

Traditional and monogamous dating is where we're supposed to start in order to end up where we're taught, we're supposed to be. For me, that's some bullshit. Nobody fucking knows what it is they really want until they come face to face with it and are willing to do uncomfortable things to keep it. In search of this or that, to me, is a colossal waste of time. People get so caught up in the so-called destination that they miss the journey……its unforeseen twists and turns, happy accidents, and the bumps and bruises along the way. It's what makes the final destination special and meaningful when in fact you reach it."

"Yeah, but what about finding your soul mate, your mister right?" J'Nae spoke softly.

"Mr. Right? That perfect guy women relentlessly search for? Who in the hell can live up to that expectation? Maybe for a moment but long term, come on, Just keep it simple. Remove the expectations society dictates one should have as the norm or how things should be and automatically the pressure is gone. Without it, oftentimes, people tend to be more open and freer with one another, embracing the natural spontaneity of their acquaintance, and who knows, it just might lead to an unencumbered and satisfying intimate entanglement or even a fulfilling relationship. Sometimes a person may say they're not looking for a mate and then unexpectedly the right person comes along under the right set of circumstances and before you know it, they're all in. You've found everything you didn't know you wanted. But when your destination is predetermined, orchestrated by societal norms and old school views of what happiness is supposed to look like, then so is your path. And when your path is predetermined your mind and your heart aren't receptive to the unambiguous nature of self-discovery on your journey of love. And when that happens, you've likely missed out on the best parts simply because you're preoccupied with making sure all the boxes are checked. Don't live for society, or what society says you want, live for self. **Find your own unique happiness!**"

"I feel you Rona, but it sounds so… casual." J'Nae concluded.

"I don't mean it to sound casual in any sense. Flexible and uninhibited while being observant and cautious would be a better way to describe it. And being smart. But most importantly just being open to the possibilities and letting things go where they may."

"Well, that sounds like some ho-ass behavior if you ask me. Be flexible, okay, so what happens after you've been flexible and open a few times or more than a few times. No man wants a used-up woman. Untouched or barely soiled, that's what my grandmother always told me." Vonne exclaimed.

"Really Vonne, so how's that working out for you? Girl, just because your shit is all fucked up, don't mean others can't find their happiness taking a slightly different path." Replied Zsasha.

"Damn, you going there, girlfriend? Kind of harsh wouldn't you say?" Rona interjected and J'Nae agreed.

"My bad." Zsasha acknowledged. "I didn't mean to come across like that, Vonne. You know I love you and I sympathize with what you're going through. But I agree with Rona. We must stop blaming others that their choices render our circumstances, including your husband, for the crap that you allow him to do. All I'm saying is, people need to relax a bit. Take a breath and stop living their lives based on what or how society stipulates they should. Find your own happiness. Put up with whatever you want to put up with but own it. Everybody needs to own their own shit, no matter what it is. It is truly the gateway to emotional freedom and inner peace. And stop worrying about what other people think. Bitches be crazy!"

"I feel you on that." Vonne said. "That's some deep shit and something to think about."

"I know, but right now I gotta go. I have some folks waiting on me and I need to get back. I'm sure lunch is over by now and if they continue without me, I'm gonna be pissed the fuck off! Y'all stay and finish the wine. There's another bottle in the top rack of the wine cooler in my office. J'Nae, here's a spare set of keys. Would you mind locking up for me when you ladies leave? It's just the front door and I'll get the keys back from you later."

18

"No problem, I got you."

"Thanks girlfriend and it was so good to see you, J'Nae. I missed you. We all missed you! We'll catch up later."

"Well, you go handle that, sista!" said Rona.

"Oh, I will. Trust and believe, I got this!"

"Bye sweetie."

"By y'all."

Zsasha left the gallery with slightly mixed feelings. Most of what she told the girls was a complete fabrication. She was usually honest and truthful with the girls when they discussed things about their lives, but there was no way she could tell them that Magda and Milo weren't investing in Ahsasz but were investing in *Ahsasz Down Under*, the adult club her and her husband operated in the basement level of the art gallery which they knew nothing about. Client confidentiality was crucial to the survival of that business and they always that part of their business on a need-to-know basis. Besides, they weren't ready for all that anyway.

Vonne, Rona and J'Nae continued to drink wine for another hour or so catching up on J'Nae's recent emotional rollercoaster including isolating herself these past weeks and whatever gossip she had missed. They laughed and drank and were simply happy to be reunited again. After hugging it out and saying their goodbye's, they all went their separate ways, except for J'Nae. She stayed back to clean up and lock up as Zsasha requested. It was her first time in the gallery alone and she took a few moments to look around and check out what additions Zsasha had made since her last visit.

The next morning, J'Nae woke up feeling a bit refreshed having gotten out of the house and reconnected with the girls. While heading to the kitchen to make herself something to eat, she looked around the house and realized what a mess things had become and just had closed off she'd allowed herself to be. She began cleaning up in the kitchen and living room while nibbling on some fruit, yogurt and toast when she heard the doorbell ring. It was Vonne.

"Hey Vonne, what's up? I wasn't expecting you, but please come in."

"Hey J'Nae, how are you?"

"I'm good. Just trying to straighten up a bit. What brings you out this way?"

"Well, I called but you didn't answer, so I just drove on over, to make sure you were okay."

"Since when, yesterday? Girl you crazy."

"Nah, for real." Vonne replied.

"What's the real reason you came all this way? My house isn't close to any of your stores so what's up?"

"Can a girl get a cup of coffee first?"

"Sure, you know where the Keurig is. Help yourself."

Vonne took her sweet time making herself a cup of coffee simply because she wasn't sure J'Nae was quite ready for the proposition she had in mind.

"You know, I've been thinking about what Rona and Zsasha were discussing yesterday, parts of it, anyway." J'Nae uttered from the other room.

"Oh yeah, how so."

"Just the whole thing about life is a journey and not to get too caught up in the destination."

Vonne couldn't believe her luck. J'Nae was going to make her reason for coming over a whole lot easier than she anticipated. She found her way back into the sitting room and rejoined J'Nae on the sofa.

"Ok, continue." Vonne remarked.

"I mean, it's time for me to start thinking about expanding my horizons, maybe getting out more and meeting new people. The kids are grown and out of the house living their lives, doing the things they want and need to do to make themselves happy. Maybe it's time I start doing the same thing. Ever since Julian passed, my life and my existence has been centered around my kids."

"Well honey that's normal, under the circumstances, especially when they were younger."

20

"Right, but somewhere in all that, I lost myself. Even after they became adults, I still made them the center of my life. He'll, I didn't even work for the most part. I made them my job, my support. Taizja was my best girlfriend and Aiden was the man in my life. That sounds so pathetic when I say it out loud."

"No, it doesn't. You're being way too hard on yourself. Most mothers would have done the same thing given the same circumstances."

"Yeah, for a while. But at some point, you adjust and begin taking care of yourself." J'Nae paused for a moment before she continued, thinking about the reality that just became crystal clear. "I didn't do that, did I?"

"Girlfriend everything you did, you did out of love, and no one can judge you for that. You raised two amazing individuals and you should be proud. And if you really feel like you've been neglecting yourself, do something about it."

"Like what?" J'Nae asked.

"Well, for starters, how about going on a dinner date with my pastor. You know he's been wanting to take you out for some time now. Why not start with him. He's not a total stranger and he is a pastor."

"You think he still wants to take me out, after all this time?"

"I'm sure of it. In fact, he asked me about you just a few weeks ago. He's always asking me about you."

Feeling brave J'Nae threw caution to the wind and ran with it.

"Well set it up. It's time I branch out a bit, and like you said, I have met him a time or two and he is a pastor so let's do it."

"Okay sista girl, with your big girl britches on, I will. I'll give him your number and you two can go from there. How's that sound?"

"Cool. Now don't you have some stores you need to go manage?"

"   Yes, I do." Vonne replied as she headed for the door. "Remind me not to stop by unannounced!"

"Girl, quit."

"I'll call you later." Vonne replied.

"Cool. Bye sweetie."

21

"Bye."

And with that, Vonne was gone. J'Nae headed to the kitchen to reheat what was left of her coffee and mulled over the idea of going out on a date. She thought it was a good idea and a great way to change up her routine.

Chapter 2

It took J'Nae a full week to thoroughly clean her house from top to bottom including washing and drying the massive amount of laundry that had accumulated while she checked out from almost everyone and everything. She was steadfast and diligent as she worked each day motivated now by a new outlook and perspective about life, hers in particular. Her primary incentives were the phone conversations she shared with Pastor Roberts. However brief, he managed to call and check in with her a few times during the week. They wanted to leave the deep dive Q & A period for their upcoming face to face meeting. They would have a little bit of a drive which would give them plenty of time to do so and then enjoy a nice dinner.

J'Nae couldn't remember the last time, if ever, she was set up on a date by anyone. But for whatever reason she allowed Vonne to do just that. The dating game has changed so much over the years, all thanks to the invention of the internet and social media. Dating sites make it seem so easy allowing you to swipe left or swipe right based solely on the profile pics or a few sentences you write about yourself or what you're looking for.

Today, at any given time and at any given place, people walk around with their heads slightly hung low with tunnel vision totally focused on their smartphones, smartwatches, or tablets. Kind of makes it hard to meet people in passing or at an event. Everybody is connected and tuned in, so it seems, young and old alike. Even children seem to prefer electronic devices over physical interactions with other kids even when outdoor activities are staring them in the face.

No one is engaging in face-to-face public meetings anymore. Times have definitely changed so reluctantly, J'Nae agreed to have dinner with Pastor Roberts, the associate pastor from Vonne's church. His full name was Demetri Roberts and he had taken a liking to J'Nae a while back when she visited his church a few Sundays with the girls. According to Vonne, he continued to seek her out asking when she planned to visit again.

Despite her new-found outlook on life, J'Nae was still a bit squeamish every time the phone rang. A man calling her of a personal nature, hadn't been part of her life since she became a widow. But after they spoke a few times, her anxiety subsided, and it got easier and eventually she began to look forward to their conversations and dates. It had been a long time since she enjoyed the company and conversation of an intelligent man. And the pastor part, definitely an added plus. She happily anticipated not having to worry about the usual games a lot of men play, regardless of their age or status. Yes, J'Nae was feeling surprisingly good about the dinner date, so much so, she allowed him to pick her up at her home.

When his gold Cadillac pulls up to her house and he gets out to open her door. "Well, Hello Beautiful." Demetri says, opening the car door.

"Hello Pastor Roberts", J'Nae replied. "It's great to see you again."

"The pleasure is all mine, young lady. And tonight, it's just Demetri."

Demetri Roberts, J'Nae thought to herself. A guy with two first names……hmm, that's different.

"Okay then, Demetri. Did you have any trouble finding my house?"

"Not at all. Your directions were spot on and of course there's this new little invention called GPS. It actually works!"

"You're funny." J'Nae replied.

"And by the way, you look lovely this evening, J'Nae. Even more lovely than I remember."

"Well thank you. Demetri. I only wanted my attire to be well matched with your distinguished taste. I remembered you to be quite the snazzy dresser."

"Well you look perfect." He replied while smiling ear to ear.

They were both dressed quite nicely for the evening. J'Nae had on a navy-blue backless Donna Karen dress, just slightly above the knee along with a pair of Laura Dunne pumps. She wore a shawl covering her backless dress so as not to be too revealing. She didn't want to appear to be too forward or too sexy on her first date with this man, this man of God and she wanted to be respectful.

He wore a tailored grayish blue suit vest and slacks, accessorized by a gray, blue and black finely checkered tie and what looked like a very expensive tie clip. He sported a black silk button down shirt with shining gold cufflinks, all matching the gold jewelry he wore on his wrists and fingers. First man she recalled wearing more jewelry than she did…. oh well.

Taking off on their journey, J'Nae thought back to their conversations on the phone, realizing he wasn't very forthcoming about his friends or the name of the restaurant they were dining at, just that it was a bit of a drive. For a brief moment, she found it unsettling that she hadn't pressed for more details but chose not to worry. Vonne knows who she's with and probably had a pretty good idea of where they were going, so as quickly as those feelings appeared, they were gone. Vonne was not one to go quietly in the night and if she turned up missing, the whole congregation would know what's up and who she was last seen with.

"So how come nobody's snatched you up yet? A pretty lady like yourself, I bet you have men falling all over you."

"Thank you, Demetri. And no, not falling over me. They might be falling behind me when I'm not looking but who's to say. I pretty much keep to herself. I've been focused on my family and completing my educational goals these past few years, so that didn't leave much time for dating. What about you Demetri, what keeps a man like yourself single and unmarried?"

"I came close once." He stated. "I was engaged but it didn't work out. I guess I just haven't met the right one yet…present company excluded."

J'Nae smiled a little smile, inside and out. So far so good. He had not yet disappointed her.

"You see, women tend to get caught up in the pastor more so than the man, if you know what I mean. I'm not looking for a churchy type of woman, one that's uptight, has to stay on the

25

straight and narrow, do things by the book and so forth. No, that's not what I'm looking for. I need a woman that can meet all my needs, be everything I need her to be, including my first lady when we stand before God. However, I live life like every other man. I do what makes me happy and sometimes there's conflict. I am a man of God, however, in that statement, man comes before God so when the time comes, my woman needs to be able to distinguish my being a man from my being a man of God, understand? It's like when I'm in church, I'm in church 100%, but when I'm not in church, I'm an entirely different man, a natural man, like any other. I try not to mix the two. I keep them separate and I'm equally committed to both, just not at the same time."

J'Nae's mouth flew open in shock at the same time she turned to face forward, as not to reveal her shock and disbelief. What did he just say? He's a pastor but he wants to leave the religious aspects out of dating and his personal life. No, oh hell no! I must have misunderstood some part of what he said. Scratching her head and trying to gather her thoughts, she hadn't noticed that he had pulled into a parking lot and was now parking the car, nor had she been paying attention to where they had pulled in.

"Isn't this the MGM National Harbor Hotel and Casino?" she asked cautiously.

"Yes, it is. There's a restaurant inside I frequent. The food is excellent, and all the servers know me by name." he stated rather proudly.

"So, your friends are meeting us here?"

"Yes. In fact, I'm quite sure they are already inside. This is something they do regularly. We all do."

"I think I've been here before, but it was quite a few years back." J'Nae commented with a bit of uncertainty.

"Yeah, they upgraded it about 5 or 6 years ago, making all types of renovations. They now host various entertainment venues and shows. It helps to keep a steady stream of cash flowing into the casino."

26

Now out of the car and walking inside they enter a long corridor which would eventually lead to a reception area where first time players register and receive a rewards card used to track their spending.

"The restaurant is just down here to the left." He said, slightly guiding her arm.

They continued to walk down the corridor, J'Nae taking it all in. Dazzling lights and illuminated signage highlighted the various restaurants, bars, ballrooms, and performance venues along the route. It seemed endless. Each sign trying harder than the last one wanting to draw you in. J'Nae didn't remember so much to do, so many options when she was here years ago. It had changed quite a bit.

As they continued towards the entrance to the ground level of the casino the décor changed. About 150 feet from the entrance, the corridor darkened and was illuminated only by the lights which were mounted directly above the individual pictures hanging on both walls. Each appeared to be at least 17" X 21" and all had a caption below showing the amount of their winnings. It was the MGM's Hall of fame.

"Hold on, is that your picture I just saw on the wall?"

"Oh, well yeah. They put pictures of some of their winners up throughout this corridor. Kind of like the casino wall of fame, if you will."

Again, J'Nae was left speechless. What the hell have I walked into? See this is why you don't go on blind dates or allow friends to set you up. They act like they don't know you at all or the person they're setting you up with. No one is ever properly vetted, and you always spend the date counting down the minutes. I mean really. A gambling pastor? One that doesn't want a churchy type of woman in his life...ah, he'll no. What was Vonne thinking?

They were almost at the end of the corridor when they abruptly made a sharp right turn into the restaurant. It was just a few feet from the casino entrance. J'Nae didn't say much as they were quickly seated at a table, and it didn't seem to bother Demetri one bit. J'Nae ordered the first thing she recognized on

27

the menu without giving it much thought. He did the same. She was thankful the salads arrived quickly as she was already eager to see this date come to an end. When the main course arrived J'Nae realized she hadn't told them how to cook her steak. The waitress, probably scared off by the 'Get me the hell out of here' look on her face, didn't take the time to ask.

They sat and ate, mostly in silence until J'Nae asked about his friends that were supposed to be joining them for dinner. She barely got a few words out before he cut her off, stating that he prefers not to conversate at the dinner table. Okay, sitting in silence, that was fine by me. He wouldn't have liked much of what she had to say anyway. The steak was fine, but no way was it worth driving fifty minutes outside of town for. And she had yet to meet any friends. Even though the entire casino and restaurant staff appeared to know him by name, no one acted like they had a pre-arranged dinner meetup with him. This all felt a bit strange to J'Nae, but she kept it to herself.

As they walk away from the restaurant, J'Nae follows alongside him without question, again taking it all in while trying to come up with a creative way to have an early end to the evening. But she soon gave in. After all, what good would it do with the long ride back. What other surprises could there be? So far, it's been ridiculous, yes, even more than absurd but physically she's safe. No one could have predicted this hot mess of a gambling, sinning, part-time preacher man unless you knew him intimately, but something tells her, there's still more to come. And she was right.

After what appeared to be a quick yet deliberate walk through a portion of the casino floor, Demetri took a seat at a high stakes' poker table without saying as much as a word to his date. J'Nae just stood behind him watching and being observant. Still in disbelief, she shook her head as he procured chips and placed his first bet. A gambling pastor, what could top that? Is gambling a sin? Maybe or maybe not. But there are a host of vices that are not necessarily sins but are surely inappropriate for a man of God. Hold on, wait...did he just order a double shot of crown and coke? I'm so done!

The ride back was a bit uncomfortable as there was not much talking. J'Nae had long ago decided this was not the man she thought him to be or anyone she had any desire to have in her life. Small talk and polite conversation were the best she could do followed up with a fake nap. Once they arrived at her house, J'Nae sprang to life. She thanked him for dinner, said good night and went inside, locking the door securely behind her.

Chapter 3

The next day, J'Nae woke up a bit later than usual. The first thing she did was block Demetri's number. The date was emotionally tiring and the quiet drive back into town was nerve racking. Ordinarily, she would be in a state of disbelief had this happened to someone else and she was hearing about it in passing. But since today's bank balance has $300 less than it did the day before, she knew this to be a real and true event, one that she experienced firsthand and at a cost. Just then her cell phone rang.

"Hello"

"Morning, J'Nae."

"Hey Rona, what's good?"

"Me? Never mind me, how are you? How did your date go last night?"

"Girl, OMG. What was I thinking to let one of y'all set me up on a blind date?"

"What do you mean, one of y'all. I have never set you up on a blind date before, J'Nae. Hell, you won't let me."

"And with good reason! Last night was proof, not that I needed any."

"Proof for what?"

"Proof that blind dates, setups or fixer uppers are not for me. It's like Vonne doesn't know me at all or at least what I would consider compatible or even acceptable."

"It couldn't have been that bad J'Nae, he's a pastor."

"Are you telling me or am I telling you?"

"Okay girl, speak."

"I don't even know where to begin. Pastor Roberts or should I say, Demetri aka Demetri Love, former radio host......

"What?"

"Yeah! Vonne left that part out. Maybe if she had shared that with me, I would have been better prepared for the evening."

"Well, weren't you guys just going for dinner?"

"Yeah, that was the plan. We were supposed to meet 2 of his friends for dinner."

"Okay, so what? No dinner?"

"Oh, yes. We had dinner all right. Did I mention that the restaurant was inside the Casino Aztar?"

"Whaaaaat?"

"Yes. And it was a lovely dinner. Personalized service like I've never seen before."

"How so?"

"Everyone and I do mean everyone knew him by name. The restaurant staff as well as the casino staff all called him by name. Of course, why wouldn't they know his name? His picture is hanging on their "Wall of Fame" in the corridor as you walk in. Apparently, he was one of their big jackpot winners at some point."

"Say what!"

"Yes, girlfriend, yes. A gambling preacher!"

"Dang girl. I didn't see that coming."

"Well hold on, there's more."

"Okaaaay……"

"Suffice it to say, he is a gambling and drinking pastor that is not looking for a "churchy" type woman on the straight and narrow."

"For real?"

"For real...pastor my ass!" The frustration and anger were still apparent in her voice. She was not happy.

"I can't believe it. Vonne knows better than to set you up with somebody that doesn't have a moral center."

"You would think. I mean, we've known each other for how many years now?"

"Yeah, but she may not have known those things about him. I have to think she knows you well enough to know that would never have worked or even been of interest to you."

"Pastor Roberts…. I don't think so."

"Well sounds like pasturing is what he does, not who he is."

"Whatchu said girlfriend, whatchu said."

"So, have you talked to Vonne yet?"

"No, not yet. She has something going on at one of her boutiques today, so I figured I'd just wait until the next time we meet up. Besides, I still need a little time to gather my thoughts and calm down a bit. As it stands right now, I might blow up on her."

"I just want to know what she was thinking with this move. I mean damn!"

"Yeah, me too girl."

"So, what if she calls you before you get yourself together. Then what?"

"Oh well, it's on then, I guess. Who knows, I mean, what am I supposed to do, not answer the phone? That would be childish. I'm not going to avoid her like that. I mean truth be told, yes, I'm upset with her right now and rightfully so, but we are talking about Vonne. And If I really want to keep it real, it's partly my own fault. I should have known better. Vonne's history has shown us that she's not the best judge of character especially when it comes to men."

"And sometimes women too." Rona interrupted. "She overlooks critical tell-tale signs, bad behavior and things that would be red flags to almost anyone else."

"That's true."

"Even at her age now she hasn't learned to read the writing on the wall. She's way too trusting."

"Again, that's true."

"And I don't know why that is." Rona admitted. "She's a beautiful, attractive, and educated woman with a lot to offer a deserving man. But she doesn't believe that."

"I know. That's why she settled for the dead-beat non-working x-ball player husband she continuously supports."

"Which is my point, J'Nae. You can't be too hard on her. You know she's going through it right now. She's not in a good place. And it didn't help much having her ass handed to her last time we met up."

J'Nae remembered all too well. "Yeah, that was bad."

"It was brutal."

"Well, the truth always is."

"Yeah, you're right, that's why you've got to cut her some slack. She meant well."

"Yeah, she did, and like I said. It was partially my own fault. I know what works for me and what doesn't. And fixer uppers never do!"

"Well, that's because you let the wrong people set you up, sista girl!"

"So that's what it is then, huh?"

"Yes, mam. The person that sets you up should know the real you quite well and know what you value in a relationship, all relationships. They should know what your goals are in life and what you want or need to accomplish them. Are you looking for Mr.Right or Mr. Right now? How important is financial wellbeing? Is religion a factor? Does he or she have children in the home under 18? If so, is it a deal breaker or not? Those are some of things your matchmaker should already know about you in order to set you up on a successful date. At the very least your matchmaker should only set you up with someone that has potential. But most importantly, the right person should be able to distinguish between what you want and what you need. 9 times out of 10, they are not the same."

"I don't know girl. I think this blind date thing is a wrap. At least for now. I have something else to focus on in the meantime."

"Oh yeah, what's that?"

"I got a job!"

"Really, cool. That's awesome."

"Yeah, it is. It's the one I'd been praying I'd get. It took them a while to compose a good offer and finalize everything but yes, I got the job with the salary I wanted."

"Great, but don't change the subject. You're still open to dating, right?"

"I don't know, I'm not really feeling it right now. I may just put that on the back burner."

"That's fine. We've always known you to be scary."

"Who? What? Me... scary? I don't think so, I'm just selective."

"Call it what you will. But when you're ready to take off your training wheels and go for a real ride, holla at a sista, okay. I got you."

"Yeah okay, whatever."

"Alrighty then, I gotta go. See you tonight?"

"For sure. Bye sweetie."

"Bye J'Nae."

J'Nae lay across the comforter on her neatly made bed, in the nude, reflecting on the conversation that just ended with Rona. A slight chill ran across her body, and she began to sneeze repeatedly. Damn it, she said to herself, realizing she'd just peed a little. She abruptly jumped up attempting to clean up her mess before it soaked through to her sheets and mattress. This had happened a few times before, so she wasn't completely surprised by it. Fortunately, she was at home in lounge wear and was able to minimize the damage to her clothing and bedding. She cleaned herself up, did some chores around the house before she washed and dressed for the evening out with the girls.

Shortly thereafter, she arrived at Ahsasz to meet the girls for wine and stimulating conversation. Walking from her car in the swanky downtown location that housed the art gallery and The Coffee House next door, she notices Rona's high-priced midnight blue beamer, proudly sporting her 'Rona Wright Realty' ' car magnet. It's the only car she recognized on the street directly in front of the gallery which should now be closed for business. Zsasha's car is almost always parked in the back alley at the rear door of the gallery.

"Hey ladies." J'Nae greeted. "Glad to see you didn't start without me."

"Wassup? Wasn't sure you were going to make it tonight." Zsasha confessed. "I heard you were 'in your feelings' earlier about your date with Demetri."

"Yeah, I was but I'm not trying to make it a big issue. After all, It's Vonne we're talking about, remember."

Zsasha snickered under her breath realizing at that moment Vonne was the last person that should have been trying to set anyone up on a date, blind or otherwise.

35

"True, true, and by the way, congratulations on your new job."

"Awe, thank you Z."

"You're welcome and you definitely deserve it."

"Excuse me, excuse me!" Rona inserted. "Have either of you heard from Vonne at all? Did she text or call?" Rona asked.

"No, not me and her car wasn't parked out front when I pulled up either." J'Nae replied.

"So no one's heard from her today?" Rona repeated. "What about you, Zsasha, you're being unusually quiet this evening, any word?"

"Nah, not anything, but it's still early, give her a minute. You know whitegirl got some drama going on. She's got stuff she needs to work out right now. If she's not here in five, we'll start without her."

As if that was her cue, Vonne walks in sporting an all-white outfit obviously fresh off the rack, her rack at 'The Boutique'.

"Where my girls at!". Vonne said as she strutted in obviously having had a head start on drinking. "I'm sorry I'm late but I wanted to stop by 'The Boutique' to get one of the new seasonal outfits that just arrived. Take it out for a spin, y'all know how I do. So, what do you think, and be honest, please?"

"You look hot sista girl, I love it." Zsasha commented.

"Yes, you do. But I'm more concerned about how you're feeling." Rona announced, always being the voice of reason.

J'Nae hadn't said much since Vonne walked in. She really wanted to talk to her about the Demetri fiasco, but it looked like she'd already sustained a beating, emotionally speaking and this just wasn't the right time.

"I'm good, sweetie. But I'll be better once I have a glass of wine in my hand."

Zsasha began to pour wine into four crystal wine glasses that she had set out earlier in preparation for the gathering. They were all seated around a chrome plated glass table Zsasha had established in what would be their corner hideaway for wine and whatever they wanted to get into.

"Zsasha, what happened to the painting of yours you had hanging on this wall right here?" J'Nae asked. "It was the one with the woman holding the..."

"I know which one you're talking about." Zsasha remarked. "I moved it to my office to make room for the next showcase. It's on the 19th and we're featuring a new and talented artist. I emailed you guys about it."

"Oh yeah, sounds interesting. Will you have any of your own work on display?" Rona asked.

"Well, this *is* my gallery, and I *am* an artist, so hell yeah, there will always be some of my shit here and there, just not that piece. It doesn't blend well with the theme of his work that'll be on display. I'll rehang it at some point."

Zsasha never really liked to discuss that particular piece of artwork. It was one of her early pieces she completed while in college or sometime after graduation; long before she met Simon.

She was in a dark place back then, starting with her last few years of college which were filled with late nights, lots of partying and heavy drinking. Those close to her were concerned she may never graduate especially as her drinking became a bigger part of her daily life. Eventually she was put on academic probation near the start of her junior year. With a stroke of luck, she was able to complete her first semester as a junior then left school that summer and took the following semester off, claiming she needed a break.

During her absence, J'Nae's relationship with her college sweetheart Julian had grown and intensified. Love was on the horizon and the two became inseparable. Julian graduated just after Zsasha returned to school and it wasn't long after that J'Nae dropped out to get married and start a new life with her true love.

It wasn't known to many at the time, but Zsasha had also graduated...from alcohol to drugs and after finishing school a year behind schedule, she lived the next couple of years spiraling out of control and getting in and out of trouble on a regular basis, actively living in her addiction. Her family tried to convince

37

themselves that she was just acting out and would pull it together at some point. But J'Nae knew better. J'Nae knew what happened to Zsasha that one night. She knew what caused Zsasha to leave school so abruptly and spend the next six months or so in seclusion, away from school, away from everyone. But it was a subject they discussed one time and one time only.

It was during one of her darkest and drug-filled years that she painted this specific portrait as well as several others, most of which were lost or left behind which she considered collateral damage. But this one, is one of the few she managed to hold on to while living fast and loose.

"So, when do you want to go out to celebrate your new job?" Zsasha asked.

"I don't know, whenever."

"How about next Saturday night? We can go to that new club down by the river." Rona replied.

"Club Nonchalant?" Zsasha asked.

"Yeah, that's the one."

"I hear it's pretty nice." Vonne mumbled.

"It is, and we'll have two reasons to celebrate." Rona recalled. "J'Nae's new job and Vonne's birthday."

"Sounds like a plan to me." Zsasha confirmed.

"What do you think, J'Nae, Vonne, y'all good with that?" Rona asked.

"I'm cool with it." Vonne replied.

"Yeah, sure, let's do it."

"Cool. Let's plan on the 5th. We'll meet up around 7 pm, maybe have a cocktail or two and head out. We'll make it a couple's thing." Rona declared. "I'll secure the tickets."

"That's fine and all for me and Zsasha, we both have husbands, and we all know you never have trouble finding a date but a couple's night...that would mean J'Nae's tight ass would need a date." Vonne remarked.

"I beg your pardon..." J'Nae replied.

"Speaking of a date Vonne, have you heard anything from Pastor Roberts?" Zsasha inquired, knowing she was forcing the issue.

"Ah, that would be a negative." Vonne replied.

"Well, that's a relief, right J'Nae?" Rona questioned.

"I wasn't half expecting to hear anything. He had to know I wasn't the slightest bit impressed or happy with his truth." J'Nae stated. "I just wonder why he waited to share those things with me in person. We spoke on the phone almost daily for a week or so before we went out. Of course, none of those conversations were all-nighters but nothing he shared prepared me for all that."

"Well did the topic of drinking, gambling and sex outside of marriage come up?" Rona smirked.

"Well, no, it did not. I guess I made a few assumptions with him being a pastor and all."

"There's your answer. I'm sure you weren't the first woman to run the other way when they found out what he was really about. He was probably hoping you'd look past all that when you saw his ugly ass picture on the casino Wall of Fame." Rona confirmed.

"That's a possibility. It could've been just that simple. There are plenty of bitches out here willing to deal with a man and his issues, regardless of what they are simply because he has money." Zsasha replied.

"Yea, but I'm not that chick! There's no way he could think I am in any way interested in what he's offering. I've closed the door on that one for sure."

"Cool. Let's toast to closing the door on that one!" Rona cheered.

"Here, here." Vonne slurred, as she refilled her glass of wine.

"But you know what they say, when one door closes, another one opens." Rona continued.

"Right, right." J'Nae said half-heartedly.

"So, let's open some doors for ya, sista girl." Rona suggested.

"You need to open one right quick and get yourself a date. Remember it's a couple's thing and stashing your battery-operated bullet in your panties in the lobby does not count as a plus one." Zsasha laughed and everyone laughed along with her.

"I don't know, maybe I'll ask L.B." J'Nae said. "He's been trying to get me to go out with him since forever. He's nice enough, I'll ask him."

"Is that the best you can do girlfriend?" Zsasha inquired.

"Well, he's not a stranger and let's face it, anybody else would be."

"You're right and that's fine but you need more prospects." Vonne insisted. "Zsasha, where's your laptop or tablet?"

"In my office. Why?"

"Can you grab it? We're going to create a dating profile for J'Nae." Vonne announced.

"A dating what?" J'Nae asked.

"Yeah, a dating profile on one of those dating sites like Date2Mate or IFoundLove.com."

"Uhm, I don't think so, Vonne. Thanks, but no thanks. I think you've helped enough."

"No really, we should do it." Vonne persisted.

"I agree." Rona stated. "It'll be different this time because you'll get to choose whom you talk to and whom you don't. By the way Vonne, great idea but you can sit this one out. I'll set it up."

"Whatever." Vonne replied.

"Besides, don't you miss it, J'Nae?" Zsasha asked.

"Miss what?"

"Dick, girl, dick! You know that thing that make-you say Umm, Umm, Na-Na-Na-Na. Na-Na-Na-Na. Make-you say, Um, um, um, Na-Na-Na-Na."

Rona and Vonne joined Zsasha in singing the chorus to the popular rap song none of them seemed to know by name. They continued laughing and singing while sitting around the computer while Zsasha and Rona created her profile. They gave her the username 'NayNay411'.

By the time the ladies were well into their third bottle of wine, J'Nae finally gives in to the excitement and mystery of the whole online dating thing and even starts posing for a few selfies. Most of them were headshots from various angles but a few of them revealed her cleavage but only in an innocent and slightly teasing way; nothing at all extreme.

Without drawing attention to herself, Zsasha slipped away needing to retreat to the safety of her office. Once inside, she paused to stare at it and quickly got lost in its story.

The painting pre-dated *Ahsasz* and most of the early artwork still in her possession. Cultivated in grayscale, it depicted a young woman of color from the waist up, crying while holding her newborn baby in her left arm. A few pale pink and blue brush strokes were perfectly blended into the varying shades of gray representing the swaddling around the infant.

At first glance, one might think the left side of the painting had been damaged by water, since a portion of the swaddling appeared to be smeared outward toward the edge of the canvas. Looking closely, an experienced artist would immediately know it was intentional; that there wasn't water damage at all, but tears stains shed by the heartbroken mother depicted in the painting. And while the streaks and smears resembled drag marks, its purpose was to illustrate how fast the baby was ripped from her arms, leading up to the most profound yet obscure meaning illustrated in this piece of art, the pink and blue streaks.

Most new mothers joyfully accessorize their newborns according to their gender, making it easy for admirers to know the appropriate compliments to make. In this case it wasn't straight forward. The light pink and blue streaks did not reveal the gender but the combination of the two illuded to the uncertainty of one sex over the other; ultimately translating to the unimaginable truth; that the mother had not yet held the baby long enough to determine if a boy or a girl.

Zsasha wasn't sure why the mention of the painting, a painting she saw almost daily, was disturbing to her at this time. Shaking it off, she took a moment to look at herself in the mirror and realized she needed to touch up her hair and make-up. She reapplied eyeliner and mascara and a bit of press powder, which she kept on her bathroom counter. She reached inside her top right drawer to retrieve a personal memento she'd kept for years; a small, silver-plated hairbrush she used to lay down her curly edges.

After she was satisfied with her appearance, she turned to leave her office when that very same painting caught her eye. Instinctively she took another moment to reabsorb the painting and all it represented. She sighed momentarily then quickly rejoined her friends. The rest of the evening was full of laughter, pretty pictures, and catchy taglines they debated on which ones to use.

That next morning, J'Nae awakens to the buzzing of her cell phone which she keeps in bed right next to her pillow. There were no missed calls or text messages, just several notifications. Turning over to turn her ringer off, intending to go back to sleep, she catches a glimpse of the notification banner and is stunned to discover she has 99 profile hits on the dating site the girls created the night before. Sitting straight up in bed, now wide awake, she thought to herself, maybe, just maybe there was something to this whole online dating thing after all. Excited as she was, she didn't let it alter her personal plans for the day. She showered, dressed, and headed out to make her first and most obvious change to date.

Chapter 4

Monday morning arrived and J'Nae was filled with excitement and a bit of anxiety as she arrived and was escorted to where she was assigned to work. This is a huge first step, she thought, as she settled herself into her new office. Typically, the first day is filled with orientation, several webcasts, and a ton of paperwork. They did not disappoint. She dug in, making significant progress, and was only briefly disturbed by her boss. A few hours later she was happy to see 12:00 noon roll around because she had lunch plans with Zsasha at a café a few blocks down the street.

It was a little quaint place tucked away on the corner of a not too busy side street just down from J'Nae's office. It had an old-world Italian décor complete with red and white checkered table clothes and a small vase with a candle inside at the table center. She made sure to arrive five minutes late hoping to find Zsasha already there waiting for her.

"Oh my gosh, J'Nae! I almost didn't recognize you. You cut all your hair off and colored it too!"

"Yes, I did. I asked my hairdresser to come to the house and hook me up before I started my new job. I figured it was the perfect time for a change. So, what do you think of my new look?" J'Nae said, looking for approval.

"Gurl, I love it! You look amazing, J'Nae! Really! That short crop style fits your face. It makes you look both professional and sexy at the same time. And the attitude you walked in here with, gurl yes, yes! Trust me, You need to carry that with you at all times!"

"For real?"

"Hell yeah. You make looking like a boss bitch effortless. You go girl!"

"Awesome! That's exactly what I was going for. HBIC, Head Bitch in Charge!"

"And you do. Like game peeps game, Head Bitches peep Head Bitches. That's you all the way."

"Cool because I was aiming for low maintenance and high performance."

"So, are you still talking about your hair or are we talking about men now?" Zsasha teased.

"I wish. In fact, I might actually have a few options on that front."

"What do you mean?"

"Well, after you all set up my profile, I had 99 hits on the dating site the next morning."

"Really, 99 hits? That's probably a record of some kind. Have you contacted any of them yet?"

"Oh no, I haven't actually viewed them as of yet. I've been too busy pampering myself and getting ready for my first day of work. Actually, I kind of forgot about it for a while, until I peed on myself again. Then for some strange reason I updated my profile pics with my new look. And please don't read anything into the peeing incident and the dating site. I know you and where your mind can go and I promise you it ain't nothing like that!"

"I'm sure, especially not with ya ass anyway. And did you say peed? You actually peed on yourself or just had a little leakage?"

"Sometimes it's just some leakage and sometimes it's a bit more. And it's happened several times already and I'm afraid it's going to happen at the wrong time."

"Honey, is there ever a right time for peeing on yourself? Wait a minute. Did I just say that? Oh damn!"

"Yeah, I know, right." They both laughed.

"Never mind all that. I'm sure we're both thinking the same thing and I answered my own question, one I never should have put out there specifically with you."

"I know...with your freak nasty ass."

"You just need to see a doctor about it. It's actually a very common occurrence for women in our age group. I personally know a doctor you can see about that and from what I know, all you need is a G-shot."

44

"A what?" J'Nae asked.

"A G-shot. It's a simple in-office procedure where the doctor injects a small amount of collagen into your G-spot. It causes swelling that ultimately results in blocking bladder leakage. They do it right in the office."

"Really. That's it?"

"Yep. That's it. There are a few different procedures you can get to address various issues. One in particular is injected directly in your G-spot. I think it swells and somehow blocks something or another resulting in little to no leakage at all. You should call my doctor and schedule an appointment for a consultation. She can probably get you in this week. In fact, I'm certain of it."

"Really, now. How so?"

"She owes me a favor." Zsasha didn't want to reveal to J'Nae that Doctor Westmore was not only her doctor but a member of *Ahsasz Down Under*, the private swinger and adult pleasure club she runs with her husband Simon. In fact, the confidentiality clause in the membership application and agreement prevents her from disclosing that information even to close friends. J'Nae has always been aware of her lifestyle but she has no idea what goes on at the basement level below the art gallery.

"I'll text her cell phone now and tell her to expect a call from you shortly. The sooner the better. I'm sure you can step away to make a quick call."

"That won't be a problem, thank you."

"Don't mention it girlfriend and I really mean don't mention it, not to Rona or whitegirl. I don't tell y'all heffa's all my business. Some know this, some know that but none of you knows everything."

"I got it, no problem. I'll give her a quick call soon."

J'Nae understood her wanting to keep that between the two of them. Everybody knew Zsasha lived a slightly non-traditional lifestyle from time to time, but they all knew she had some secrets. One of which they both shared. So J'Nae was all too happy to comply.

Zsasha did as she promised and sent a text message to Dr. Westmore with J'Nae name and number and a short description regarding the nature of her visit. They finished their lunch, paid the check and exited the building going their respective ways. J'Nae could see Zsasha on her phone as she walked towards her car. A minute later she received Dr. Westmore's contact information, proving her friend to be true to her word.

Later that evening, J'Nae decided to check her online profile and review her matches. Sorting through the list she finds that she didn't receive 99 hits from 99 different individuals. One of her matches had liked the photo array the girls posted the other night and commented on each of them several times. Stalker! That's an automatic delete. But as she read through the remaining matches, she found one in particular that caught her eye.

His profile displayed his name as VinScent, an African American male 48 years of age. He was tall, handsome and of medium build, appearing to weigh about 210 pounds. His tag line read 'I enjoy life and all it has to offer. I take time to smell the roses and appreciate the scent of all the flowers in bloom. If you are a beautiful flower, please visit my profile to learn more. From there we can meet for coffee for a pleasant exchange. Hope to see you soon.'

Right at that moment, J'Nae was abruptly interrupted by a phone call from Zsasha.

"Hey sweetie, what's up?"

"Nothing girl, just scanning through some of my matches on the app you all set up for me."

"Any prospects?"

"Maybe one or two."

"Well don't be shy girlfriend, go for it."

Without giving it any more thought, J'Nae sent a quick message asking to meet Vinscent at The Coffee House the next day. He promptly responded suggesting a time and she agreed. After all, it's just coffee.

"Anyway, I was just calling to see if you'd made contact with Dr. Westmore's office yet."

"I did, yes, and I'm seeing her the day after tomorrow at 6:00 pm. She has late hours that day and said she could fit me in for a consultation."

"Cool. Do your research and ask her whatever questions you have. She's cool. I'm sure you'll like her."

"Are you really sure about her? I mean, she's got her shit together, right? She knows what she's talking about, right?"

"No doubt, she's on point. You'll see for yourself when you go in for your consultation. You're not committing to anything, just judge for yourself."

"So, you really trust this chick, huh?"

"Yeah girl, I do. I've been seeing her for several years now. Stop stressing."

"And she's the one who told you about this procedure?"

"Yes, just relax and trust me, she's done wonders for me and several women I know personally."

"Oh yeah, how so?"

"Well, some people call it vaginal rejuvenation, I like to refer to it as Pussy Pilates."

"What?"

"Pussy Pilates, it's like exercise for your pussy without actually doing any work. You just get the benefits and girl, with my lifestyle it was inevitable, hell it still is. But don't worry about it. The g-shot procedure was initially developed for women like you. Nowadays, you can get the g-shot or the o-shot depending on your issues. They are all pretty much the same as far as I know. They may have a mild side effect for a short time. I like to refer to them as happy accidents."

"Back up, women like me...what do you mean?"

"I mean women with your issue. Damn girl, stop being so sensitive. You'll be alright. Besides, you can't go on peeing on yourself every time you laugh, cough or sneeze, now can you?"

"I suppose not."

"Alright then. I don't wanna have to start handing you disposable diapers every time you walk in the gallery."

"Ha ha, real funny."

"I ain't playing." Sasha replied. "Yo ass will have a designated seat with your name on it and it'll be covered in plastic just like grandma's furniture was back in the day." Zsasha giggled.

"Girl you stupid!"

"I'm just saying relax, damn. She knows what she's doing, it's been her primary focus for several years now, and she's performed those procedures over a thousand times. Look her up online. I promise, you're in good hands."

"Okay. I'm trusting you, just know that."

"Cool and you know I wouldn't steer you wrong. Let me know how it goes and how you feel about it then. Okay?"

"Yeah, okay."

"And ask her some questions alright sista-girl, we'll talk later."

"For sure. Goodnight Zsasha."

"Night sweetie and get some rest."

Chapter 5

Taking a step inside the world of online dating J'Nae pulled up to The Coffee House, excited about the prospect. From the outside, confidence was clearly reflected by the look on her face and the way in which she carried herself. But as each step brought her closer to the mystery waiting behind door number one, her dynamic confidence gave way to the nervousness and uneasiness one would expect to feel for a first timer. But she kept it in check and proceeded on her way.

She was wearing a cream-colored snug fitting Marc Jacobs dress that came just past her knees. It was sleeveless and boasted a low-cut V-shaped neckline that showed just the right amount of cleavage. Her feet were clad in a pair of Jimmy Choo 3" inch heel pumps, matching in color dawning the same buckle and bow tie combination found on her handbag, also matching in color.

Walking into The Coffee House, she felt a bit overdressed for the occasion and realized she should have consulted her advisory panel for input and final approval. But it was too late for that now. She read somewhere online that it was important to convey your personal level of class and status on the initial meet, regardless of where you're meeting so that your potential mate knows what to expect and how to come at you if he or she is at all interested. It sets your level of expectation; no scrubs allowed sort of speak.

Taking a seat facing the door, J'Nae looked around and didn't see anyone who resembled the photo Vinscent had on his profile. She noticed a few African Americans seated by themselves throughout The Coffee House, but no one stood out. She did, however, catch a glance of a couple she passed on her way in. The gentleman was wearing a brown suede suit jacket, button down shirt and tie with exceptionally large cuff links at the end of each sleeve. Seated across from him, was a woman wearing a long floral house dress and flip flops, with her hair pulled away from her face. She was cute enough, but they seemed like an unlikely pair. As they both stood up as if to leave, it appeared the woman was a bit more anxious to leave than the man. She was reaching over to hand him something when J'Nae was startled by the barista and took her eyes off the pair momentarily.

"Hi Ms. Carter, good to see you again. May I take your order?"

"Hi, and yes you can. May I have a vanilla latte with soy milk if you don't mind." J'Nae replied.

"Coming right up."

As the barista walked away J'Nae turned her attention back to the couple at the table near the door but they were nowhere in sight. She glanced around the room just in time to spot a man waving to her and calling her name as he approached her table.

"Good evening, Nay Nay, right? I'm VinScent. May I sit down?"

J'Nae was at a loss for words. This was the same guy she just saw seated at a table with the woman in the house dress. That was strange, she thought.

"Oh, hi VinScent. Yes, I'm Nay Nay, but you can call me J'Nae. Nice to meet you."

"Mind if I have a seat?" he asked.

Without waiting for an answer, he sat down at the table with a freshly brewed cup of coffee he had obviously just picked up at the self-serve counter. He was beaming a big smile, full of eagerness and excitement.

"Wow, you look good enough to eat, girl." He said leaning forward. "Did you bring them, or do you still have them on?"

Totally confused J'Nae frowned.

"What? What did you say? Did I bring what?"

"Your panties." He stated while handing her two crisp one-hundred-dollar bills. "The bathroom is right there so you can go in there to take them off if you're still wearing them."

J'Nae, completely caught off guard and floored, could only utter a few words.

"Excuse me, there must be some mistake. I'm supposed to have a meet and greet with a gentleman named VinScent that I connected with online. I don't know what you're talking about."

"You're NayNay411, right?"

"Yes, that's my screenname."

"I'm VinScent, that's V-i-n-S-c-e-n-t with a capital 'S', emphasizing Scent, get it? The deal is I pay you $200 for a pair of your dirty panties. How else will I know if I want to date you."

"Motha fucker please!" she yelled as she stood up to leave. "Obviously, you've mistaken me for some trick-or-troll like the one who just left here. Get away from me you freak! And lose the digits. Oh yea, that's right, I never gave them to you! Note to self…. Remind me to thank God for dodging that bullet!"

VinScent remained seated as J'Nae turned to leave. Walking out the door she thought her exit looked a lot like the one she all but witnessed a few minutes earlier with him and the other young woman that J'Nae now knew was also anxious to get away from him. She didn't look happy at all but must have been desperate since she did hand him something she was certain were her panties before her abrupt exit. This fool is running around town trying to buy dirty panties. Damn! Freak nasty SOB, just freak nasty!

Shaking it off, J'Nae walked next door to Ahsasz and could see a hint of light peeking through that appeared to be coming from the back where Zsasha's office was located. Without giving it any thought, she pulled out the key to the gallery Zsasha forgot to collect a few weeks ago, and let herself inside, locking the door securely behind her. Glad to be away from that freak, she headed towards Zsasha's office fully expecting to see her seated behind the desk. Instead, what she found was another door which she always assumed to be a closet of some sort. It was partially ajar and obviously not a closet but a door leading into a hallway she'd never knew existed,

Noticing Zsasha's handbag on the credenza behind her desk, she figured Zsasha was here probably working on inventory or something.

Eager to share her ordeal with her girlfriend, J'Nae went through the door, and followed along the hallway which led to a short flight of stairs. She continued, while thinking this is an odd place for storage but kept walking anyway. A minute or two later she began to hear the faint sounds of music playing just beyond where she stood. It was an odd type of music; unlike anything she'd known Zsasha to listen to. Curiosity got the best of her, and she continued to walk towards the sound and what she could now clearly identify as a red light shining through from underneath a door that was now right in front of her.

Instinctively she reached down to open the door and found it unlocked. Without a moment's hesitation, she stepped inside what appeared to be the backside of a storage room that didn't appear to store any artwork. She took a few steps forward toward another door also revealing a bright red light. Opening the door, she continued until she was in full view of an ongoing event involving multiple people and multiple things. At that moment, she froze where she stood. What she saw was beyond her wildest dreams and imagination.

It was a dark room with red fluorescent lighting glowing on the skin of everyone and almost everything she could see. The dark room held a small crowd of people in various attire. Some were in costumes, some talking and drinking with one another, while others were hugged up in an embrace and quite touchy feely. Several of them were scantily dressed, men and women alike. To the left of her was a full-scale bar, the front of which was covered in purple leather with matching purple leather seats with a gold-plated frame.

The large room contained 4 stripper poles strategically placed throughout the room as well as two cages dangling from the ceiling with people in each. There were round tables of various sizes situated throughout and most were taken. Looking around at the obvious nature of things J'Nae could think of only one possible scenario that made any sense...Zsasha, Zsasha and Simon.

"Girl! What are you doing down here and how did you get in? A voice called softly. Zsasha hurried over to where J'Nae stood, grabbing her arm, and pulling her in close.

"Zsasha. What's this all about?" J'Nae inquired. "I was just next-door meeting..."

"We'll talk about that later." Zsasha interrupted. "Right now, I just need you to go with it. Just follow my lead!"

"Huh, what?"

Before Zsasha could repeat herself, she turned her attention to the attractive couple walking up just a few feet behind her.

"Alice, Ralph, this is my friend and business associate Madame J. She backs me up from time to time when I'm unavailable and assists me in keeping things running smoothly. Most of the time she functions behind the scenes, so you won't see her much."

"Nice to meet you." Both Alice and Ralph spoke politely.

J'Nae did her best to hide her shock and confusion while playing along as requested. Whatever questions she had for her friend would have to wait. She was smart enough to know that now was not the time to ask them.

"Likewise." J'Nae replied while nodding her head in acknowledgement. "Anytime I can be of assistance..."

"I was just finishing up a private tour for our first-time guest. Why don't we all head back to my office, shall we?"

With that, Zsasha led the group back the same way J'Nae had entered but with very little dialogue. Once inside, she directed her guests to have a seat.

"I'll be back in a moment. I need to get some files for Madame J and they're in the other office. Just give me a minute. Madame J, follow me."

The two of them left the office and headed into the main showroom before uttering a word.

"Damn girl, I had no idea you were getting it in like that. And right here up under our noses!"

"Actually, you know very well Simon and I swing. That's been our chosen lifestyle since before we got married."

"Yeah, but this is different. What was all that?"

"Sista girl, you ain't supposed to know none of this."

"Well, it's a little late for that now, don't you think?"

"Ah, yeah."

"So, what's up? What is all that?"

"Well, that's *Ahsasz Down Under*. The swingers club Simon and I own, operate and manage under the gallery."

"Ahsasz, Ahsasz. Oh, I get it now. Asses Down Under. Oh my! And who were all those people"

"Now that ain't none of your business. Our clients pay an extremely high price for confidentiality and anonymity. You need to forget everything and everyone you saw in there. And you can't share this with anyone, not even Vonne or Rona. Understand?"

"Yeah, sure. Of course. I got you. But seriously, Rona doesn't know?"

"Not anyone, ya hear! I can't have you fucking up my money, chasing folks away and shit. And stop asking questions. I have no answers for you, for real."

"Okay, okay. I got it. Don't worry, I won't say a thing, ever."

"And how the hell did you get inside anyway?"

"The key you gave me a few weeks ago when you wanted me to lock up."

"Damn, I forgot about that. Why didn't you say anything?"

"I didn't think about it. I mean we're here all the time anyway, I just figured it wasn't a big deal."

"Well, it is, that's my bad. That one's on me."

"But look, it's all good. No need to stress yourself. I won't say anything, I promise."

"I can't deal with this right now. I got people waiting. I gotta go."

"Alright, go handle your business, whatever it is."

"I mean it J'Nae, not anyone."

"Of course, of course, but we're gonna talk about this some more later, right? I got questions and I want answers." J'Nae said, grinning.

"Fine, whatever girl. Now go. Go."

"I'm going, I'm going. What are you about to do now?

"Damage control sweetie, damage control."

J'Nae walked out the front door of the gallery headed towards her car key still in hand. Despite the shock and awe, she was feeling, her senses kicked in and she immediately turned around intending to return the key. Instead of going back inside interrupting whatever Zsasha had going on, she made the quick decision to lock the front door, leaving it as she found it. Unbelievable. Ropes, chains, swings 'Oh my' she uttered as she walked past a car that was parked behind hers. Once inside she glanced up at her rearview mirror and saw a man sitting in the driver seat. Even in the dark she could clearly see VinScent with a pair of lady's panties on his head and face. He sat there smashing the crotch of the panties into his nose, rubbing them back and forth across his face. She recognized the brown suede jacket and large cuff links from earlier that evening. It was him; it was VinScent all right. The first freak show she saw that night.

Shaking it off yet again, she started her car and headed home. Throughout the entire drive, her mind kept going over everything that happened that day. She wasn't totally surprised about Zsasha and Simons' involvement in an adult club. No, not at all. It was the fact they owned, managed, and operated it, and did so right under her nose, literally.

Just how many times had she been seen coming or going or even inside the gallery sipping wine and such? Did everyone know about it but her? What kind of people game through the club and the gallery for that matter? Exhaling, she turned the corner onto her street with her mind still twirling from the images of the past few hours; those of VinScent sitting in his car with panties on his head, the ropes, chains, and swings under the gallery. Damn, everybody has lost their damn mind.

Pulling into her driveway, she didn't notice her neighbor, L.B. across the street, out walking his dog. He spoke to her, but she didn't speak back, overwhelmed and preoccupied with the events of the day. She made a mental note to reach out to him the next day and ask him to be her date the following week when she was scheduled to go out with the girls. But with everything that had happened that evening, it would have to wait. Once inside, she decided to go straight to bed and shut it down for the night. She needed to process everything that had occurred. She quickly drank a full glass of wine and went straight to bed. For tonight, it was a rap.

Chapter 6

The next two days had been mostly uneventful for J'Nae. L.B. accepted her invitation to Club Nonchalant on Saturday and her consultation with Dr. Westmore was this evening. She arrived on time and felt good about the information Zsasha shared with her about the procedure along with the information she researched on her own. Even though she found herself momentarily feeling less and less confident about her choice, she believed Zsasha was right about one thing, that she is too young to have this issue, especially since the problem will only get worse over time. She knew she had to do something, so she might as well listen to what Dr. Westmore had to say. Afterall, it's just a consult.

She entered the lobby of the small clinic, checked in and took a seat. A short time later her name was called, and she was ushered into an exam room and given a few forms and instructions followed up with a traditional gown given for most gyn appointments.

"Is this really necessary?" J'Nae asked the nurse. "I'm just here for a consultation."

"Yes ma'am, it is. Usually, Dr. Westmore will give you a quick exam to make sure you're even a candidate before you go any further. It saves time in the end." The nurse replied.

"Um, okay then."

J'Nae did as requested. Now partially disrobed and sitting on the exam table waiting patiently for Dr. Westmore, to her surprise, the Dr. didn't keep her waiting for long. In fact, she was like a whirlwind. Suddenly she was there, introducing herself, going over the procedure and what it entails etc. Asking if there were any questions she could answer or concerns she could explain. Then, just as quickly as she appeared, she was gone. But not without saying she'd be right back to give me a quick pelvic exam to make sure everything was in order and that her nurse would be in shortly. J'Nae tried to relax even though she felt a bit rushed. The nurse came in and guided her into the normal position for a pelvic exam. J'Nae, like most women have been in this position many times, was still a bit nervous. She didn't have a history with this doctor, so it was to be expected. Lying back, she watched the nurse setup the tray table next to her with a speculum and other gynecological devices she had seen before. Moments later Dr. Westmore came in, holding her sterile and gloved hands upright in front of her. The nurse continued setting up the tray table while Dr. Westmore positioned herself at the end of the exam table.

"Ms. Carter, this won't take long, and it will be completely painless, I promise." said Dr. Westmore. J'Nae smiled and nodded. She just wanted to get this part over with. Although pelvic exams are not painful, it's always a bit unnerving with a new doctor.

"Okay, you'll feel something cold, it's just the speculum."

"Okay." J'Nae said.

"Now just a slight pinch." Dr. Westmore finished. After a bit more poking and prodding it was over.

"Okay Ms. Carter, we're done, alright. You're good to go. No sexual intercourse for the next 48 hours and no douching and don't submerge your body in water. Showers only. If you experience any bleeding, painful swelling or discomfort of any kind, call us right away. The procedure was...." Dr. Westmore was abruptly cut off by J'Nae sudden outburst.

"The procedure? What do you mean the procedure? This was a pelvic exam, right?"

J'Nae, obviously blindsided by Dr. Westmore's statement, began to ask herself what was different about this exam. She'd had them a few dozen times over the years but found herself questioning what was different about this one? She knew it was something. Something was a bit off, but it didn't register at that moment.

"Ms. Carter, the procedure I just administered was a G-shot. It will be perfectly normal to experience certain changes in how your body responds to stimulus. Intentional or unintentional. Some of the common yet short term side effects from this treatment may include a sense of urgency to urinate; injection site tenderness with or without pain; feeling bloated along with pressure on the bladder; headaches and lastly some spontaneous orgasms of varying intensity and duration. These will only last until your body has time to adjust to your amplified g-spot. It shouldn't be more than a few weeks, at the most but it can vary for everyone."

"Oh my God! I came in for a consultation; to simply discuss the procedure. Your nurse insisted on the pelvic exam to see if I was a good candidate. I never said I made up my mind to actually have the procedure. Are you kidding me! You actually gave me the G-shot?"

"Yes, Ms. Carter. I did. You signed the consent form. It's right -----"

Realizing she had just been injected with the collagen-based filler by accident, J'Nae was furious. She hadn't made this decision. The decision had been made for her. None of this was supposed to happen, at least not like this. She was just doing her due diligence on the product and its side effects.   "Now what? You injected me prematurely. What exactly am I supposed to do now?"

"Prematurely", said Dr. Westmore. Were you planning on getting the injection anyway?" asked the doctor. "Did this just happen a bit sooner than expected?" Dr. Westmore sounded hopeful. Maybe, just maybe the situation unfolding would resolve itself.

"Ms. Carter, …. Ms. Carter…."

J'Nae hesitated before she answered, thinking long and hard. The truth of the matter is that all the research she'd done indicated positive results. Nothing she found about the procedure was negative or indicated any significant long-term risk. Everything had pointed towards going forward with the injection.

"Yes, I probably would have consented to the injection sometime in the future. But the problem is that I hadn't consented. You took that choice away from me. And now, it's done. It's been done."

"I apologize for the confusion." Dr. Westmore spoke in a sympathetic voice.

Did this bitch just apologize for the confusion? Is she for real, J'Nae thought? An apology seemed useless in this situation. This bitch needs her ass beat. A good ole' fashioned beat down, sister to sister, kick your heels off and remove your hair piece, beat down. Right here in her office so that every time she walks through the office doors, she'll remember the spot where she got her ass beat and why. And that's really what the takeaway from this should be. Why and how this shit happened. And what she should do to make certain this never happens again.

J'Nae rushes home furious about what just occurred. She couldn't believe what had just happened and was still in shock when she picked up the phone to call Zsasha.

"Zsasha!"

"Hey girl, what's up?"

"I just left Dr. Westmore's office."

"How did it go?"

"How did it go? Let me tell you how it went! It went too damn far, that's how it went!"

"What's going on? Why are you so upset?"

"That bitch did more than answer my questions, she actually gave me the G-shot!"

"Oh really? So, you decided to get it then, huh?"

"Hell no! That crazy doctor gave it to me by accident!"

"She did what?"

"Yeah, by accident."

"How the hell did that happen?"

"I don't know Zsasha. She was in then she was out then she was back in again. It all happened so fast."

"Well wait a minute. We ain't talking about a shot in the arm. You had to assume the position. Care to explain?"

"Nurse ratchet said she had to give me a quick exam to see if I was even a candidate or not. That's why I assumed the position."

"Oh, I see. So, what are you gonna do now?"

"I don't know girl, it just happened. I'm all over the place right now."

"But you're okay, right?"

"Yeah, yeah I'm okay."

"Probably just need to get some rest and see how you feel about it tomorrow."

"Yeah, you're probably right." J'Nae sighed.

"It'll be okay."

"I guess. Hey, I gotta go, somebody's at the door."

"Okay. Well call me later if you want to talk, otherwise I'll see you Thursday evening at the gallery."

"Oh yeah, we'll talk...about this and that other situation."

"Yeah, yeah, okay."

"But look, don't mention this to Rona or Vonne. I haven't told them anything, not even that I was considering the shot. I don't even remember which one she gave me."

"Damn girl, my bad. Dr. Westmore always has her shit together. I'm so sorry."

"Me too, just keep it to yourself for now, okay?"

"Okay, no problem. I got you."

"Goodnight Zsasha."

"Goodnight sweetie."

Hanging up the phone, J'Nae headed towards the door with little to no enthusiasm. She could hear her visitor knock for the second time. Peeping out the side window, she could see it was L.B. and he was carrying something with him. J'Nae opened the door but made no effort to smile or seemed pleased.

"Hey J'Nae. How are you? Hope I didn't catch you at a bad time."

"Actually, you did. I've had a stressful day and just want to eat and go to bed. I'm sorry."

"No problem. I just wanted to drop this off for you. It's just a little something to celebrate your new job." He said as he passed her the gift bag. "I didn't see any reason to wait until Friday since you've already started working. But I'm sorry to have intruded." He mumbled as he turned to leave.

"Hold on a minute L.B. That's very sweet of you, you didn't have to do that."

"Well, I wanted to."

J'Nae shrugged a moment while scratching her head indicating she was contemplating what to say next.

"Well thank you. Would you like to come in for a drink before I turn in for the night?" she asked.

"I don't want to intrude."

"It's fine, really. I need to get out of this head space I'm in. Please, come in and join me. I could use the company and the distraction. Come, have a seat."

"Don't mind if I do."

"Dark or light?"

"I'll have whatever you're having, how about that." He smiled.

"Okay, suit yourself."

With that, J'Nae walked to the kitchen, retrieved some glasses and ice then made her way to the bar. She poured each of them a shot of bourbon and took a seat on the sofa next to her guest.

"So, tell me, who pissed off my baby today? Give me their name, address, and social security. I'll make sure they never bother you again." He joked.

"Ahh, that's sweet but not a good idea. It's a situation I need to work out for myself."

"Well, I hope it's not work related."

"No, not at all."

"Cool, because it's a bit too soon for all that, you just started."

"Yes, I did, and thank you for the gift. It was very thoughtful of you."

"You're welcome, but you haven't opened it yet."

"Right again."

"Why not open it now?"

"Okay."

J'Nae picked up the gift bag she had placed on the floor next to her feet. Inside was an inspirational desk sculpture of a person pushing a large ball uphill. The quote on the base of it read: The best way to predict the future is to create it yourself.

62

"That's so cool. Thank you again, really."

"You're welcome."

"I have the perfect spot for it on my credenza."

"Great. I hope it inspires you to go after the things you want in life."

"It's nice, really." J'Nae reiterated.

"I'm glad you like it."

"I do, I really do."

"Cool. Now I'm going to leave you to do what you do. We're still on for Saturday night, right?"

"Yes, of course."

"Okay. I'll see you then."

"Goodnight L.B. and again, thank you."

"You're more than welcome. Goodnight."

Closing the door, J'Nae sighed a bit of relief. It was a good idea to ask him in. The anger had subsided to the point she was able to get a good night's sleep. Whether or not it was him or the bourbon was yet to be decided but nonetheless she was relaxed.

As she prepared for bed, her mind continued to drift towards L.B. and she wondered why she'd waited so long to give him the time of day, outside of being neighborly and their professional relationship. He really seemed like a nice guy. Climbing into bed, she cut the TV on and turned to the Lifetime channel where she knew she would find a good drama. She cut the volume down low enough to hear but not high enough to disturb her sleep. Within a few minutes she was out, resting comfortably no longer distraught by the events of the day.

* * * * *

Thursday evening, J'Nae and Vonne arrived at Ahsasz at the same time. Zsasha was busying herself in the gallery as they came in and sat down where they always sit. Zsasha already had wine glasses and her choice of wine at the table.

"Hey girl. I see you're ready for us tonight." J'Nae commented.

"Yeah, to what do we owe this special treatment?" Vonne asked as she poured herself a glass of wine.

"Nothing special. I'm just dealing with a few things tonight and can't stay as long as I planned."

"What's going on?" J'Nae asked.

"For starters, I may have to postpone the gallery showing."

"Okay, well that's not so bad, is it?'

"Yeah, it is. Making changes this late in the game causes all kinds of problems, especially when you're dealing with the media and the date has already been announced."

"Oh, I can see where that could be problematic." J'Nae acknowledged.

"Why not come on over here and have a glass of wine, might help relieve some stress." Vonne suggested.

"I wish it were that simple."

"Well, do you want to cancel? We can leave if you're not feeling it, we understand." J'Nae replied.

Zsasha thought about her options for a second and decided to take the approach 'shit happens' and let it go.

"Hell no! In fact, go ahead and pour me a glass. I'm on my way!"

Vonne didn't hesitate to do just that, topping herself off to boot.

"So girls, what y'all got going on? Anything to take my mind off my own shit would be great."

J'Nae was anxious to talk more about her recent discovery but knew that had to be a one-on-one conversation. And since Zsasha was already stressed out about something, she didn't feel good about getting in her ass about Dr. Westmore and her screw up; it just wasn't a good time. But there were other issues she could share openly with the girls like L.B. and his congratulatory gift and the time they spent talking on a more personal level. But before she could utter a word, Vonne had a verbal outbreak she obviously couldn't contain.

"Lee's been acting secretively these past few days and I don't know why."

Lee Hall was a former NBA basketball player who was forcibly retired in his prime as a result of a severe injury that deemed him unsuitable to play ball. The 6' 5" tall African American had trouble dealing with the sudden loss of his career which inevitably led to all sorts of inappropriate behavior including bad investments, gambling debt and infidelity.

"Really? Just out of the blue?" Zsasha inquired. "So what do you think that's about?"

"I don't know, but I'm determined to find out... tonight."

"Are you sure you want to do that right now? Why not wait until you have some evidence or indication of what's going on." J'Nae suggested.

"No time like the present. Besides, I'm already liquored up!"

"Precisely a good reason to pick another time. Don't you want to be in your right mind, have your wits about you?" J'Nae asked.

"Oh, it's happening sista girl, it's happening tonight!"

"Um, hey Zsasha, what happened with Rona?" J'Nae said purposely changing the conversation. "Why isn't she here?"

"She said she had to meet up with somebody tonight, said it couldn't wait and that she'd see us Saturday night."

"Oh wow, okay."

J'Nae was a bit puzzled with Zsasha's explanation. Rona is the most reliable one among the group. Anytime she needs to change plans, she always calls or texts letting everybody know. A creature of habit for sure, especially when it came to us. Why would it be any different this time, she thought?

"Well did she say anything specific?" J'Nae asked.

"   No, not really. She was real casual about it. She just had to meet someone. I'm sure everything's good."

"If you say so." J'Nae responded.

"Hell, call her yourself if you're so concerned." Vonne slurred.

"You can do that J'Nae, but if you ask me, you're over analyzing it." Zsasha remarked.

"Well, you do whatever you feel you need to do. I'm out. I've got my own issues to deal with tonight. You did say you couldn't stay long so I'll see y'all later."

"Night Vonne." J'Nae replied while Zsasha just nodded her head and mumbled something under her breath. Vonne gathered her things and left the gallery.

J'Nae sat in silence for a few minutes, still bothered by Rona's absence. Zsasha was definitely preoccupied and said she wanted to keep things short, so she decided to follow Vonne's lead.

"Well, it is late, and you said you had something to do, so I'd better go too. If you're ready, I'll walk out with you. Where's your car parked?"

"Out back where it always is. But no girl, I'm good. There's a few things I need to take care of really quickly, but I'll see you Saturday night... with bells on!"

"Bells...you...I don't think so but yeah, see you then. Be safe sweetie. Love you."

"Back at cha."

J'Nae made her way to her car without incident and Zsasha continued the work she had started before Vonne and J'Nae arrived. She hated keeping secrets from her friends, but they didn't need to be all up in her business knowing everything going on. Especially J'Nae now that she knows about the *Ahsasz Down Under*. She needs to be even more careful about her affairs so she can protect her clients and her business.

Chapter 7

Club Nonchalant was situated between club H2O and the convention center, all beachfront and located near the heart of downtown DC. Inside Club Nonchalant were several bars and dance areas spread throughout 3 floors. Each area had its own theme and color combination, yet all were designed and decorated with elegance. The owners spared no expense in the setup and layout of Club Nonchalant. Even the patio area had the finest décor including covered tables on the patio level and fire pits for those exterior tables on the ground level.

Soft music and a somewhat familiar voice of Jill Scott filled the room as she finished singing one of her classic songs. It was the end of her first set before Leela James or one of the other well knowns took the stage. Everyone was there. Vonne and Lee, Zsasha and Simon, Rona and Ricardo and J'Nae and L.B. were all seated at a large table in the VIP section. Rona had arranged and secured the tickets, and everyone was impressed with the outcome.

The night felt magical. Everyone looked superb and appeared to be getting along quite well. Vonne and Lee seemed to be happily enjoying each other's company and most shockingly Simon was exceptionally nice to J'Nae. Ever since her late husband and his BFF passed away, he had become quite distant and even unfriendly to her a lot of the time but tonight, he was almost his old self. It was going to be a good night, a great night and everyone was relaxed and having a good time.

The lineup consisted of various well known artists including Jill Scott, Leela James, Marsha Ambrosius and Ledisi plus a string of other female artists. It was unusual having so many top-notch artists performing on the same stage on the same night, but Rona explained this was a benefit concert they all volunteered to perform at in support of victims of sex trafficking.

The crowd clapped for quite a while and most audience members gave a standing ovation as the second artist finished her set and left the stage.

"Intermission is starting. Ladies, now would be a good time to visit the powder room." Rona stated.

"I'm already there." Vonne replied, leading the pack in that direction.

"I can't believe the lineup tonight. This is amazing, Rona. Thank you. All of you, thank you for doing all this."

"You're welcome, besides, I had the hookup. It's for a good cause and you're a good cause so it's a win-win situation." Rona teased.

"So that's what I've become, huh, a cause?"

"Girl, we're just happy you're out of the house, working and even dating a bit. All of which are long overdue by the way." Zsasha confirmed

"And so is this trip to the restroom. Excuse me."

Zsasha and J'Nae headed straight for the stalls while Vonne and Rona leaned in at the counter to freshen up their makeup. VIP guests have a private restroom not open to the general audience and no line to wait in. Inside an attendant stood ready to assist the ladies with anything they needed during their visit.

"You and Lee seem to be getting along well." Rona commented. "Things must be going well."

"Girl, he's been really sweet since he landed his ass in the doghouse…. trying to make what he did alright."

"What did he do this time?" Rona asked.

"Well, he told my dad it was ok to come visit for a while, and he did it without talking to me first."

"He did what?"

"Uh huh, and during the week of my dinner party."

"Ouch!"

"Yeah, he answered the phone the other night, intoxicated of course and dad took full advantage of him, chatting him up knowing he was drunk, and Lee fell for it."

"I would have thought he knew better than that after all this time."

"So did I, however my dad convinced him he was coming to make peace. He swore he had changed, and things would be different this time and just wanted the chance to be a better father."

"Well, do you believe him?"

"Hell no! I want no part of that bullshit. I've had enough of his lies and delusions to last two lifetimes. When he's around me, I don't function well. I become discombobulated and every part of my life suffers as a result. I just can't handle him and the way he treats me, and I certainly don't want to be dealing with all that bullshit while trying to expand my business. I have a dinner party scheduled where I'm planning to schmooze and entertain some very influential people I may or may not need to open a few doors for my expansion plans. The last thing I need is to be distracted by him and the way he always manages to get under my skin. It's just a bad idea, all the way around, just a bad idea."

"I get it, trust me, I understand. I've heard the stories more than once and I sympathize with you. It really is a bad time for him to be here."

"It is. The last time he showed up was devastating for me. It took me a long time to pull myself up out of that dark hole."

"Was that before or after you met and married Lee?"

"Right after we met but before we married."

"Makes sense." Rona mumbled.

"What does?" Vonne asked.

"Never mind."

"No, say it. What makes sense?"

Rona wanted to tell Vonne what she was really thinking. That basically she substituted one asshole for another when she married Lee. But she thought better of it and being quick on her feet, she came up with another plausible explanation without hesitation.

"It makes sense why Lee said it was okay for him to visit. He's never witnessed the destruction that comes with that relationship firsthand, has he?"

69

"No, not really. They've only met once, at the hospital when my mom was sick. That was about the same time Lee was dealing with his own shit with the team. He wasn't really tuned in at the time."

"Well, there's your answer. He didn't really know."

"Trust me when I tell you, Lee is well informed about dear old dad!" Just then, J'Nae exited the stall in time to see one of the performers enter the restroom.

"Hello ladies. I hope you're all enjoying the show."

Vonne and J'Nae were speechless.

"Rona dear, it looks like your friends are at a loss for words."

"Hey sista girl." Rona said, giving her friend a big hug. "It's so good to see you. Look at you, you look amazing!"

"Ah sugar, you're so sweet. Life has been good."

"I bet...you've been living your life like it's golden, huh..." Rona chuckled.

"Yes, I have, now you ladies hurry on back to your seats now, ya hear. The next set is about to begin."

A moment later, Zsasha exited the stall, having missed the entire conversation. After washing her hands, she put on a bit of lotion and handed the attendant a few dollars for her services and looked around noticing J'Nae and Vonne's faces.

"What, did I miss something?" she asked.

"Ah, yeah." Vonne stuttered. "That would be ---."

"We're all about to miss her." Rona interrupted. "She's about to be back on stage. Let's go."

J'Nae was still obviously in shock and had no idea Rona was personally acquainted with her and never said anything about it. More secrets, she thought to herself.

"Yeah, I met her sometime back through the course of my real estate business." Rona explained.

"Well, you could've said something, especially taking us to an event she'd be headlining." J'Nae said, finally able to open her mouth and speak.

"My bad, but y'all know I meet famous people during the course of business and sometimes it involves confidentiality agreements. Y'all know what's up."

"Don't worry about them silly bitches." Zsasha remarked. "They still don't know what they wanna be when they grow up!"

"Whatever." Vonne said, rolling her eyes at Zsasha.

"But hey, before I forget ladies, I set a new date for the Gallery Showing."

No one said a word or even acknowledged what she said.

"Hello? Are any of you silly bitches listening to me?"

No one was paying any attention to Zsasha and her comments as they were all two anxious to return to their seats for the next musical ensemble. They made it back to their table just as the next artists walked on stage.

"I've had a blessed life thus far. God's been good to me. Good friends, a wonderful husband....my girl Rona......My life is Golden. I'm living it and I'm loving it!"

Just then the music began to play and in moments her amazing voice filled the room. The girls now ready for their third round of drinks were all feeling entertained and in full swing of the evening. J'Nae volunteered to snag the waitress once she caught sight of her again. And amid the crowd, she recognized a former classmate across the room at the bar closest to the VIP area. He smiled and nodded as he was obviously staring back at her.

His name was Rick Mosely, and he was a bit younger than J'Nae. He was 6'2" inches tall, honey brown skinned with dimples on his cheek. His body was athletically toned with muscle definition more than worthy of the tight shirt he wore underneath his sports jacket. His deliciousness was oozing from every orifice of his body and in that moment, J'Nae's body shuttered. He signaled to her to come over and she could not resist, completely disregarding her date sitting next to her. Getting up suddenly to get the drinks was all she could do to thwart the magnetic attraction pulling her in his direction.

"I see an old classmate of mine at the bar. It'll be quicker if I order the next round at the bar instead of waiting for our server. Is everybody good with the same thing?"

Nobody paid any attention to her and what she was talking about. Ol' girl was singing, and their table was just ten or twelve feet from the stage. Even though she was the guest of honor, and they were there to celebrate her, she took a backseat to Jill Scott, Leela James and the other A list performers appearing on stage.

Walking towards the bar, she felt his eyes on her burning right through to her inner core, revealing the sinful thoughts that were going through her mind. What's wrong with me, she thought to herself. I know better than this. He is way too young for me and I have a date. But those thoughts left as quickly as they came and no matter how many excuses she tried to tell herself, she kept coming up with more and reasons to move forward, such as 'hot young man' and 'good looking motha fucker', 'sexy son of a bitch'...what the fuck?

"This ain't me." She said to herself.

"Mam?" remarked the bartender, looking perplexed.

"Oh, my bad. I was just singing out loud." J'Nae uttered, unable to think of a more appropriate excuse for her apparent outburst. She ordered a round of drinks for her table and asked for them to be delivered. Momentarily she wondered if the bartender could read her mind, or had she really blurted out what she was thinking. After handing off her credit card she sat down on one of the wooden bar chairs and waited for it to be returned.

Within moments, Rick, her former classmate approached and was standing directly to her left. She had no chance to gather herself before he sprang into action.

"Hey J'Nae, it's so good to see you." He said while extending his hand.

"Rick, right?" she replied, struggling to hear him over the music. "I remember you from class a while back."

"Wow, you look amazing! How have you been J'Nae? Its obvious life's been treating you well."

"Thank you, yeah, everything is good. Started a new job recently. How about you? How have you been?" J'Nae asked, trying to talk over the music.

"Not as well as I'm doing now." He said, leaning in, all the while grinning. "Are you here with anyone?"

"Yes, I am. A few of my friends, and um, my neighbor friend of mine. Just out celebrating my new job."

J'Nae knew she was giving off a vibe that didn't reflect her immediate thoughts and feelings. Her mind was saying one thing and her body something else. Just then, Rick leaned in even closer, his cheek to her cheek, in a voice somewhat unsettling he whispered. "Are you ever going to let me take you out, Ms. fine and sexy?"

J'Nae took a deep breath and exhaled. But before she could get her words out, he spoke again.

"I don't know what you're afraid of. I'm not going to hurt you or take anything from you that you do not want to give freely. I'm only asking to spend some time with you. Get to know you on a personal level. Enjoy each other's company, outside the classroom environment we shared some time ago. Can we do that?"

Crossing her legs, J'Nae felt a shiver down her spine and a sudden tingle in her groin area in response to his hand gently grazing hers. Instinctively she repositioned herself, uncrossing her legs and then crossing them again, switching the position of her right and left legs. Looking directly in his eyes she wondered why she had been denying herself all this time. Afterall, he's an adult and she is too. Uncrossing her legs once again, her left leg dropped off the bar stool and she rested her tippy toe on the floor. Without noticing, she scooted up and over to the left of the bar stool so that her crotch was resting on the left edge of the stool, all the while having moved much closer to her former classmate.

"I've been admiring you for some time now, J'Nae Carter, and I must say, you are a divinely beautiful and sexy woman."

J'Nae now, fully aroused, started to breathe heavier as he continued to flirt.

"I can tell you're feeling the same attraction as I am. Your mouth ain't saying much but your body language is. Let's have dinner soon."

As he continued to speak, her body continued to react. As each nerve ending in her body was stimulated and fully aroused, the intensity increased enough to disrupt her normal breathing pattern making it difficult for her to speak. She knew he was waiting for a response, but she was unable to give one.

"No need to hold out on me J'Nae, relax and just go with the flow."

"Oh." She said, barely audible. "I...I--" she took a breath as she tried to regain her composure. She was unsuccessful. Not realizing she had leaned to the left and slightly forward shifting her weight accordingly while pressing her left tippy toe to the floor which provided the resistance she needed as she inconspicuously grinded her crotch along the outer edge of the bar stool enjoying the hardness and the pressure on her clit.

"What's the matter?" he whispered as he noticed her facial expression change.

"I can't. No, no, I can't...uh um." she mumbled.

And there it was., She climaxed right there where she sat, nearly cheek to cheek with this hot young man that had been after her affection. After she exhaled and began to regain her focus, she could hear his voice becoming clear.

"Are you okay?"

"She jumped up from the bar stool, a bit out of breath and obviously flushed and said, "I can't, I can't. I gotta go."

J'Nae turned to leave but Rick reached out and slightly tugged at her arm pulling her back in towards him. Handing her his card he said, "In case you change your mind, beautiful."

J'Nae walked back to her table, tucking her credit card in her purse. Caught up in her physical feelings of what just transpired, she was unaware the set was ending. Everyone stood for a standing ovation just as J'Nae rejoined her group.

"I was beginning to worry about you, girl. Everything alright?" Zsasha asked.

"Oh yeah, sure. It's just a busy night. You know how long it takes to get a drink on a night like this. It's packed in here."

The group was soon served the last round of drinks while the D.J. played various soulful melodies. While they sat around drinking and discussing their favorite songs of the night as well as songs from other artists in which they shared mutual admiration, J'Nae faded in and out, making every effort to hide her distraction or lack of interest in their conversation.

The ride home was filled with the soft sounds of Floetrys' album Floetic. 'Say Yes' was currently playing at a volume high enough to enjoy but low enough to hear each other speaking. J'Nae, still in a state of arousal and buzzed from the fourth lemon drop she downed that evening, allowed the music to free her mind and body and relax. She looked over at L.B. while he drove and wondered what he was waiting for? I'm so ready, she thought. That episode back at the bar was just an entrée to what she really wanted to indulge in. Her body was more than ready to take the next step. And why not him? After all, they've known each other as neighbors for a few years. L.B. was certainly no stranger. And now that she dipped her toe in the sand, she was eager to dive straight into the water, the deep end.

"The show was awesome, don't you think?" he asked.

"Absolutely. Jill Scott is amazing." J'Nae replied. "You know she came into the VIP restroom between sets and introduced herself while we were in there freshening up."

"Really?"

"Yeah. Apparently, she knows Rona quite well. Sorority sisters or something."

"And Rona never said anything to you guys?"

"Well, no, not specifically. She actually met a few famous people through the course of business."

"And what business is that, again?" L.B. asked inquisitively.

"Her business. Rona Wright Realty."

"Oh, yea, yea, yea. So, which one was she now?"

J'Nae looked suspiciously out of the corner of her eye letting the look on her face answer his question.

"Sweetheart, I was just making small talk. The reason why I can't distinguish one of your friends from the others is because the only woman I saw in the room tonight was you." L.B. said as he pulled up to the traffic light and stopped.

J'Nae blushed at his remark. Realizing they were about to turn on the main road into their subdivision she decided to seize the opening he gave her. She impulsively leaned over and kissed

L.B. with a full open mouth and plenty of tongue. He returned her enthusiasm and embraced her, cradling her left cheek in his right hand. The kissing continued and the passion she felt earlier in the evening began to resurface between the two. They would have sat there in the car, at the traffic light making out if the intensity hadn't been interrupted by the blaring horn of the car just behind them, also wanting to turn at the light.

L.B. pulled the car in front of J'Nae's house putting it in park and shutting off the engine. He rested his right hand on her left thigh looking directly in her eyes. He froze for a moment then whispered to her how beautiful she looked in the moonlit glow of the night. Opening his car door and getting out of the vehicle, he walked around to her side of the car and opened her door, all the while watching her shift her legs from the cross-legged position she held while seated to the moving positions necessary to exit the car. He extended his left hand to her, and she abruptly put her right hand in his as he guided her out of the car.

They walked up to her front door, stealing glances of one another, all smiles with each step. J'Nae, extremely excited and still reeling from the spontaneous explosion at the bar could think of only one thing. What all women think just before they get it for the first time...what does it look like? How big is it? I hope he knows what to do with whatever he's packing. But no matter what she thought, or how stimulated she may be, her demure and reserved nature would never allow her to utter the words aloud.

Even still, her body was revealing what her mouth would not say. With her nipples hard and her panties moist, she opened the door, attempting to step inside while slightly tugging at his forearm intending to lead him in. But she felt him resist and quickly turned toward her companion.

"I had a wonderful time this evening. I'll call you tomorrow. Good night, J'Nae." L.B. said.

For a split second, J'Nae looked both surprised and perplexed at his response. But it wasn't obvious, even with her level of intoxication and extreme arousal, unless you had the ability to watch her in slow motion, you wouldn't have been the wiser. Her quick wit and natural ability to pull it all in at a moment's notice did not disappoint.

"I'll expect you to."

"I've got an early morning tomorrow. But I would love to take you to lunch. How does that sound sweetie?"

To J'Nae, it sounded like she wasn't getting any tonight. And after all this time he'd been pursuing her, she thought it was a sure thing. Oh well, maybe it's for the best.   They   said good night and exchanged a brief kiss then retreated to their respective homes. J'Nae was in a state she rarely found herself in, drunk. She peeled herself out of her clothing and wasted no time jumping in bed. She slept hard and heavy for the first time in a long while.

Chapter 8

The next morning on her way inside The Coffee House, J'Nae could see the eagerness on the faces of Rona and Zsasha as she came in and took her seat.

"Hey, good morning." J'Nae said, looking around the room. "Where's Vonne?"

"Look at her, coming in the door deflecting. You know we want the scoop about last night." Rona said.

"Yea girl, about last night." Zsasha inserted with an obvious reference to the movie title. "How did things go with my man L.B.? Did you do some housekeeping, get those cobwebs dusted off?"

"Well not exactly." J'Nae replied.

"Spill!" Rona said firmly.

"Wait, now. Give her a minute. Can't you see the girl is embarrassed and obviously struggling with what happened." Zsasha said half-heartedly trying to sound sympathetic.

"I'm fine, Zsasha." J'Nae replied. "Where's Vonne?"

"Where's Vonne?" Zsasha repeated. "I'll tell you where she is, she's somewhere other than here. Now what's up?"

"Yeah, quit stalling J'Nae." Rona replied.

"I'm not sure. I mean, I thought things were going well. I was certainly ready to take it to the next level and all."

"Really?" said Zsasha, sounding pleasantly surprised by her comment.

"Yes. And I thought he was too. We were definitely feeling each other. We were kissing and everything. Then suddenly, we weren't. He just kissed me at the door and said good night."

"For real?" Sasha asked.

"Well maybe he didn't know you wanted to go there." Rona proposed.

"No, it wasn't that I'm almost certain of it." J'Nae said.

"Well, what do you think it was?"

"I don't know, I mean, well. I ran into Rick while I was at the bar."

"Rick who?" Sasha inquired.

"Just a guy from class." J'Nae answered.

"You think maybe he saw the two of you talking?" Rona asked.

"Well, that...or something else.?" J'Nae said, sounding elusive.

"What do you mean or something else? What happened?" Rona questioned. "Did he kiss you?"

"Well what else could it have been?" Sasha demanded.

"Uhm, no, he didn't kiss me. In fact, he didn't do anything other than stand there looking all fine and sexy while whispering in my ear."

"Baby girl, that's how it's done when you're in a club. How else are you supposed to hear each other?"

"Never mind all that, what happened after the kissing and such? What could have turned L.B. off after he was so warmed up?"

"Well, while I was at the bar, I had a bit of a side effect from that shot."

"You had what?" Rona inquired.

"A side effect from a G-shot or O-shot, I don't know which."

"Girl, what are you talking about?"

"I was accidentally injected with one of them at the doctor's office. I'll explain the details later."

"Side effects...like what?"

"I um...had a spontaneous orgasm while I was at the bar talking with Rick, my former classmate."

"Get out...really?" Sasha exclaimed.

"Yes, really."

"Well so what. What does that have to do with L.B.? He was at the table with us the entire time." Rona asked.

"Yes, but he could have easily seen us chatting at the bar. And anyone paying close attention could have seen me and what I was going through."

"You mean having an orgasm?" Zsasha jokes. "Girl what were you doing, playing with yourself out in the open for all to see?"

"No, no, of course not."

"Then what? I don't get it."

"I don't know. Maybe I'm just being paranoid. I mean Rick didn't really know what was happening and he was standing right next to me."

"And I always had you pegged for the quiet type, definitely not a screamer!" Rona teased.

"I'm so embarrassed. There was nothing I could do to stop it from coming on."

"Well why would you want to? It's been such a long time, right? Don't you feel better now that you've relieved some of that pressure that's been building up all this time?" Zsasha asked.

"Yeah, a little bit, I guess, but I didn't want it like that!"

"I'm sure you didn't, Miss Conservative. Whatever you were injected with must have done a number on you. Especially if you thought you were ready to handle some business. Girl you know that ain't you." Rona declared.

"I thought I was ready, and I thought he was too, even after we left the club. He was romantic and spontaneous and passionate."

"So, what happened?"

"I don't know, Rona. When we got to my front door, he just kissed me and said good night."

"That's it?"

"That's it.

"I believe things tend to work out the way they're supposed to."

"Yeah, Rona's right. You weren't in your right mind for all that." Zsasha reinforced.

"I suppose, but it's still weird. He didn't seem to mind my level of intoxication on the way home."

"Did he say anything else?" Rona questioned.

"Yeah. He said he had an early morning but wanted to take me to a late lunch."

"He probably had to get up early for church or something. Today is Sunday." Rona reminded.

"There's your answer. He's a choir boy just like you." Zsasha determined. "So, are you going to go...to lunch?"

"I don't know. I'll just have to see how I'm feeling if and when he calls."

"If?"

"Yeah, if."

The girls sat in silence for a moment, not knowing what else to say when Vonne arrived cheerful and smiling and obviously in a good mood.

"Hey, sorry I'm so late. Waitress, can I get my regular, to go please?"

"Well look at you! Smiling, upbeat and shit; happier than a sissy with a bag of dicks." Zsasha remarked.

"I'm always happy and upbeat, girlfriend."

"Ahh, no, not really." Zsasha replied.

"So, you're implying that I'm usually sad, miserable and somewhat of a drag, huh?"

"Well..."

Rona interceded before Zsasha could finish whatever it was she was about to say.

"You're definitely in a better mood, much better than you were last night."

"Whatever." Vonne replied, you could hear her voice cracking a smile when she spoke. It was obvious she could barely contain herself or the news she was eager to share.

"So, what gives?" Zsasha asked.

"Lee and I decided to sleep in."

"Really now? Did that have anything to do with the magic and seduction of last night?" J'Nae chimed in.

"For sure. And the magic lasted all night long!" Vonne said, barely holding back her excitement.

"You go girl!" J'Nae remarked.

"Yeah, well, I'd still be enjoying that black magic if I hadn't been interrupted."

"By whom?" Rona inquired.

"One of my store managers had an emergency. I've got to be there in time to open and handle things until she arrives. I just stopped in to say 'hey' and grab some coffee and see how y'all made out. So, what did you guys think about the show? I bet the magic reached out to y'all too. The Ladies put on a show! They turned up."

"Ah, yes they did. As always, Jill did not disappoint." Zsasha confirmed.

"Leela was pretty solid too." J'Nae added.

"Can't say that for L.B. though." Rona revealed.

"What do you mean?" Vonne asked.

"Long story short, he bailed at the door. Said he'd call her for a late lunch today, but we'll see. J'Nae's not too hopeful at this point. Her self-confidence has taken a hit." Rona explained.

"Well not for long, I promise. He could barely take his eyes off her the whole night." Vonne replied.

"That's probably true, in fact I know it is. The whole time when he should have been facing the stage, he was staring at you J'Nae, most of the night. I saw it with my own eyes." Rona added.

"Well, it doesn't matter at this point. He bailed on me. It is what it is."

"Oh well, I wouldn't worry sweetie. From what I saw there's already someone waiting in the wings." Vonne revealed. "I saw you at the bar, more importantly, I saw him up on you all close and personal. But more on that later, I gotta go."

"I'm right behind you." J'Nae stated as she got up from the table to leave. "I'll holla later."

Following behind Vonne, J'Nae left The Coffee House with no real destination in mind. She just wanted to get out of there and avoid reliving the events of last night. Driving around, she noticed it was nearly 1:30 pm and still no word from L.B. Determined to get her mind on something else, she reached for her phone to check her email when she noticed two missed calls. They were both from L.B. Without hesitation, she hit the call back button.

"Hey. It's J'Nae. I saw I had two missed calls from you this morning."

"Hey babe. How are you today?"

"I'm good. How about you?"

"Good, good. So, I guess you forgot to turn your ringer back on this morning, huh?"

Realizing he was correct, J'Nae was suddenly smiling and beaming realizing she hadn't been dissed. He'd been trying to call her just like he'd said.

"I guess I did. My bad."

"It's all good sweetie. Actually, I kind of forgot about something I put on my calendar at the last minute."

"Oh?"

"Yeah. Could we possibly make lunch, dinner instead? Maybe candlelight, a little soft music, and I'll even cook my favorite meal, just for you. And to top it off, I'll follow it up with a foot massage that'll make your hair curl!   My way of making up for having to step away this afternoon. What do you say, babe, is it a date?"

J'Nae hesitated for a moment trying not to sound too eager at his dinner proposal, wanting him to feel the uncertainty she had experienced earlier. But she was more than tempted. All those things he described sounded a whole lot like foreplay and after the past few days she was more than ready. Without further hesitation, she agreed.

Hanging up the phone and full of anticipation, her self-confidence had now been restored. She decided to head to the spa for a nice relaxing massage in preparation for the evening. Once again feeling the excitement from the night before, she could hardly wait.

* * * * *

J'Nae arrived at L.B.'s promptly at 7:00 pm. She was wearing a beige bandage style form fitting V-neck dress layered fringe at the hem of the dress. Her back was exposed down the center also in a V-shape making it impossible to wear a bra. Her feet were partially covered in a pair of bronze colored Gucci sandals with a matching handbag and her hair was pulled back away from her face. She looked stunning as she approached the front door. And just like magic, the door opened, and her date appeared.

"J'Nae, come in." L.B. said with excitement and awe.

"Don't mind if I do." J'Nae said as she stepped inside. "It smells amazing."

"Thank you. Just a little something I thought you might enjoy."

"Well it smells delicious."

"So do you." L.B. remarked. "Have a seat, make yourself at home."

"Don't mind if I do."

"Did you have any trouble finding the place?" he asked jokingly knowing full well J'Nae was a close neighbor.

"Sort of. I got a bit confused when I passed the mulberry bush, just left of the rose garden. I thought I needed to stay on the main street, but something was pulling me in the other direction."

"That would have been me guiding you in my direction, at least I'd like to think so." L.B. said smiling. "Can I pour you a glass of wine?"

"Yes, please and thank you."

"Red or White?"

"Whichever you prefer."

They settled on white wine at his choosing and engaged in conversation that included highlights from the night before. Unlike the dialogue earlier that day with her friends, it was quite pleasant remembering the night before.

The meal he prepared consisted of grilled chicken breast, asparagus sautéed with minced garlic and bacon bits, along with roasted new potatoes with parmesan and fresh herbs. Taking her first bite, J'Nae was pleasantly surprised with the flavorful taste of the chicken breast.

"Um, that's delicious."

"Thank you."

"Did you make this yourself?"

"Of course I did. It's a recipe I found on the food network. In fact, the entire meal was inspired by my favorite chef. He was runner up last season."

"Well it's absolutely delicious. You've outdone yourself, L.B."

"And I'm hoping to outdo myself again...one of these days."

85

"Careful tiger. You don't want to bite off more than you can chew."

"I think it's a bit late for that." L.B. said, as he wiped his mouth with his napkin, indicating he was done with his meal.

"Finished so soon? It barely looks like you ate at all." J'Nae commented.

"For now. I want to leave room for dessert."

L.B. sat across from J'Nae watching her eat the rest of her food. When she was done, he stood to gather the dishes and clear the table.

"Dinner was delicious. Thank you for cooking for me. Here, let me help with that." J'Nae said as she gathered a few dishes.

"I've got it." L.B. said, taking the dishes from her hands. "Why don't you have a seat in the living room, and I'll join you shortly."

"Okay."

J'Nae took this opportunity to look around the living room and do what most women do the first time in the home of a man they are dating...snoop. Even though she was fairly new to the dating scene, she'd picked up a lot of tricks of the trade from her girls and their love tales over the years. It took no time for her radar to zero in on some pictures of what appeared to be his family.

"Is this your sister?" J'Nae asked when she saw a photo of L.B. with a much younger female.

"Is she wearing a pink dress?"

"Um, yeah, she is."

"That would be my niece."

"She's a pretty girl."

"Yes, she is. And we are very close. My sister used to let her spend summers with me when her and her husband first separated and later divorced."

"When parents separate and are no longer together, for whatever the reason, it's often difficult for the children to adjust. Even when there's no obvious disconnect. A child's world is reshaping and it's never easy."

L.B. knew in his heart that J'Nae was not only talking about his niece, but her children too. The impact of having lost her

86

husband, the father of her children appears to still be with her and based on her comments still with her children as well. L.B. had never experienced that sort of loss. He wanted to be sympathetic and understanding without changing the mood he'd worked hard to set. He also knew he had to act fast or he was going to lose the momentum of the evening. He had to do something. Returning to the living room, he grabbed the remote control and began playing Jill Scott's latest album beginning with a song she sang live at Club Nonchalant where J'Nae was obviously turned on.

"Remember this?"

"Oh yeah."

Setting down both glasses of wine, L.B. took J'Nae by the hand, and pulled her in close. They began slow dancing as the sultry voice of Jill Scotts' 'Can't Wait' filled the room. She could feel his heart beating as he pressed on her back pulling her even closer. It was romantic and enticing as it seemed to go on for quite a bit of time.

"I've waited a long time for the opportunity to spend time with you like this." L.B. whispered. "You're a very beautiful woman."

"Thank you, you're too sweet."

"I really hope we can do this again soon, if that's okay." He asked.

Did he just say maybe we can do this again soon? That sounds like he's ready to wrap up the evening. I'm still reeling from the other night. That damn shot has my hormones going full speed ahead.

"Sure."

Pulling away, L.B. gave J'Nae a gentle kiss on her forehead and squeezed her shoulders.

"Can I walk you home?"

"That's not necessary. I drove my car."

"Yes, I did. I didn't want to walk on the pavement in these shoes."

"I really enjoyed your company tonight, J'Nae."

"I did too. I'll call you."

"Great. Goodnight beautiful."

"Goodnight L.B. We'll talk soon."

J'Nae hurried along and was at home in no time. She poured herself a glass of wine and headed to her bedroom. While undressing, she realized breaking things off early was for the best. Making the decision to be intimate with someone should be made with a clear head, not with alcohol or hormone intoxication.

* * * * *

The next morning, Zsasha walked into The Coffee House and sat down where Rona and Vonne were already seated. Rona was the first one to speak.

"Good morning Zsasha."

"Hey y'all, wassup?" replied Zsasha.

"Where's J'Nae?" Vonne asked. "I thought she was meeting us this morning."

"I spoke with her for a hot second on my way here. She said she needed to get in the office early this morning and wouldn't be able to join us. She ended up oversleeping and running late...something about a rough night."

"I wonder what's up with that?" Rona inquired.

Zsasha opted to ignore the innuendo since it was in reference to J'Nae. Instead, she turned her attention to Vonne who seemed unusually quiet.

"What's wrong with you? Pick your face up off the table and pull yourself together, you look a mess."

"I'm tired, Zsasha. My dad arrived last night." Vonne replied with little to no enthusiasm. "With my dinner party coming up, it's a really bad time for family drama and it weighed on me all night. This event is extremely important for my expansion plans and it's too late to reschedule."

"I get it, but how did it go, with your dad I mean?" Zsasha pushed on.

"Not what I expected. I mean, he was polite, cordial and very talkative."

"I bet." Rona interrupted. "You haven't had more than a 5-minute conversation with him in years, right?"

"Right." Vonne replied. "And with good reason."

"Well did you all make any progress last night?"

"Not as far as I'm concerned. I really wasn't interested in what he had to say. He was shit for a father and nothing can change that."

"No argument here." Rona confirmed. "But how did he behave? Was he mean towards you and belligerent like he's been in the past?"

"No, at least not yet. He said he was just here for a quick visit and that he'll be gone in a few days."

"Well, don't let your guard down." Zsasha stated while fidgeting in her purse.

"I won't."

"Good, because the minute you show a bit of sensitivity, he'll take that as a sign of weakness and fall right back into his old habits again. And you need your head in the game for all those high-profile people that'll be waiting in line for you to kiss their asses. That requires skill. It's one of those things you do without looking like you're doing it. Your head has to be in the game, period."

"As it stands now, he'll be long gone by then, don't worry. I know I look a bit rough right now but that's because all this caught me off guard, thanks to Lee's drunk ass. But I've been down this road one too many times to let his bullshit affect what I need to do. Truthfully, I don't think it's going to be a problem. It may have been because he was tired from the trip, I don't know, but something was a bit off with him. He didn't seem quite like the old asshole I've always known him to be."

"What do you mean exactly?" Rona asked.

"Well, it was almost as if he was weaker, less confident and commanding. Basically, he didn't look like he had any fight left in him."

"Really now. That's strange. What do you make of it?" Zsasha inquired.

"I don't know." Vonne replied. "But that mean spirited old man that took pleasure in belittling me, constantly comparing me to my ½ sister Kiera, just wasn't there, at least not last night."

89

"Maybe he's sick and he came here to seek absolution and forgiveness."

"I guess anything's possible, Rona."

"So, would you be willing to give it to him if he asked?"

"I don't know, maybe...probably not. He doesn't deserve it."

"I'm witcha girlfriend." Zsasha chimed in. "Besides, that's God's job, not yours. We got your back. None of us want to witness him tearing you down. It took a lot of love and care to pull you up out of that black hole of darkness he drove you to."

"Yes, it did, and I love you ladies for it."

"And we love you too, Vonne." Rona confirmed.

"Yeah girl, we got you. Don't sweat it."

On that note, the ladies left The Coffee House and headed to the separate destinations. Vonne went to one of her boutiques to begin working on inventory, Zsasha headed next door to Ahsasz, and Rona went to show a property she had listed.

Chapter 9

Vonne's home was situated in an upscale suburb of Falls Church, VA, not far from the Potomac River. The house stood on about 2.5 acres of land and was a 2-story colonial. She had purchased the home after the successful opening of her 5th boutique which was long after Lee retired from the NBA due to an injury he suffered during the playoffs.

The purpose of this dinner party was to serve as an opening and opportunity for her to get better acquainted with certain individuals in the political arena. Some of which were on the planning board or the zoning committee who may one day become useful as she continues to grow her. Others were business owners, local politicians and people of influence that would do her good to be more than a casual acquaintance.

The guests began arriving and were scattered throughout the first floor of her home. Several waiters and servers walked deliberately through the crowd topping off drinks in the hands of socially charged guests while others carried trays with champagne trays and a variety of appetizers. The choices ranged from bacon wrapped dates stuffed with blue cheese to stuffed mushrooms and liver pate. All of which were delectable and prepared by Chef Roget, a personal and dear friend of Rona's and a former client.

Rona arrived early prior to all other party guests so she could make sure Chef Roget had presented an elegant dinner menu from the options she herself recommended. It was Vonne's first time using Chef Roget and had to be certain everything went as planned. Since he came highly recommended by Rona, her help was essential in management of the kitchen staff as giving off the right impression was necessary for this and future endeavors.

Vonne thought it prudent to become acquainted with those in local government that may have influence that could one day be of importance in her line of work. With the opening of two new stores in the Washington DC area, mixing and mingling with members of city council and other local politicians of influence was essential. Among her guests were Governor Olmstead, Mayor Brinkley and Commissioner Moore. 'The Boutique' was doing far better than Vonne could ever have hoped. And its continued success hinged on forging new relationships with many of the dinner guests of the evening.

Zsasha and Simon were among the last to arrive, not too far behind J'Nae, who is usually prompt. Gazing into the room of guests, Zsasha and Simon were met with friendly smiles and pleasantries from several party goers Vonne was unaware they knew from aspects of their own business. Something most of them chose to keep under to themselves.

Walking over inconspicuously, Vonne greeted her friends while snagging two glasses of champagne from a server then handed them to J'Nae and Zsasha, motioning for Simon to grab one as well.

"You're all late, but you're all here." Vonne Said.

"That's all that matters. By the way, you look amazing, Vonne. Confident and empowered." J'Nae bragged.

"Thank you, my lady."

"And your dad's gone, right?" Zsasha teased. "...Lee, is he behaving himself as well?"

"My dad ended up staying for just a couple of days, freeing me up to focus on this event, making sure everything went as planned and Lee, well he's not quite out of the doghouse just yet. In fact, he's on the patio talking with one of our very special guests. Make sure you make your rounds and introduce yourselves. This party is all about mixing and mingling."

"You're absolutely right. Zsasha agreed. "Let's mix it up a bit, shall we."

Zsasha, having a clear view of Simon on the patio, who appeared to be on his phone, headed in his direction. In less than a minute, her journey was interrupted as she was swept up in the gathering of people chatting and enjoying drinks and pulling her into their conversations.

J'Nae found herself standing just outside the kitchen next to the food table the servers and waiters used to replenish their serving trays. Feeling a bit out of place, she focused on Chef Roget's appetizers while glancing around the room at the party goers. Caught up in her own thoughts, she was completely unaware as Rona crept up behind her tapping her shoulder.

"Oh, dang girl, you scared me. I didn't see you walk up. How are you?" J'Nae said as she embraced her girlfriend with a hug.

"I'm a good girl, you look great. Where's L.B.? I thought he was your date for the party tonight?" Rona said, lying through her teeth. She was fully aware that J'Nae decided to push the pause button on that situation, once she realized he was a man of convenience and not someone she had a real romantic interest in. She had shared her revelation with Zsasha who, without her knowledge, shared it with both Rona and Vonne.

"He was unavailable this evening." J'Nae replied.

"Really, prior commitment I suppose?"

"Well, no, not really. The truth is I didn't invite him."

"What?"

"Yeah. It would have been a bit awkward since I decided to keep things platonic."

"I'm sure. It certainly would have been extremely awkward for him too." Rona said, nodding her head pointing towards Lee, who was standing next to Rick, chatting him up.

Following her lead, J'Nae could see Rick looking directly at her. He smiled and nodded. Without further provocation, she could feel the intensity of his stare burning through her flesh. Her body suddenly warmed up and she began to blush, turning her attention back to Rona who had a devilish grin on her face.

"What is he doing here?" J'Nae asked her friend. Unaware, her facial expression revealed more 'pleasantly surprised' and less 'annoyed and pissed-off' which is what she wanted to convey even though it wasn't what she was actually feeling.

"I invited him." Rona admitted. Her voice was intentionally loud enough for others nearby to hear.

"We invited him!" Zsasha and Vonne announced simultaneously as they appeared to already be part of the conversation.

"Yes, we invited him to the party because we knew you wouldn't." Zsasha confirmed.

J'Nae stood there not knowing exactly what to say or how to respond. The truth of the matter was she had been contemplating taking him up on his offer. She hadn't had a one-night stand ever before and well, hell, she just needed to get laid. Damn that G-shot! And why not him? He wasn't exactly a stranger. He had been in some of the same classes with her and on one occasion they were both part of the same study group. He's as good as any other prospect she had recently, maybe even better.

J'Nae turned toward Rick and this time when their eyes met, she didn't turn away. Again, she felt his stare burn through her flesh and immediately felt the need to find a private place. She excused herself and rushed to the restroom knowing what was to come. She effortlessly journeyed to her happy place giving in to an explosion more intense than the others.

She returned to the gathering just as everyone was taking their seats. Vonne, with her multiple agendas had strategically seated those who could potentially impact specific hurdles with others with similar influence. She made certain to seat the Chairman as close to herself as possible and purposely arranged her personal guest in close proximity with one another.

After dinner was served, J'Nae and Rick appeared to be two longtime friends to any outsider looking at the two of them. Once again, the spontaneous orgasm an hour or so earlier left J'Nae open minded to the charms of her former classmate. Fully captivated by one another, the two seemed inseparable for the remainder of the evening. Hanging on each other's words and finishing each other's sentences. They couldn't take their eyes off each other for more than a few seconds. They also didn't immediately hear the commotion at the front door or notice Vonne racing towards the foyer to deal with an uninvited guest.

"Vonne! Vonne! It's me, Kiera! Aren't you gonna give your little sister a big hug?" Vonne froze right where she stood, at least for a moment. Vonne recognized the voice, the southern accent as well as her slurred speech. OMG! Vonne thought. Not tonight, Kiera, not tonight. Caught completely off guard, she rushed to the front door and grabbed her drunken sister by the arm ever so gently, guiding her through to the kitchen. Realizing she couldn't do this without acknowledging her arrival Vonne just simply shouted out a few words while escorting Kiera to the kitchen. "Hey everybody, this is my sister Kiera, up from Louisville. We'll just be a moment."

The crowd resumed their chit chat that for some had now become soft whispers and innuendos. It was obvious the topic of discussion had changed, and no one said it out loud, but everyone was thinking it. Who was this drunken fool that just crashed the party? And why was she whisked away to the kitchen.

"What was that about?" Zsasha said to Rona and J'Nae. "Tell me that wasn't her sister Kiera."

"I'm quite sure you heard her as well as I did. She said her sister Kiera is from Louisville." Rona replied.

"Did Vonne know she was coming?" J'Nae asked

"I doubt it." Zsasha said. "She would never have let that happen especially on a night like this." Just then Zsasha's phone began to ring. Perfect timing, she thought to herself as she stepped away to answer her call. "Excuse me, I need to take this."

"Ladies, is everything okay?" Rick asked as he walked up to J'Nae, gently placing his right hand on the small of her back.

"Yeah, maybe, I don't know. Maybe we should check on her."

"Nah, give her a minute." Rona said softly. "It's just her sister. What harm can she do?"

J'Nae took a moment to reflect on what Rona just said about Kiera. Thinking back to the many stories Vonne shared about their relationship over the years, it only took a few more seconds before J'Nae replied to Rona's comment.

"That's it. I'm going in. I'm going to check on her myself."

Zsasha caught up with Rona and J'Nae as they walked towards the kitchen together. They could hear Vonne and Kiera's voices getting louder as they approached.

"You cannot stay here Kiera. It's a bad time for me and Lee right now. We are trying to work on our issues."

"Please, Vonnie, I have nowhere else to go."

"I'm sorry. My relationship with my husband cannot sustain our family dysfunction any longer. Dad was here for a few days, and it was just too much for us. I'm sorry. We just can't do it."

"Dad said he had worked it out with you and Lee; that it was okay for me to come."

"Really, well he lied. And that shouldn't be too surprising. He was always good at that sort of thing." Vonne said with obvious resentment in her voice.

"Okay, fine, I'll leave. And on my way out, I'll just tell everyone that dear St. Vonne is putting her homeless sister out on the street! I'm sure that will go over well with you fancy DC friends."

At that moment, she realized she had been set up by dear old dad. It wasn't an accident that she showed up tonight, they planned this shit. And Vonne knew she was stuck. Her sister was fully capable of carrying out her threat and Vonne couldn't afford what that would cost her.

"Okay, okay, you can stay, but not for long. I can't have your shenanigans affecting my life anymore or my business."

"Thank you, thank you. I promise to be on my best behavior."

"You'd better. And don't get it twisted, this is just for a few days. The first sign of trouble and your ass is out of here!"

Just then, Rona walked in the kitchen after having heard much of the conversation eavesdropping at the kitchen door.

"Everything alright, Vonne?" Rona inquired.

"Yeah girl. Everything's fine. This is my sister Kiera. She'll be staying with us for a few days."

Rona's mouth said hello, but her mind was screaming 'what the fuck'.

"Hi Kiera. Nice to meet you." Said J'Nae as Zsasha walked into the kitchen standing alongside their girl. She didn't say anything, she just stood there facing Kiera who now, observing the posse that had formed, responded with little to no enthusiasm inspired by her obvious intoxication.

"Anything I can help you with?" J'Nae asked.

"Damn. Yes. Can you show Kiera to the spare room just behind the laundry area? Can you help her get set up? I need to apologize to my guest." Vonne said.

"Don't worry about that. We'll take care of that." Rona said, nudging Zsasha through the door.

Walking out of the kitchen, they passed Rick just a few feet from the kitchen door. As Vonne trailed a few steps behind them, Zsasha tugged at her arm to get her attention.

"Is everything ok, girl?"

"I'll have to fill you in later. I just need to say a few words to my guests."

"It's a little late for that, sista girl. Most of them have left already and the stragglers are on their way out the door now. But it's all good. I took the pleasure of thanking them for coming and apologizing for the interruption. Most of them were so buzzed they'll forget about it anyway."

"You think?"

"Yes, I do, for sure. Everything is fine. You wanted to have a meet and greet, and you did, and I didn't hear any chatter as they were leaving, none at all, so don't worry. As far as I'm concerned, you made quite an impression, besides, you'll have other opportunities to expand on the connections you've made. I'm sure all is forgotten. Besides, I know some of them and trust, they got their own shit to worry about, you feel me." Zsasha stated rather convincingly.

Vonne may have been stressed and unnerved by her sister's unexpected and poorly timed visit, but she picked up on everything Zsasha had just said. She had suspicions about Zsasha's dealing for some time now, so her assurances were taken to heart.

Zsasha was more than happy to see Vonne's guests to the door. She knew almost everyone in attendance, quite a few of them from her club. She wanted to give them a gentle nudge making sure they were aware of her presence and her relationship with the host. She really didn't have to do much at all other than show her face and she did that. At the end of the day, all is well, for Zsasha, anyway.

Rick patiently waited for J'Nae to return. When she finally emerged guilt and distress was not only on her face but in her voice as well.

"I'm so sorry I kept you waiting for so long."

"Don't worry about it. Is everything okay with your friend Vonne?"

"Not really, at least not at the moment, but it'll pass."

"Well maybe it'll work itself out."

"Maybe, but right now she needs me, so can we pick this up later?"

"Yes, absolutely. I'll call you."

"Great. I appreciate your understanding."

"Not a problem. I'm glad we had this time together. I'll call you soon."

Rick, being a gentleman, showed himself out so as not to pull J'Nae away from her friend who was obviously going through something personal. She returned to her friends who were gathered in the kitchen to help Vonne decompress after the shock of the evening. Lee finally showed his face but didn't say much to his wife. Letting her father come visit without talking to her first was bad enough, but adding her sister into the mix, he knew he was in deep. And it didn't matter whether he had any knowledge of Kiera's arrival, he knew Vonne would never believe him no matter what he said, not now anyway. All he could do was just retreat for the night and hope that tomorrow he'd wake up better prepared for what was ahead.

Chapter 10

Coffee with the girls had become a habit much like wine at the gallery. Often an unplanned event and something J'Nae looked forward to on a regular basis. The mornings were usually filled with a few quick laughs and brief updates and relationship laundry that would often be cause for a wine and cheese evening event. There were also times when the conversations were on a much more serious level where they discussed the not so humorous details of their intimate lives. But they were always there to support and encourage one another, no matter what the situation and they did it without judgement while at the same time keeping it real. And once again J'Nae, Rona and Zsasha sat around the table of the very familiar Coffee House waiting for Vonne to arrive to assess the damage and help her navigate through it.

When she walked in, she looked a bit out of sorts and somewhat disheveled. As the owner of her own string of boutiques that was something you just didn't see. Making her way to the table she signaled for service and plopped down with her friends.

"Vonne, baby, how are you?" asked J'Nae.

"Girl we weren't sure you were going to make it with all you got going on at home. Are you alright?" asked Rona.

"I'm beyond stressed. That was a bit much to handle unexpectedly even from her. I mean Kiera showing up like that, intoxicated and with her usual drama was too much. I didn't see that coming."

"So, what's going to happen now that she's here? Do you have a plan?" asked Zsasha.

With a bit of emotion, Rona interrupted Zsasha's line of questioning.

"Girl, give her a minute to process all this shit. What kind of plan can she have at this point? It ain't been but a minute since all this went down. Give her a chance to exhale and get herself together first."

"She ain't got a minute." Zsasha remarked.

"Ahh, there won't be any exhaling going on here, not anytime soon. Hell, I've got daddy drama, sister drama and Lee is being Lee...with his shady behind. Can't afford to exhale or relax. With all of this mess in my house right now, I'm liable to lose everything if I take too long to blink. Y'all know what's at stake. I'm trying to align myself with certain political people that may help me bypass some of the hurdles I might run into trying to open DC stores and those who I may need to vote in a way that would be favorable to my expansion plans."

"It'll all work itself out in the end, you'll see." J'Nae's kind words offered little comfort to Vonne as she sat there sipping on her coffee while engrossed in her new reality.

Feeling like it was time to change the subject, Rona turned her attention toward J'Nae.

"J'Nae," Rona asked, "Would you be interested in house sitting for me for a few days? I'm going out of town to celebrate my birthday." Rona finished.

"Really now? Which mystery benefactor is accompanying you on this sudden getaway?" Zsasha inquired.

"That would be Ricardo. He wanted to take me somewhere special for my birthday, however some business came up that he couldn't postpone so he asked me to join him."

"Is that right? You go girl witcha bad self. Jet setting around the world with all those rich ass men you seem to find with no trouble. I wanna be you when I grow up!" Zsasha said jokingly."

"I don't know why." Rona said dryly. "You got Ahsasz money all day long, a get out of jail, 'I can't cheat' card good for a lifetime with that fine ass 3-legged freak you call your husband."

"Trust and believe, he can walk on that 3rd leg too!" Zsasha said proudly. "But hold on sista, how is it that you know about that? Yeah, we're freaks and all and we swing like monkeys, but we also have rules. And I don't recall any liaisons involving you!"

"No sweetie, it ain't nothing like that. I'm just messing with you." Rona quickly diverted the conversation in another direction. "J'Nae, are we still going to the gym?"

"Yeah, yeah, I'm going. Just struggling for motivation today."

"Well let's go girl. The bike ain't gonna ride itself!"

"Whatever."

Rona and J'Nae made their way out of The Coffee House leaving Vonne and Zsasha at the table contemplating their next steps. They both drove their own vehicles to the gym, with J'Nae following behind Rona for the short distance to the Vida Fitness Center Rona used regularly. As J'Nae parked her car, she received a text message from Rick asking her if she was free for dinner on Monday evening. Frowning at the impersonal text message request, J'Nae did not respond. She tossed her cell phone in her bag and entered the gym just seconds behind Rona.

Finding two treadmills side by side was easier than Rona anticipated. It was late morning and the usual crowd had come and gone. The apple fritters they ate at breakfast had settled along with a bit of guilt and they were both feeling the need to clear their conscience.

"I hope Vonne is going to be okay." J'Nae said.

"Yeah, me too. She'll be alright if she doesn't let her father get inside her head. He has a knack for doing that and the aftermath is never good." Rona replied.

"You're right about that. She was devastated the last time he wormed his way into her life. But Vonne is stronger now than she was back then. She's got a greater sense of self-worth and her confidence level is through the roof. Look how successful she is with her boutiques."

"She's successful, yes, but sometimes we let our demons disrupt everything good we have going on in our lives and they take center stage."

"That's true. Sometimes our past isn't as far behind us as we think."

"So what's going on with you and Rick? I saw you chatting with each other up most of the night. The two of you looked kind of cozy, like old friends catching up. Did you guys hook up after the party or what?"

"No, nothing like that. We talked about our lives and our careers and such. He's actually in communications now."

"Really, well that sounds like a promising career path for a young man."

"I'm sure you've heard of him before. He's a late-night radio host, who goes by the name Rick Moss on air."

"Oh really, yes, I've heard of him, we all have."

"Yeah, and he seems focused."

"And what did you guys do after Vonne's party? Did y'all hookup?"

"I went straight home. But I will say I thought about it, if only for a hormonal minute."

"Huh?" Rona replied in a tone revealing her lack of understanding.

"It happened again." J'Nae mumbled.

Looking over at Rona she could still see the confusion on her face. As she was

now fully in the throes of her file-mile run took a deep breath in so she could respond with the appropriate emphasis.

"It, girl, it!"

"Oh, wow! I didn't realize that was still going on. How long are the side effects supposed to last? Have you reached out to Dr. Westmore about IT?"

"Yes, I did. She said they could last anywhere from a few weeks to a few months."

"Is that right? Wow! I don't know whether to feel sorry for you or feel sorry that it ain't happening to me, shit." Rona said jokingly.

"Well, It's not bad, it's just inconvenient."

"I'm sure." Rona said as she stepped off the treadmill then grabbed a towel.

"You'll never guess what Dr. Westmore said I could do so *IT* won't happen as often."

"Uhm, wanna bet?"

"She said if I had sex on a regular basis, it would reduce the pressure that's building up on my G-spot and it would basically stabilize for lack of a better word."

"So what's the problem?"

"The problem is I'm not in a relationship with anyone and that's not a reason to go out and have random sex!"

"I don't see why not. You're a grown ass woman with grown ass needs. And you got this young hottie chasing you like a lost puppy. Girl, he wants you, and I know you know it."

"He's an attractive young man with a lot of promise, I'll give him that."

"No, sista girl, give him that!" Rona declared, pointing towards J'Nae's crotch.

J'Nae, looking like her true feelings had been outed, said nothing. The truth is she found him very attractive and has been thinking about him quite a bit. She was just unsure if it was her true desire or if it was influenced by the G-shot.

"Stop acting so uptight and just go with it for once in your life." Rona grabbed her towel and motioned towards the locker room. "You're still house sitting for me, right? Ricardo is adamant about us taking this time so he can spoil me for my birthday. We might even be away longer than planned. You know how it is with him and his spontaneity. So can I count on you to watch the house and feed Annabelle?"

"Yes, of course."

"Cool. The plan is to be back late Monday or early Tuesday evening but like I said, you never know. Here's a thought...why not invite Rick over to the house to keep you company?"

"It's something to think about but I don't know, it might send the wrong message, you know, having him over to the house, any house. We haven't had a proper date yet."

"Stop being so hesitant and uptight. This isn't nineteen fifty, besides you're the one who said you were more than tempted, remember?"

"Yeah, yeah, that's what I said."

"Well then, what's the holdup?"

"He's so young."

"Is he over 21?"

"Yes, he is, but would you believe he texted me out?"

"What?"

"He texted me out. He asked me out to dinner via text message."

"And?"

"Don't you think that's a bit immature?"

"Nope, not nowadays. Besides, maybe he was at work or something."

"I don't know. Maybe."

"Times are changing girlfriend. Maybe you should just go out with him anyway. How old did you say he is?"

"37-ish."

"That's perfect. He's old enough to handle a mature relationship and young enough to knock it out the park. Now go get it girl and quit stalling! I'm tired of talking about this…"

J'Nae didn't say much more about Rick after that. They showered and dressed and headed to their cars. The decline in chatter and noticeable preoccupation made it obvious that J'Nae was giving it some serious thought. Rona planted the seed and provided an opportunity for J'Nae to be spontaneous. All she had to do was to unwind a bit, free herself from a few outdated stereotypes and let nature take its course.

Zsasha and Simon were dropping Ms. Honey off at Ahsasz. Ms. Honey had been employed by Zsasha and Simon for several years and had been overseeing staff at Ahsasz in preparation for gallery showings and other events, including *Ahsasz Down Under*. Since she hadn't yet given her a new key, she had to get out to unlock the doors to let her in.

"Ms. Honey, one of us will be back to help you lock up and put everything away in about 2 hours. Is that enough time?" Zsasha asked

"That should be fine Ms. Zsasha." Ms. Honey replied.

"Call me if you need anything before then. Okay?"

"Yes, mam. I'll call if I need anything."

Ms. Honey went inside the gallery and Zsasha locked the door. In the background, she thought she heard someone calling Ms.

Honey by name but when she looked up, she saw no one and didn't hear it again. She got in the car where Simon was waiting, and they headed for lunch.

"This ought to be interesting." Zsasha said to her husband. "This will be the first time we've seen Magda and Milo since the sleepover at our house."

"Yeah, but what's so interesting about that? We've been sharing with them for years. What's the big deal?"

"I don't know. It was just different last time. Don't you think?"

"Aside from them staying over that night, not really."

"Not just that night, the next day too."

"Yeah, but that was your doing if I recall."

"Yeah, I know but it was a special occasion. Closing the door on a physical relationship and opening one of a professional nature."

"So, what's the problem?"

"There's no problem, it's just..."

"It's just what?"

"Never mind, forget I brought it up."

Pulling up in front of Fiola Mare, Zsasha and Simon got out of their silver Q70L Infiniti where they were met by the valet.

"So, you don't open doors for me anymore, dear? Just have somebody else do it for you." Zsasha states matter-of-factly.

"I believe I've opened quite a few, don't you think." Simon said with a crooked smile on his face.

"I guess that's why we're here, isn't it?" Grinning at her husband, Zsasha knew she had walked right into that one. She accepted her defeat and they continued into the restaurant.

"Why do you think they wanted to come here?" Zsasha asked. "This establishment is known for its privacy."

"And that's a problem? I would think you'd be grateful for their discretion."

"I am, but it's not necessary. We've dined with them in public many times."

"What's with you all of a sudden? Did I miss something?"

"Ever just get a feeling and you can't figure out why or what it's about?"

"Uhm, not with our lifestyle." Simon stated firmly.

Zsasha and Simon were seconds away from reaching the Maître d when Magda appeared having discreetly come from the opposite direction.

"Darling, you look marvelous." Magda said, as she embraced Zsasha. "Absolutely divine. How are you dear?"

"I'm good." Zsasha said as she returned the embrace and topped it off with a kiss on both cheeks. Magda turned her attention and enthusiasm to Simon and didn't hide her affection for one minute.

"Simon dear, always the best-looking man in the room. How are you?"

"Direct as always...I'm good Magda, thank you. Where's Milo?"

"He went to the little boys' room. Our table has been reserved and it's ready, follow me."

Simon and Zsasha did as she said and followed her to the table she and Milo had procured before their arrival.

"I've already ordered some appetizers." Now looking directly at Simon, she added, "I figure I have a pretty good idea of what you have a taste for."

"Good gosh woman!" Milo teased as he approached. "Calm down. We all get it!"

"We all do get it, don't we!" Magda declared lightheartedly.

Her comments made everybody giggle at the obvious joke and lighten the already pleasant mood.

"Shall we order?"

Shortly after everyone ordered, lunch was served followed along with light conversation of various topics. None of which seemed to lead to anything of significance which had Simon and Zsasha curious and wondering what the reason for the gathering was. Simon was willing to play their game until they were ready to disclose but Zsasha's personality was much less patient and always direct and upfront.

"Okay, what's up guys? You've been buttering us up and basically kissing our ass for the past hour. What is it that you want? I know it's something." Looking at Magda and then Milo, Zsasha continued. "Go on, spit it out. What is it?"

"Well, we just wanted to ask a favor of you. Both of you."

"Quit dragging it out and ask already."

"Well, we have some new friends we want to introduce to you."

"What exactly did you have in mind?"

"Well, her name is Ellie Porter. We've been spending some time with her, and her partner Adam Russo and we wanted to invite them to Ahsasz for the next gallery showing."

"Really, now."

"Yes, full disclosure, they share the lifestyle and have an interest in exploring it further. However, they know nothing about *Ahsasz Down Under*, but are aware of the two of you but not by name."

"I would hope not. Our members pay top dollar for privacy and anonymity and with our shared business venture on the horizon, you'd better know that too, both of you."

"So, are you open to it? Can they at least attend the gallery showing?"

"Sure, but only the showing. And before you get ahead of yourself and start revealing too much information about our business, remember the rules. You can have them as guests but only to open events. Beyond that it's an entirely different process. We decide who gets invited in and when, period."

"Yes, of course."

"Exactly what is it that you wish to accomplish by inviting them to a gallery showing. That event isn't tied to anything related to *Ahsasz Down Under*."

"I thought it would be a good time for you to observe them on your own turf. A background check doesn't tell you everything you need to know about a person." Magda stated.

"Mine do and I pay good money for it."

"Good to know."

"Now, you guys are picking up the check right!" Zsasha said, chuckling at her friends.

"Sure, why not."

The four of them said their goodbyes and headed their separate ways. Simon and Zsasha headed to Ahsasz to retrieve Ms. Honey and check on a few things. As they entered the gallery, they were pleased with what she had accomplished in such a short time.

"Wow, it's looking pretty good here, Ms. Honey. You did a lot and in such little time." Zsasha said. "How did you pull it off?"

"I had a visitor." More than one, Ms. Honey said to herself, but I'll never tell. "John Lee came by for an hour to help out. I couldn't have done as much without him."

"Well I'll be sure to thank him when I see him later."

John Lee was married to Ms. Honey and also worked for Zsasha and Simon at their home and other properties. He took care of the grounds, vehicles, and general maintenance and whatever else they needed. Ms. Honey was responsible for overseeing the household staff as well as those that assisted in Ahsasz and *Ahsasz Down Under*. She was the only other person that knew as much about anyone coming through the door. Other than Zsasha and Simon, some would say she knew more. They did this for a considerable salary in addition to the comfortable detached living quarters the Stewarts were more than happy to let them occupy. Of course, they were also subject to a strict confidentiality agreement, given their surroundings.

"Ms. Honey, why is my private entrance to the club unlocked? You know I prefer you to work in one area at a time. We had the renovations done on both floors so you can have a full kitchen in both areas and expanded supply cabinets for supplies and whatever else you might need. What am I missing here?"

"I'm sorry, Ms. Zsasha. I must have opened it while I was cleaning your office bathroom."

"Well please try to be more careful with that. Security is very important here."

"Excuse us, Ms. Honey." Simon interrupted. "Zsasha, aren't you being a bit hard on her? There's no one here, what's the big deal?"

"Simon, you know as well as I do this only works if privacy is guaranteed. We can't afford careless mistakes like this. I have all sorts of personal and private stuff in my office and my door to the club should never be left open and unattended."

"I thought we agreed to keep the client records in the safe. Why would anything critical be in your office?"

"It's mostly my own shit, that's it and that's all."

"Well, we're good then. Are you sure you're okay? You've been a bit off all day today."

"I'm fine. Let's head home."

Zsasha knew she was lying the moment she said she was okay. The truth of the matter was she had been feeling a little uneasy all day but didn't know why. It wasn't any one thing she could put her finger on, just something that had been gnawing at her all day.

* * * * *

Looking through her closet, J'Nae was contemplating what to wear on her dinner date with Rick. She took her time contemplating which dress and what look she wanted to portray. She decided on a tan colored cotton blend snug fitting dress accented by black knee-high boots and a black pea coat that hung about 4 inches longer than the dress. She wanted to be sexy and conservative all at the same time. Her phone rang just as she was putting on her jacket to head out.

"Hello."

"Hey girl. What are you up to?" asked Rona.

"On my way out. I'm meeting Rick for dinner downtown on K street. What's up with you?"

"So, you finally decided to give in, huh?" Rona said with excitement.

"It's just dinner and some conversation. That's all. Nothing serious."

"Yeah, just have fun. So, are you taking him back to your place afterwards or are you going to his?"

"It's just dinner, sweetie."

"So you said. Hey, I got an idea. I'm going to be leaving a bit earlier than I thought, so you can have him over to help you house sit a day or two if you want. It'll be more intimate. I'm sure Ms. Honey would be more than happy to prepare a meal for you guys. It'll be my gift to you, for finally getting back out there and taking a chance."

"I don't know, maybe, we'll see."

"Okay, fine. Whatever you decide. I'll call you when we're on our way back. Oh, and use the guest room at the top of the stairs on the left, if you need it or want to stay over."

"Cool."

"And don't forget to feed Annabelle, even if you don't see her, be sure to put her food out every day. And if you do stay over, sleep with the door closed, otherwise you might wake up with her tail in your face. She likes to sleep on the pillows."

"Alright, will do. Be safe and you guys have fun."

"We will. See you in a few days."

J'Nae ended her phone conversation just as she was pulling up to the restaurant. Rick was standing outside where the valet is usually waiting to open your door.

"Good evening." Rick said as he opened the car door. "You look lovely as ever." Extending his arm towards her, J'Nae stepped out and took his arm as he closed the door.

"You're looking very handsome as well."

"Thank you. Shall we?" Rick asked as he handed the keys to the real valet and took J'Nae inside.

The restaurant had an elegant feel to it but a contemporary décor. Rick escorted J'Nae to the elevator which took them to the second floor. They were met by a hostess who seated them in a private dining room completely cut off from any other guest. It provided them with a private and exclusive dining experience.

"Wow, where are we? Where's everybody else?" J'Nae asked.

"We have the floor to ourselves."

"Just us?"

"Yes, just us for as far as your eyes can see."

J'Nae was impressed. She didn't say it but the look on her face said it all. A waiter arrived at their table carrying a bottle of wine, opened it and poured them each a glass.

"I took the liberty of ordering a bottle of Red Bordeaux. I hope you find it to your liking."

Taking a sip, J'Nae was quite pleased with his selection.

"It's delicious. You never said you were a wine connoisseur."

"I have many hidden talents, all of which I welcome the opportunity to share with you, if you allow me."

"Well let's see how the evening plays out."

"That's fine." Rick said, smiling like he had a secret. The two continued to make small talk eyeing each other as dinner was served.

"This looks delicious, but did we order?"

"Already taken care of. I took the liberty of ordering for us. You mentioned how much you like a good steak, so I had a special meal made for us. The chef is a dear friend of mine, I could introduce you."

"Oh, that won't be necessary."

"Why not. I'm sure Alex would love to meet you."

"Well, maybe later."

Sampling her plate, J'Nae was impressed with his choices. The steak was seared to perfection, sided with new potatoes and bacon wrapped asparagus. Washing it down with a superb glass of wine was the perfect finish to a delectable meal.

"That was delicious. Please thank Chef Alex for me."

"No need. You can do that yourself." Rick said. "Here she is now."

Walking towards their table was a tall, fabulously attractive woman, donned in an all-white non-traditional chef's uniform. A skirt 4 inches above her knees replaced the slacks most chefs wore while in the kitchen. Her hair was long and wavy and bounced with each step she took in their direction sporting shiny white patent leather pumps. Smiling as she approached, Rick removed his napkin and stood to greet her.

"Alex, how lovely to see you. It's been too long."

Both Alex and Rick reached out to embrace one another. Since it had been a few years since they'd seen one another, their embrace was tight and warm and lasted long enough for J'Nae to begin feeling insecure. A slight bit of uncomfortableness rose up from the pit of her stomach to her chest area when they didn't let go of each other right away.

They shared an embrace reflective of the family inspired love they'd grown to have for one another over the years. A normal person on the outside looking in wouldn't see anything that resembled a relationship, past or present, romantic in nature. But when it comes to men, bitches are anything but normal.

"Way too long! It's good to see you too, love."

"This is my friend, J'Nae."

"She's every bit as beautiful as you said she'd be. Hello J'Nae. How are you?"

"J'Nae paused for a moment without speaking, completely caught off guard by her gender and beauty, recovered quickly and uttered a simple hello. Aware of her obvious snafu, she came back with more appropriate conversation.

"Forgive me, I'm J'Nae. The meal you prepared was absolutely delicious."

"Thank you. Rick mentioned you were a lover of steak, so I prepared this meal especially for the two of you. It's one of my specialties."

"Well, it was divine." J'Nae said smoothly. "You too obviously know each other well. What am I missing here?"

"Not much." Rick inserted. "Actually, Alex dated my sister back in college. We ran into each other a few years ago when she relocated to this area, and we've kept in touch ever since."

You could see a sigh of relief on J'Nae's face even though she tried not to appear happy about the revelation that just unfolded. Rick and Alex couldn't help but grin at each other at the obvious joke.

"Don't worry, he's all yours!" Alex remarked jokingly. "It was a pleasure to meet you, J'Nae. Rick, good to see you again love. Take care you two."

With that, Alex was gone. J'Nae was a bit embarrassed at how she was feeling and her inability to keep her emotions under wraps was something they laughed about several times throughout the remainder of the evening as Rick took a great deal of pleasure in teasing her about it every chance he got. They said their goodbye's and J'Nae headed home.

When she arrived home, there was a text message waiting for her on her cellphone. It read: 'Jealousy becomes you!' J'Nae laughed and kicked off her shoes and clothing then stretched out across her bed. She replied, 'You got me, didn't see that coming.' Before she could get comfortable, Rick replied, 'I'd like to see you coming...' Caught off guard she replied with a smiley face emoji without giving it much thought. She had a great evening with Rick and found him enticing. She replied again. 'Tomorrow, come by the house for dinner...8:00 pm'. Without hesitation, she texted the address and almost instantly received his confirmation.

She was more than excited lying in bed, fully engulfed in her fantasy sexcapade. She could feel the onset of another spontaneous orgasm and this time, she was in the right place, and it was the right time. Lowering her right hand to her groin and welcomed the release of the sexual tensions that had been building up all evening. She exhaled, then drifted off to sleep.

Chapter 11

The next morning, J'Nae was awakened by her cell phone which she usually kept on the bed next to her pillow.

"Hello?"

"Girl get up! What are you still doing in bed? It's almost noon. Get up!" Vonne's voice came through the phone loud and clear. Looking at the alarm clock, J'Nae could clearly see Vonne was not telling the truth. It was just after 10:00 am.

"Girl quit it. It's too early for this nonsense."

"I got Zsasha on the other line, let me click over."

"What's up girl?" Zsasha said. "How was your dinner date with Rick last night?"

"It was good, secluded and intimate...special."

"Oh yeah, do tell girlfriend, do tell." Vonne inserted.

"I can't believe y'all are waking me up with all these questions right now. I'm not going to tell you what you want to hear."

"Girl, we've been waiting as long as you." Zsasha said. You could almost hear her grinning as she spoke.

"I'm afraid you'll have to wait a little longer for those details. It was just dinner, a very nice private dinner and with our own personal chef, Chef Alex."

"That sounds romantic, was it?"

"Yes, but not in the way you're thinking. He was a perfect gentleman."

"Well just holla at me when you get there." Zsasha stated. "I'm tired of waiting, damn girl."

"Whatever...So what are you two up to today, anything in particular?"

"I'm still taking care of last-minute details for the artist exhibit. In fact, I'll be doing a bit of that daily until the day of the showing. What about you Vonne? What you got going on today?"

"Taking Kiera on a tour to see a few of my boutiques so she can start getting familiar with the inventory and how that's handled."

"Why?" J'Nae asked.

"Yeah, I thought she'd be on her way out by now Girl.

"Well, she has nowhere to go. No job or money coming in, she can't possibly support herself. And the last situation she was in was more than toxic."

"And why is that your problem?" Zsasha asked.

"Because she's my sister. I can't just put her out on the street and turn my back on her. She has nothing, absolutely nothing."

"So instead, you're going to give her a job, huh? Opening your home wasn't enough, so now you're opening your business as well?"

"And your bank account too." J'Nae added.

"It's just for a little while." Vonne spewed.

"Look here girlfriend, I don't say much, well yes I do, but I'm gonna say this anyway because woman to woman, you need to hear this and hear this loud and clear. Letting her move in your home where she's around your husband was a bad idea to boot. You can't allow another woman in your home, especially one known for causing drama, cutting up and shit. You know better than this. And then to bring her into your well-established business, that's next level. What did Lee have to say about all of this?" Zsasha questioned.

"Truthfully, he feels somewhat obligated because of how all this went down, ya know, him bringing dad here. So, he's okay with it...for now. We have to do what we have to do for family, that's the bottom line."

"You sound like you're trying to convince yourself this is a good idea. It's not, Vonne, trust me." Zsasha reiterated. "This is gonna come back and bite you in the ass."

"It might." Vonne admitted.

"If you feel so strongly about it, find some other way to help her, just keep her away from all you've got going for you."

Vonne didn't respond to Zsasha's comments right away. Instead, she paused and took a minute to acknowledge what her

116

friend said but only for her sake. She knew if she didn't appear to pay attention to what Zsasha said, she would only come back more harshly and Vonne just didn't want to hear it.

"Vonne, sweetie, we're just worried about you. We've all seen what your family has done to you in the past. Your father was here then left, leaving your sister behind who is living with you and your husband. Lee on his own is more than a notion most of the time. I'm with Zsasha. I think you're going to be in over your head." J'Nae shared.

"Well, it's what I have to do for now, anyway." Vonne said, without much enthusiasm.

"Well, we're here for you sweetie, always."

"Yeah, we got your back." Zsasha added.

"I appreciate that."

With that, the conversation ended. J'Nae was not happy about Vonne's revelation but she wasn't going to let it put a downer on her mood. Nope, it's her life. Vonne's a big girl and she can handle herself. If it goes south, we'll be there to pick up the pieces like we always do for one another. With that, J'Nae showered and dressed and headed to Rona's to feed her cat and enjoy some of the amenities of Rona's custom-built home. On the ride over, J'Nae reached out to Rick, and he answered.

"Hey sweetie, how are you today?"

"I'm fine. I was just thinking about you and thought I'd call to confirm our plans for this evening."

"It's a date. I wouldn't miss it for the world." He replied.

"Just so you know, we'll be hanging out at Rona's house. I'm house sitting for her and taking care of her cat while she's out of town for a few days. It'll just be the three of us. Is that cool?"

"A cat, huh?"

"Yeah. What's the matter? You're not afraid of a little pussy cat, are you?" J'Nae knew full well she had stepped out of her comfort zone with that remark. But she couldn't take it back now, nor did she want to. Being flirtatious and sexually suggestive was not something she had embraced much in her past, but she was now willing to take a different approach. He was different, and that G-shot had awakened parts of her

117

creating a desire for him that was strong and overbearing. The personal rules and standard of behavior that guided her in the past were no longer relevant. It was a new day for J'Nae Carter, a new day indeed.

"Me, afraid...nope, never that. See you at 8:00."

"Can't wait."

* * * * *

Later, back at Ahsasz, the staging of the new exhibit took the rest of the day. Planning and preparing the gallery for a showing was a huge deal, on the surface, however the big money came from *Ahsasz Down Under*. All the kinks had been worked out including the layout and setup which had been slightly modified to accommodate some of the artists' larger pieces. The date of the exhibit had been postponed once already but the start of the event was drawing near.

Aside from the catering, the last step would require the featured artist, Andre DeSimone to give his final stamp of approval once he made certain everything was secure and properly mounted and showcased according to his vision, for the most part. He was scheduled to arrive the next day so getting everything in place tonight was crucial.

That evening, J'Nae had spent a considerable amount of time rummaging through Rona's closet looking for the perfect dress to wear for dinner date with Rick. The meal had been prepared by Ms. Honey at Rona's request and had just been placed in the warmer moments ago.

She didn't want the dress to be formal or elegant since they were staying in; however, she wanted the dress to reflect all that she was feeling inside. Daring, excited, enticed, sexy and stimulated were all representative of the vibe that consumed her body, inside and out. She was ready for what was to come next.

Fully dressed and looking at herself in a large mirror hanging over the bar she thought to herself...this is it...this is happening, this is happening tonight. Her reflection revealed a backless Donna Karen form fitting dress she borrowed from Rona's closet. It was Couture and she was certain to be one of Vonne's pieces. Continuing to stare in the mirror, she was happy with what she saw.   She had long ago accepted the fact that Rona has a banging body, for sure, but seeing is believing and this dress…was made for her, without a doubt she looked much better in it than her girl.

As she returned to the large foyer area right off the front door, J'Nae did her best to find a seductive position on the small bench positioned to give off the appearance of a waiting area. But it wasn't very comfortable and much too small for anything else, much less sitting seductively. She gave up in less than a minute and headed toward the sofa making sure to leave the door unlocked for easy access.

Before she positioned herself on the sofa, she reached down between her legs and quickly stripped herself of her panties. If I'm going to do this, I'm going to do this right, she thought. And without any further consideration, she tossed her panties behind the couch, claimed her seductive position, and anxiously waited for her friend.

When he arrived just seconds later, she could barely hear him knock on the door over the sound of her rapid heartbeat pounding in her ears. As she became more aroused, the pounding in her ears grew louder and louder causing her to fumble for a few seconds. But she quickly regained her resolve and told him to come on in.

Rick entered, looking divine and entirely edible and she was more than ready for her seat at the table. She knew this would be an amazing experience and she was ready to embrace it fully and let herself go. It was they're third date and she no longer wanted to hide the fact that she had been secretly coveting him since they first reconnected at Vonne's dinner party. It had been hard for her to openly admit, but she had moved past her hang-ups. No longer was she conflicted about age differences and potential ramifications of their lust, but more concerned about being self-indulgent and determined to give herself, her mind, body, and soul whatever the fuck it needed and whenever it needed it. And she needed it, now.   Not the spontaneous orgasmic burst that tantalized her body throughout the day and night. But the touch of his hands caressing her; his strong

119

unyielding member guaranteeing that head spinning, teeth grinding, bing-bang-zoom, knock it out the park, hella sex game she so desperately knew was just moments away.

Rick swiftly walked toward her, taking in her position on the sofa. She could see the desire in his eyes, a hunger or thirst that was equal to her own. What am I doing, she thought...this man is just a few years older than her adult children? But just as quickly as that question entered her mind, it exited. The next thing she knew, he was close up on her. So close, she could hear him breath and feel the warmth of his breath on her face.

"Hmm, you smell good sweetheart."

And just then, forcefully and without notice, his tongue pried her lips apart then danced vigorously around the inside of her mouth. Consuming her as she yielded to his direction, she allowed him to lead and guide the sensuality of their kiss. His hand was on her breast cupping one, then the other, caressing them gently at first and then a bit more aggressively he massaged them, one at a time, flicking her hard nipples as he passed from left to right and back again. Scooping her breast out of her dress, he gently bent down and ran his tongue across her right nipple sending chills up and down her spine. She moaned, so turned on that she didn't notice he surreptitiously dropped to his knees, positioning himself for his next move, kissing her down the outer part of her thigh while pushing her dress upwards and out of the way. Fervently his tongue was between her legs, licking gently around the outer part of her pussy then aggressively sliding his tongue across her clit, massaging it in harmony with the simultaneous flicking of her nipples. She was in ecstasy. Instinctively her legs spread apart welcoming his face, begging for his mouth to tightly embrace her whole pussy. She raised her leg slightly, perching it on the arm of the sofa to make her pussy completely accessible. As he sucked with his full mouth, her juices began to flow down her inner thigh also trickling back towards her ass. Oh my goodness, his touch was electric, sending shocks all thru her body. His tongue continued to work its magic and her clitoris began to swell from the excitement. Just then, she climaxed, squirting her love

120

juice all over his face and hair, leaving trails dripping from his nostrils. He grunted but he continued, licking, and sucking her pussy with his whole mouth……. Pulling and massaging, more vigorously and aggressively than before. Intermittently flicking his tongue in and then back out, again and again while sucking in a circular motion. She felt his tongue slide once, then twice, gently across the rim of her asshole sending shock waves through her body. The sensation was beyond words. Suddenly his tongue changed focus and was back licking and flicking ever so gently over her clit. Her juices flowed so heavily at this point, she could hear his lips smacking and making suckling noises as he continued to work his craft. All the while, lifting her, holding her, ever so gently over him at an angle perfect for the task at hand. Without notice, he rose slowly but steadily, at first lifting her with him while continuing his salacious attack on her pussy. Then as his body rose upwards, he slowly lowered her downwards, then he slid his dick inside of her with a force and passion that demanded she climax at once. And she did. He continued to thrust his dick in her now saturated pussy. All she could think of is how beautiful his unseen dick must be to yield such an incredible feeling. Amazing!!!! Again, she moaned that moan he was now accustomed to hearing. The thrusting continued…in and out, in and out while her body began to shake. With each stroke she came closer and closer to ecstasy, and he was prepared to make sure she got everything she could possibly get out of it.

Just as she began to climax in sync with his rhythm, he abruptly lifted her up off him then covered her entire pussy with his wide-open mouth sucking the rest of the orgasm out of her until the shakes and trembling were no more. Breathing heavily, she collapsed on him in total and complete exhaustion. She began to feel his cool soft breath over her face and neck as he carefully tried to cool her down. She tilted her head backwards so his cool breath could be felt on her cleavage, cooling her breasts instantly. Instinctively, she reached for him and reciprocated along his forehead, neck and chest area, holding ever so tightly to his masculine shoulders. Gently she relaxed in his arms.

They lay there, in their nakedness, embracing the extraordinary sweetness of their now depleted love. He looked at her and she looked up at him. Lovingly he smiles and runs his hand through her sweat-soaked hair. They allow exhaustion to take over and they both surrender to sleep.

Chapter 12

Opening her eyes, Zsasha looked around the gallery for Ms. Honey whom she found asleep on the sofa in Simon's office.

"Good morning, Ms. Honey."

"Good morning Ms. Zsasha."

"What time is it Ms. Honey? Andre should be here at 10:00 am."

Looking at her watch, Ms. Honey announced it was 8:30.

"Damn, well I'd better shower and dress right quick. You can use my private bathroom to shower when I'm done if you want too. We've been here before, so you know the routine."

"Yes, I do, Ms. Zsasha, thanks but no thanks. John Lee is picking me up to take me home. He should be here any minute."

"I hope he wasn't worried about you last night. Did you tell him you were staying here all night?"

"I think I sent him a drunk text message late last night. He knew where I was and why I was here. He even offered to come help. I'm sure everything will be fine."

"Cool but let me know when you're leaving so I can double lock the doors." Zsasha warned.

"Of course, but isn't Mr. Simon coming?"

"I don't know, maybe. I think we spoke last night, but I have no idea what we talked about. By the way, what did we do last night? I don't remember us drinking that much."

"We drank nearly four bottles of wine between us."

"Really, so that explains the headache, huh?"

"Yes mam."

"Damn, so how do you feel now?"

"I'm good.   I didn't drink quite as much as you did sweetheart."

"No surprise there." Sasha smirked.

"You were in your feelings about a few things and needed to vent. You talked, I listened blah, blah, blah."

"Like so many times before." Zsasha recalled.

"That's for sure." Sasha grunted. "You know more of my secrets than anyone."

"I don't know what you're talking about." Ms. Honey insisted. "Coffee?"

"Hell yeah, but I need to freshen up first, thanks."

Zsasha headed into her office toward her private bathroom, undressed and jumped in her private shower. It took no time at all for the aroma of freshly brewed coffee to make its way into her office, mildly stimulating her senses while putting a little pep in her step. She recognized her husband's voice approaching but couldn't make out who he was talking to, it was further away. Stepping out of the shower, she was instantly greeted by her husband, who as usual, was dressed impeccably, all day, every day and she loved that about him.

"Morning, love."

"Morning sweetie." Zsasha said leaning in for a kiss. "Is Andre here yet?"

"No, not yet. I'll take care of him when he arrives. Go ahead and indulge yourself. You look like you had a night."

"Didn't do too bad, two bottles of wine and a shot or two."

"I heard it was more like four bottles of wine and a fifth of bourbon." Simon teased.

"Whateva." Zsasha shrugged.

"So, you got a wine hangover huh, that's the worst one, baby."

"I know! I don't know what got into me last night. I can't remember the last time I drank so much and on an empty stomach."

"I know you know better than that. Something must have been weighing on your mind for that to happen."

"I think it's just anxiety, sweetheart. We arranged, delayed, re-arranged and still opening night has yet to come and go."

"You're always stressed when featuring a new artist. You never know how well they'll be received."

"Yeah, probably so." Zsasha conceded.

Fully dressed now, she walked toward the mirror to see what she could do with her hair. Lucky for her, she spends hella money at the hairdresser and buys only the finest hair weave.

"What are you looking for, Z?"

"My hairbrush. I always keep one in my bathroom for times like this."

"Did you check your purse?"

"No. I never take it anywhere."

"Well just check anyway. You were drinking last night. Maybe you dropped it in your purse and forgot about it."

She checked it and saw nothing. At least not what she was looking for.

"I wonder where it could be?"

"I don't know sweetie. But I can run to the store and get another one. It'll only take a minute."

"Nah, don't worry about it. I have a rattail comb I can use to flatten my edges. A little water and it'll be fine. Besides, we need to be in the showroom when he gets here, both of us, together."

"I agree."

Zsasha and Simon left her office to take one last look at the exhibit layout hoping Andre would be happy with their changes. Once he arrived, Simon took the lead on showing him the layout while explaining their staging choices and reasons for deviating from his specific plan.

Zsasha, having returned to her office, was distracted by her missing hairbrush and wondered if someone had been in her office snooping, maybe trying to get access to her client files or something and took the brush as a memento. It had no monetary value but was something she hung onto for sentimental reasons and had it for many, many years. She shrugged her shoulders and put the matter out of her mind, certain it would turn up later.

* * * * *

Kissing him good morning, J'Nae could still taste their love on his lips as well as hers. It was sensual and enticing, causing the memory of the past several hours to linger throughout the day.

125

"Are you rushing off so soon?" J'Nae asked.

"I'm afraid I have to work today sweetie. I'm filling in for my partner who's on vacation."

"You never mentioned much about your job. What exactly do you do?"

"I'm in communications."

"That sounds intriguing. Care to elaborate?"

"I'd love to, but I've got to go. Can I see you later?" Rick asked as he kissed her ever so gently.

"Sure thing."

"Great. Have a good day baby."

"You too, sweetie."

Once the fog cleared her mind, J'Nae was also running a bit behind schedule. She needed to tidy up the place and drop Rona's borrowed dress off at the dry cleaners. As she began gathering her things, she picked up her phone and noticed she had several missed calls from Vonne. She immediately dialed her back.

"Hey Vonne, what's going on? Did you like but dial me nine times or were you really trying to get a hold of me?"

"No. I've been trying to reach you since last night."

"Is everything alright? What's going on?"

"It's dad. Ever since Kiera showed up, he can't help himself. He's constantly on video chat with her and purposely where I can hear their conversation. He's fallen back into his old ways."

"How so?" J'Nae inquired.

"He's been on one of his rants about Kiera as a child and teenager. Kiera did this and Kiera did that, remember honey."

"Well maybe he's just proud and wants to remind her of better days. You know she's going through it right now. It makes sense that your dad would try to lift her spirits."

"That may very well be the case but it's not necessary to put me down in order to lift her up. It's the same shit, different day. And Kiera is always going through something, so I've seen this skit before and trust me, I know how it plays out."

"Well, aren't you the pessimistic one today."

"Ah, not really. I told you I've been down this road before, a few times. First dad will dwell on the highlights of her past and then he'll commit to her constant praise, and right there in my face!"

"I assume it's unwarranted, right?"

"Absolutely, but he won't stop there. He'll start focusing on a short period of time where some might say Kiera was more together than I was, which if you ask me, never existed but he'll continue down that road. The more liquored up he is, the worse he gets. That's usually when I make my move to the next room, however depending on who else is around and his level of vulgarity and of course my mood, I might just get in his face and go toe to toe with him, no matter how hurtful he is. He'll be sure to belittle me every chance he gets, and he'll continually say I should be more like her. Kiera was doing great when this and Kiera was doing great when that….and so on. And if at any point I make the decision to walk away, they always seem to find themselves where I can hear them clearly. It's all done on purpose."

"I don't know girl. Are you sure you're not overreacting? Maybe this time will be different."

"And maybe my tits are as perky as a twenty-year-old."

"Girl you need to quit. History doesn't always repeat itself, don't let him get to you before you see what's going on. You own several boutique's, have more on the horizon and a gorgeous home to boot! He can't possibly complain about your achievements and if he does, he's just hating."

"Yeah, whatever. So anyway, why the hell are you so damn happy and in a good mood, J'Nae?"

"What do you mean?"

"Uh Oh! You did it. You finally went and did it!"

"Did what?" J'Nae teased, barely able to keep a straight face.

"You got laid!"

"I don't know what you're talking about." J'Nae claimed, turning her back to her friend.

"Yes, you doooo…!" Vonne replied rather slowly with a coyness about her.

127

"No, I don't."

"You got fucked!!! And by a young man no less!"

"I don't kiss and tell, girl."

"You don't have to. I can hear it in your voice, better yet, I can see it all over your face! I don't know why I didn't sense it sooner, It's so obvious!"

"Is it now?"

"Yes, it is, and it's about damn time! That pussy couldn't have been locked up any tighter if it was guarded by Homeland Security, I mean it, for real for real!"

"Yeah, whatever."

"Whatever my ass, don't you feel better?"

"Actually, I do!"

"Well good for you. It's about time you let that cat out the bag."

"You're too funny." J'Nae laughs.

"And we're talking about Rick, right?"

"Yes, and OMG is all I can say!"

"You go girl!"

"Yes, and that's what I'm about to do. Go! Holla later sweetie and don't stress yourself."

"Easier said than done." Vonne stated firmly.

"Look, if it gets too stressful, come over and crash with me. A few hours or a few days, whatever you need, I got you."

"Thanks, girlfriend!" Vonne said in a somber voice.

"I told you I got your back." J'Nae reiterated. "Now call me if you need me, okay?"

"Okay, bye."

"Bye sweetie."

Vonne decided to head downstairs to find her sister. She was determined to make the best of the current living arrangements and not allow family drama to damper her day. She found her sister relaxing in the family room watching TV.

"Hey Kiera, I'm going to be working on inventory today, would you like to come with?"

"Doesn't sound like much fun, I'll pass."

"You sure? You'll get first look at some of the latest fashions right off the rack."

"Is lunch included?"

"Sure, why not."

"Okay, I'm in."

"Cool, let's do it."

The two gather their things, lock up the house and settle in Vonne's car for the ride into the city. Not long after they took off Vonne noticed Kiera was steadily sipping from a tumbler she pulled out of her bag.

"Kiera, what's in your cup?" Vonne asked, half acting like she already knew the answer.

"Iced Tea. I had it shipped here from Long Island." Kiera responded in a joking manner.

"Are you kidding me? You got in my car with some alcohol? Kiera, I told you when I agreed to let you stay here that I wasn't having none of your foolishness. You know I could get a ticket for having an open container if we get stopped."

"Ah, hold your horses, I was just messing with you. You're always so serious and you can't take a joke."

"I can take a joke. Just not that particular joke with that particular subject matter and not with you."

"You always gotta go negative." Kiera said.

"Gee, I wonder where I get that from." Vonne said with sarcasm. But once she thought about her last remark, she thought better of it. She had many memories of how she felt when it was done to her.

"Sorry Kiera. It was wrong of me to throw your past in your face like that. Dad's done it to me a thousand times and I know exactly how it feels."

"I guess you're more like him than you thought."

"I guess so. And I should know better. My bad."

"It's fine, it's not that serious, Vonne."

"Actually, it is. You're here to get a fresh start and you won't get one if I don't give you the benefit of the doubt and let go of your past mistakes, some of them anyway."

"I appreciate that sis, I really do. And I appreciate all the help you're giving me.

Vonne couldn't believe the words that were about to flow out of her mouth, but it just felt like the right thing to say at the time.

"I'm happy to help. But this offer has conditions, and you absolutely have to be working towards getting your life on track."

"I am Vonne, really."

"I'm serious, Kiera. I have a husband and a business to run. I don't have time for drama and bullshit, okay. We'll sit down tomorrow and come up with a plan. A solid plan we can put on paper. Maybe we'll start it today over lunch."

"Is that necessary?"

"I think so. If you can see your plan daily and track your progress, it will help you stay focused on the task at hand."

"You think?"

"Yeah, I do. Because as you begin to check off your tasks as you complete them, you'll see how much closer you are to your goal. And those results will help you stay motivated. Before you know it, your plan becomes your new reality, and you'll feel empowered and confident about yourself and what you can achieve. Trust me, you'll see."

"Okay, okay." Kiera said, sounding enthusiastic at the prospect of getting her shit in order. "I'll let you lead the way."

Arriving at the Boutique, the sisters headed towards the back of the store where the new inventory was stored.

"Vonne, I think I hear a phone ringing. Is that you or me?"

"Uhm, it's me. Hello?"

"Hey wassup?"

"Hey Z, what's going on? Wasn't expecting to hear from you today. Thought you'd be knee deep in gallery prep. The showing is tomorrow, right?"

"Yes, it is. Everything is pretty much done. Ms. Honey and John Lee helped me out a great deal over the last couple of days. So, we're pretty much set."

"Oh yeah, okay cool."

"Yeah, well that's why I'm calling, to see which one of you heffa's is free tonight. We can sample some of this fine ass wine Simon ordered, recommended by one of his business associates. It comes in at $500.00 a bottle. You in?"

"Hell yeah, oh but wait, right now, Kiera and I are at the Arlington store working on the new inventory that just arrived. What time are you talking about meeting up?"

"Kiera is with you?"

"Yeah."

"I didn't see that coming. You sure you want her all up in your business like that?"

"It'll be fine. And it's just for a little while anyway. So, what time are you trying to do this?"

"A little earlier than usual with the show tomorrow and everything, how's six o'clock?"

"I don't know. I'd have to drive Kiera back home and come back out."

"Nonsense. Just let her drive herself home and I'll pick you up. You're way too close to Ahsasz to go back to the house just to come back out this way."

"Seriously, let her drive my car?"

"Hell, you got her in your store and up in your house. Letting her drive your car is not that much of a stretch and anyway, what's the worst that can happen?"

"Yeah, but I don't know if she's ready for all that."

"Well, you got her around all your high-end merchandise at the store, right?"

"Yeah, I do."

"Well, I've shopped in your boutiques before and some of those dresses cost as much as a good car."

"You're exaggerating, but I get it."

"So, I'll pick you up at 5:45. Just lock up then and send her on her way, cool?"

"Okay cool. See you then."

* * * * *

J'Nae had just finished her phone call with Zsasha about meeting up that evening when she received a phone call from Rick.

"Hey sweetie, how's your day been? You miss me yet?" Rick asked.

"It's only been a few hours, sweetie." J'Nae replied, trying not to sound too harsh.

"Every minute I'm away from you feels like a lifetime."

"Seriously?"

"Yeah, seriously."

"That's so sweet of you to say, baby. I can't wait to see you too."

"How about later?"

"Uh, later...I'm meeting the girls at the gallery soon, sorry sweetie."

"Oh well, I'll have to figure out other ways to entertain myself in your absence."

"Don't you go getting too creative now, sweetheart. I might start thinking it's something I want to be in on... you getting creative and all."

"OMG, your inner freak is showing."

"I didn't mean it like that."

"Sure, you did, and it's all good."

Laughing, J'Nae realized she set herself up for that joke and decided to just roll with it.

"Actually, I'm on my way to meet Zsasha and Vonne at the gallery right now. We're previewing the featured artwork and sampling some wine they're serving at showing. Although I don't know what the point is, most of it we've already seen."

"Well, it sounds like fun."

"It should be. It always is, but without Rona, who knows how it'll go."

"I'm sure you ladies will be fine. Text me when you're heading home, okay?"

"Okay Rick, talk to you soon."

"Bye, baby."

* * * * *

Pulling up to Ahsasz, J'Nae could see Zsasha and Vonne letting themselves inside. As she walked up to the door Zsasha was holding open, she could see an unusual look on her friend's face as she walked past her to go inside. She looked troubled.

"What's wrong with you? Are you okay?" J'Nae asked Zsasha.

"I'm okay." Zsasha replied unconvincingly.

"No, you're not, spill it. What's going on?"

"Yeah girl, you look preoccupied or something." Vonne confirmed.

"I don't know. Just now, when I was unlocking the door, I had the strange feeling that I was being watched. That's crazy, right?" Zsasha asked.

Vonne and J'Nae looked at each other in sync. Both were thinking exactly the same thing.

"I don't think it sounds crazy at all." Vonne protested. "There are all kinds of strange and deranged people in this world. Plus, you own this beautiful art gallery that just happens to be filled with expensive artwork."

"True. But check this, this isn't the first time I've felt like this lately."

"Have you mentioned it to Simon yet?" J'Nae uttered.

"No. He'll just say I'm being paranoid. Besides, after our most security upgrades it's like Fort Knox in here. Nobody is breaking in here."

"You still need to tell Simon. Both of you encounter so many different types of people through the course of business. It's for your own good to tell him about it." Vonne persisted.

"She's right, it can't hurt any." J'Nae seconded. "Better safe than sorry."

"Alright. I'll tell him tonight and see what he says."

"Good." J'Nae said.

Walking towards her office to get the high-priced wine and the glasses she had set out for the evening Zsasha felt a wave of relief come over her. Knowing that her girls supported her, and she wasn't being paranoid took the edge off and her anxiety began to fade. They were right. During the course of their regular business activities, they encountered all sorts of people from Ahsasz and *Ahsasz Down Under*, some of which are from various walks of life and potentially from all over the world.

For the most part, if they don't have a criminal history and do have a considerable amount of wealth, they can probably pass the background check required for access *Ahsasz Down Under* provided they have a referral and a sponsor. In reality, it's not far-fetched that her businesses could draw some negative attention from some unsavory individuals even with all the protection and privacy in place. J'Nae may have some ideas about what Simon and Zsasha are into, but she will never have a full understanding of the intricacies in managing and maintaining a business of that nature.

"Love what you've done to the place, Zsasha."

"Well thank you Madame."

"It must have taken days to create and engineer the new layout. It looks absolutely amazing!" Declared J'Nae.

"We've been working on this for a while now which you would have noticed on your last visit if you weren't so preoccupied with Rick." Zsasha said annoyingly.

"She ought to be preoccupied with Rick." Vonne exclaimed. "Have you taken a good look at that fine ass caramel coated chocolate drop lately?"

"Yes Vonne, I have. He's kind of hard to miss." Zsasha answered.

"You can say that again! I mean damn! I love my unemployed husband and he's fine and all but ooh la la!"

"I agree girl, even I'm guilty of eye fucking his fine ass a time or two!" Zsasha confessed.

"Alright y'all, that's enough." J'Nae warned.

"I don't know Vonne, what do you think? Can baby girl handle all that? I think she might have bitten off more than she can chew."

"Well, you can just ask her, you know."

"No way! For real? I don't believe it." Zsasha said jokingly.

"Yes, she did it, she did it alright!" Vonne exclaimed.

"Why do you sound so surprised? You've been riding me harder than anyone about being so uptight and picky." J'Nae insisted.

"Harder than Rick!" Zsasha said while laughing. "Girls, we ought to go out and celebrate. This is a big deal!" Zsasha said. "And I'm not trying to be funny, really. I'm happy that you finally took real steps to get on with your life!"

"Finally?" J'Nae asked suspiciously. "Albeit unsuccessful, I've been dating for a few months now."

"   Yeah, that's what you said." Uttered Vonne. "But truth be told, I didn't believe all those dating horror stories you told us. Especially the panty bandit. That was way over the top!"

"Yeah, it was." Said J'Nae. "And so was he. Sitting in his car with a pair of panties over his head and face. Just nasty, I tell you, just nasty!"

"Oh yeah Vonne, it happened. I believe it happened just like she said and it's not as strange as you think. Men crave the smell of pussy. And not all of them like it fresh smelling, either." Zsasha explained.

"What do you mean not all men like it fresh?" J'Nae asked with confusion in her voice.

"Sweetheart, some men like pussy to smell and taste like pussy, in its natural state. You got some brothers that like it spring cleaned right before sex and then those that want it marinating in its own natural juices all day long. They call that seasoned." Zsasha explained.

"Oh my gosh!" J'Nae uttered, feeling like she had been found out.

"Girl where have you been? Surely you and Julian had oral sex on some level. From the stories I've heard, he was no boy scout!"

"Excuse me," J'Nae said softly as she stood up. "Zsasha, I need to use your bathroom."

J'Nae walked away with her glass of wine in hand without waiting for an answer. She hurried along to Zsasha's office and into her private bathroom where she stood in front of the sink looking at herself in the mirror. Only to see the very same

135

feelings of uncomfortableness that caused her to abruptly leave her friends, make their appearance across her face. Unsure why she felt embarrassed by the conversation only intensified her anxiety. She'd experienced oral sex before, as the giver and the receiver, but only with Julian and now she felt exposed. And the idea that Rick craved her natural smell and taste was more than unnerving simply because she enjoyed the slightly seasoned taste of herself on his lips and didn't want to admit it.

Although the girls often discussed intimate details about sex and oral sex J'Nae was pretty much on the side lines. She had to admit that while at first, listening to all this pussy talk was a bit uneasy, it was a turn on and she felt herself become warm, moist and aroused. Once again, the G-shot had her totally discombobulated and five seconds away from climax. A minute later or two later she splashed water on her face, patted it dry then slowly made her way back to her friends.

"Wow, what was that about?" Vonne asked. "I knew what was up with young boy before you arrived, but I promise you, I didn't see that coming." Vonne said.

"I did...think about it, Vonne. J'Nae has always been uptight and by the book, a goody two shoes, we all know it. Now, she's stepped outside of her comfort zone not once but twice and on top of that, she had a GYN doctor, one I referred her to, who accidentally injected her with a substance that temporarily increased her sexual desire. Yes, it helped her issue, but she doesn't know that she can trust what she's feeling when her hormones have been manipulated."

"I do, if it has anything to do with Rick, she's good." Vonne replied.

"Do you really? Because I don't know how you can justify that. First off, the dating profile we convinced her to create that led to her encounter with the panty creep right out the gate. Before that, she almost gave it up to L.B., a man that's been after her for a few years now simply because her hormones were out of sync."

"I get it, but I think this is different. I think there's more to it with Rick."

"I don't see why. Not only is she having sex with him, but he's about 10 years her junior. I'm sure the age thing has been on her mind, and I think all this talk has made her feel like a relic or out of touch, maybe even irrelevant. Maybe that's why she ran off."

"Well, she's definitely feeling something. I think she really likes Rick, more than she's letting on."

"Maybe, maybe not. She'll let us know when she's ready."

"For sure."

"Maybe it's nothing." Zsasha mumbled. "Hey J'Nae! Are you alright?"

"I'm fine. I was just admiring the portrait hanging in your office. I remember when you painted it back in the day." J'Nae, now back with Vonne and Zsasha, was now relaxed and at ease. She helped herself to another glass of wine determined to alter the focus of conversation.

"Yeah, that was a long time ago." Zsasha reiterated. "Almost feels like another lifetime. So, have either one of you heard from Rona? I'm wondering how her trip is going." Zsasha asked.

"I'm sure she's having the time of her life." Vonne replied.

"She's actually due back late this evening." J'Nae interrupted. "Something about Ricardo having to cut his trip short; some kind of work emergency."

"Well good. Maybe she'll be able to attend the gallery showing after all. With her high standards and refined taste, I look forward to showing off what we've done. I think she'll be impressed."

"Absolutely. If not, I'm impressed enough for the both of us. You and Simon did an amazing job. And this artist, very talented, don't you agree, Vonne?"

"I do. So, what time is this shindig anyway?"

"We open the doors at 4:00 pm but the fun doesn't start until around six. So, what do y'all think about this wine?"

"I love it." Vonne replied.

"No surprise there, girlfriend. J'Nae, what about you? Is it worth the $500 price tag?"

"Not $500 of my money but yes, it's good, very good."

"Cool but don't y'all heffa's get used to it. Next time, we'll be back to drinking our usual."

"For sure." Vonne replied. "We need to get going so you can rest up. We can't have you looking tired and worn out at your big event tomorrow, now, can we?"

"Nope, not at all. Let me lock up my office and we can all walk out together. Vonne, I'm assuming that since I brought you here, you're riding with me, right?"

"I am."

"Ok, cool." Goodnight Zsasha, see you tomorrow. Look Fab!"

The ladies all exited the gallery while Zsasha set the alarm and locked the gallery doors. While J'Nae and Vonne were chatting on the sidewalk, J'Nae pulled out her phone and texted Rick letting him know she was just leaving the gallery.

"Damn girl, he got you logging your arrival and departure times already?" Vonne teased.

"Sweetie, it's not like that. We were supposed to hang out tonight, but he was called into work to cover for a no-show, so he cancelled. Sometime later the no-show shows up and in his mind our plans are suddenly back on. So, then I told him about my backup plans with ---"

"Back up plans?" Zsasha interrupted as she approached. "Oh, so that's what we are now, you're back up plan? Girl you got it bad, real talk. He slid his way in the number one spot, and we didn't even see it coming. Umm um, he got you girl, he got you."

J'Nae didn't respond verbally but she knew in her mind her friend was right. She had overcome her issues with their age difference and was really feeling Rick. She just wasn't ready to admit it, to herself or anyone else.

Chapter 13

The changes at Ahsasz were splendid. All the featured artwork was perfectly staged to showcase an array of Andre DeSimone's talent in a way that captured the essence of each piece, no matter where you stood. There were upwards of 80 attendees during the first hour with many more to come. Each expressing their interest in one or more of the many pieces on display. There were sculptures, paintings and photographs covering the walls, both functional and nonfunctional. The turnout was just what Zsasha, and Simon anticipated. Many of their top buyers were present with checkbooks in hand. Zsasha and Simon stood proudly in the center of the main gallery taking it all in as if this was their first time at the rodeo.

"Zsasha! Simon! This is absolutely amazing!" Rona said, walking up to the two of them.

"Hey sweetheart, so glad you made it back in time. I thought you would be gone a few more days."

"That was the plan initially, but Ricardo had a last-minute deal go south and needed to return to try and rescue it before it was a total loss, so we needed to return earlier than expected."

"And you're okay with that?"

"Oh, absolutely. This sort of thing happens all the time in his line of business, international business."

"Yes, yes of course."

"Has J'Nae arrived yet?"

"Yes. She arrived a few moments before you did. She should be easy to spot. She's the one with that young boy trailing behind her like a lost puppy."

"Stop it, you're being silly."

"I mean it, really. Those two have been inseparable since Vonne's dinner party.

"Really?"

"Yes. And she finally broke him off too and I think it was at your house."

"Well good for her. Now maybe she'll stop being so anti-social and maybe open her mind up to new things."

"I've been trying to get her to do that for years now."

"I know you ain't talking about that wicky wacky shit you and Simon got going on. J'Nae is as strait-laced as they come. Even the most adventurous people ain't prepared for that shit."

"Whatever bitch, but don't knock it until you try it."

"Hard pass, thanks."

Just then, J'Nae and Rick approached, each holding a glass of champagne and smiling like high school sweethearts.

"Zsasha, Simon, you two outdid yourselves this time. Everything looks wonderful and Andre is an incredibly talented artist." J'Nae stated with excitement in her voice. "But I don't see very much of your work, Zsasha. Was that one of his demands or something?"

"No sweetie. I just removed the pieces that clashed with Andre's theme. After all, it's his showing and I wanted everything to be about him."

"That's very generous of you, considering this is your gallery and you always have some of your work on display."

"Yes, it is and you're right, I usually do but right now, I need to discover how generous my guests are going to be with their wallets. We'll catch up later, okay?"

"Yes, of course. Congratulations again."

Zsasha walked off to catch up to Simon who had already wandered off to greet potential buyers and first-time attendees. It was important to the success of the showcase they make their presence known; them and the artist Andre DeSimone.

"Why do you think she ran off so quickly?" Rick asked J'Nae.

"I just think she's wanting to mingle, promote her artist and make money. Look at the size of this crowd. It's ridiculous!"

"I had no idea this many people would turn out for this event." Rona exclaimed. "Andre DeSimone is an unknown artist. Maybe I'd better get more acquainted with the world of fine art. I see a lot of possibilities here."

"Rona, dear, I think you got enough going on with Ricardo, Damien and what's-his-face."

"Jon Paul."

"Yeah, that one, Jon Paul."

"Well, if that were the case, then I wouldn't be flying solo tonight."

"True, true. Hey, have you seen Vonne yet? I thought she and Lee were coming tonight."

"I thought so too. It's still early though, maybe they're on the way."

"Yeah, maybe."

The evening continued with guests coming and going, trays of hors d'oeuvre being carried around accompanied by fine wine. Soft tunes from a pianist floated through the room along with the verbal exhilaration from the small grouping of individuals throughout the room. The gallery showing was proving to be a success. Just a few hours into the showcase, Andre DeSimone had sold numerous pieces of his work and there was still time for buyers to explore and make purchases. For a young new artist, he did extremely well for his first major showcase, as did Simon and Zsasha.

"Simon, Zsasha darling, you both look splendid this evening. Everything looks spectacular." Magda greeted. "How have you two been?"

"Fine, fine. Magda, how wonderful to see you both again. Milo, you look well this evening. Glad you both could make it to our event."

"Wouldn't miss it for the world. Allow me to introduce our personal guest this evening. This is Ellie Porter and Adam Russo. Ellie, Adam, these are our dear friends Zsasha and Simon Stewart. This is their gallery."

"It's a pleasure to meet you both." Ellie said, Adam echoed.

Ellie's eyes were focused on Zsasha and Zsasha alone. Her voice exuded excitement yet was slightly seductive. She was enamored with Zsasha and made no attempt to hide it. It was there for all to see, if you were paying attention.

"The pleasure's all mine." Simon replied. "It's wonderful to see interest from your generation."

"Yes, it is." Zsasha confirmed. "Welcome Ellie, Adam. Please, enjoy some wine and hors d'oeuvres." Zsasha said softly as she turned and walked away. Simon, realizing that his wife was headed away from the crowd came back with a quick explanation in an attempt to deflect from her sudden departure.

"Zsasha just needs to check on the kitchen inventory and make sure wine is flowing and being chilled at the right temperature. She's a perfectionist that way. Please, take your time viewing the magnificent pieces on display and let me know if I can answer any questions for either of you."

"Actually, I was looking to purchase a watercolor painting I had my eye on when I was here a while back." Ellie conveyed.

"This is the first day Andre's work has been on display. Exactly how long ago was it?" Simon asked.

"About 2 or 3 months ago."

"I don't recall any artist we featured during that time period that worked with watercolors. However, we've had a few other works on display from time to time. Various artists we've worked with in the past will sometimes bring just one or two pieces to add to our regular ensemble. It might have been one of Zsasha's original pieces. Could you describe it?" Simon suggested.

"I'll just look around and see what I see, you know, take it all in, for now. Thank you, though."

"You're most welcome. Please let me know if you have any more questions about any piece you may find intriguing."

"We will, thank you Simon."

With that, Adam and Ellie nodded and were soon lost in the crowd. Simon, glancing around the room looking for his wife, excused himself leaving both Magda and Milo looking perplexed. He found his wife at the opposite end of the gallery standing alone staring out at the crowd of people that had now grown a bit larger.

"Zsasha, what was that all about?"

"What?"

"Why did you just walk away so suddenly? You didn't engage Ellie and Adam like you usually do our guests."

"Sorry. I was just feeling a bit uneasy for some reason."

"Is it because they're young and are interested in our lifestyle?"

"Yes, no, I don't know what it is. I just suddenly got this overwhelming feeling of uneasiness. I can't explain it, but I felt it and it was strong and powerful, so I took off."

"Well don't worry about it. I'm sure it was nothing. And anyway, just because they're interested doesn't mean we have to invite them into our inner circle. We include who we want to include."

"You're right. I'm overreacting. Shall we mingle with our guests?"

"Yes, let's."

Simon took his wife's hand and led her back to the center of the showroom. The rest of the evening proceeded smoothly. Aside from the general enthusiasm directed at Andre, the crowd was quieting and dwindling down as the hours passed. A few guests were waiting to complete their purchases or try their hand at negotiating a better price; you always had those that never wanted to pay the sticker price. Those deals would have to be approved by the artist and the gallery owners. Nonetheless, Zsasha and Simon were more than pleased with the outcome, including the higher-than-expected attendance and revenue especially for a relatively unknown artist. They did quite well for themselves, better than expected. And from the looks of it, the extra labor and expenses incurred to please the artist were well worth it. The record-breaking sales were proof.

As the night was coming to a close, Zsasha was beyond tired, pretty much exhausted from the evening and everything leading up to it. So much so, she completely forgot that Vonne never showed up.

Chapter 14

Vonne arrived home after a long and tiresome day at work. She had been working out of the Tysons Corner location. New inventory had begun arriving over the last few days and the receiving and allocation process was long and tedious. Having her sister Kiera helping with inventory and stocking ended up being a better idea than she thought. She was surprised her sister was such a quick study and seemed to have a knack for retail. Overall, Kiera had been doing a great job and Vonne appreciated the help, so much so she'd given her sister the day off.

Walking in the house Vonne could smell the aroma of Italian cuisine coming from the kitchen. From the look and smell of things, giving Kiera the day off was proving to be a good idea. It was obvious she had been busy in the kitchen and since Vonne was starved, she couldn't resist investigating what was cooking and smelling so good and oh so familiar coming from the stove. She lifted the lid and stuck a spoon inside to steal a taste of nostalgia. Wow, it was delicious. It Tastes like mom's recipe from back in the day. She was delighted with the familiarity and the memories that flowed through her soul.

Looking around the kitchen she saw a freshly made salad on the table, a bottle of chilled red wine and untoasted garlic bread that just needed to go in the oven. Maybe I've been too harsh on my sister, misjudging her and her intentions, Vonne thought to herself. She hasn't really been a bother to me, in fact she's been quite helpful.

Happy that her sister was taking positive steps and showing signs of improvement miles beyond her normal selfish behavior was pleasing which allowed Vonne to exhale, igniting a moment of reflection. Working at The Boutique and cooking a nice meal wasn't the only way Kiera made herself useful in Vonne's home. As Vonne relaxed, she realized her sister had been doing some laundry, probably unaware the housekeeper usually takes care of that. And since it was her day off, it had to be Kiera's laundry because Lee doesn't lift a finger to do much of anything in the house.

Inspired by her sister's good deeds with dinner, Vonne decided to finish up the laundry her sister had started earlier once the dryer came to a stop. She emptied the contents of the dryer into the laundry basket atop the dryer just to get them out of the way so she could insert the wet clothing that had just finished washing. She picked up one piece at a time so she could determine if it was dryer safe or if it needed to hang dry. The load was filled with lace tops, cotton tank tops and bras in all styles and colors. Unsure of her sister's preference, Vonne decided that only the cotton tank tops could go in the dryer. The rest should probably be hung up.

Starting the dryer, Vonne began to fold the clothes she removed from the dryer and planned to place them on Kiera's bed in return for her nice gesture cooking dinner. And mom's marinara sauce was no 30-minute task. It took 2-3 hours to prepare and simmer. Vonne was halfway through folding Kiera's clothes when it dawned on her that she hadn't folded any panties. She had folded shorts, skirts, short skirts, fitness wear, t-shirts, socks, bras, sport bras and several items she would classify as lingerie, but no panties, period.

Her mind did a quick recall of the wet items she tossed in the dryer and again, didn't recall seeing in that load either. Nothing but bras and tank tops in that load and Vonne simply didn't know what to make of it. She thought it was weird but shrugged it off and continued folding the rest of her sister's clothes.

"Hey Vonne, when did you get in?" Kiera said as she entered the kitchen area from upstairs.

"Oh, hey. About 20 minutes ago. I see you've been busy today." Vonne said. You could hear her smiling as she spoke. "That smells like mom's marinara sauce, my mom's marinara sauce."

"Well, it should, it's her recipe."

"I'm starving and I can't wait to eat it."

"Good, I'm glad. I wanted to do something nice for you and Lee for all that you're doing for me. Really, it means more to me than you know, letting me stay here and giving me a job at your Boutiques.   I know you struggled with both decisions, and I wanted to show my appreciation."

"Yes, you're right. I did struggle a bit. Your track record hasn't been…."

"You don't have to say it. I know better than anyone the sins of my past. I'm just saying that I appreciate you doing what you're doing. I promised you I wouldn't be any trouble to you and all my drama is in the past. I want more for myself and in order to achieve that, I must expect more from myself. And that all begins with gratitude.   I'm grateful for you and your forgiveness and the chance we have now to be close, real close, like sisters are supposed to be."

"Well let's not get ahead of ourselves just yet. We all have a past and for most people, it includes a thing or two we're not proud of. So, the forgiveness you're speaking of, doesn't come from me, it must first come from you. You have to forgive yourself for your personal transgressions. Once you're truly able to do that is when you are truly able to heal and allow change. That's something that starts within, Kiera.

"I appreciate you saying that Vonne. And you didn't have to finish and fold my laundry either."

"I didn't mind. You didn't have very much anyway. Speaking of which, I saw a lot of sexy bras and lace tanks, but I didn't see any panties.   What do you do, wash them by hand or something?"

"No, I just don't wear panties."

"What do you mean you just don't wear panties?"

"I mean I don't wear panties, at all. That's not unusual. Lots of women go bottomless."

Vonne had to take a moment to breathe and process what her sister had just revealed before she could formulate an appropriate response, if there was such a thing. Although she was certain she'd heard right, she didn't want to ruin what was turning out to be a decent moment between sisters, something the two of them rarely ever shared. But she couldn't let it go. She knew she'd heard correctly, and it was much too serious to overlook. It had to be addressed.

"So, hold on a minute. All this time you've been living in my house, a house I share with my husband who graciously allowed you to stay in and you're telling me that all this time you haven't been wearing underwear of any kind?"

"Yeah, that's right, so what?"

"So, you've been walking around my house this entire time without panties!" Vonne said with obvious anger.

"I don't understand." Kiera replied. "What's the big deal?"

"The big deal is this is my house! And the man that sleeps upstairs is my husband! You've been prancing around my house leaving your nasty ass scent all over my sofas and chairs and cushions and you don't think that's a problem? Bitch, are you crazy? The only scent of pussy that should be left around this house is mine! My husband sits in these chairs and lays on these sofas and all the while smelling yo ass all over the place! Have you lost your fuckin mind!"

"Vonne, relax. It's not that serious, okay. I'll stay out of his way like I try to stay out of yours."

"That's not the point and has nothing to do with what I'm saying! You're a grown ass woman and I know you know better. How could you be so disrespectful to me, to my home and to my husband and not even know it?"

"Vonne, I'm sorry. I never meant to be disrespectful to either of you. I never thought anything of it."

"Well, that's because you ain't never had a real man, a husband that respects you, which makes sense because you obviously don't respect yourself!"

"Vonne, that's not true. I'm sorry. I'm so very sorry." Kiera pleaded.

"Yeah, you're that alright, sorry. But you're right about one thing. All bitches go panty-less from time to time. As mature women, we know that. When we go out to dinner, at the club and such, mostly in their own homes, yeah, all bitches do it. But all bitches know better than to be in another bitches' house

148

dropping their scent all over the place, in front of their man and shit; where he lays down to take a nap.

You know damn well a man can smell the scent of pussy a mile away! And you got yours all over my furniture and shit, my couch cushions, and chairs. What the fuck were you thinking, Kiera! What?"

"Vonne, I'm so sorry. I had no idea you felt this way."

"Every bitch feels this way, Kiera! I swear you act like you were raised by street walkers."

"I'll take care of it, I promise. Please don't be angry with me. We were making such progress for once. I don't want to ruin that."

"Bitch that ship has sailed. Get the fuck out of my face! Shit! I knew I was gonna regret taking you in. I knew it."

"You don't mean that, Vonne."

"Yes, the hell I do! Now get. GET!"

Kiera did as her sister directed and retreated to her room. Vonne grabbed the bottle of wine that had been chilling, a corkscrew and her cell phone and headed for the patio. This was too much, she thought to herself. Too fucking much too fucking soon.

* * * * *

The next morning, Vonne was up and dressed a few hours earlier than usual for a day like today. With her purse and keys in tow, she noticed her sister sitting outside on the patio just off the kitchen as she walked through headed towards her car. Although Kiera's back was facing the kitchen, she heard footsteps and turned to meet Vonne's glare as she passed. It was as if Kiera could feel the negative energy beaming from her sisters' glare and burn straight through to her back. They both turned away from each other in sync.

As Vonne got in her car, she reached in her purse and pulled out her cell phone to charge it. That's when she noticed a text message from the night before that went unanswered. It was a message from J'Nae reminding her the girls were meeting for coffee in the morning. Vonne read the message and dropped the phone as quickly as she picked it up. She had her own agenda

149

for the day and meeting up with the girls for coffee wasn't part of her plan.

Inside the house, Lee had just entered the kitchen to do some juicing. He was wearing a pair of red and white Nike jogging shorts, a matching white tank top, white socks, all matching a pair of red and white Nike running shoes. As usual, he was dressed for his day.

"Morning Kiera, where's Vonne? I need to talk to her about something before she leaves for work."

Kiera stared at Lee for a moment trying to tell if he knew about last night. Surely, she went to her husband bitching about the events from the night before, telling him everything in a way to make her look bad. But for some reason, based on his present demeanor, he appeared to be unaware and unaffected. So, Kiera just went with his coolness and responded as if it were any other day.

"She left already." Kiera said as she made her way out to the patio.

"Wow, really? That's unlike her." Lee replied, trailing slightly behind her.

"Yeah, well, she's got inventory to process and distribute. She's been at it for the last several days...keeping her busy and all."

"Well not that busy, your ass is here. Isn't that why she hired you in the first place? To work in the boutiques, helping with inventory and everything?"

"Yea, that's right. But I'm not scheduled to be in until later today."

"Oh, okay. So, what, you plan to be sitting out here chilling, enjoying this beautiful weather in the meantime?"

Before Kiera could answer, Vonne walked into the kitchen toting a few bags purposely being noisy to make her presence known. She walked up to her husband, who had been standing in the patio doorway talking to Kiera and planted a kiss.

"Kiera, I picked up a few things I thought you needed. I'm just going to lay them on your bed. Do you think you can be ready in 30 minutes? I want to get an early start and we need to do a few additional things at the Arlington store. You good with that, right?"

"Sure. I'll be ready to leave in a few. Lee, there's some spaghetti in the fridge from last night, in case you get hungry."

"Oh, okay, cool. Thanks."

Vonne continued her way upstairs to the master suite so she could gather her thoughts and gain perspective on the situation. Awkward and uncomfortable as it may have been, there was just no way she was prepared to tell her husband what really went down last night. Kiera without panties. There just wasn't an upside to sharing that information.

Chapter 15

Afew days had passed since the gallery showing and orders were still pouring in. People were stopping by to make an alternative choice when their first pick had been sold to the person willing to pay a higher price. Either way, Andre DeSimone was no longer an unknown artist. He'd definitely made a name for himself and was surely on the rise.

Later that morning, Zsasha sees Simon talking with Ellie Porter in the main gallery. Walking towards them, she felt none of what she'd felt when she first met Ellie Porter the night of the showcase. She was more than happy with the success of the showcase and anyone around her could tell.

"Zsasha, there you are." Simon declared. "This is Ellie Porter. She was a guest of Magda and Milo's at Andre's exhibit."

"Yes, of course. Hello Miss Porter, how are you?"

"Hello Mrs. Stewart, I'm fine, and please call me Ellie. It's a pleasure to see you again. You have an exceptional gallery."

"Thank you, Ellie, and you may call me Zsasha. We work hard at showcasing the best talent in the area. It is our honor to give the unknown a chance to be seen. What did you think of Andre DeSimone's work the other night?"

"It was splendid, absolutely splendid. However, I'm more interested in another piece I've had my eye on for a minute."

"I thought this was your first visit to our gallery."

"Actually, I visited a few times before with my father. It was a while back."

"I see."

"May I ask, how much of what I see is your work?"

"As of right now, not very much. But I can claim each piece on the back wall."

"You're very talented, Zsasha."

"Thank you, Ellie."

"Do you mind if I look around for a bit?"

"Please do. Take your time. One of us will check on you shortly in case you have any questions."

Zsasha retreated to her office to gather the completed orders awaiting Andre's final approval. Taking a pause when she entered her office had become a new habit she'd developed shortly after she relocated one of her portraits from the gallery to her private office. Standing there, directly facing the portrait she once considered her masterpiece, she stared and quickly got lost in her own thoughts. For several minutes, her mind transcended to the events that initiated this particular painting, including the pain and emotions she felt and revealed with every brush stroke. She was shocked and startled by the sudden interruption that ripped her from her mental retreat.

"There it is. That's the portrait I've been looking for."

"Pardon me?" Zsasha said, gathering her thoughts.

"Yes, that's the one, right there. You previously had this portrait hanging in the gallery, right?"

"Yes, I did. I moved it, along with several other items to accommodate Andre's artwork. Some of the existing items clashed with his artistic style and since he was the main attraction, I moved them."

"I see." Said Ellie. "What is the list price for this piece?"

"I'm sorry Ellie, this piece isn't for sale. It's one of my first pieces right out of college. I was extremely inexperienced and the materials I used were less than top of the line. I keep it around because it shows how much I've grown as an artist over the years."

"I think it's amazing! Yes, it's raw, no doubt, but that's the beauty of it. It coincides with the delicate story the portrait depicts. I think it's one of your best pieces that I've seen so far."

"Thank you, I appreciate your sentiments, however, it's not worthy of sale."

Reaching into her purse, Ellie pulls out a cashiers' check made out to Ahsasz and hands it to Zsasha.

"I beg to differ." Ellie remarked with confidence. "Maybe this will change your mind."

Zsasha was shocked by the enormous amount of the check. She had received many offers over the years, but this was substantially higher than all the others put together as well as most any item she'd sold in her gallery.

"Why on earth would you pay so much money for a painting like this? Most people can't tell this, but it's not complete. It's not finished."

"Well, neither is the story it reflects." Ellie whispered. "Maybe that adds to its appeal."

"I beg your pardon."

"Perhaps the story is still unfolding, and the outcome has not yet been determined."

"Perhaps."

Simon enters the office where the two ladies stood discussing the painting.

"Miss Ellie has purchased 'Forsaken'. Can you make the delivery arrangements for her? Thank you, sweetie." Zsasha didn't wait for a reply. "Ellie, it's been a pleasure. I hope you find this piece to be complimentary to your collection. Take care, love."

Simon was in complete shock at his wife's request. The portrait had been heavily guarded by her heart for many years. For Simon, the thought of her selling the portrait was inconceivable. Zsasha and Simon had compiled a considerable amount of wealth from building both Ahsasz and *Ahsasz Down Under*. So the hefty price tag in no way influenced her decision, it had to be something else. Simon made a mental note to keep tabs on Ellie Porter. She was young and she had resources. Resources that could once again find their way to Ahsasz. At the end of the day, it's just business.

Chapter 16

Later in the week, the girls met up at The Coffee House for a standing meetup that had every week at the same time. Zsasha was the first to arrive and was eager to question Rona and J'Nae about her recent event.

'I'm so glad you all enjoyed the showcase. It went better than we anticipated." Zsasha said.

"Yes, it was pretty well put together. We had a delightful evening." J'Nae commented.

"I did too." Said Rona.

"Cool. So, have either of y'all heard from whitegirl? She said she was coming but –"

"No, not me. But I'm not really surprised." J'Nae said. "She's been dealing with a lot of family drama lately."

"I told her not to let that girl move into her home, even if it is her half-sister. I know how bitches can be." Zsasha boasted.

"I'm sure you do." Rona said with a bit of sarcasm.

"Wait a minute now, little girl." Zsasha fired back.

"Little girl?" Rona questioned.

"Yeah, Money, little girl! Because the grown woman I know you to be knows me better than that. Well enough to know exactly how I get down and how I don't. So, talking out your mouth sideways, you must be somebody's child, because you got me confused, Money. And yes, I called you Money. Because every man, notice I didn't say nigga, every man that you honor with your presence got to have plenty of it. And in case you are still confused, I'm referring to Money, honey. So, talk about what you know and not what you don't!"

"Ladies, ladies, enough. I'm sure Rona was just being facetious, that's all."

"You know I didn't mean anything by that shit. The real issue is why are you being so sensitive all of a sudden?"

Zsasha paused for a moment reflecting on what she had just said to her friend. She knew she went way overboard but had no idea why.

"Damn. I don't know why I went off like that." Zsasha confessed. "My bad, girlfriend. I don't know what got into me."

"It's all good. Let's just forget about it. I've got an open house I need to prepare for anyway." Rona said as she got up from the table, coffee in hand.

"Are we straight?" Zsasha asked.

"We're good." Rona replied. "I'll catch up to both of y'all later. Bye."

Both Zsasha and J'Nae said goodbye to Rona as she exited The Coffee House. J'Nae immediately turned her attention to Zsasha and everything she was feeling was written all over her face.

"I know J'Nae, I know. You don't have to say anything. I know I was tripping."

"Girl, what's going on with you? I haven't seen you get like that with Rona, ever. Not one time. What's going on?"

"Nothing, girl. I just had a few busy days and I'm not well rested. I'm good though, really, I'm good."

"Say what you will, but I know better. That was odd behavior even for you. And that's saying something."

"You just can't give a sista a break, can you?"

"It's just way too easy with you. I can't help myself. But seriously though, you got something going on. What is it girl? You can tell me. What's up?"

"You're right, J'Nae but I don't know if I'm tripping or not. I'm not sure if my mind is playing tricks on me or what."

"That sounds serious."

"It might be girl, I don't know."

"Okay, okay, so what happened? What's got you so discombobulated and high strung?"

"Well, it's been a couple of things, a couple of little things."

"Yeah, so tell me about them."

"It's just that a few times…." Zsasha kind of drifted, not wanting to appear crazy to her friend.

"A few times what? Come one Zsasha. Let's keep it real. I got you. You're one of the strongest, most confident women I know. Whatever it is, it's got you."

Zsasha was touched to hear the concern and support from J'Nae. And momentarily, she felt at ease drawing on the strength of her bestie, but it was short lived. Responding to the sudden change of expression of Zsasha's face, J'Nae pushed a bit harder.

"Well sweetie, this is getting a bit..."

"Somebody's watching me." Zsasha said.

"Watching you, what are you talking about?"

"Well, there have been a few instances where I have felt like I'm being followed or watched by someone. One day I even thought someone was in the gallery with me when I thought I was there alone."

"For real? Zsasha, that ain't nothing to play with. You can't take that lightly."

"So you don't think I'm tripping or overreacting?"

"Not at all. You've always had good instincts since I've known you, so if you feel like someone is watching you or following you, go with your gut."

"Wow. And here I thought you were going to think I was half crazy."

"Oh well wait a minute. You are half crazy, that's for sure. But what you are not paranoid. If you feel like you're being watched or followed, then I say, there's a real strong possibility you are."

"You really think so?"

"I do. I mean you encounter all sorts of people that have all sorts of sexual perversions. Folks from all walks of life."

"Yeah, but my investigators are top notch."

"And they might be, but we've both been around long enough to know that people can hide whatever they want to, especially in this fast-paced era of technological development we live in. You can pretty much be whoever you want to be whenever you want to be them and not leave a trail."

"Honey, that's not making me feel more secure."

159

"And that's not what I'm trying to do. You're like a public figure, somewhat. Lots of people know who you are; recognize your face and what not. Plus, you never know if your clients are sharing privileged information or not. Talking about you, your business or other prominent people they encounter or simply revealing things they shouldn't."

"We have pretty strict rules for all members. It's very secure."

"Well maybe, but that's not always enough."

Zsasha sighed while she contemplated J'Nae's remarks.

"Girl, you kind of got me scared a bit. You said you think someone was in the gallery with you when you thought you were alone?"

"Yea, but I never saw anyone actually in there. I just thought a few things had been moved that I was certain were in a different place when I came in early that day."

"Well, do you think Ms. Honey could have moved things around?"

"No, no. It wasn't her. I spoke with her already."

"Well, you need to be careful."

"I'm trying to be. I already made a few changes to my security protocol after you stumbled in here like Dora the Explorer. What else is there for me to do?"

"Let's see. You can hire 24-hour armed security or get yourself some protection."

"You mean a gun?"

"Yes, no, well maybe."

"We have plenty of those."

"Well, do you carry one?"

"No, I don't, but 24-hour armed security is an option. That could benefit Ahsasz especially since we have a lot of valuable art here. And it may even reduce my insurance premiums. But it may be problematic for *Ahsasz Down Under*. My clients pay very well for privacy. I'll have to check into that."

"Well good. Sounds like you've got some work to do."

"Yes, yes I do."

"Well come on. I'll walk with you to the gallery and help you check things out."

"Oh, so, you're my bodyguard now?"

"No silly. You know I'm way too pretty to fight!"

"Yeah, you are." Zsasha said smiling. "But that's necessary. I'll be fine."

"You sure?"

"Yes, and thanks sweetie."

"For what?" J'Nae asked.

"For listening to me without judgement and for just being a good girlfriend."

"Awe...You know both you and Rona could take a lesson out of my play book."

"I know girl, I know."

"Just call her. Explain everything you got going on. She'll understand."

"I know. I just don't like saying I'm wrong to a mother fucker."

"Put your big girl britches on and handle it. Besides, you owe her. Yo ass was dead wrong!"

"Yes, I was."

"So just do it, and sooner rather than later."

"I will sweetie. Take it easy."

"You too, call me if you need to, got it?"

"Yeah, I got it."

"Okay. Bye sweetie."

"Bye, hun."

J'Nae left and jumped into her car. She was a little bit behind schedule for the early part of her day. She needed to pick up Rona's dress from the dry cleaners and return it to her and stop by and check on Vonne. She thought about postponing lunch with Rick but decided that wasn't a viable option. Instead, she headed straight to Vonne's house and put off picking up Rona's dress for another time.

* * * * *

Inside the gallery, Zsasha closed and locked the front doors behind her. She knew she would be the first to arrive but decided not to let the fact she was alone get the best of her. Getting situated in her office, Zsasha tucked her handbag away neatly in her desk drawer and briefly looked at the pile of approved sales waiting to be scheduled for delivery. It had been a week since the showing and the pending items needed additional payment instruments or delivery instructions. She decided if they waited this long, they could wait a bit longer as she had more pressing things to address. Security.

Zsasha spent the next 30 minutes or so compiling a list of private armed security agencies she believed offered the services she required. She printed off her list just as she heard the alarm beeping indicating someone had entered. It was her husband, Simon.

"Zsasha baby, you here?"

"I'm here, I'm in my office."

Simon entered her office and immediately gave her a long intimate kiss.

"You left a bit early this morning. I didn't have a chance to give you a proper good morning."

"Sorry baby. I had coffee with the girls this morning. One of our standing morning meet ups, plus I wanted to know what they really thought about the showcase."

"I know you care a great deal about what they think, so tell me, what did they have to say?"

"They loved it. They were impressed with the layout and staging, the artwork, everything. They all had a really good time."

"Cool. I'm glad they were here to support you."

"They always do that; you know what it is."

"So, what about Vonne? I noticed she never made it. Everything alright with that one?"

"Who whitegirl? I really don't know. I haven't heard from her yet and her ass missed coffee this morning too.

"That's unusual."

"Yea it is. J'Nae said she would stop by her place and see what's up. With that crazy ass family of hers in and out of her house, ain't no telling what's going on over there."

"I'm sure y'all will figure it out, whatever it is."

"We always do, them my bitches!"

"True that. Anyway, John Lee is supposed to be here this afternoon to help me with the deliveries scheduled for today."

"Baby, why don't you hire a crew? Your ass is getting too old for this shit."

Before Simon could respond, Zsasha was interrupted by a call on her office phone.

"Hello, this is Zsasha speaking."

"Good morning, Zsasha. It's Ellie Porter. How are you today?"

"Oh, Ellie, good morning. I'm fine, how are you?"

"Lovely. It's a wonderful day. The weather is nice and I'm looking forward to getting out a bit today. Which brings me to why I'm calling. I want to invite you and Simon to join Adam and myself for dinner along with Magda and Milo this evening. I know it's short notice, but the reservations were made a month ago and the other party just cancelled. Magda thought it'd be a good chance for us to get to know each other a bit. Please say you'll join us?"

"Well. I'd have to talk to Simon first. I don't want to commit without doing so. You understand, don't you?"

"Of course. The reservations are at Rotunda in downtown DC at 7 pm. Could you just drop me a line say by 5 pm?"

"Sure, I can do that."

"Wonderful. I'll talk to you soon."

Zsasha hung up the phone and immediately dialed Magda's personal cell phone.

"Hello."

"Magda, it's me, Zsasha."

"Hey Zsasha, we were just talking about you."

"We? We who?"

"Ellie and me. We were hoping for you and Simon to join us for dinner this evening."

"Is she with you right now?"

"Yes."

"And she knows it's me on the phone, right?"

"Yeah, yeah."

"Well this is awkward. I have no choice but to accept the invitation."

"Wonderful. We'll see you at seven then."

"Magda...."

"Bye Zsasha. Wear something pretty!"

Furious for being blindsided, Zsasha hung up the phone. Magda knows better than to put her on the spot, especially in this business. There's a protocol for recommending new members. Everyone has to go through the same process no matter who sponsors them. Otherwise, it jeopardizes the safety and privacy of the other members.

"What was that about?" Simon asked as he approached.

"Oh, that was Magda and Ellie inviting us to dinner tonight."

"Oh, so what's the problem? You already knew Magda was pushing her as a potential member, right?"

"Yeah, but I don't like being ambushed."

"Magda caught you off guard, huh?"

"Yeah, she did."

"You should've seen it coming. She's been pushing that young woman in our faces for a minute. You just haven't been paying attention."

"Maybe so."

"Besides, we need to continually grow our business."

"True, but we don't know anything about Ellie and Adam."

"We don't know anything about a lot of our clients until we do a deep dive. We'll get our investigator on it. Besides, referrals from existing members is how we've grown our business. It's nothing new. They know what's at stake and most of them have more to lose than we do."

"You're right, of course. It's just..."

"It's just what? Ellie and Adam are harmless. Besides, they've survived Magda and Milo and you know how intense they are."

"True, but..."

"You worry too much. As long as they survive our background checks, investigators and membership fees, it'll all be fine. Besides, she's hardly more than a kid and so is he. Relax."

Zsasha heard her husband and decided to do just that. Relax. She laid down on her office sofa and allowed the comfort of her sofa to embrace her.

* * * * *

Walking up to the front door, J'Nae hesitated and thought it might have been a good idea to call first. Vonne certainly has her hands full with her family and she might just need a bit of privacy. But as she turned to walk back towards her car the front door opened.

"J'Nae, hey girl. What's up? Looks like you were about to leave."

"Vonne, how are you? No, I was just headed back to the car to get my phone."

"Stop lying girl and get in here." Vonne gave her girlfriend a warm embrace. "What brings you by?"

"Well, you do. You've been missing in action for a minute, and we're concerned. Is everything alright?"

"Ain't nobody dead if that's what you mean...at least not yet anyway."

"That's a good sign, so what's going on?"

"Oh girl! What was I thinking? I should have known better than to have my sister staying up in here. She's burned me before and I should have known she'd do it again."

"Well wait a minute. I thought things were going well. You said her attitude had improved and she seemed to be more mature and everything, you even gave her a job, right? So, what's up? What's the problem?"

"Bitch don't wear no panties."

"Say what?"

"I said, my nasty ass ho-ass mother fucking sister has been living in my house, walking around pantie free."

"You mean she doesn't wear any underwear?"

"That's exactly what I mean. Prancing around my husband, leaving her stank all over my furniture and shit. She got me fucked up. I ain't with that shit no kind of way!"

J'Nae could only think about the rendezvous she had with Rick while house sitting for Rona's, specifically the things they did and the places they did them. She felt like a hypocrite but decided to keep that secret to herself.

"Damn girl, you have been going through it, huh. We knew something was up, but I promise you in a million years we would've never guessed that, at least not me anyway. Doesn't she know better? She's a grown woman and has been that way for more than a minute."

"Girl, she tried to give me all kinds of excuses to justify herself. She even acted like there wasn't anything wrong with it. Like it was somehow a normal thing to do."

"No, she didn't."

"Yes, she did. Then we had it out."

"I'm quite sure you did. So where is she now...packing her stuff?"

"No, she's in Arlington working on inventory. I haven't been back very long from dropping her back off at the store."

"So, you took the day to regroup and pull it together, huh?"

"Hell no. I'm here supervising the cleaning crew steam cleaning my furniture, carpets, drapes and shit, anything her nasty ass might have left her stench on."

"I know that's right, but drapes?"

"Oh, it was just included in the package."

"I see, but for real girlfriend, what was she thinking?"

"Who the hell knows! But one thing's for sure, this arrangement is coming to a swift end, that shit ain't cool."

"Girl I'm so sorry you're going through this mess. We need to take a trip, maybe get out of town for a few days or something."

"There's an idea I can get down with. What did you have in mind? Where would we go?"

"I don't know...the Catskills, maybe Martha's Vineyard...somewhere far enough to feel like a getaway but close enough to drive to...but not real close."

"New York...I could do New York. We'll make it a couple's thing, now that you got a man!" Vonne said, smiling so hard you could hear it in her voice. "Nae Nae's got a maaan, Nae Nae's got a maaan."

"Girl you silly, but you're right, I got a man, and right now he is patiently waiting on me, so I'm gonna have to cut this short."

"Okay girlfriend. You don't want to keep that young man waiting."

"Call you later?"

"Sure, but don't worry about me, I'm fine. I'm good, really."

"Okay sweet pea. We'll talk again soon."

J'Nae hugged her girlfriend, kissed her goodbye, and walked to her car. Getting inside, she immediately noticed the time. She wasn't late for lunch, but she wouldn't have time to pick up Rona's dress from the cleaners. It'll just have to wait. She put on her seat belt, started the car and began pulling out of the driveway as her cell phone rang. It was Rona.

"Hello."

"Hey J'Nae, it's Rona."

"What's up girl?"

"Did you catch up to Vonne?"

"Yes, I did. I'm just leaving her house now."

"So, she's okay?"

"Yeah, but girl, um..."

"What? What is it? What's going on now?"

"It's deep girl. Wait, hold on, that's Rick calling. Let me call you back in a minute."

"Bump that, just meet me at Marilyn's in about 30 minutes. Can you do that?"

"Yeah. Okay, I guess...but Rick will be with me."

Rona had already ended the call just before J'Nae could explain she wouldn't be alone. Clicking over, she answered Rick's call.

"Rick, hey sweetie. Sorry it took so long to answer. I was on with Rona."

"That's cool, baby. So, are you on your way to meet me?"

"Yes, but can we meet at Marilyn's instead? Rona wants to meet up for a minute and get an update on Vonne. It's a good halfway point."

"Baby you don't have to sell me on the idea. I don't care where we go as long as we're together."

Instantly J'Nae began to blush. She was more than smitten with her handsome new beau. She felt amazing. With Rick a part of the equation, she had a new and zestful energy about life, love, and all things J'Nae. Her confidence was through the roof. And she really enjoyed the looks of jealousy and envy across the faces of most women they encountered. Rick Mosely was no scrub, no sir. There was nothing about him that was average, and everyone knew it, except him.

"Is that right?" J'Nae replied with a tad bit of innocence in her voice.

"You know what it is, baby."

"Yes, I do. And it goes both ways sweetie."

"For sure. So how far out are you?"

"About 15 minutes."

"Okay, see you then."

* * * * *

Vonne was ready to head back out to the Arlington store where Kiera was just as soon as the cleaners finished up. She poured herself a glass on Pinot and walked out to the deck. Having worked through the drama of the recent days she was ready to get back to her normal routine. But since she had some time to kill, she thought it was a good idea to check and see if Kiera had worn any of the panties she'd given her. She ran upstairs and into her sister's room to snoop and right away could see several pairs in her hamper. She sighed a bit of relief and thought seriously about taking a real thorough look around. At the same time, she could hear one of the cleaning crew call out to her, so she'd have to put a pin in those plans for later, maybe.

"Hey J'Nae, Rick, how y'all doing?"

"Fine." Rick replied. "Good to see you again Rona." He said smiling.

"Dang girl, you couldn't wait on us before you got started?" J'Nae uttered.

"I just ordered some appetizers. I was hungry and you guys are late." Rona confirmed.

"By like 5 minutes." J'Nae replied matter-of-factly. "You could've waited."

"Like I said, I was hungry. Here, help yourself. I ordered enough for all three of us. Our waitress will be here in a minute to take our order."

"You mean you haven't ordered yet?"

"No, silly, I haven't, but I did look over the menu. They have a few new items. You should check out the salads."

"Okay, I will."

"So, what have you two love birds been up to lately?"

"Just the usual, hanging out, spending time together, when our schedules permit."

"Yeah, I work a lot of second and third shifts so we're not both off at the same time very often. Eww, ouch." Ricked mumbled as he grabbed his head.

"What's wrong, boo?" J'Nae asked. "Are you okay?"

"My head is suddenly pounding."

"Are you alright?" Rona inquired. "Can I get you anything?"

"No, I'm afraid not. What I need isn't here. I'm gonna have to cut this short, ladies, my apologies. J'Nae, I'll call you later."

"Well at least let me drive you home."

"No sweetie, I'll be fine, not to worry. I'll text you when I'm home."

"Okay boo, be careful."

With that, he kissed her and was out the door. Rona and J'Nae looked both shocked and concerned about his sudden issue and quick departure. They sat in silence for a bit. Rona didn't want to be the first one to speak on what just happened. But J'Nae hadn't said a word since he'd left, and the silence was becoming awkward.

"J'Nae what was all that about. He was here one minute and gone the next. He hadn't even ordered yet."

"I know. It's those headaches he gets. They're awful, almost debilitating."

"I'm guessing this has happened before?"

"Yes, he said he sometimes gets these intense migraines, maybe every couple of months or so, but I've never witnessed it before now. He looked like he was really in pain."

"No doubt about that. I saw the color drain from his face."

"Really?"

"Yeah, really. I'm sitting right across from him, so I noticed when it came on."

"I should've driven him home."

"You heard what he said, and you know how men are about that sort of thing. They feel like letting someone help them, anyone, male or female, is a sign of weakness."

"That's ridiculous."

"Yes, it is but it's true. Just call him later in the day and see how he's doing. If he's been dealing with this for a while, I'm sure he knows his limitations and how to treat it. Try not to worry. Let's order some lunch."

The two ordered their lunch and tried to enjoy some girl talk. J'Nae did her best not to focus on Rick's issue and was happy to bring Rona up to speed on how well things had been going for them. When she found herself feeling anxious, she turned the conversation towards Vonne and her recent drama. That's enough to distract anybody. Afterwards, they parted and went their separate ways.

* * * * *

Zsasha and Simon arrive at the Rotunda and are seated rather quickly at a table with Magda and Ellie.

"Zsasha, Simon, you glad you could join us."

"Magda, it's good to see you as always. Hello Ellie."

"Hi Zsasha. So glad you could make it on such short notice. Simon, it's always a pleasure to see."

"Hello Ms. Porter."

"Please, call me Ellie."

"Ellie." Simon replied, turning his attention to Magda. "Where's Milo? I thought he was joining us?"

He's in the men's lounge with Adam, Ellie's friend. You remember Adam, right Simon?"

"Yes, of course."

"You can join them if you'd like."

Simon stood up, leaned over to kiss his wife and headed towards the men's lounge to join Milo and Adam.

"More wine, madam?" the waiter asked. "Ladies?"

"Yes, thank you." Magda replied.

The glasses clinked together as Magda began to speak.

"Here's to new friends, good food and the start of a new relationship."

"I'll drink to that!" Ellie said with enthusiasm.

"Cheers." Zsasha chimed in.

Magda was the first to speak, knowing she was responsible for the outing, thus making it her job to keep the conversation going.

"Zsasha, Ellie has been boasting about a piece of artwork she recently took off your hands. She says it showcases your rawest talent."

"She's exaggerating."

"No, Ms. Zsasha, I'm not. You're very talented, and the portrait is a real treasure."

"Well thank you, dear. I hope you enjoy it."

"Zsasha, we took the liberty of ordering some appetizers. I hope you find them to your liking." Magda explained.

In the distance, she could see their waiter heading towards them carrying two plates of appetizers. Zsasha knew Magda had a peculiar palette consisting of anything non-traditional. As the waiter placed the appetizers on the table, Zsasha made no effort to hide her displeasure.

"How delightful. Toasted ravioli with spinach and goat cheese tartlets. It looks amazing."

"I told Magda not to order that and to go with something safe and traditional, like oysters."

"Well that wouldn't have worked either. I prefer my food a bit more solid and firm. But I will try the toasted ravioli. It looks like it might actually taste good."

"We'll we can order something else if you'd like. Franco, I'm afraid this isn't going to work for my guest. Can you bring her something more traditional, if you don't mind?"

"Yes, madam, of course. Would smoked salmon crostini be to your liking?"

"That sounds wonderful." Zsasha replied. "Thank you. So, Ellie, how did you come to learn about Ahsasz and *Ahsasz Down Under*? Most of our members are a bit older than you and have no issue with the financial commitment involved. It's been my experience that the younger generation has a multitude of more desirable ways to spend their money."

"And I do, as well. However, Adam and I have been in the lifestyle for two years now and we are very happy with it. So much so, we'd like to broaden our horizons and explore it further."

"Two years, huh?""Yes, we're looking for a place that offers many options to meet our various tastes. One that values privacy and discretion above all else."

"Has Magda explained our process for potential new members? We have quite a rigorous application and verification process. And there are no refunds on your initial fee, should you fall short of our requirements."

"Yes, we're aware of that. I have our application completed along with half of our initial application fee, $50,000.00 each."

"Wonderful. I'll be sure to review and distribute to my staff as soon as the check clears."

It was at that time Adam, Milo and Simon returned to the table. Everyone had a drink in their hand while the chatter and laughter grew. Dinner soon followed and the evening ended with ease. There was no further talk about the gallery or the club. Magda knew Zsasha was the one in charge, more or less, and much more stringent than her husband. She was the one they had to win over no matter how positive the background check came through.

"I'll drive, sweetie." Simon stated. They were the first to have their car retrieved by the valet.

"I'm actually kind of glad we came." Zsasha admitted. "I had a good time and I'm no longer in the funk I've been in the last few days."

"I can see that, sweetie." Simon replied. "It looks like you and Ellie really hit it off, or am I seeing something that's not there?"

"No, you're right. I had her pegged all wrong. She's cool, and I feel totally ridiculous for overreacting. She's harmless. In fact, she reminds me of myself back in the day."

"Is that right?" Simon said, sounding somewhat facetious. "That's quite a leap from where you were before. And all that changed over dinner?"

"Baby I'm not saying she's my new best friend, I'm just acknowledging that I may have been hard on a sista and didn't give her a fair chance. That's all I'm saying. And anyway, she'll soon get to know me and how I get down, so I ain't worried."

"You ain't worried?"

"I ain't worried. She don't want none of this!"

"I beg to differ." Simon said jokingly. "Isn't that why they're here?"

"Membership will give her access to the club, but access to me and you, uh, I don't think so, besides, we have our rules. We don't shit where we eat."

"I know that, but does she?"

"If she don't know already, she'll know soon enough. Besides, they're young and inexperienced...you know what it is boo, you know what we are."

"Absolutely."

"Say it baby, say it."

"We're game changers!"

"You damn right!" Zsasha said firmly while looking at her husband. "They can't handle this!"

Simon in turn looked seductively at his wife and without warning, suddenly turned the car down a deserted street. Pulling over, he barely had time to put the car in park before Zsasha

173

was straddling him in the driver seat, coming down intensely on his hot and firm erection.

A short time later, the windows were completely fogged, and the moaning grew louder as their intensity increased.

"Oh baby." Zsasha uttered. "I'm almost there."

Gripping her waist and pulling her into him with a bit of force, Simon could feel the pressure building as his penis began to throb bringing him closer and closer to climaxing. No matter how much sex they had with others, Zsasha was his one true weakness and could get him there in record time.

"License and registration, please!" an officer said after three quick taps on the window.

"Damn, baby. It's the police."

Zsasha didn't bother returning to the passenger seat. Feeling and looking perturbed she let the window down about halfway before the police officer shouted one more time.

"My goodness. Zsasha, Simon, don't you two have a club for this shit! What is wrong with you two?"

The officer's voice sounded familiar, but his face wasn't clearly visible. Nonetheless, it was clear the officer was not a stranger, he had called them by name.

"Murphy, is that you?" Simon asked.

"Yes, and you better be glad it is. I could ticket you guys for this shit. In fact, if it were anyone else, I would!"

Simon and Zsasha just started laughing as they realized it was Murphy, a police officer that moonlighted as security for them a few years back.

"This is unbelievable! You're not even that far from the club!"

"Murphy," Zsasha said, starting in a low voice. "Can you turn around and walk away, please!"

"Yeah, ma'am."

"We're just gonna head on home. You mind stepping back?"

"Oh, yeah, of course. My bad. But just keep driving until you get there, okay, geez!"

"By Murphy!" Zsasha said as she rolled the window up. Looking at Simon, they both just fell out laughing as she found her way back to the passenger seat, his erection was long gone. "Damn, can't get away with nothing these days!"

"Nope, and you ain't getting away from me either." Simon assured.

"We'll let's go, daddy!"

Not long after the run in with Murphy they were home. Much to their surprise, they weren't alone. J'Nae's car pulls up right behind them. Their home was situated on 5 acres of land yielding a mansion with three levels above ground and one below. Large floor length windows replaced portions of the exterior walls covered with a chrome finish giving the house a metallic yet polished and sterile look. The yard was meticulously manicured and green all the way around.

Getting out of the car, Zsasha takes a few steps toward J'Nae, the two of them meeting each other halfway.

"J'Nae, hey what's up?"

"Hey sista girl." J'Nae said as she gave Zsasha a hug. "Simon, how are you?"

Simon half-heartedly nodded his head in acknowledgement purposely avoiding making eye contact with J'Nae. Whatever animosity he had harbored in the past

was still there.

"Did you guys have a good dinner?"

"Yeah, dinner was fine. What brings you out this late? Don't you have to work in the morning?"

"Yeah, I do. I was just running some errands and doing a little shopping, trying to keep the blood flowing. I thought you'd passed me a little ways back but it must have been someone else. I was headed home and had to go this direction anyway so I thought I would say a quick hello. I won't keep you though, it's late."

"Nonsense." Zsasha insisted. "Let's go inside."

"You sure? I'm not intruding, am I?"

"Yeah, you are, but so what. Come on. I'll get us some wine and we can chat for a bit."

Walking through the front door, the look on J'Nae's face was that of a child walking inside a large toy store for the first time.

175

"You act like you've never been here before.   Nothing's changed."

"I know but it's been a while. I forgot how amazing your home is."

"Well never mind all that. Are we having red or white?"

"Red please, thank you."

"So, what's up J'Nae? You don't usually just show up like this, what's going on?"

"I'm waiting for Rick. He had a migraine and took the day off work. He said he feels fine now and is meeting me at my place in a little while."

"So how are things going between you two?"

"You can't tell? OMG! I can't get enough of him!"

"Baby girl, from what I see, he can't get enough of you either. You two are always together, like almost every day."

"Um, it is every day. Either he's staying over at my house or I'm staying over at his."

"And you look happy, happier than I've seen you in a very long time."

"And you know, we have a standing lunch date every Wednesday at the park, if his schedule permits."

"So you've said, so you've said.   So, what's the problem then?"

"Nothing with us. He's great and I'm good. It's Vonne."

"Vonne?   What's whitegirl got going on now, more family drama?"

"You really need to stop calling her that."

"No can do, so did something happen?"

"I guess you could say that."

"Girl, quit beating around the bush and tell me what's going on."

"Okay, I will. But only because I'm sure she'll be telling you and Rona herself."

"Well, what is it?"

"It's Kiera. Vonne just found out she doesn't wear panties, at all!"

"Come again?"

"You heard me. All this time Kiera's been in her house, she's been panty free. Vonne says she doesn't even own a pair of panties."

"Wow, un-fucking believable!"

"And Vonne is very upset about it."

"Upset enough to put her ass out?"

"I think she's seriously considering doing just that."

"I told her not to let that bitch move up in her house. Especially with her dead-beat ass husband who doesn't work and is home all the dang on time. That's just trouble waiting to happen."

"I agree but you know Vonne. She's going to do whatever she wants to do. She doesn't listen to anybody."

"She just doesn't know how to say no. That's been her problem since I first met her white ass way back in the day."

"I know but this is serious."

"Yes, it is, and I'll be the first one to admit I go without panties sometimes, quite often actually. But only when it's appropriate."

"Well, did you have some on tonight, while you guys were out?"

"Well, see it's like this, I did, but then on our way home, we kind of pulled over, blah, blah, blah. You feel me, like right now, I'm sitting in my house on my furniture juicy as hell."

"I didn't really need to know that Zsasha."

"Hell, you asked. And I was just trying to prove my point. There's a time and a place for everything. And any real woman knows that you don't be up in another woman's house with the windows down like that, period. Especially in their situation; living with her sister and her sisters' husband, hell nah! I'm surprised whitegirl didn't beat her ass for GP. You know she can fight."

"I suppose, I don't know. But I know she's stressed. At least her father went ahead and left."

"He started all this mess, him and Lee. I feel for her."

"Do you really?"

"Yeah girl. Look, I got an idea. Let's me and you go over there and straighten Kiera's ass out ourselves. I know I joke a lot about her, but that's my girl."

"Your whitegirl."

"Girlfriend, she's only white on the outside."

"Girl you crazy, you know that, right?"

"Yup, so you down or what?"

"Whatever, you ain't doing nothing. But on a side note, Vonne and I were talking about taking a trip together. Like a long weekend or something."

"Hell yeah! I could really use some time away. These past few weeks have been hectic and emotionally draining. Where are you thinking about going?"

"Somewhere we can get to by car and less than an 8-hour drive."

"Okay. How about Martha's Vineyard or the Catskills?"

"Either one of those sounds good. We need to see what Rona has to say about it. If she's on board, it's a go."

"Sounds good to me. So, when are you thinking about taking this trip?"

"I don't know. But soon. We need to consider everybody's schedules and availability. I'm hoping we can do it in about two months or so. If we go to the Catskills, it'll be perfect for skiing."

"Sounds like you've been thinking about this for a minute."

"Well yes and no. I've been thinking about planning a romantic weekend getaway with Rick for sure. However, a couples' trip will not only be romantic, but fun too."

"I see you don't need any convincing."

"Nope, not at all."

"And Vonne is cool with this also?"

"Yes, absolutely. And they need it. Vonne and her husband have had troubles in the not so distant past. This might give them a chance to reconnect without any negative influences around them. Even though we'll take the trip together, we'll all be with our significant other."

"Ok cool. Let's talk more about it the next time we all get together."

"Tomorrow night at the gallery. It's on your calendar."

"Yeah? How do you know?"

"I put it there so there's no excuse."

"Cool." Zsasha commented. "And I won't try to get out of it. I think it's a great idea and long overdue, not just for Vonne and her husband, but for all of us. And this will give us all some up close and personal time with Rick so we can investigate his ass."

"You mean interrogate, don't you?"

"No, I mean exactly what I said, investigate."

"I'm fine with it either way. I know it comes with the territory, dealing with you."

"So, we're good?"

"Yes, we're good."

"Okay then, because I really need to finish fucking my husband."

"Finish?" J'Nae looked perplexed. "You guys pulled in right before I did."

"Yeah, we did. But look sweetie, I told you we pulled over on the way home."

"Say no more. I have my own personal business to attend to. I can see myself out."

"Yeah, but I got to see you out too."

"Girl you trippin."

"No I ain't. We get down up in here."

"Girl bye."

"Bye now, drive carefully. And pace yourself, homeboy ain't going nowhere."

J'Nae smiled and left. She ignored the advice Zsasha had just given her and hurried home. As she pulled up to her house, she could see Rick was already there, patiently sitting in his car waiting for her, like a good man should. She was pleased.

Chapter 17

Meeting at the gallery had once again become a regular outing for the girls and all four were present. The wine had been poured and all were eager to share the recent events in their lives. As usual Zsasha was the first to start off.

"So glad you could join us, Vonne. It hasn't been the same without you."

"Nice to know I was missed. You could've called a sista, you know."

"You were in my thoughts every day, plus I wanted to give you and your family space to work out your issues. So, what's been happening on the home front?"

"Like you don't know. I'm sure y'all all know about my sister and her underwear issues. We all know J'Nae can't hold water."

"That's not true." J'Nae politely stated. "But that shit was crazy. There's no way I could've kept that to myself, even if I tried."

"No worries honey bunny, I wasn't trying to keep it a secret, at least not from my girls."

"Well, who else is there?" Rona asked.

"My husband, that's who."

"I take it you're not planning on discussing her inappropriate behavior with Lee, huh?" Rona reasoned.

"The way I see it, there's just no upside in sharing that bit of information with him, if you know what I mean. The only thing that would do is to give him something specific to think about and occupy his penis brain day in and day out. He's a man like any other, and if you put that kind of temptation right up in his face, we're gonna have some real problems."

"Sounds like you already do." Zsasha warned. "I tried to tell you that shit was a bad idea."

"Yes, you did, and I had to go and do it anyway. Woe is me."

"Woe would be her ass if it were my sister...bump that!" Zsasha proclaimed. "I wouldn't be having none of that shit in my house or anywhere around my man, even coming from you bitches."

"Moving on," J'Nae interrupted, "I thought we could all take a trip together. A couples outing for a long weekend, maybe to the Catskills. What do y'all think about that?"

"You already know I'm in." Vonne replied. "Lee and I need some one-on-one time together."

"That could be nice. When did you have in mind?" Rona asked.

"Definitely this winter while the mountains will be covered with snow. We could get a cabin, do some skiing or whatever." J'Nae replied.

"I don't know girl's, y'all know my schedule towards the end of the year. I have the Masquerade Ball and holiday events to plan for."

"Speaking of the Masquerade Ball, have you confirmed a date yet?" Rona inquired.

"Yeah, I have, but I don't know it off hand. I'll have to check my calendar. It's not on Halloween but it's usually around that time, hence the theme, *Masquerade*."

"We get it, we get it." Vonne insisted.

"But y'all bitches know you're not invited, right?"

"We know Zsasha, we know." Vonne uttered.

"And don't you also have the Silent Charity Auction around that time?"   Rona asked, purposely trying to steer the conversation in a different direction.

"That's a bit earlier in the season but if we're gonna do this, we need to do it after the ball. My calendar should free up a bit from January to March and I'll be able to block off some time." Zsasha replied. "Y'all really want to do this, huh?"

"Yes, we do." Rona confirmed. "So here's what I'm thinking, I've got contacts in property management all over of course and some of them have deluxe rental properties in the Catskills. Let me reach out to a few of them, see what's available during our time frame, yadi, yadi, yadi, and then we can get together and make a decision." Rona suggested.

"That works for me." J'Nae replied.

"Cool, I'm in. Lord knows me and my husband need some time away from my sister."

"So how soon can you nail down a time period? The sooner the better." J'Nae stated.

"I got you girlfriend. I'll have some dates in a minute." Rona assured.

"Well, we all know who'll be joining J'Nae, what about you Rona, who are you thinking about bringing on our winter getaway?" Vonne asked.

"Girl, it's way too soon to be thinking about that. You know I have options, so we'll just have to see how I'm feeling at the time."

"What you really mean is who you're feeling at the time." Vonne jokes.

"Can't argue with that." Rona admitted.

"I envy you and your freedom." Vonne confessed. "You live as free as a bird with no restrictions other than the ones you place on yourself."

"You're right about that." Rona conceded. "I wasn't happy and fulfilled in my prior life but endured for the sake of the kids, until they were of age. Reggie and I, having been best friends for years, made it manageable. And on top of that, he was as happy to end the marriage as I was. We both shared the same feelings about our marriage and each other and when the time was right, we made the decision that was right for our entire family."

"And you're both the better for it." J'Nae shared.

"Absolutely, that's the main reason why we're able to be such good friends now. There was no drama."

"Lucky you." Vonne replied. "I believe I've got enough drama for everybody at this table."

"Yes, you do, honey bunny, yes you do."

"So, J'Nae, have you told Taizja and Aiden about Rick yet?" Zsasha asked.

"Yeah, have you?" Rona seconded. "I'm sure they'd be happy to see you getting on with your life."

"I think it's way too soon for all that. We're just dating and it's still early, don't you think?"

"Early? Hell no! It's late, late as hell for your ass... just getting started." Zsasha laughed.

"I'm serious."

"Me too. It's been several months now? Aren't you guys exclusive?"

"Yes, we are."

"Well, I would think it's kind of serious, wouldn't you?"

"I don't know. We haven't actually had the talk yet?"

"So, he hasn't said he's all in?" Rona asked.

"No, not yet."

"Well you'd better find out now." Zsasha exclaimed. "You don't want to wait until you're too far gone and then get your heart broken because you guys aren't on the same page. Just ask him. Put your big booty shorts on and just ask him. I bet you'll be pleasantly surprised."

"You think?"

"Girl, we all have seen how he looks at you and only you." Vonne stated. If you keep on messing around, I'll come get him!"

"Vonne, you have a husband." J'Nae stated firmly.

"Yes, I do, but he don't look like that!"

"Girl, you need to quit." Zsasha declared. "But you're right in theory. J'Nae, If you don't lock it down, one of those evil bitches that's been giving you the side eye is gonna end up with your man. Watch what I say."

"J'Nae, ignore her, in fact, ignore both of them thirsty heffas." Rona insisted. "That's your man. You do what feels right to you when you feel it's the time is right. Don't let these emotionally scarred bitches scare you into messing up this relationship. He ain't going nowhere, no time soon, trust me, I've seen it with my own two eyes. That man is in love with you!"

"I'm not worried about them. Rick and I are in a good place, and I like it just how it is."

"Good for you. Do you, make yourself happy." Rona reiterated. "So, ladies, ready to call it a night?"

"Yeah, I am. I've got an early morning appointment and I'm tired of you motha fucka's." Zsasha jokes.

"Whatever, I've got to be in the office by 7:00 so I'm out." J'Nae replied.

"I still have inventory." Vonne stated. "So yes, let's wrap it up. Zsasha, you want me to stay behind and help you clean up?"

"No, just leave your glasses in the sink and we can all walk out together. I'll deal with it in the morning."

The girls all said good night and exited the gallery together, each looking out for one another as they made their way to their cars.

* * * * *

It was just a bit after 10:00 pm and J'Nae was busy in the kitchen when the house phone rang.

"Hello."

"Hey mom! How are you?"

"I'm fine Aiden, how are you doing sweetie? I miss you."

"I miss you too, ma...hadn't talked with you for a while. What have you been up to?"

"Me, not much really. My new job has been keeping me busy but other than that nothing much."

"Does this new job have you working past 10 o'clock at night?"

"Huh?"

"I've called you several times and left a few messages over the past several weeks. Now I know you're bad at checking messages on the house phone but dang ma, it's been a minute."

"Oh, well like I said, the job has been keeping me busy. And sometimes I hang out with the girls at the gallery. It's best to reach me on my cell phone nowadays."

"Yeah, I guess so because you seem to be out of the house all times of the day and night."

"It's just work and stuff, nothing much."

"Don't give me that, what's up? You better not be out there wild'n out with some knucklehead dude mom, I mean it."

"Boy please, I'm all the way grown, and I do indeed have a life."

"I'm serious mom, you know I can track your phone just like you were tracking mine, a few years back."

"Boy, quit!"

"So that's a yes then, huh?"

"Yes, to what, Aiden?"

"You out there wild'n out with some knucklehead dude, ain't you?"

"Boy, I don't have to answer to you, and you don't need to know all that. You just need to worry about you and what you got going on. Now have you spoken with your sister lately?"

"Yeah, Taizja and I video chat all the time. She's doing fine, you should reach out to her!"

"Maybe I have already and maybe I haven't."

"Mom, what's with all this secrecy? You're being real cloak and dagger all of a sudden. Maybe you're ashamed of him? Is he fat and ugly? Is he young? Are you out there cougar-in, mom? Ma?"

"Well, I am dating someone."

"I knew it. What's his deal, is he younger than you?"

"Yes, a bit."

"It better not be Tyshawn!"

"Who?"

"Tyshawn, from the neighborhood. He lived around the corner while I was in junior high and high school. He would always say inappropriate things about you and try to be slick about it. I wanted to break his neck."

"Is that why y'all stopped being friends?"

"Our friendship ended because I stomped his ass for talking about you like that."

"What? And why haven't you ever told me about this before?"

"Because mom, you didn't need to know everything going on out there in the streets. I ain't no punk, never have been and never will be. I handle my business."

"Well, the answer to your question is no, it's not Tyshawn. His name is Rick, and he is quite a bit older than you."

"Mom, you're quite a bit older than me, so that's not saying much."

"Too bad because that's all I'm saying right now so this interrogation is over."

"Alright mom, I love you and I'll talk to you soon."

"I love you too, son. Bye baby."

"Bye mom."

J'Nae hung up the phone and returned to the meal she was packing up for Rick. He was working 3rd shift 9:00 pm – 5:00 am filling in for a colleague immediately following his regular 1:00 pm – 9:00 pm shift. Working a double made it hard for them to have dinner together or share uninterrupted quality time so she decided to bring dinner to him. Her agenda wasn't completely unselfish, bringing dinner to his place of employment would also give her a chance to see where he works and maybe watch him live on the air for a bit.

With everything neatly packed, J'Nae locked up the house and headed to her car. Pulling out of the driveway, her cell phone rang. It was Rona.

"Hey Rona, what's up girl?"

"Not a whole lot. I was expecting your voicemail, thought you would be tied up with Rick about this time. What are you up to?"

"Actually, I'm just heading out to drop dinner off for him at the station. He's pulling a double working both second and third shifts tonight. What's up with you?"

"Well, I just wanted to run something by you."

"Okay, what's up?"

"Is it me, or has Zsasha been spending a lot of time with Ellie Porter lately?"

"Um, yeah, they've been hanging out, lunching, shopping and such. I haven't really thought much of it."

"I'm not surprised. You've been busy working that young man you're seeing. I'm sure he takes a lot of your focus and attention."

"Yeah, but I'm not ignoring her or any of you guys for that matter, not on purpose."

"I know girlfriend, lighten up. I was just busting your chops. I'm happy for you, really, more than you know. But I'm a bit concerned. We don't know anything about this girl, where she's from or who her people are. I mean she just showed up and slipped right in. I don't know why Zsasha is entertaining her and spending all this time with her. I just think it's weird."

"I understand and I feel you. I haven't noticed anything that would give me concern at this point but maybe I'm missing something. Maybe I have been a bit preoccupied with Rick and even Vonne's drama to an extent."

"Well, I could be overreacting."

"No, I don't know. I don't think so, at least not entirely."

"Why do you say that?"

"Well, not too long ago, Zsasha shared with me a concern of hers."

"Really, about what?"

"She thought someone was watching her."

"Is that right?"

"Yeah. She even thought someone had been in the gallery one night when she thought she was there alone."

"That's nothing to take lightly. Does Simon know?"

"I'm not sure. She thought she was being paranoid, so she was reluctant to tell me about it. But I let her know that whatever she was feeling, she probably had a good reason for it."

"This is getting a bit scary."

"Yeah, she said she was going to increase security, maybe have onsite security

24/7 or something."

"If it was that serious, I would think she'd tell Simon about it."

"I don't know, just ask her. She'll talk to you about it."

"Yeah, I guess."

"Well look, this is something we should definitely discuss together, share our concerns and let her know we're here for her. However, I just pulled into the parking lot at Rick's job and he's on a schedule. He can only take a break when there is coverage or when he pre-records a portion of the show, so we'll have to continue this conversation later."

"Absolutely. I am more bothered now than I was when I reached out to you."

"I'm sorry, that wasn't my intention, Rona."

"I know. We'll talk again soon. Love you."

"Love you too. Bye."

As soon as J'Nae hung up the phone she began gathering up the portable thermal lunch bags she stored everything in. Even though dinner was all that she'd prepared, she came equipped with three separate portable items, each packed with something edible, or something required for him to eat. The main dish was a seafood pasta alfredo where she had carefully packaged the seafood, pasta, vegetables, and alfredo sauce individually. A garden salad and small containers containing ranch dressing, bacon bits, croutons, onions, cucumbers, tomatoes, and cheese filled the second thermal lunch pouch. The last one consisted only of garlic bread wrapped in aluminum foil, silverware, and napkins. The only thing missing was a beverage which she was certain he could get on site.

Walking inside the station, J'Nae was escorted to the studio area where Rick was broadcasting live on the air. Three sides of the studio were partially made of glass leaving little privacy for whomever may be inside. Rick sat facing forward leaving his back facing J'Nae rendering him unaware of her arrival. While she stood there watching her man at work, someone approached from the right end of the hallway causing J'Nae to take a step backwards so they could pass. In doing so, she accidentally bumped into a young man trying to walk around her.

"Oh, I'm so sorry." J'Nae said to the stranger.

"Oh, you're fine. Are you here for Rick?"

"Yes, I am. I'm J'Nae Carter."

"Nice to meet you. I'm Paulie. I'm the head sound engineer for the station. If you'd like, you can wait in the next room where you can see and hear him live. How does that sound."

"Wonderful!"

"Great, follow me."

The two walked just a few feet down the hall and into a smaller room adjacent to the booth where Rick was broadcasting live. When he saw her enter, his face lit up, he nodded and continued on. Paulie and J'Nae made small talk and just a few minutes later they were joined by Rick.

"Hey sweetheart." Rick said while giving J'Nae a kiss. "You're a sight for tired eyes and just the stimulation I need to keep going. How are you, baby? Is this guy bothering you?"

"No silly, I'm good. You sound even better in the studio than on the air."

"The smooth sounds of Rick Moss." Paulie said. "That's why he makes the big bucks."

"I wish." Rick replied.

"Well, I'll leave you to it. Sounds like the pre-recorded portion is on point so my business here is done."

"Nice to meet you, Paulie."

"Likewise. Enjoy."

"I bet you like having two last names, don't you?" J'Nae teased.

"I do, especially when I receive certain perks and benefits using one over the other."

"Wow, the life and times of Rick Moss Mosely. I'd love to be you when I grow up."

"You don't have to be me, baby, just be with me."

"I'm right here, boo."

The two laughed as they headed towards the break room area where they shared the meal she'd prepared, small talk and a few intimate kisses. Periodically, J'Nae caught the stare from several station employees out the corner of her eye. She wasn't sure if they were looking at her because she was a bit older than him or if they were just looking at her. Either way, she tuned them out and continued with her one-on-one time with her man.

Chapter 18

After a few long days at the gallery, the breakfast meetup with Ellie had almost slipped her mind. Zsasha arrived at Miss Maples Restaurant just a few minutes behind schedule. Thursdays were usually busy days for Zsasha who'd make an effort to wrap things up so her weekend would be free even when there wasn't anything on the books. Ellie was already seated, and coffee had been poured.

"Hello Zsasha." Ellie said as Zsasha took a seat.

"Good morning. So sorry I'm late. Had a hard time getting out of bed this morning."

"Would that have had anything to do with your gorgeous husband?"

"Watch out little girl. We do what we do but Simon is off limits."

"My bad."

"And to answer your question, no. I tossed and turned quite a bit last night and didn't get much sleep. I finally fell off around 3 o'clock this morning. That's why I'm dragging today."

"Well you don't look like it."

"Thank you. So, what do you have planned for today?"

Not a whole lot. I'm planning on visiting my father for a bit and who knows what I'll get into after that."

"Are you guys close?"

"You ladies ready to order?" a voice interrupted.

"Yes. I'll start." Zsasha replied. "I'll have the country breakfast with country ham and a side of bacon."

"How do you want your eggs?"

"Over hard." Zsasha replied.

"Toast or biscuits and gravy?"

"Biscuits and gravy, please."

"And you ma'am?"

"I'll have the cottage cheese and fruit plate." Ellie answered.

"Anything else, ladies?"

"No, we're good." Ellie said.

"Girlfriend, you could've had a cottage cheese plate at The Coffee House and any number of other places. What's the point of coming to Miss Maples' if you're not gonna eat?"

"I'm just selective about what I put into my body. I have my cheat days of course, but this isn't one of them."

"I get it, for sure, but this is a cheat day for me. I usually eat a much lighter and healthier breakfast but every now and then I like to enjoy comfort food."

"As you should."

"I used to eat here all the time like clockwork but as I got older, I had to slow it down a bit."

"I'm sure."

"Weren't you about to say something about your father when the waitress interrupted us and took our order?"

"Yeah, you were asking if we were close."

"Were you?"

"Not exactly. He tried his best to fill the void my adoptive mother left when she passed away."

"Oh, I'm sorry to hear that."

"It was a long time ago and we weren't close either. My mother and I had nothing in common, we were cut from two distinctively different clothes. If they hadn't already told me I was adopted, I would have figured it out on my own. I am nothing at all like either of them."

"So, you and your dad didn't grow closer after your mom passed?"

"No, we didn't. He tried his very best to connect with me the only way he knew how. His idea of father daughter bonding consisted of a series of ridiculously lavish gifts he'd give me to fill the void created by the lack of an emotional connection. It was easier for him to avoid me and my questions and eventually he just sent me off to boarding school."

"Wow, really? That's so sad."

"I guess he was dealing with his own grief and just wasn't available for me."

"And how old were you when your mom passed away?"

"I was pretty young, 9."

"Really? So where do things stand now for you and your father?"

"Nothing much has changed. We keep in touch once or twice a month and occasionally I'll visit and see how he's doing."

"Well at least you two are on speaking terms."

"Here you go, one country breakfast with country ham, a side of bacon along with biscuits and gravy. And your cottage cheese and fruit plate."

"Thank you."

"Enjoy, ladies."

"So, what about you, Zsasha? Are you close with your parents?"

"Like you, my mom passed away when I was young. Since I was the oldest and the only girl, I pretty much had to raise my three brothers if we wanted to survive. My dad was always at work, at least it seemed like it to us. I did the shopping and cooking and most of the household chores."

"And now? What's the relationship like today?"

"Well, I left out the part about him cutting me off and out of his life."

"Really? Why did he do that?"

"Basically, he didn't approve of my lifestyle choices and certain other decisions I made. And him being who he was, no longer had a place for me in his life."

"Really?"

"Yes, and it got worse after we opened *Ahsasz Down Under*."

"That's sad. How long has it been now, since the two of you spoke or had any interaction?"

"Girl, it's been more than ten years. But I don't think about it much, I can't. It was his choice and his decision. If and when he wants to talk to me, he will, but until then, I'm doing me."

"And you should, you absolutely should!"

Zsasha smiled then nodded in agreement while she finished the last bites of her country breakfast. Talking about her family issues was not something she did often, especially with someone outside her inner circle. But what the heck, Zsasha felt drawn

193

to Ellie and had been learning just how cool and low-key she was. She was an easy person to like and Zsasha had no qualms with her at all.

"Ellie, do you have time to talk with me about something before you leave? I don't want to make you late for your visit with your father."

"Sure, I've got a bit of time. What's up?"

"Every year we host a Silent Charity Auction, and I was wondering if you'd be interested in helping me out with it?"

"I could do that. What exactly do you need?"

"I could use your help in contacting some of my top clients and reaching out and developing new resources. You never can have too many."

"No problem."

"I would need you to remind them of the upcoming Silent Charity Auction in hopes they'll have a generous amount of money earmarked for this year's event."

"Have you scheduled a date for the auction?"

"No, in fact, that's on the top of our list as far as things to do."

"I'm cool with it either way."

"Awesome!" Can you come by the gallery at 9:00 am so we can sit down and hash it out?"

"Absolutely."

"Alright then, I'll see you tomorrow."

Cool, tomorrow it is and Thank you, for breakfast."

"You're welcome, sweetie."

Zsasha was more than thrilled that Ellie had agreed to help with the Silent Charity Auction. Usually, the city councilwoman would head up this event, calling on local politicians, business owners and other people of wealth and influence for donations to be auctioned to the highest bidder.

In recent years, Zsasha's function was purely to assist in the setup and staging process as well as administrative functions before, during and after the event. What she liked most was the task of reviewing bids to determine the winners and act as one of the narrating hosts along with Simon and Councilwoman Weatherly.

But this year, Councilwoman Weatherly had her own problems to deal with. She had been caught in a college cheating scandal where parents were paying a professional test taker an absurd amount of money to take the SAT tests for their children, a misguided attempt to secure acceptance in a prestigious college or university. As a result, Zsasha became the chairperson and needed someone to assist her. Ellie was all too eager for the task.

* * * * *

The store was locked up for the night and Vonne was more than ready to be at home. Inventory at the Arlington store took longer than she'd anticipated even as a solo project. She nearly regretted sending Kiera to the Capitol Hill location earlier in the day but needed someone to cover the front of the store while the manager attended to a private shopper that required concierge style service; something The Boutique was known to provide.

The ride home had been shorter than usual even for this time of night and Vonne exhaled a big sigh of relief as she pulled into her driveway. Peeling out of her car, she sighed a sigh of relief. Kicking her shoes off just as she stepped through the door, she could hear Kiera and Lee's voices coming from the patio area. They were both seated at the patio table which had been moved a few feet closer to the outdoor firepit they had going to take the chill off the night air.

"Hey, what's up?"

"Hey Vonne. You're home early. I thought you were meeting up with the girls tonight?"

Vonne hesitated to respond right away but made it a point to walk over and lean into Lee, planting a kiss on his lips as if to stake her claim.

"No, not tonight. I was doing inventory at the Arlington store. Something smells good. Looks like I'm just in time for dinner."

"I'm so sorry, Vonne. I thought you had plans with the girls, so I only made enough for us."

"Us? What do you mean, us? Us is me and my husband who own this home.   Us is me and my husband who pay for everything in this house. So what exactly is your definition of us in this scenario?"

"Come on Vonne. Do you really have to do this again?" Lee questioned.

"I apologize, sis. I didn't mean to exclude you. It's just you meet up with the girls quite often and I just got your schedule wrong. I can make more, just give me a minute."

"Just forget it.   It's really too late to eat anything heavy anyway. I'll just make myself a salad or something."

"Let me do it." Kiera insisted.

"No thanks, sis. You've done enough already." Vonne replied as she headed into the kitchen, Kiera trailing right behind her.

"I really don't mind, Vonne. It's late and I know you're tired, besides, I feel terrible leaving you out on dinner. Let me make it up to you or at least try."

"Alright, fine. There's probably a bowl left over from what I made last night."

"Yep, there is." Kiera replied as she retrieved the pre-made salad bowl and the homemade dressing Vonne liked. "Here you go sis. The toppings are on the table where I left them this evening."

"Thanks, Kiera."

"I wish I could do more." Kiera said as she walked over to the laundry area just off the kitchen.

"No, you're fine. It's just been a long day and I'm exhausted."

Kiera returned to the kitchen with a laundry basket of what looked like Lee's sportswear.

"Oh, my goodness! So you're doing my husband's laundry now too? Do you not have a good understanding of boundaries, Kiera?"

"Yes, I did his laundry earlier this evening but not before doing yours which you'll find neatly folded in your room. And I didn't consider this a boundary issue. It's just my way of helping out around the house. My bad."

Vonne shrugged and sighed and got up from the table, leaving the salad without another thought.

"I can't deal with all of this right now. I'm going to bed."

Kiera stood there and watched her sister leave the kitchen and head upstairs. She had no words for what just happened, nor did she have the desire to figure it out. She was coming to realize that she couldn't win with her sister, no matter how hard she tried.

"Hey, where's Vonne?"

"She got upset and went upstairs."

"What about?"

"The laundry. She feels like I overstepped her boundaries by doing your laundry."

"She's just had a rough day. I'll talk to her."

"Well, my advice is to make that sooner rather than later or she'll have an issue that you're down here with me. In fact, I'm going to bed too. She left this mess, so she can clean it up herself. Good night, Lee."

"Good night, Kiera."

Chapter 19

Sitting at The Coffee House, Zsasha was interrupted by the ringing of her cell phone. It was Ellie Porter.

"Hey, good morning."

"Hey Ellie, what's up?"

"Well, I had an idea. Why don't the four of us go out on my yacht this weekend and spend a few hours on the water."

"On your yacht?"

"Yes. We can sit around the deck, eat and drink a little and discuss the Silent Charity Auction. You did ask for my help, right?"

"Yes, I did, but we'll begin before then."

"No problem. I'm sure they'll be plenty to discuss, personal and professional."

"I guess that'll be okay, but I'll need to run it by Simon first, just in case he's not available."

"Cool, just let me know. See you at 9:00."

"And you will. Bye Ellie."

"Was that Ellie?" Rona asked as she walked up to the table Zsasha was seated at. "What did she want this early?"

"Well good morning to you too, Rona. What's got your panties in a wad this early?"

"Nothing, I'm fine."

"Try again, girlfriend."

"It's just Ellie, Ellie, Ellie every time I turn around. What's that about?"

"You tripping, Rona."

"No, I'm not. I know you're spending a lot of time with her all of a sudden. Why is that?"

"You know the deal. She wants in and I'm vetting her personally."

"Don't you have people for that?"

"Yeah girl, I do…"

"I hear a but in there. What's up?"

"Nothing. Sometimes I handle the vetting process myself. This is one of those times"

"Any particular reason why?"

"No, not really, besides I like her, she's cool."

"So, you are getting personal with her?"

"It's kind of hard not to. I did ask her to help with the Silent Charity Auction, now that I'm replacing Councilwoman Weatherly, I need an assistant. And she happens to be free."

"Right, whatever."

"Why do you have a problem with her?"

"Why do you not?"

"It's not like you to be so distrustful, Rona. Something else is up."

"I just think it's strange the way she showed up out of nowhere. She paid a ridiculous amount of money for your portrait and finagled her way into your life. Something about her just doesn't sit right with me. It's like she has an agenda maybe or she's after something."

"I'm sure you're overreacting. She's harmless, but in case you forgot who I am, I'm nobody's fool."

"I know that but just know, I'm keeping my eye on her and her friend, Adam."

"If that's the case, then maybe you should join us this weekend when we take her yacht out for a few hours. And before you trip, it's business. We need to discuss the upcoming Silent Charity Auction."

"Go out on the water on her yacht where she'll have home field advantage, thanks but that's a hard pass."

"You're over the top with this one, Rona."

"You just be careful, love."

"Careful about what?" Vonne asked as she took a seat with Zsasha and Rona.

"Hey Vonne." Rona said.

"Hey. My bad for being late. I had a long day yesterday and a rough night when I got home."

"Is that right?" Zsasha asked.

"Yeah, and it was a Xanax night too, so no need to ask, I'm disclosing."

"Relax sista, ain't nobody judging you. Ah, where's J'Nae? She's not usually this late. Is she coming?"

"She's not coming." Vonne replied.

"Oh, so she called you, huh?" Zsasha asked, not hiding her surprise. "Well, what in the hell did she say?"

"Stop hating. You're not always the go to girl getting the 411 on everybody and everything."

"Yeah, whateva, and?"

"She didn't call me; she didn't have to. I just think she's a bit preoccupied at the moment. She's got her hands full if you know what I mean. I'm quite sure everything and I do mean everything is fine!"

"Girl, you need to quit drooling over her man. We all get it. We see the same thing you see." Rona reiterated.

"Yeah girl, we're just not trying to be all obvious about it. We'll catch up with her on Friday night at the gallery. Give her a little wine and she'll spill."

"Whatever, but admiring his physical perfection is a happy distraction for me. A much needed one at that!" Vonne confessed.

"Really? Why is that? Rona asked.

"Just go ahead and tell us what's going on in your world these days." Zsasha demanded. "I'm sure it's got something to do with Kiera, right?"

"Doesn't it always?"

"Yeah, it does, so get to the point. I've been here for nearly an hour listening to this chick moan and groan and I've got things to do."

"Well this won't take long. In fact, let me get my order to go." Vonne signaled to the waitress and made her request. "Here goes, and please tell me the truth. Tell me exactly what you think in case I'm overreacting."

"You're not." Zsasha determined.

"Give the girl a chance to tell us what happened." Rona insisted. "Go ahead Vonne."

201

"Well, I got home kind of late last night, around 10 o'clock. And I found Lee and Kiera on the patio chilling with a bottle of wine after having finished eating a meal Kiera cooked."

"Alright, we're with you so far. What then?"

"She only made enough for the two of them. Gave me some excuse, said she thought I was out for the evening with you all."

"I could see how she might think that Vonne." Rona confessed. "We do meet up quite a bit in the evenings as well as coffee in the morning a couple times a week. I can see it."

"Well I can't." Zsasha admitted. "Sounds to me like she was getting a bit too cozy with your man and that's disrespectful."

"And that's exactly how I felt. I told her she doesn't understand or respect my boundaries and that's a problem. But it gets worse. After I calmed down, I let her make me a salad in the kitchen which was actually left over from the day before. It was her attempt to make it up to me and show that excluding me from dinner was a simple miscommunication."

"Do you believe her?" Rona asked.

"I did, for about five minutes, that's when I realized she'd done Lee's laundry and was about to fold it all up."

"And how did she explain that one?" Zsasha asked.

"She said it was just her way of helping out around the house. She had done mine as well."

"I still don't like it." Zsasha reiterated. "But you know that already because I told you not to let no bitch in ya house! But you wouldn't listen and now you got all these damn problems. So, what are you gonna do, Vonne? What's next?"

"Hold on a minute Zsasha, Vonne, you probably don't want to hear this, but you could just sit down with her, Lee as well, and just tell her what she can and can't do. Explain the definition of boundaries as well as what is and isn't appropriate. Sounds to me like she just doesn't know any better and I don't say that lightly. I only know what you've shared with me about her upbringing, her struggles, issues and the tumultuous relationship you guys had over the years. I don't think anyone in her life has ever held her accountable for her actions, not really. I mean her only consistent influence was your father and we all know what not to expect from that. I just think she needs to be around people that act appropriately, so maybe she can learn how to behave better. Sometimes you don't know what you don't know."

"That's some bullshit if I ever heard some. That chick is old enough to know how to act around your husband so I'm not cutting her no slack. If you wanna take Rona's suggestion, fine, I'm cool with that. Invite her to coffee with us or plan some other outing, I'm good with that too, but she can't come to the gallery to hang out. Not at any time or for any reason. I don't want her ass nowhere near it or anywhere else I do business. She keeps too much drama around her, and I can't have that."

"I get it. And yeah, you were right. I should've listened better, but I didn't, so now I've got to make the best of it. I'll talk to her after I talk to Lee. He's partially responsible for this too and I do not plan to let his ass off the hook."

"Well good, I'm glad. "Rona stated. "It's nice to know my words didn't fall on deaf ears."

"No, they didn't. But morning coffee is not the best time to hang out with her. It's early, most days we are not on the same schedule and it's usually a bit rushed with everybody off to start their workday. So, let's do wine one night, like we usually do, we'll just do it somewhere else."

"I'm up for it." Rona replied.

"Yeah, ok, whatever." Zsasha breathed, sounding a bit uninterested.

"Well don't sound so happy about it. How about we invite Ellie to come along? It'll give us all a chance to get to know one another." Rona suggested.

"Look here, business is business sista girl, ain't no need for all of that."

"Says you." Rona uttered. "Be sure to let me know when that changes."

"For sure."

"What are y'all talking about?" Vonne asked.

"Nothing really. Rona tripping on Ellie."

"Oh, I see. I'll come up with something and let everybody know. You guys can invite whoever you want. The more the merrier."

"You pretty turned up about this, huh?" Rona asked.

"Yes, I am. Coming home to stress and bullshit does not a happy home make. So yeah, I'm willing to do whatever I can to make this better for everybody, especially me."

"You wouldn't be you if you didn't girl." Rona replied.

"I know, right. So, let's get out of here. I made Kiera go in early to cover for me so I can talk to Lee. He should be back from his morning run by the time I get back to the
house."

"You go girl, you handle that."

"Yeah, call me and let me know how it goes." Rona remarked on her way out.

"And Zsasha, behave yourself and quit messing with her. She's got enough to deal with. I'll holla at you ladies later."

"Bye Rona."

"Yeah, bye heffa." Zsasha mumbled under her breath as she followed Vonne out not far behind Rona.

Vonne had her phone in her hand ready to call Lee as she drove off from The Coffee House. But the element of surprise made her feel more confident and more in control of the situation. She knew her husband very well and anticipated he would try to minimize the recent issues and her overall concerns when it came to her sister.

In the past, Vonne would most likely call Lee on the phone about any concern she had. Whether it was about the house, The Boutique's or some random woman clapping at her on social media. In doing so, Lee always had a heads up and a chance to work up a charming solution or charismatic lie to deflect responsibility or defend his actions. This time, he would have no time to prepare a bullshit story and he was not known for thinking on his feet. Not that he should need it, he was present last night and should have known what was coming. But like most lazy, spoiled, and overconfident men, his arrogance precluded him from seeing what was building on the horizon.

As she pulled into her driveway going to the rear of the house, Vonne could see his running shoes parked by the door leading to the laundry area. Her car purred like a kitten so unless he saw her pull in, he wouldn't have known she returned home. She got out of her car and entered the same way he did and found him taking off his sweaty clothes and throwing them in the wash.

"You sure you don't want to leave that for Kiera to take care of for you?"

"Vonne! What are you doing back home?"

"Do I need a reason to come home?"

"Of course not, but you've been knee deep in inventory so you've said, complaining about it every five minutes, I wouldn't have thought you could spare the time."

"Well, I needed to come home so we could talk. It's important."

"Okay, but can I get a shower first?"

"Yeah, sure, but don't take all day. I do need to get back at some point."

Lee retreated upstairs to shower and change into a pair of Lakers basketball shorts and matching tank. Vonne reheated what was left of her coffee and grabbed two mini muffins which served as her breakfast. Barely finishing, she noticed Lee's wallet, cell phone and keys on the counter. Like most women, she was tempted to go through his cell phone and see what he'd been up to, but she knew from past experiences and biblical teachings, 'seek and ye shall find'. And odds are, you will find something that you probably won't like. Choosing to refrain from violating his privacy seemed like the best option at the moment. One thing at a time.

"Hey, so you wanted to talk about something, what's up?" Lee asked, walking into the kitchen.

"Yes, I do. It's about Kiera. She's not respecting appropriate boundaries and you are part of the problem."

"What? What are you talking about?"

"For starters, Kiera shouldn't be playing wifey to you in my absence. She shouldn't be cooking private meals, doing your laundry or sitting around chilling, sharing a bottle of wine with you in a romantic setting or any setting at all if I'm not present."

"Hold on, don't you think you're making too much of this? She's your sister and you're the one who invited her to move in."

"Yes, she's my sister but I did not invite her to move in. Her being here was a direct result of you scheming with my father. I promise you this was their plan all along. But that's neither here nor there. You're my husband and I expect you to support me in dealing with her and her issues. You're allowing her to do all these personal things for you, private dinners and hanging out; it's encouraging her behavior and I feel disrespected in my own home!"

"Oh yeah, that's right, you're home. I forgot I'm just a guest here."

"You know exactly what I'm talking about, Lee. You don't need to be spending so much time with her when I'm not around. By not calling her out you're working against me, against us and it needs to stop."

"Well what am I supposed to do, just ignore her because you're not here? Cook my own meals and go eat in our bedroom or something? This is crazy. Nobody is trying to disrespect you. I think you're letting your own insecurities cloud your judgement, and maybe you're a little jealous of her and her relationship with your father!"

"Jealous! You must be out of your mind! The only thing she has going for her is me! Why the hell would I be jealous? I'm tired of having issues with her, especially issues like this. This type of shit could be avoided if you would just have my back and respect me as your wife. If you did that, I mean really did that, she would have no choice but to do it too. And dad has absolutely nothing to do with this, at this point."

"You need to take a chill pill, Vonne. As usual, you're overanalyzing every little thing. You'd have a problem no matter what I'd say or not say to Kiera. It's too much. Either you'll say you're getting too close and personal with her, or you don't talk to her, you're freezing her out and making her feel unwelcomed.

No matter what I do, you'll find fault with it. You always do and I'm tired of it!"

"You're tired of it? Can't you see what you're doing right now? I'm your wife and if I'm telling you that I feel disrespected, even if it's unintentional, a supportive husband would be asking what he could do to change how I feel."

"We're not even here together that often. What could I possibly change, Vonne?"

"You could start with maintaining healthy boundaries with her and when she crosses the line or even gets too close to it, tell her. Let her know. You need to consider how I'd feel in any situation that occurs when I'm not present."

"Healthy boundaries, huh? You need to sort out your issues with your sister yourself and stop putting me in the middle of your shit. I'm not gonna go out my way to be rude to her or avoid her because of your unresolved issues. I'm not gonna do it!"

"Uh, do we have a problem, me and you?"

"I don't know Vonne, maybe, maybe we do."

Lee grabbed his keys, wallet and the cell phone he'd left on the kitchen counter earlier and walked out of the house. Vonne could hear him revving the engine on his red 2015 Porsche Boxster just before peeling off down the road. She stood in the kitchen, frozen for a moment replaying their recent conversation against the one she had previously envisioned in her mind. Nothing about the two scenarios were similar and she was left feeling hurt, betrayed, and disappointed at his total lack of understanding and support. Her only comfort was that Kiera wasn't around to witness it.

* * * * *

"Are you planning on taking the entire day off or just showing up half-a-day?" Rick asked.

"Neither sweetie, I'm working from home today."

"Oh yes you are. I can attest to that, in fact, how about another lesson?"

"A lesson, huh? What subject did you have in mind?"

"Uhm, how about The Science of Making Love." Rick answered.

"That sounds like a class I definitely want to be in, but can I enroll in the next session? I've got some work I need to get started on that just can't wait."

"Absolutely. Class is always in session. You just need to let your instructor know when you're ready."

"Count on it." J'Nae leaned in for a kiss and proceeded to grab a robe while looking around the room for her panties. Once found, she slipped them on then sat down at her computer and powered it on.

"Baby, what are you doing?"

"I told you, I'm working from home today. I just need to email a few reports I completed last night while you were at work, so they'll think I've been working all morning."

"Ah, no, that's not what I mean. Why did you put your panties on and cover up with your robe? There's nobody here but us."

"I know. But I don't trust the PC camera when I'm logged in. Big brother could be watching or some foreign ally snooping around doing Donald Trump's dirty work."

"Yeah okay, but why your panties? No one on the computer can see that far down while you're sitting."

"Oh, I just don't want to get my chair dirty, that's all."

"Dirty you say?"

"Yeah." J'Nae replied, giving him the side eye. "It wouldn't be easy trying to get my scent out of the fabric on this chair you know, the cover doesn't come off."

"Why would you want to? This is your house and it's your scent and I find it intoxicating."

"Is that right?"

"Yes, it is. I think about your scent and your taste on my lips every day, many times a day baby. I love the way you smell and taste, anytime."

"I'm surprised by that."

"Why is that?"

"Because I douche before we have sex, every time."

"Really?"

"Well, almost every time. If I get the chance to."

"Babe, I'm gonna need you to stop doing that. I want to taste your natural juices, all of them, just as they are."

"Ew."

"I love it boo, and soon you're gonna love it too."

"I don't know about all of that."

"Trust me, you'll see. Just follow my lead when the time comes, you'll be turned on by your inner essence too."

"I'm already familiar with all that."

"No, not really. Trust me, it'll change you."

"Whatever. Now how about a little breakfast while I get a little work done and maybe I'll show up for class sooner than you think."

"Okay love, I got you. Coffee?"

"Of course, thanks sweetie."

"Thank you."

* * * * *

"Hey Zsasha, did you enjoy breakfast?" Ellie asked as she entered the gallery.

"Yes, I did. I was just getting started. Thanks again for helping me out."

"No problem. Whatever you need."

"Well let's start by giving you some background on the event. It's a Silent Charity Auction that's held every year. Councilwoman Weatherly has been the organizer in the recent past but due to some extenuating circumstance- "

"Everybody knows she's involved in the college cheating scandal and as I've heard, at more than one university."

"More than one, huh?"

"Yeah, but no one is confirming to what extent, but she's stone-cold busted, I'm certain of that."

"Well anyway, I usually reach out to some of my friends, local government officials and people I do business with. Each year, we ask them to donate something to be auctioned off. It could be a piece of artwork, a weekend getaway, anything really. 100% of the proceeds will go to charity. The charity is determined by the board, and they usually make their decision for the upcoming year right after the current auction is completed, more or less."

"Okay, and who is this years' recipient?"

"Against All Odds. It's a charity centered on providing medical care, lodging accommodations, meals etc. for sick children and their families."

"That sounds like a much needed and deserving cause."

"It is. The thought of children coming into this world and having to struggle with illness or disease is unsettling to me and Against All Odds is one of the charities I hold near and dear to my heart."

"I can see that. So, what's first up? Has a date been determined?"

"Not yet, that's actually one of the things I wanted us to take care of today. Since we hold the auction here, I select three available dates in the order of my preference and submit them to the board for review. They usually have a decision back to me in two or three days. I just need to check my calendar to make sure there aren't any showings or other events scheduled to begin or end within 5 days before and after each of the potential dates."

"That must be hard, with everything you and Simon have going on here."

"It can be challenging, but it's for such a good cause that I'm willing to block off 10-12 days for the auction."

"Why is that necessary?"

"Because the artist showcases and other events require time for delivery, setup, staging and artist approval before the doors open and afterwards, time for sales confirmation, inventory count, packing, pickup and re-placing any house artwork that may have been removed prior to the show. So that everything goes smoothly, and nothing is rushed, I require 5 days on the front and back end."

"I see. I didn't realize how much preparation is required to put together a showcase, but I get it now."

"Cool."

"So, I guess we just need to view your calendar to see what's open."

Zsasha proceeded to unlock her laptop and open her calendar. She only had time for a quick glance before her phone rang. It was Simon.

"Hey hun, what's up?" Zsasha asked.

"Are you with Ellie by chance?"

"Yes, why?"

"I just received the investigative report on her and her partner."

"I see, well hold on a minute." Zsasha requested. "Ellie, I need to take this in my office, I'll be back in a minute."

"No problem. I'll just take a glance at your calendar for potential openings. Is that cool?"

"Sure, knock yourself out." Zsasha replied as she turned and headed for her office.

"So, what did the report uncover? Short version, please."

"Basically, nothing scandalous or criminal is in either of their backgrounds. Ellie's father, Daniel Porter is the source of her wealth. He owns many companies in the US and abroad and his net worth exceeds 100 billion."

"Really, I'm impressed."

"Yeah, me too. Sadly however, her mother, Lynette Porter passed away when she was just 9 years old. Ellie was their only child which by the way, they adopted shortly after her birth. She has no other known siblings."

"Interesting. Anything about Adam?"

"Not much. His background was unremarkable. He has no living family to speak of. He met Ellie during their freshman year in college and he graduated the same year she did. Her father was his benefactor for his last two years so they must have become very close during that time. His finances are miniscule, mostly non-existent except for some property he inherited from an aunt, and a stipend he receives monthly for living expenses and property maintenance."

"Do either of them have any children?"

"No, neither of them has any known offspring."

"So, the report shows no valid reason to deny them membership, huh?"

"No, it doesn't but we haven't always relied totally on investigative tools. We've also been known to use our judgement and intuition. What is your gut telling you?"

"My gut says it's a go, but I'd like to see how things play out with the Silent Charity Auction she's assisting me with. I'll make my final decision in a few weeks."

"Cool. Now you can continue growing your relationship with her. You should feel better about it now."

"Yeah, right."

"Don't act like you don't know what I'm talking about. Everybody can see it. I'm surprised your girls haven't picked up on it yet, with all the time you two have been spending together in the past weeks."

"Goodbye Simon."

"Bye baby."

Hanging up with her husband, Zsasha returned to the gallery and her meeting with Ellie. When she sat down beside her, she was surprised to find that Ellie had taken some notes and scribbled a few dates beside them.

"I see you found something to keep yourself busy."

"Yes, I did. Is everything alright, with Simon, I mean?"

"Yes, it was just business. Anyway, let's see what you got here."

"Well, I wasn't exactly sure what month you typically hold the auction; however, I found the following dates that fit your criteria in August, September and October."

"Great. First off, August is just too soon. We usually try to find a time during September and October. Let's nix the August dates and focus on September and October."

"Okay then, it looks like the last week in September would be a good time as well as the first week of October. You have two weeks blocked leading up to Halloween, but I didn't see any notes regarding why. Is there an event you're planning but didn't pencil in?"

"Yes, that would be the Masquerade Ball.   It's likely the biggest event of the season."

"I see. So, the last week of September or the first week of October? What are your thoughts?"

"Well, I thought I had something on the books at the end of September." Zsasha revealed.

"Nope, you're completely open."

"Well, I'm thinking September is probably the best time since I'll be busy finalizing the plans for the ball in October."

"Then let's go ahead with the last week of September."

"Not so fast, sweetie. We need to submit 3 dates to the board, remember? They have final approval."

"Of course."

"So, we'll go with the first week of October, the first week of November, which I know they'll never go for being so close to the holiday season and my first choice of course, the last week in September."

"Sounds good but don't you want to make it a bit more specific?"

"Yes, and you can do that now while I run to the bathroom. You isolate the dates of every Thursday through Sunday of each of those weeks and highlight them on my calendar. Title it 'For Board Consideration – Silent Charity Auction'. And be sure to double check there's nothing going on for the 5 days before each Thursday and the 5 days following each Sunday. Then we're good to move on to the next item on the list."

"And what would that be?" Ellie asked.

"Letter writing." Zsasha replied, her voice trailing behind her as she disappeared to her office.

Ellie did as Zsasha asked and reviewed the dates under consideration and found no reason to eliminate any potential dates. She created an event and titled it as instructed blocking off the dates in questions. When Zsasha returned she had a few ideas about the letters needing to be constructed.

"So, about the letters, are they directed at previous donors or who exactly?"

"For starters, we have a specific letter for each group. The first being previous residential donors who may or may not have attended or donated in the past. Secondly, we have who's who in our local political arena including past, present or potential future seat holders."

"That sounds impressive."

"It is. We don't play around when it comes to raising money for a charitable cause."

"I see."

Thirdly, we reach out to our local business owners, most if not all won't fall into category 1 or 2. And last but not least, in conjunction with the Chamber of Commerce, we reach out to them to address the non-local business owners they're working on attracting their business to our area."

"Sounds all very professional and specific."

"It is. Don't let the hood girl in me fool ya. I can turn it on and off like a light switch sweetie."

"I can tell, I can tell."

"And of course, if you have some professional colleagues with deep pockets you want to invite, make a list and present it to me. I'll review it and let you know who's approved."

"That'll work."

"So how about you work up a draft for each of these categories and we can review them tomorrow?"

"Alright, sounds like a plan?"

"Same time?"

"No, let's meet here at 11:00 and I'll have lunch brought in for us."

"As long as it's not that heavy country food from Miss Maple's, I'm good."

"I got you. I know you don't eat like that. I have a few local places that will set us up nicely. You can look them over tomorrow and decide then. Okay?"

"Okay, well I'd better leave you to it. See you tomorrow."

"Bye girl and thank you for your help. Don't forget the letter drafts, I'll be looking for your best work."

"And you shall have it. See you then."

214

Chapter 20

G ood morning Zsasha."

"Hey, good morning." Zsasha replied as she entered the main gallery. "I hope you haven't been waiting for too long. Did Simon let you in?"

"Yes, he did and no, I just arrived. Shall we get started?"

"Aren't you the anxious one. Don't you wanna take a few minutes to order lunch before we dig in?"

"I'll make it simple for you. Any meatless salad with balsamic vinaigrette dressing is fine with me."

"That's it? That's all you want?"

"That and a glass of wine, if I may?"

"You may indeed." Zsasha smiled. "Simon, can you order lunch for us? I'll have a grilled chicken salad with honey mustard dressing, and she'll have a mixed green salad with balsamic vinaigrette dressing, both with bread sticks."

"Sure sweetie, no problem. Pickup or delivery?"

"Delivery, please."

"Got it."

Simon retreated to his office to place the order while Zsasha turned her attention back to Ellie and the project at hand. She could see the obvious excitement on Ellie's face and saw no reason to prolong her agony.

"So alright, let's see what you got."

Ellie took no time in pulling out her thumb drive, connecting it to Zsasha's computer and retrieving her documents. She was feeling confident that her drafts would surpass Zsasha's expectations hoping to ingratiate herself even more. Zsasha reviewed the documents carefully, one after the other, making mental notations of the changes she would need to make. Her face was serious and did not reflect any emotion that might indicate her feelings one way or the other.

"Well, what do you think?" Ellie asked anxiously.

"I think you did an excellent job on these."

215

"Really?"

"Yes, I do. I'm impressed."

"Great. Now all I need is the list for each group, and I can go ahead and create the mail merges and print them out."

"We're getting a little ahead of ourselves. First off, I need to tweak them a bit, add a few words I feel necessary and specific to each group and of course, a few of them are confidential. Therefore, I'll be handling the mail merge and sending out. You understand, right?"

"Yes, of course. Not sure what I was thinking."

"It's all good. You were just excited and proud of your work and rightfully so. You really did an excellent job on these. I should have them in the mail within the next few days."

"Then you must've heard from the board already."

"Yes, I did and with the options I gave them it was an easy choice. They decided on the last week in September. The 26th to be exact."

"Great, that'll give us ample time to arrange everything else. So then, what's next?"

"I'm going to put you in touch with my personal assistant, Ms. Honey and the two of you can create the menu. It'll be light of course and it should include a variety of wine, beer and a few specialty cocktails that should blend well with whatever hors d'oeuvres and meal options we serve. Of course, I'll need to approve whatever you two come up with."

"Absolutely. Do you have a caterer in mind?"

"Yes, I do. A long-time trusted chef I've worked with many times in the past. He has his own staff, and they do everything. All I have to do is provide the check."

"Wonderful."

"And while you two are busy with that, I'll be monitoring the replies and descriptions of the items being donated so I can plan for the delivery, setup and staging of each item."

"I didn't realize so much work went into prepping and planning an event like this."

"Yeah, most don't. But we've made progress and we're on target so relax for the next day or two and I'll have Ms. Honey reach out to you after that."

"Cool. Sounds like a plan. I'll wait to hear from her and touch base with you then."

"Awesome. Thanks Ellie. I'll see you later."

"You will indeed."

* * * * *

J'Nae had left work an hour early so she could prepare for the Wine and Cheese night with the girls, plus Kiera. Since Zsasha was not on board with Kiera coming to the gallery the decision was made for J'Nae to host the gathering at her house. It was a unanimous decision and an easy one as well. Rona doesn't entertain at her home much at all and having it at Vonne's house seemed more like Kiera was included as a resident and less like she was an invited guest, which was the reason they were getting together with her in the first place.

Most of what J'Nae planned to serve had been pre-ordered early in her workday and prepared by On the Go Catering, a locally owned establishment she'd used many times for things of this nature. Using On the Go Catering would allow her time to stage the seating area, organize and plate the items just the way she wanted without the mess and stress of preparing it all herself. She even had a few games in mind to play but planned to place them nearby yet out of sight. Something they could do if things began to go south.

Turning onto her street she checked her watch and saw she had 20 minutes before the food was scheduled to be delivered. That was good. It would allow her plenty of time to do what she needed to do before the girls would arrive. Pulling into her driveway she sighed realizing the excitement she was now feeling wasn't related to the outing with the girls. It was of a personal, more pressing nature that required her immediate surrender. And she had no problem with that at all.

She parked her car, cut off the engine, and leaned back to welcome the orgasm building in her groin. Reaching downward, she gently ran her hand over her upper thigh area moving swiftly

217

to the crotch of her slacks. She began to put pressure on her clitoris while massaging it in a circular motion. Closing her eyes, she let out a subtle moan as the pressure continued to build. She thought of her lover and could almost hear him calling her name as she rode her pleasure wave to the end.

"Hey J'Nae, didn't you hear me calling you?" LB said just a few feet from her car.

"I didn't mean to interrupt you while you prayed but I didn't realize what you were doing until I got up close."

J'Nae could barely form her words realizing how close she came to being busted.

"Hey LB, my bad. I was in deep thought, and I guess I didn't see or hear you."

"It's all good. I just wanted to see how you're doing. Haven't seen much of you lately. The new job must be keeping you busy. Love to catch up with you sometime."

"Yeah, sure, but right now I'm expecting company and I need to prepare really quick. I'll call you." J'Nae said walking inside.

"Sure, okay."

J'Nae didn't purposely intend for her remark to sound like a brush off, but it did, and she knew it. LB was also painfully aware that his time with her was over and unlikely to come again. He had seen the same guy spending time at her house for a while now and she was almost never at home, alone anyway. Yeah, that ship has sailed.

On the Go Catering had delivered on time and everything was fresh and ready to be served. Since it was a wine tasting and the girls would have a few different wine options, J'Nae decided to have a few different appetizers that should pair well with at least one or two of their wine choices.

Zsasha and Rona were the first to arrive, each toting a bottle of wine of their choosing. J'Nae took Rona's jacket and hung it up in the closet.

"Are you sure about this, sista girl? It's not too late to back out. White girls aren't even here yet."

"It'll be fine, Zsasha. We're doing this to support our friend."

"And you would do well to remember that Zsasha." Rona announced. "I know you'll be tempted to mess with her but the objective here is to make her feel welcome and maybe teach her how to behave and interact with women you're close to."

"Oh, I got it, for sure for sure. When she leaves here, she'll know how I get down and how I look out for mine."

"I figured you were gonna say something like that. Just don't ride all night, okay?"

"I won't. I'll be sweet as pie." Zsasha smirked. "I think I hear them at the door now. I'll get it." Zsasha walked purposefully to the door before anyone had the chance to cut her off. "Hey Vonne, come on in. You must be Kiera. Hi Kiera, welcome."

"Thanks for the invite. You have a lovely home." Kiera said.

"Oh, this isn't my home. This is J'Nae's spot. I'm Zsasha. Me and Vonne go way back. I was there when she opened her first boutique."

"Really, so you're the one with the art gallery, right?"

"Yeah, that's me. Why don't y'all ladies come in and have a seat. J'Nae put a few things out for us to nibble on. Follow me."

Zsasha hell bent on steering the conversation away from Ahsasz led them to the area where J'Nae and Rona were fussing over the hors d'oeuvres. With all the shenanigans and undesirable situations Kiera has found herself in over the years, it's unlikely her social circle would cross paths with any of theirs, but Zsasha didn't want to take any chances.

"Hey, y'all remember Kiera." Vonne said.

"Hello Kiera."

"Hi Kiera, welcome to my home. Please make yourself comfortable."

"Thank you J'Nae. I was just telling Zsasha you have a really nice house."

"Thank you. I see everybody came with a bottle of wine. Rona, can you help me put these on ice?"

"Sure, no problem."

"Ladies, I already have a bottle of white and rose on the table. Help yourselves and please excuse us for a moment."

Rona and J'Nae made their way to the kitchen and placed the bottles of wine in the wine cooler.

"Is it me or is Zsasha going out of her way to be nice?" J'Nae asked.

"Oh, she's definitely laying it on thick."

"I guess she took your advice after all."

"Nah, I don't think so. In fact, I think she's up to something. I think she's laying on thick so she can catch Kiera off guard. You know how she is."

"In that case, we'd better hurry back."

Rona and J'Nae returned to the group just in time to hear Zsasha talking about her lifestyle. No one expected Zsasha to be open with someone she barely knew so the girls were all curious to see just how much of her private life she was willing to disclose. They were shocked to get their answer as they returned to the group.

"We've been swinging since before we were married."

"Wow, how do you do it? How do you keep him interested in you when he can go out and have any woman he wants?"

"Well Sweetie, for starters, he can't go out and have any woman he wants. We have rules that we must follow and boundaries that must be respected at all times."

"Like what?" Kiera asked.

"For starters, there is no independent sex outside the marriage. Our relationship is primary, and we both have to agree each time we share our bed."

"I see."

"Also, we limit the number of times we connect with the same couple. That's so nobody gets attached or tempted to cross the boundaries we've established to protect our marriage. You see, it's important in any relationship to know the boundaries. You must determine what is acceptable and what is not in order to protect, maintain and respect the primary relationship, which is our marriage. I'm sure that since you live with your sister and her husband, you're familiar with boundaries and expectations, right?   How to live peacefully and stay inside the lines. Otherwise, y'all would be going down through it all the time."

"J'Nae, this is tasty. What exactly is it?" Vonne interrupted.

"On the Go Catering calls it Scamputto. It's one of their original recipes. It has shrimp scampi stuffed with goat cheese and something green then wrapped in prosciutto. Also, I have Hot & Creamy Crab tartlets, spinach balls and cucumber bites, with a variety of cheeses, crackers and fruit as well as a bit of chicken salad."

"It all looks delicious." Vonne remarked. "You didn't have to put yourself out like this."

"It wasn't any trouble at all, like I said, On the Go Catering. And they're really good too."

"And everything goes well with the wine too. Speaking of wine, we're a little low. Do you mind?"

"Not at all."

As the drinking continued, it became more challenging for the four of them to sound less like an interrogation panel and more like interested parties. Nonetheless they managed to keep Kiera talking about herself and perspective on all things Vonne and Lee. By the end of the evening, they'd learned that Kiera suddenly became in possession of a very nice car and was purposely vague when asked about it. They also learned she was definitely jealous of Vonne and everything she had, including her non-working, X-NBA ball player husband. They also learned that both Kiera and Vonne contributed to the discord in their relationship with each carrying their own set of baggage and harboring ill will from the past. Overall, the night went well, but not well enough to change how any of them felt about her.

Chapter 21

Bella was beyond exquisite. It was built in 2010 and fashioned after the Dilbar, one of the largest yachts in the world at that time. It slept up to 28 comfortably in 14 cabins of varying sizes not including the accommodations below deck to house a crew of up to 14 members. The master was a split-level suite fit for a king and his queen. Beginning on the back end of the top deck and continuing down to the back end of the deck directly beneath. It included a private lounge area with a dedicated luxury grill platform attached to a private kitchen, a private pool, hot tub, and bar, all of which included 24-hour staffed concierge service to cook, clean and accommodate any and all related needs the occupants may have.

Additionally, there were junior suites throughout the yacht, some of which we split-level and some were not. Although exquisite in layout and design, none of them were as luxurious as the master suite. Every suite was designed to be slightly different than the next. Each of them offered a few of the top-of-the-line amenities found in the master suite but none of them had it all. Some shared a kitchen or a lounge area whereas others shared a bar or deluxe patio and grill. But one thing they all had in common was direct access to 24-hour concierge service. Whether it was a long cruise or a short one, every guest was catered to and made to feel special.

Throughout the many decks there were countless lounge areas both formal and informal, a game room with a league size pool table, a sports bar eatery with an abbreviated bowling alley, a deluxe cinema, and a club-styled dance hall. There was plenty to do while cruising on the extravagant vessel.

As they boarded the immense beauty known as Bella, Zsasha and Simon were greeted by the captain and his cruise director.

"Welcome Mr. and Mrs. Stewart. I'm Captain Reed. My job is to ensure the safe operation of this vessel, manage the crew members and make certain your cruise is safe, pleasant, and enjoyable. This is Renee, she'll be your Cruise Director for the day." She will show you to your cabin where you can change, relax and/or get comfortable. You will find everything you may need hanging in your closet. If there is anything else you need at any time, please don't hesitate to let us know. We leave port in 15 minutes."

"Thank you, Captain Reed, and Renee. Where can we find our host, Ellie Porter?"

"Here I am Zsasha!" Ellie screamed as she approached them on the main deck.

"I'm so thrilled you both agreed to join us for the evening."

"This is amazing, Ellie! I could live here all year long." Zsasha proclaimed.

"I do, sometimes. It's beautiful and relaxing but after a while I start to feel a bit cutoff from the world if I'm out here too long."

"I don't know sista, that looks like a check mark in the plus column for me, a definite win."

"Well, you are welcome to use her anytime you'd like, both of you. Just reach out to me and I'll make it happen."

"That's way too generous of you." Simon remarked. "But thank you."

"You're more than welcome. Let me show you where you'll be staying."

As she turned to lead the way, Ellie's cell phone rang and by the ringtone she knew it was her father. It was a call she needed to take.

"Zsasha, Simon, please excuse me for a moment, that's my father calling, and I need to take this. Renee, please escort them to their cabin and make sure they have everything they may need."

"Yes ma'am."

"You two go ahead and get settled in. I'll come up and get you shortly, cool."

"Cool." Zsasha replied but not before Ellie had turned and walked away to take her call.

"Right this way Mr. and Mrs. Stewart."

Even though it was a large luxury yacht, the walk to their cabin was short. It was up one level and towards the rear of the yacht. Inside was decorated with varying shades of gray, silver and black. It had a polished sterile look and feel to it similar to their own home. The bed was king sized, and the mattress was a very comfortable memory foam, a quality higher than any of their own.

The closet was fully stocked with swimsuits, robes, sandals, and slippers as well as various outfits in their sizes to accommodate any occasion. Toiletries were stocked in the bathroom along with curling irons, a blow dryer and various hair care products. Ellie obviously thought of everything.

"This is something else, Simon. Who the hell is this girl and where did she come from?"

"You know as well as I do, you read the report."

"I did, but damn, this yacht had to cost several million dollars at least."

"That's about right, sweetheart. That was in the report also."

"Oh, right, Bella...I get it now. Her daddy sure spoils her."

"He can afford too."

"I'm sure he can."

"Why don't you get comfortable while I take a quick look around and I'll meet you back here in twenty?"

"Okay, don't get lost, baby. I don't want you too far from me."

"Awe, what's the matter sweetheart, you scared?"

"Ah, yeah, a little bit. I would prefer you be by my side when we pull out. This is a lot of ship."

"It's not a ship Zsasha, it's a yacht. A very large yacht."

"Just don't go too far."

"Alright, I'll see you in a few minutes."

Simon kissed his wife while embracing her tightly. As he turned to leave there was a knock on the cabin door. It was Ellie and Adam.

"Hey guys, Adam, I was just coming to look for you. How's it going?" Simon asked while shaking Adam's hand.

"Great man. Good to see you both. I trust you'll be comfortable here?" Adam asked.

"If not, we can put you in a different cabin." Ellie offered. "Maybe one with---"

"Nonsense. This is perfect and absolutely stunning." Zsasha revealed.

"Wonderful. Why don't you two change and we'll go sit out on the rear deck. We'll get a nice breeze, have a drink and chat. We'll just step out and give you a minute to change."

"Okay. We'll be right out." Zsasha replied.

Zsasha and Simon quickly did as she suggested and appeared just outside the door. Ellie and Adam were true to their word as they were waiting just a few feet away with big smiles and a crew member standing next to them waiting to be of service.

"Now that's better. You look relaxed and comfortable. Like you belong on a yacht." Ellie laughed. "This is Jared. He'll take your drink order and bring it to us on the main deck. He can make anything you'd like. He even has a few specialty drinks he created on his own if you're brave enough to try one of them."

"I'll take that challenge." Simon boasted. "How about it, Z?"

"I'm in."

"Good. Jared, please make us an assortment of your specialty drinks. I'll have my usual. Adam, what are you having dear?"

"I'll have whatever is left over. You know I'm not picky and I do love them all."

"Okay then. Shall we?"

Ellie led the way towards the designated lounge area at the rear of the main deck. It was the largest lounge area with extended seating suitable for a large number of guests. On their walk down, they passed several other seating areas, some with enclosures and some without. There were several bars and places to eat, and drink scattered throughout the main deck with a considerable amount of open space perfect for displaying auction items.

"There's a fitness center and a spa if you want to get a personal and private massage. You'll find them just a few feet from your suite, if you're interested."

226

"I appreciate that Ellie, we appreciate that, but we should probably get down to business."

"Relax Zsasha, we have plenty of time for that. Here we are. This is one of my favorite places to entertain. It's open and accessible to the things I use most often. And lounging out here taking in the breeze while feeling the engine's hum is beyond relaxing."

"It's perfect." Zsasha said, taking a seat. Looking out at the Potomac she just noticed the yacht was moving. "I didn't realize we had left port. It's such a smooth and quiet ride."

"It is. Only the best for daddy's little girl." Ellie jokes.

"You did say this was a gift from your father." Zsasha confirmed. "What was the occasion, if you don't mind me asking?"

"He was feeling guilty about sending me off to boarding school and moving on so quickly after my mother died." Ellie replied.

"I see. But this yacht isn't very old. She's been gone for many years now, right?"

"Yes, but this isn't the first one. He upgraded once he got involved in a serious relationship."

"Oh, okay."

"Remember, our communication hasn't always been good. He's not one to open up and talk about his feelings so instead of dealing with his or mine, he put distance between us to avoid what he was uncomfortable with, and some years later began to regret it. It's his version of trying to undo the damage he caused in our relationship. He's very remorseful now and shows love the only way he knows how."

"Awe, that's so sweet."

"I know, right. I still give him a hard time every chance I get. I know he loves me, and I've forgiven him for the past, but I'm just not ready to let him know just yet. He still needs to suffer a bit. I may not always take his calls or talk to him often, but I love him very much."

"I'm sure you do."

"He has his ways of getting my attention though." Ellie revealed.

227

"Oh yeah, how so?"

"He wanted to buy me my own private jet."

"Really? I don't get it. Your own luxury yacht is okay, but a private jet is too much?"

"He already has three of them and there's only two of us in the family!"

"Oh wow, okay."

"Yeah. I had to reach out to him at that point. When I need to travel, I just use one of them. It's like having my own anyway."

"That's awesome. It's obvious he loves you very much."

"Yes, he does."

"Sista girl, you are blessed and don't you forget it."

Jared returned with the drinks and another crew member followed behind with appetizers.

"Those look delicious Jared, thank you, but why so many, there's only four of us here?"

"There for the two of you to sample and you and Mr. Stewart may have the same preference."

"Thanks, Jared. I appreciate that." Simon said. "So, what's what?"

"Well, I could explain," Jared replied in a serious tone. "But then I'd have to kill you."

Everyone laughed at the obvious joke.

"Just sample each one and then decide. If none of them are to your liking, I'll be right over there to make you whatever you want."

"I'll go first." Zsasha said as she selected a red colored drink and took a large sip. "This is divine. What is it? Never mind, you can't tell. Try this one, sweetie." She passed the glass to Simon then selected a different drink that was purple in color. "Oh, that's a bit sweet for me, let me try one more."

Eventually she settled on her first selection as did Simon, but before long all of the drink variations were gone. Adam and Simon wandered off for a tour of the yacht while Ellie and Zsasha continued to chat.

"I just want you to know, I really enjoy hanging out with you, you're like the big sister I never had."

"Back atcha, little lady."

"I really hope our relationship continues to grow and develop beyond business. Adam really likes you too."

"Does he now? So how long have you guys been together?"

"It's really hard to say. We met at school and became fast friends. My dad kind of took to him and acted as a surrogate father, helping with his tuition and other expenses after his aunt passed."

"So, he has a real bond with you and your father, then huh?"

"My father kind of saw him as my guardian for a few years and he kind of was, until you know…"

"How did that news go over with your dad?"

"I really don't know, he never said much to me directly. He stepped back a bit from the financial support but eventually he came back around. He's known him for so long, that eventually he realized with the amount of time we'd spent together that it was bound to happen anyway, so he got over it."

"That's great. You guys seem happy together, in sync."

"We are, and on so many levels and we're both eager to join *Ahsasz Down Under* and fully embrace the lifestyle."

"Are you sure about that because it's not as easy as you think to swing and maintain your primary relationship. You need to have rules and boundaries that must be respected at all times. Otherwise, you'll have all sorts of relationship problems and once you do, things will never be the same again. Just be sure you want to take on the lifestyle and the risks that come along with it. It's more than a notion."

"It works for you and Simon, right?"

"Yes, it does. But we've been at this for a very long time, and we stick to our guns and enforce the rules, no matter what. What's your endgame, with Adam and this lifestyle? That's important to know and establish beforehand so you'll know what rules to put in place to preserve the primary relationship."

"What are they, the rules I mean?"

"Our rules are just that, our rules. It's the framework or structure we established and swore to abide by for the purpose of exploration while protecting our marriage."

"Please continue."

"They fit our lifestyle and are not for anyone else. It's not a one-size-fits-all situation. This is something you'll need to sit down with Adam and discuss and come up with what works for the two of you."

"I was hoping you could guide us with that. Maybe you and Simon could share some of your experiences that helped you guys create the rules and do things in a way that works for the two of you."

"I'll speak with him about it later, but I can't make any promises."

"Here he comes now." Ellie said. Adam was right behind him.

"Zsasha, do you have your phone with you? Ms. Honey has been trying to reach you. She says it's a 9-1-1."

"No, I left it in the cabin, on purpose."

"Here sweetie, use mine. She sounded like it was really urgent, you should call her back right now."

Simon handed his wife his cell phone and signaled for Jared to come over and refill their drinks. Both men sat down at the bar behind them to wait for their drinks and to see what all the urgency was about. At the same time, Ellie took a few steps away but tried to remain close enough to hear what Zsasha was discussing on the phone. She ended the call very quickly. The face that moments ago looked relaxed and worry free was now replaced by stress and panic resulting from the unfortunate news at hand.

"What's going on Z?" Simon asked as he approached. "What was so important that she had to interrupt us here?"

"Ms. Honey received a call from Al Hadley, the President of the NBCC. He was calling to set up a time to review the platform and table layout for this year's NBCC Meet & Greet their holding at our gallery on the 25th of September."

"Okay, so what's the problem?"

"For some reason, it's not on my calendar and as of last week, that chunk of time has been reserved for the Silent Charity Auction. Now how in the hell did that happen?"

"Maybe you just forgot to put it on your calendar." Ellie suggested.

"That's not it. I remember logging it in, I remember actually typing it out. I just don't remember the dates. It was put on the books at least two months ago. I don't know how this happened." Zsasha sighed now suddenly sober.

"Well, can they move it to the following week or another day? Or maybe the board can pick one of the other available dates." Simon suggested.

"That's not possible. The NBCC has already sent out their invites, so they're locked in, no changing that. And it would be impossible to get the board together again to consider another date at this point. And if I did, do you know how that would make me look? I'd never chair this event ever again."

"Well, we're going to have to come up with something, Zsasha and quickly." Simon warned.

"I have an idea." Ellie interrupted with enthusiasm. "We could hold the Silent Charity Auction here, right here, on the yacht. There's plenty of space for us to display the donated items in a few different places throughout the yacht. Maybe we could have a theme for each level complimented with matching themed drinks and appetizers. We'd need security, of course and signed waivers of liability from everyone on board but we could definitely pull it off. I think it's a great idea! What do you think, Zsasha?"

"I don't know Ellie; I mean it sounds great and all but an auction on a yacht?" Turning to her husband. "Could we really do this, Simon? On a yacht?"

"I think so. Look around Z, this isn't just any yacht, this is huge. I think it's a really good idea; a step up from what we've done in the past. The guests will love it and have a great time. What's the quote...everybody loves a cheerful giver...or something to that effect."

"I know you ain't trying to quote scripture."

231

"No, but Ellie's right, there's more than enough room on each level to host the event, make the guests feel comfortable and display all of the wonderful items up for auction. About how many guests are invited?"

"Last year and the year before there were between 50 - 70 invited guests so I would say 65 - 100 guests plus the catering staff."

"Consider it done!" Ellie announced. "And my staff will be here to support and assist the chef you've hired for the event. Of course, if he would prefer his own team, that's understandable and I could make that happen as well. We could work it a number of ways."

"It all sounds good and I'm grateful to have this as an option, but I will need to discuss it with the board and get approval. Since this event involves board funding, would you be open to signing a contract?"

"Absolutely. Whatever you need. I'm glad to be able to help. I know how important the auction is to you so whatever you need, just ask."

"Wow, you continue to surprise me."

"I just like to pay it forward as much as possible."

"You're doing that in spades, Ellie." Zsasha proclaimed.

"Thank you, now we'd better head to dinner. Chef's a bit temperamental if we're not on time and his food gets cold."

"Well let's go then, I'm starved!" Zsasha replied.

"I'll second that." Simon followed.

Now that the stress level had returned to normal, the four friends were able to enjoy an Asian inspired dinner and upbeat conversation centered around anything and everything except the auction. With both Simon and Adam passing on a low carb, low sugar dessert, the girls were left alone to chat while they found their way to the theater room to search for some type, any type of sports entertainment.

"Looks like we're almost back at the port." Zsasha observed. "This has been quite an evening, Ellie. Thank you, thank you so much. I had a wonderful time and I appreciate you looking out for a sista."

"That's what we need to do for each other, more and more. Everybody needs help every now and then. No one can do it all, it's just not possible."

"You're right about that. Simon just asked me to consider hiring a coordinator, someone to handle the logistics and coordinating special events so I can focus on discovering and booking talented artists."

"That sounds like a good idea to me."

"Yeah, but I'm not entirely sold on the idea, at least not yet. I've always had some control issues and as you know confidentiality is not something I can afford to take lightly. Hiring someone to help even if it's limited to the gallery operations still poses a threat. There'd be another set of hands and eyes I'd have to look out for and frankly I'm not sure if I want to take that on right now."

"What about Ms. Honey? Can't she help you with any of this?"

"She's already got her hands full coordinating all the home staff as well as the staff for the club. She also works the club on most event nights, and she handles special projects for me and the girls. Now that I'm saying it out loud, I don't know how she does it all."

"She certainly has her hands full. It doesn't sound like that's an option."

"No, it's not but right now I'm not going to worry about it. Done enough of that tonight already."

"Do you mind if I ask you something personal?"

"If I do, I'll let you know, what's up?"

"Why don't you and Simon have any children?"

"We have our reasons and tonight ain't the night for that conversation. But we do enjoy life, our life. He's my best friend and my lover and I wouldn't be me without him."

"That's so sweet. I can see that he feels the same way about you." Ellie confessed. "It's obvious you two were made for each other."

"He's special but keep that to yourself. He'll never hear that coming out of my mouth. Otherwise, he'll think he got me twisted, and I still need him to work for it the same way he did back in the day. Always working for it."

"This right here...this is what I like; talking with you like a big sister trying to school her little sister. I really like you, Zsasha. I hope we grow our friendship for

years to come."

"I'm up for it." Zsasha replied.

"You sure about that because I'm sensing a bit of jealousy from your girls. I know they don't care for me very much."

"That's not true." Zsasha said, barely able to keep a straight face. "Well not entirely anyway. They'll come around once they get to know you."

"Maybe, maybe not, we'll see."

"You ladies trying to spend the night here or what?" asked Simon.

"Yeah, we better get going. Thank you both for a wonderful evening. Your yacht is exquisite, and I can't wait to experience it again."

"Anytime Zsasha, anytime."

"I'm holding you to that. Goodnight, Ellie, Adam, we'll talk soon."

"Good night you two. Be safe."

Chapter 22

The past few weeks came and went without event. The fall leaves were covering the ground and the temperature had cooled a bit as summer made way for fall. Traffic had increased with the start of school now in full day session, and the busy day to day of ordinary life seemed to consume everyone and everything.

There were no wine and cheese nights at the gallery nor morning coffee at The Coffee House to speak of. The girls who usually gathered several times a week found themselves caught up and busy with their own lives. Aside from the occasional sightings, Zsasha speeding past Vonne hurrying out of The Coffee House, or the time Rona stopped in and had a 3-minute conversation with Vonne, who was waiting in line, there hadn't been any in depth dialogue between the girls, any of them. And that was okay.

J'Nae had several days of work-related travel that spanned over the course of the past two weeks and spent whatever free time she had with Rick in person or on video chat whenever their schedules allowed. Vonne was busy completing the fall display setups at each of her boutiques, something she liked to do personally. Although she had help from Kiera and the rest of her staff, she preferred to show off her own flare while making sure each location had its own appeal. Rona was simply doing Rona and Zsasha had her hands full preparing for the NBCC Meet & Greet as well as the Silent Charity Auction. But when J'Nae returned and all their schedules opened up, wine and cheese at the gallery was back on and everyone had something to share.

"This is the first time we've all been together since our last gathering, and I wanted to say thanks for including Kiera. It has made a difference in our relationship, and I feel as though she has a better understanding of what's expected of her while she's in my house and in my business."

"Glad to hear it, hope it lasts."   Zsasha remarked with sarcasm.

"That didn't sound sincere." Rona advised.

"It's the best I got, unless you want me to be honest."

"Never known for you to hold anything back so don't start now." Vonne demanded.

"Since you asked, that night let me see a bit of the real Kiera and let me tell you, she wants everything you have, Vonne and if you continue with this ménage à trois you got going on, ole girl just might get what she wants and then some."

"I'm sure Lee is aware of how her behavior is affecting Vonne." J'Nae proclaimed.

"Really, you think.   Have you noticed Vonne hasn't said anything about that?   Let me be direct.   Hey Vonne, how are things with you and Lee? Are they any better?"

"You're being a real bitch right about now and so early in the evening." Rona declared.

"No, she's right. Things may have improved slightly with me and my sister, but they've gotten worse with me and Lee. We still haven't recovered from the fight we had about her cooking and doing his laundry and shit."

"And there it is, the fall out, or the start of it anyway. Y'all still not following me?"

"I'm listening." J'Nae said.

"I definitely have to hear this too." Rona agreed.

"Okay Vonne, you felt as though your sister was not respecting you, your home and your husband then you discussed it with him and his part in it, whether he was aware or not and now you and Lee have barely spoken since then? Honey, she's already causing problems in your marriage and it's going to get worse."

"You don't know that for sure, Zsasha." J'Nae stated.

"Oh yes I do, and the reason is Lee is not backing his wife. Even if he disagrees with her, he should never let it be known to Kiera because in doing so, it gives her power and influence. He's not protecting the primary relationship and when that happens, all kinds of shit gets fucked up! Watch what I say." Zsasha declared.

J'Nae shook her head in disbelief.

Vonne wanted to be hopeful, but she knew better.

Rona didn't say a word.

"So wassup bitches, cat got your tongues? No one has anything to say... Rona?"

"Unfortunately, I agree." Rona admitted. "If it happened like Zsasha said it did, she's probably correct and you need to straighten things out before they get worse."

"I don't know what else to do. I'm not comfortable just up and putting her out."

"If you can't get her way from him, get him away from her. Take him somewhere where y'all can spend some time together." Rona suggested.

"Like the Catskills?"

"Yes, but no. You need to act a lot sooner than December. Take a long weekend. You have staff to cover whatever needs to be done at the boutiques for a few days. Just do it. Do it for you and do it for your marriage."

"Excellent idea, Rona. I knew you'd come around to seeing it my way. And please understand Vonne, you're my girl. We've been through a lot over the years, some of which these two heffa's don't know anything about. I got you, I do. It might sound harsh when I'm pulling your coattail but that's only because it's serious and I'd rather hurt your feelings by telling you what's up and putting you on game then to see you hurt by either of them down the road if shit really goes sideways. Real talk girlfriend, I love you."

"I love you too, Zsasha."

"Great. Now that you've had your kumbaya moment Zsasha, would you mind getting another bottle of wine please. I think we all could use another drink right about now."

"I'll get it." J'Nae offered.

"There's a bottle chilling in the small wine cooler as you walk into the kitchen." Zsasha explained. "Grab the bottle on the top rack. I was ready for this one."

"Why is that?" Rona asked. "You didn't know what Vonne was going to say, did you?"

"No, no, it's me. I fucked up. I really fucked up."

"What happened?" Vonne asked.

"Long story short, I scheduled the NBCC Meet & Greet the same week as the Silent Charity Auction."

"No way, girl. How did that happen?" Rona questioned.

"Yeah, that's not like you at all. You're always on point with your business."

"I second that. I can't see you making that kind of mistake Zsasha." J'Nae agreed.

"Isn't that girl helping you plan the auction, Ellie something? Maybe she had something to do with that mix up." Rona suggested.

"I don't see how." Zsasha replied.

"I do." Rona explained. "But what I can't understand is how you can see so clearly through other people's bullshit every time, unless it has something to do with you."

"I know you don't trust her Rona. I doubt any of you do."

"Because I don't have a reason to. She showed up out of nowhere, with a wad of cash wanting something of personal value to you. Then she wanted in on your club."

"My what!"

"Get over it Zsasha. We all know about the club! Truthfully, Vonne and I have known for years. J'Nae on the other hand, I don't know how she knows or when she gained that knowledge, but the cat's out of the bag so knock it off."

"Alright."

"Anyway, if that wasn't enough, now she's trying to be your best friend. I'm almost certain she has an agenda. You have allowed her in your business and have been spending a lot of time with her. How do you know she wasn't responsible for the over booking? Does she have access to your calendar?"

"No. Nobody can log on to my computer other than Ms. Honey and Simon."

"Did you ever leave it open while you guys were 'working' and walk away for a minute?" J'Nae asked. "It only takes a second to delete an entry."

"Yeah, maybe but what would she get out of that?"

"I don't know, why don't you tell me."

"Huh?"

"What happened as a result of the overbooking? How did you resolve it?"

"Ellie offered to hold the auction on her yacht and the board approved it."

"You don't see it, do you?" Rona asked.

"See what?"

"She is trying to ingratiate herself in your life."

"Seriously Rona, you're tripping. The only thing she wants from me is membership to the club, that's all."

"Yeah Rona, I'd say that's a bit of a stretch." Vonne said.

"I agree." J'Nae conveyed. "I don't see any real benefit in her doing that."

"I just don't trust her." Rona repeated.

"We know." Zsasha, Vonne and J'Nae said in unison.

"Alright ladies. I'm going to let y'all have at it. I still have my own business to take care of before my trip later this week."

"Trip? Where to?" Vonne asked.

"Business or pleasure?" J'Nae questioned.

"The business of pleasure. Now goodnight, ladies, I gotta go." Rona replied as she gathered up her belongings.

"Yeah, it is getting late, and I do have a meeting in the morning with Al Hadley from the NBCC. Just leave everything as it is, I'll deal with it tomorrow."

"You sure?" J'Nae asked.

"Yeah, I'm sure, I'll have one of the staff members clean everything up."

"Must be nice."

"It is girl, it is. I'll holla tomorrow."

Zsasha walked the girls to the door making sure to lock it securely behind them. After taking a quick walk around the gallery to make sure everything was as it should be, she grabbed

239

her purse and laptop and headed out the rear entrance where she parked her car earlier that evening. Nothing looked out of the ordinary at first glance but as she walked around to the driver's side door, she thought she caught a glimpse of someone standing in the shadows, but she wasn't sure. Once in the driver's seat, Zsasha mounted her cell phone and plugged it into the charger she kept in her car. Latching her seat belt, she looked in her rear-view mirror and saw someone that appeared to be staring at her. Then as if he was discovered, the unknown figure abruptly crossed the alley and disappeared in the darkness. She wasted no time in driving off.

* * * * *

The next morning, Rona reached out to J'Nae from the airplane having just sent out some information on their upcoming trip. She'd already spoken to Zsasha who was a bit preoccupied with her own stuff, so she felt the need to touch base with Vonne and J'Nae on her own.

"Hey Vonne, how's it going love?" J'Nae asked.

"Good girl, what's up?"

"Is this a good time for you to chat for a bit? I've got Rona on the line wanting to firm up the details for the trip."

"Yeah, cool."

"Rona, you there?" J'Nae asked after conferencing her in. "I've got Vonne on the line."

"Hey Vonne. So are y'all ready for this trip?"

"I'm in." J'Nae announced.

"You mean you and Rick, right?"

"Right, we're in. What about you and Lee? With everything that's been going on are you guys up for it?"

"You know our temperature runs hot and cold all the time. I'm sure we'll be in a good enough place to enjoy ourselves on the trip, if not then the trip will help us get there."

"Cool." Rona confirmed. "And everybody's good with the dates and everything I emailed you, right?"

"Yeah, everything's straight." J'Nae replied. "Have you confirmed with Zsasha yet? "

"I spoke with her earlier this morning right before her meeting with the NBCC. Her schedule is the hardest to lock down but to answer your question yes, she and Simon have blocked off the time on both of their calendars so there won't be any mishaps." Rona explained. "It has to be after the NBCC Meet & Greet, Silent Charity Auction and the Masquerade Ball. I'm quite sure our girl will be more than ready for a vacation by then."

"I agree." Vonne confirmed.

"So, we're all good then. I'll have my assistant email everybody the final details as soon as she books the cabin."

"Great. Can't wait! Lee and I really need this."

"And I'll let Rick know it's a go so he can secure his time off work."

"Alright then, later you two."

"Bye Rona."

"Have fun on your trip." Vonne said.

"For sure."

* * * * *

The following morning, Zsasha was a bit behind schedule. She had slept so well that she missed her morning wakeup call and was in no rush to get out the door. Once she did, she headed straight for the gallery intending to walk next door to The Coffee House a bit later. She had barely locked the doors behind her when she saw Ellie approaching.

"Hey Ellie, come on in." Zsasha greeted while opening the door. "I wasn't expecting you today. Is everything alright?"

"Yes of course, everything is fine."

"Good. I just thought I'd stop by to share some ideas I came up with that might make things run a bit smoother at the auction. I hope that's okay."

"Sure. Let's go next door and grab a coffee."

"Even better. So how was your meeting with the NBCC? Everything set and ready to go?"

"Yep, got final approval on the layout and seating arrangements so they're all set."

"Sounds good."

"Let's sit over here." Zsasha said, nodding to the server she recognized. "Could I have a large coffee, black with two sugars, and Ellie?"

"I'll have a Honey Nut Macchiato."

"I'll have it for you in a minute."

"Thank you. So just black coffee for you today, huh?"

"Yeah, I'm not feeling anything fancy, I'm just trying to keep it simple."

"Well, you'll be happy to hear my suggestions, maybe they'll make the rest of the planning a bit easier on you. That's what I'm here for, right?"

"Right, whatchu got for me?"

"According to you, we're expecting 60-75 attendees and the event should end by 11:00 pm, right?"

"Right."

"Well, instead of dedicating space to have everyone eat at the same time, why not reserve the space for the items being auctioned and stagger dinner?"

"I'm listening."

"We could split the attendees into 2 groups, group A and group B, placement would be determined based on time of arrival or any criteria you have in mind. We could serve dinner to group A at 7:00 pm while group B peruses the items up for auction and places their bids. Then at 8:15 pm group B will be seated for dinner while group A places their bids."

"So far it sounds good."

"All bids are final and cannot be accepted after 9:15. The auditors would have from 9:15 until 10:00 pm to review and announce the winning bid for each item. I figured the dessert bar would start at 8:15 and end around 9:45 with the bar open for after dinner drinks until 10:30 pm. That allows plenty of time for everyone to socialize."

"Sounds like you've given this a lot of thought." Zsasha remarked.

"I have. I know we discussed seating approximately 20-25 at each of the main dining areas but I think that might be a little cramped. And if we stagger dinner and the bidding process it

242

will add mystery and suspense because you won't know the last person who placed a bid."

"I agree, let's do it!"

"Really?"

"Yes, that's an excellent plan."

"Awesome!"

"What about the menu selection my guy put together, is your staff on board with his choices and do they feel comfortable assisting him with meal prep?"

"Yes, everything's a go."

"Cool." Zsasha replied.

"With all of that done and out of the way, is there anything else we need to worry about?"

"Let's see, I'll need to meet with the auditing firm to go over the changes we just made, and I'll finalize the list of donors and the items donated. Other than that, all we need to do is show up."

"Alrighty then. But if anything comes up and you need my assistance, you got it."

"I know and thank you. You really came through for me and I appreciate it."

"Enough to let me get at your- "

"Nope! Not a chance in hell, little girl. Simon is mine, all mine!"

"You keep saying the same thing, over and over." Ellie jokes.

"Well quit asking the same question, dang." Zsasha smirked. "Look, I need to head back. I've got other business to take care of today. You good?"

"I'm fine. We'll talk later."

"Okay, bye Ellie."

With that, Zsasha grabbed her purse and headed out the door. Walking the short distance next door was something she'd done a thousand times, but never did she return to find the doors unlocked. She was sure she'd locked them, but the more she thought about it, she couldn't actually remember doing so. Must be the stress from all the back-to-back planning she thought, she really needed the Catskills trip, sooner rather than later.

* * * * *

Driving on I95 in a heavy downpour of rain made J'Nae begin to regret that she'd agreed to drive out to Rona's house to hang out. It wasn't something Rona did often, but she wanted the two of them to have some one-on-one time before she took off with Ricardo and Jon Paul. But J'Nae sensed Rona had a different reason for asking her over for dinner so she continued with their plans.

"Hey sweetie." J'Nae said, answering her cell phone.

"Hey love, how's my baby today?" Rick asked.

"I'm good. How are you? I thought you'd be tied up all evening. How did everything go?"

"Everything went fine. Are you driving right now?"

"Yeah, I'm on my way to Rona's house."

"I don't like you going that far out by yourself in weather like this. I should be with you boo."

"I'm fine. I've driven out here many times before. It's no big deal, really."

"Well make sure you text me when you arrive, so I'll know you're safe, okay?"

"Okay sweetie, I will."

"Alright then, I'll see you later this evening."

"Oh, you're getting off early tonight?"

"Yes, since we had meetings scheduled that ran into my shift, they went ahead and had someone cover for me."

"You mean live? Someone else was actually doing your show?"

"Yes, someone else did my show."

"I never thought I'd see that happen. I know how particular you are about your show and how closely connected you are to your listeners. Maybe we'll listen to it tonight."

"Yeah, we can do that . . . for about fifteen minutes, I've got other plans on how we'll spend our time this evening."

"Do you now?"

"Yes, I do, so go on and do what you gotta do with your girl and I will text you when I'm heading to your house."

"Okay baby, see you later."

"Bye sweetie, and don't take a shower before I get there."

"You little freak!"

"No, I'm a big freak, baby. Now just do as you're told."

"Yes, sir."

"Don't call me sir, call me daddy."

"What!"

"You heard me."

"Bye Rick."

Shaking her head, J'Nae ended the call. She was smiling ear to ear as she parked behind one of Rona's cars in the driveway. She could see her at the door with a girl come on look on her face. She grabbed her umbrella, got out and ran inside.

"Hey, how long were you standing at the door?"

"Just when you turned down the street. You know I track your phone, right?"

"What?"

"Yeah, I installed the app on your phone when you were going through your online dating phase. Give me your jacket."

"I had no idea."

"Well now you do. Can I get you something to drink?"

"I'll have what you're having."

"I'm drinking Pino tonight."

"Sounds good to me."

"Cool. So, are you and Rick attending the auction?"

"That's the plan."

"I'm surprised he's interested in that."

"Truthfully I'm not sure that he is."

"Oh my gosh, the sick puppy phase, girl he's got it bad."

"Yeah, he does, and so do I."

"I can tell and it's really good seeing you happy like this."

"I feel wonderful when I'm with him. I don't even think about the age difference anymore."

"Good for you. So, what have you told him about your wrist tattoo? Surely, he's asked about it by now."

"He has and I told him the truth. That Julian and I got matching heart shaped links around our wrist when we were in

245

college and that they were to represent that we were linked together for life."

"How did he react?"

"He just said it was very sweet and that I should treasure it always."

"Really? That's a first."

"It caught me off guard when he first asked about it because I wasn't sure what he was going to say but he just acknowledged that Julian was a very important part of my life and that he understood and respected the life I had before we met."

"Damn girl, he just keeps getting better and better."

"I know, right!" J'Nae smiled. "Now why aren't you participating in the auction?"

"I am participating in the charity auction by way of my assistant, but I won't be in attendance."

"Because you're going out of town, right?"

"I am going out of town, but that's not the reason why I'm not going to the auction. Real talk, I have no desire to be anywhere near Ellie Porter. I don't like her, and I don't trust her at all."

"You've been pretty open about your feelings, and I get it."

"Why doesn't Zsasha get it? She's all over Vonne and her 'sister issues' and she doesn't let up. She's constantly telling Vonne that Kiera has an agenda, it's obvious and staring her in the face. And despite the warnings she still chooses to let her in. And really, that's the exact same thing Zsasha's doing with Ellie!"

"If you're suspicious of her and her motives, why not show up at the auction if only to support Zsasha?"

"I can't. It's not like Zsasha to have blinders on when it comes to her personal or professional life, she's got way too much to lose. She can't afford to be bamboozled by anyone and the more I bring it to her attention the closer they seem to get. Look how she has our girl out there right now with this auction. The Zsasha I know is a professional. She never would have over booked events. I'm certain that bitch had something to do with that mess, but I can't prove it. More wine?"

"Just one more glass for me. I'm meeting Rick later tonight."

"That's what your problem is, Rick. He's the reason why you're not as concerned as I am. He's keeping your body busy and your mind distracted, in a good way, of course, but you still need to keep up with what's going on with your girls and keep an eye on Ellie especially when I'm not around. Any sign of her trying to be meddlesome in our sister circle, I want to know about it, no matter where I'm at or who I'm with."

"That's actually been in the back of my mind because she hasn't tried to befriend any of us, and that's strange to me. I know she's aware of our sisterhood."

"She is, for sure. She knows we're beyond close, we're family and in our family, we go hard for each other, without a doubt. If she don't know, somebody better tell her."

"There's not a lot we can do other than keep a watch on her and see what unfolds."

"I guess that's it, for now anyway." Rona uttered.

"What does that mean, for now?"

"I got people I could put on her?"

"Put on her, how?"

"Investigate. Zsasha and Simon have a reputable team of investigators they pay a hefty price for, but I have something they don't."

"Oh yeah, and what's that?"

"Ricardo."

"Oh really, how so?"

"With his US and foreign based holdings, he has some of the most impressive security firms on payroll, retainer, or whatever and they're all at my disposal. All I have to do is reach out."

"Wow, you go girl!" I almost did go, move forward with it but I didn't. I stopped myself before I did anything that could jeopardize my relationship with Zsasha. I don't want to jump the gun, but rest assured, when the time comes, I'm on it. Her daddy money can't match my daddy money."

"Girl you stupid." J'Nae laughed.

"No, I'm serious, him I checked out, kind of."

"You're being too cryptic for me. How did you kind of check him out?"

"When I gave Ricardo's guy the name Daniel Porter, they already had a file on him. It had been completed just six months prior. Therefore, I really didn't have to get my hands dirty if you know what I mean."

"I know what you mean, and I knew what you meant when you were bragging about your daddy's money. I knew you were talking about Ricardo and that even though her father is extremely wealthy, he's not in Ricardo's league, by any means."

"That is true."

"Changing the subject, how long will you be gone this time and I'm guessing you need me to house sit?"

"I'm planning on five to nine days, depending on how things go. Dating both of them at home is very different from dating them abroad. So much to do, so little time plus I need my rest."

"What?"

"Never mind. It's complicated. Aren't you meeting Rick tonight?"

"Oops. I was supposed to text him when I arrived. He's probably left a few messages by now."

"It's nice, isn't it."

"What's that?"

"Having someone to love who loves you back."

"Yeah, it really is. I better get going. See you later, love."

"Girl, get over here and give me a hug. I'm leaving in a few days, and I'll be gone for a while."

J'Nae walked over and happily gave Rona a big girl bear hug, squeezing her tight.

"Now that's better. You drive safe and make sure you let me know how things go at the auction. I don't want to have to come back and hand out an ass whooping, but I will if I need to."

"I know hun. Love you."

"Love you too."

J'Nae made her way to her car and called Rick right away. After getting his voicemail, she decided to send him a text message to let him know she was heading home. On the drive home, Rona's comments about having someone to love echoed in her mind over and over again. Having someone to love. Was she in love with Rick? Was he in love with her? Neither of them took the leap to say those words to one another but her feelings were strong, so very strong and deepening by the day. When she pulled up to her house, he was there, waiting for her in his car and smiled at the sight of her face.

"Hey love." Rick said, kissing her lightly on her lips. "You forgot."

"I forgot. What's that case for?"

"Something to help you remember to do what I ask."

"Oh my, that sounds intriguing. Am I in trouble?"

"Yes, you are. Now open the door."

"Yessss, daddy."

"That's more like it."

Chapter 23

J'Nae was one of the first guests to arrive and board Bella. She was wearing a solid black lace covered V-neck dress that dipped all the way down to her navel. She walked in a pair of black lace Jimmy Choo 3-inch heels that made her look sleek and elegant. She was quickly greeted by a member of the crew who directed her to Zsasha who was busy repositioning some items up for auction.

"Watch out there now." Zsasha said while the ladies embraced. "You look absolutely divine. Has your man seen you in this dress? And where is he?"

"Thank you and no he hasn't seen me in this dress, but he will soon. I told him to arrive at 6:30. I wanted to get here early to see if you needed help with anything before everyone began to board."

"That's sweet of you, but no, I'm good."

"You look amazing in that color, and it matches the décor."

"Simon and I did that on purpose. We wanted to stand out and be noticeable to all of our guests so they wouldn't be confused about who their hosts are."

"Well form fitting gold lace will definitely do that for you. And you've got the body and personality for it, so you go with your bad self!"

"Champagne?"

"Don't mind if I do." J'Nae replied.

"Is whitegirl still coming?"

"Last I heard but you never know with that one lately."

"Well, I hope she makes it, and without her sister. It's cool that she's trying to reconnect with her and all, and her heart is in the right place no doubt, but that situation is not going to end well for her. I hate to say it but I know what I know."

"Oh well, hey there's Ellie. Hi Ellie, you look lovely this evening."

"As you do also, Rona."

"I'm J'Nae. Rona won't be attending this evening. But I believe she's sending her assistant in her place."

"Wonderful. I'll be sure to introduce myself. Please enjoy champagne and hors d'oeuvres and be sure to let a crew member know if you have any special needs."

J'Nae's face couldn't have turned any redder from her remarks and inside she wanted to explode.

"What was she talking about, special needs? Does she know about my side effects from the G-shot? Please tell me you haven't discussed my personal business with her!"

"Girl please. I really haven't discussed you, any of you with her. What we share in our inner circle is between us. She ain't in that and never will be."

"I can't tell, none of us can."

"For the most part it's business but we are getting friendly."

"From the outside looking in, it looks like it's more than that. It looks like she's purposely trying to get close to you and involved in your affairs, personal and professional."

"Really?"

"Uhm, look at her now? Shouldn't you and Simon as the hosts be greeting the guests as they arrive? She has assumed the position right next to the captain, just lying-in wait."

"I don't even know why he's there. He needs to be invisible or at least, seen but not heard. Hold on, I got this."

Zsasha made her way to the boarding area just in time to greet the next few guests to arrive. J'Nae stood back to observe what was taking place and although she couldn't hear what was being said, the body language told her that her girl checked her girl and moments later, the captain relocated himself elsewhere with Ellie not far behind.

Among the second group of guests were Vonne and Rick, both obviously excited to be on board Bella, a luxury yacht like nothing either of them had seen before. J'Nae was happy to see them chatting and getting acquainted.

"Wow J'Nae, I'm speechless. You look breathtaking in that dress." Rick declared.

"Thank you, sweetie. I was hoping you'd like it."

"I do, I really do."

"Well, what about the rest of us?" Zsasha teased. "How do we look?"

Rick answered without taking his eyes off J'Nae.

"You all look lovely."

"He's so far gone." Vonne whispered.

"If y'all need a room, you can use mine."

Rick and J'Nae stood there staring into each other's eyes and didn't hear or acknowledge any of what was just said.

"Look, y'all move it along, I have other guests to greet."

The three of them made their way further along the main deck. While enjoying champagne and hors d'oeuvres Ellie reappeared and reclaimed her position next to Zsasha.

"I hope the captain is okay with stepping back a bit. As the host, I should be here greeting our guests, most of which I know by name." Zsasha declared.

"Oh, he's fine with it. He just wasn't sure where he needed to be for this occasion. No harm, no foul."

"Cool."

Zsasha continued to greet the guests as they arrived and introduced Ellie Porter as this year's assistant and co-chair. Once all the guests had boarded and had time to mingle a bit, it was announced that group A is now being seated for dinner and guests should make their way up one floor at this time. Group B instructions followed right after.

Vonne, J'Nae and Rick were all seated with group A which meant they were the last to review the donated items up for auction.

"I hope it's okay that I don't really want to win any of these items and that I just make a donation." Vonne confessed.

"Yes, of course it is. You write the check based on what you want to donate to the charity choosing an item of interest, however the losing bids aren't refunded, they are just treated as cash donations. The winning bid wins the items of course but it isn't really about winning the item. Whoever wins will be paying 3 or more times what the items are worth anyway. That's the idea. That's why it's a fundraiser."

"I know, I know, I just wasn't sure of the protocol."

"Well now you are. Just pick an item and write down the amount and the number you were given when you arrived. But hold on, we still haven't viewed the items in the other area. It's this way."

J'Nae led Rick and Vonne to the area where Zsasha was arranging placement earlier when she'd first arrived. They took a few moments to review the items which consisted of a variety of things. Rick and J'Nae stopped to investigate a 3-day private cruise for a party of 10 on Bella. It was obvious who made the donation, so they moved on to other items. They were reading the details of a weekend getaway for 2 at the Poconos when they heard Vonne's voice from a few feet away.

"Oh shit!"

"Vonne, what's going on?" J'Nae asked as she turned her attention to Vonne. "Oh shit!"

"Why would she...I don't believe it." Vonne said. "Does Zsasha know about this?"

"I don't know." J'Nae replied. "I highly doubt it."

'Wasn't she in charge of the donations?" Vonne asked.

"I believe so and they were made directly to her at the gallery."

"Then she must be aware of this already."

"I do know about that Vonne. I saw her staging this area when I arrived, and this painting wasn't here."

"Are you sure?" Vonne asked.

"I'm positive." J'Nae answered.

"Can somebody fill me in on what's going on here?" Rick asked.

Before J'Nae or Vonne had a chance to consider how to answer Rick's question, they were joined by both Zsasha and Ellie and the look on Zsasha's face revealed that she had no knowledge that one of her beloved pieces of art would be auctioned off to a random person with the highest bid.

"Rick, all I can say is you're about to find out everything firsthand."

Vonne and J'Nae and Zsasha stood silently in shock, with obvious pain on their faces. Zsasha, feeling somewhat betrayed and blindsided by this young woman who had acted as her friend, had no words to speak, just emotion on her face. She looked at Ellie for a moment, as if waiting for her to say something, anything, but nothing came. And when she could no longer take the silence, she ran off.

Chapter 24

Hey J'Nae, thanks for rushing over."

"No problem Vonne, I figured we needed to sit down and discuss what happened at the auction."

"Yeah, me too. Lee is at the gym, and I had Kiera back me up this morning and go in early, so we have the house to ourselves."

"Have you heard from Zsasha yet?" J'Nae asked.

"No, I haven't heard a word and it's been several days now." Vonne replied.

"After she ran off to compose herself at the auction, she returned and carried on like the professional we know her to be and that was that. That night, she didn't say anything about it at all, not that I'm aware of."

"Me either. I'm worried about her though. You know her as well as I do and it's not like her to be silent about anything, especially something like this."

"That's true. Maybe she's waiting to talk to us when we're all together Saturday for lunch. It's on the calendar."

"Yeah, I know. I just hate it for her, that she's going through anything with Ellie. I hadn't realized just how close they'd become." J'Nae admitted.

"I didn't either, but Rona did. She had a bad vibe about that girl from the beginning."

"She must have a sixth sense. Hold on, that's her calling me now. Hey Rona, how's it going over there? Are you having a good time?"

"Everything's cool. I just called to see how the auction went. Did Zsasha raise the money she anticipated?"

"I'm not sure just yet. I take it you haven't spoken to her at all, huh?"

"Nope, just checking in on my girls. Why, what's up?"

"I'm at Vonne's house. I'm going to put you on speaker."

"Hey Rona, wassup?"

"Not shit considering there's obviously something going on with the two of y'all clicked up so early in the morning. So, tell me, what happened? What exactly did that bitch do? I know she did something."

"Hmm, let's see..." J'Nae mumbled. "Ellie made a few unsuccessful attempts to take the lead from Zsasha, since it was her yacht and all."

"Now you're messing with me girl, just go ahead and tell me what really happened. You know what, never mind, I'll just call Zsasha and ask . . ."

"Okay Rona, my bad. You'll find out anyway."

"You're right, so spill it."

"Well, here it goes. Do you remember how Little Miss Ellie begged Zsasha to sell her that painting she kept in her office, making all kinds of promises about how she'll treasure it and keep it close to her heart forever and so on?"

"Ah, yeah...and?"

"Apparently, she just goes and donates it at the auction behind Zsasha's back. She did it at the last minute without even a word or a heads up to our girl."

"Are you kidding me?"

"I wouldn't joke about that. That shit is fucked up, Rona."

"You're right, it is. I knew she had an agenda but even I didn't see that coming. How did Zsasha react? I know it wasn't pretty."

"She was blindsided of course. After the shock wore off, she just ran out."

"Damn. That's rough."

"I know, but she wasn't gone too long, maybe 15 minutes or so and when she returned, she was professional and unscathed by the event." J'Nae replied.

"That's right and no one other than the five of us really saw what happened so it didn't impact her hosting the rest of the auction. And as far as we could tell, the board was totally unaware of what went down." Vonne added.

"That's good to hear. She worked very hard to impress the board and we all know this was very important to her. And because of that, I have a theory..." Rona stated.

"We're listening." Vonne whispered.

"Like I said before, I think this was part of Ellie's plan. Twice now something has gone down that has undermined Zsasha as the Chair of the auction potentially making her look incapable or unqualified. I hate to say it, but this just supports what I've been saying all along. That girl has an agenda, and it involves destroying our friend."

"I'm inclined to agree with you." Vonne admitted. "I can't see any other explanation for what happened."

"Me either." J'Nae chimed in. "However, we should talk to Zsasha and get the full story. If it's like you say, I would think she'd waste no time cutting her loose."

"I agree. Let's see what she has to say about it in a few days."

"Awe, you're cutting your trip short sweetie?"

"No. Ricardo is wrapping up his business soon and we'll fly out in a few days."

"Looks like you'll be back in time to meet up for lunch on Saturday. That'll give us a chance to see where's Zsasha's heads at with all this."

"Count on it."

"Okay ladybug, give us a shout when you get back and get settled."

"Will do. Bye y'all, and let me know if anything changes, I mean it."

"We got you. See you later, love."

After ending the phone conversation with Rona, J'Nae said goodbye to Vonne and headed over to Rick's house to hang out. Some things had been on her mind about their relationship, and she wanted to sit down and have a conversation. It was too early for either of them to have a drink, so it was a good time to discuss the aspects of their relationship.

Things had been heating up with the two of them for quite a while, so much so, that they each kept clothing and personal hygiene products at the other's homes. Because Rick worked the second shift, he was at J'Nae's house more than she was at his place, but they were almost always together. When she knocked on his front door, he was right there to greet her with a kiss.

"Good morning, beautiful." Rick said as he embraced her tightly.

"Hey sweetie." J'Nae mumbled.

"What's the matter baby? Did you get everything worked out with Zsasha?"

"No, not really. Vonne and I were just discussing everything and trying to make sense of it all, Rona too."

"Give it some time. It'll work itself out."

"I'm sure you're right. But I can't help but wish it was easy, like it is for us."

"Oh, so you think it's easy?"

"Yes, I do. Everything is easy with you."

"I feel the same way about you, baby."

"I'm glad to hear that because I wanted to talk to you about us, about our relationship."

"What's on your mind?"

"It's been a really long time since I dated and neither of us are seeing anyone else, right?"

"Of course not, you know that."

"Well, yeah, but we've never actually discussed it, in detail."

"Like put a label on it, that's what you mean right?"

J'Nae struggled to find the words to fit all of what was running through her mind and before she could get it together Rick had the answer in hand.

"Let me make it easy for you, sweetheart. "Let's be exclusive, officially. I'm your man and you're my woman. It's just us, no one else. Can you rock with that?"

"You know I can rock with that."

"See, easy, just like you said."

The two of them shared a deep and passionate kiss marking the next phase in their relationship.

* * * * *

Saturday came quicker than expected for the girls. Rona arrived home but not as early as she'd planned and barely had time to regroup before she was work-stalked by her office staff with questions, concerns and general confusion, a bit more than usual. J'Nae was coming down ever so slightly from a natural love high born from the intense and intimate nature of the last few days she spent with Rick. Vonne was the only one lacking a unique experience over the last few days which is why she was the first one to arrive at Borealis for lunch.

Borealis is an Italian restaurant tucked away in the east end of Tysons Corner, part of an up-and-coming community that caters to the financially well-to-do professionals living and working in the surrounding area. Borealis is famous for their dining without a menu experience in which your perceived aura determines what you will be served. Each table has an assigned chef that will greet you and converse with you and maybe ask a few random questions. The purpose is to give the chef insights into your inner self or aura in which he or she will then turn into a meal you didn't know you wanted.

Shortly after Vonne was seated, she spotted J'Nae and Rona trailing behind a well-dressed waiter. As they approached the table, Vonne could see J'Nae was beaming ear to ear, glowing and cheerful in her expressions and cross conversation while Rona, not so much. She decided to play it safe as they were seated at the table and greet them equally with compliments and attention.

"Well look at you ladies, you both look so radiant this afternoon. Now J'Nae, I can figure out why you're glowing and looking like you're ready to burst at the seams, but Rona girl, what you got going on over there?"

"Not a damn thing. Even though I was on a mini vacation, the minute I returned, my office staff and lead agents acted like they were still in training, blowing up my phone with questions they knew the answers to and other kinds of foolishness. I taught them better than that; got me stressed over some nonsense."

"I can't tell girlfriend, you look hot!" Vonne declared.

"Well thank you, love. Has anyone heard from or seen Zsasha? Isn't she usually the first to arrive?" asked Rona.

"Yes, she is, but that's because we're always meeting up at her spot." J'Nae replied.

"Yeah, but it's not like her to be incommunicado."   Vonne determined.

"Usually, she'll send out a group text if something were to come up. She probably just needed to take a breather with all she's had going on lately. I'm sure she'll be here soon."

"Any minute now our wait staff will arrive with our drinks." Vonne announced. "In fact, here they come now."

"Looks like somebody planned ahead and ordered for us."

"I did, and by the way, I took the liberty of opting for the alcohol blend. I'm sure you ladies don't mind."

"Not at all, but I'm so hungry I could eat just about anything right now." Rona confessed.

"I don't doubt it." J'Nae replied. "You've never been one to skimp when satisfying your pallet."

"Damn girlfriend, you make it sound like I eat just any old thing."

"Well sweetie, I didn't mean to imply that, however when you want to eat, you really eat."

"Yes, I do. I enjoy food from all over."

"And we can tell." J'Nae snickered.

"Uh uh girl." Vonne interrupted. "Don't be including me in that mess. Besides, it sounds more like you're describing my eating habits not hers. Y'all know I throw down."

"Yes Vonne, we're aware of that, how could we not be."

"Good, because the only person at this table that's shy about eating is you, J'Nae."

At that precise moment, two male servers appeared with varying plates of food. Vonne was served a very large meatless Asian salad with all the vegetarian toppings imaginable accompanied by 2 warm breadsticks. J'Nae was served a bowl of bowtie pasta with chicken, andouille sausage, and shrimp covered in half marinara sauce and half alfredo sauce. Rona was served a 6-ounce sirloin, 5 asparagus stalks covered in minced garlic, bacon bits and parmesan cheese. There was also a small salad wedge drizzled with oil and vinegar on a small plate. Rona wasted no time digging in while Vonne and J'Nae stared at what was before them.

262

"Not exactly what I was expecting." Vonne declared.

"Me either." J'Nae echoed.

"Let's trade." Vonne suggested.

"Sure." J'Nae was more than eager to comply. "Here you go sweetie."

"That's much better, thanks."

The three ladies enjoyed their lunch selections while amusing themselves with gossip and general conversation totaling losing awareness of their absent girlfriend.

"I've got an idea." Vonne exclaimed. "How about we do something we haven't done in a while."

"Like what?" J'Nae asked.

"Let's go shopping. Yeah, we could get our nails done, grab a massage or catch a movie...something. You guys don't have anywhere you need to be right now, do you?"

"Not me." Rona replied. "I just returned from a vacay and after being greeted with all that unnecessary office drama, I'm feeling like I need another day off or at least the rest of this one. I'm in. What about you, J'Nae?"

"Oh, I'm good. Rick is working second shift tonight, so I have nowhere I need to be. Let's do it! Should we call Zsasha and ask her to join us?"

"We should. I'll give her a call." Vonne replied.

"Cool. I'll pay the check." Rona said as she signaled for one of their waiters and handed him her credit card. "Thank you, young man."

"So, what did she say? Is she going to join us?" J'Nae asked.

"She didn't answer, it went straight to voicemail. But no worries, I left her a detailed message so maybe she can meet up with us later. For now, we can hang without her. Are y'all up for it?"

"Absolutely! One monkey don't stop no show!" J'Nae asserted.

"Y'all ready to go?" Rona asked.

"Yep. Let's go...but where are we going?" J'Nae asked.

"How about we start in Crystal City?" Vonne suggested as they left the restaurant. "It's a nice area that we don't usually

263

visit and it's not too far off the beat and path. I spotted a few new shops that look interesting. So, how about it?"

"Oh, so that's the story you're going with Vonne?" J'Nae asked with sarcasm.

"Girl ain't nothing wrong with checking out the competition. That's how you stay relevant and on top." Rona revealed. "I do it all the time, and y'all know my record, it speaks for itself."

"Yes, it does." Vonne and J'Nae replied in harmony.

"Whatever....so where do y'all want to meet? You know I gotta have my own car, just in case something unexpected comes up."

"Sure, but I can still ride with you, right?" Vonne asked.

"Uhm, that would be a negative."

"Really?"

"Yes, really. Y'all know I just got back in town and came straight over to meetup with y'all. I haven't had any rest, therefore when I'm ready to go, I'm ready to go."

Vonne dropped her head while releasing a sign of frustration. J'Nae knew what was coming next and took less than 3 seconds to interject.

"And before you ask, I can't help you either. I'll be heading in the opposite direction over to Ricks' house when we leave here, at least that's the plan as of now."

"Whatever. Let's just meet at the Arcade on Crystal Drive, near the shops. There's a parking structure right next to it. Park and meet out front on the ground level."

"Okay cool." J'Nae confirmed. "See y'all in twenty."

The ladies parted ways, and each got in their own vehicle intending to meet up at the designated spot in Crystal City. Rona was the first one to pull off and did so like she was in a hurry or late for an appointment. J'Nae followed not far behind her but at a normal speed. However, Vonne took a minute to sit in her car contemplating why she had to drive herself. After replaying the last few minutes of their conversation in her head, she realized she was tripping. Rona did just get back from a trip and J'Nae and Rick are together just about every day. And this was a spur of the moment thing, so she started her car and headed out as well.

Pulling into the parking structure next to the shopping center, Vonne could see Rona and J'Nae waiting by the ground floor elevator just north of the entrance. Vonne quickly found a parking spot and joined her friends.

"Hey, what happened back there? I noticed you didn't leave out right behind us. Is everything okay?" J'Nae asked.

"Yes ma'am, everything's fine."

"What did I tell you, J'Nae? You were worried for no reason. She probably just got a phone call or something."

"Did you hear back from Zsasha by chance?" J'Nae inquired. "You left a voice message or text earlier, right?"

"No, I didn't hear back from her and yes, I followed up my voicemail with a text message. I didn't pull off right away because I was having a moment. It's all good, trust me."

"Sure, if you say so." J'Nae remarked. "So where are we heading first?"

"Let's start at this new shop called Realm, it's just a block away." Vonne replied.

"I'm guessing this is one of the shops you've had your eye on for a minute, huh?" Rona questioned.

"You are correct. According to my source, it's a specialty, high-end boutique that caters to the DC elite. Not much different than mine."

"I can see why you would want to check it out." Rona replied.

"Yesh, well I have a few designers that are contracted to work for me exclusively. It'd be nice to know if any of them are side-stepping, know what I mean?"

"Sure, we got you." Rona stated. "Wait a minute, isn't that Zsasha leaving that very same store we're heading to?"

"Yep, that's her." J'Nae confirmed.

"And who is that she's with?" Rona asked.

"Girl, you know who it is just like I do. I just can't believe she is out hanging with this chick after what she did at the auction." Vonne replied.

"Wow, I can't believe what I'm seeing." J'Nae confessed. "She must have an explanation for this. There has to be something more going on here. This just doesn't make sense."

"You mean the fact that she blew us off for a luncheon she scheduled and didn't bother to cancel. Oh, hell no!" Vonne shouted.

"That's crazy." Rona admitted.

"And the heffa didn't even answer the phone when I called earlier or respond to my text. "Vonne acknowledged. "Unfucking-believable!"

Rona continued to shake her head from side to side as the three of them continued to look on in disbelief.

"So how do y'all want to play this? Should we just let her go on her way and deal with this later or make contact?" Rona asked.

Vonne was the first one to respond verbally and physically and didn't wait for confirmation or approval from the others. She put some pep in her step and headed straight for Zsasha and Ellie making sure they saw and heard her coming.

"Oh, hey y'all. What's up? What y'all doing out this way?" Zsasha asked, slightly startled by their arrival.

"We could ask you the same question heffa."

"What?"

"Uhm, we just thought you were meeting up with us today, for lunch, remember...you scheduled it and put it on our calendar."

"Really...my bad...I don't know what happened."

"Kind of like what happened before, you know, with the NBCC and auction mix-up."

"Well, yeah...just like that, I guess."

"That seems a bit unlikely when you think about it, wouldn't you say, Zsasha?"

"I don't know, maybe. I probably just need to have my computer checked out or maybe upgraded or something. J'Nae, you're the software developer, maybe you can take a look at it. You know how these things are."

"Yes, I do, more than you know."

"Well, we were just heading over to the Crystal City Grille, you guys want to join us?" Ellie offered.

Vonne and Rona continued to ignore her presence and refused to acknowledge her offer. J'Nae, a bit more reserved than her counterparts yet equally pissed off, reluctantly spoke out, instinctively ending the standoff.

"No thanks, you two go ahead and enjoy. Zsasha, we'll just meet up with you tomorrow, maybe at the gym. I'll text you later with the info."

"Yeah, sure. See y'all later."

With that, Vonne, Rona and J'Nae walked off without another word. Completely unaware and unconcerned they passed their intended destination.

"Well, what about that!" Vonne exclaimed.

"I know, right."

"No Rona, you don't get it. J'Nae and I were there to witness the auction fiasco and we saw the embarrassment and humiliation on Zsasha's face firsthand. There was no way possible to hide it. And seeing her like this, with Ellie right now, I am totally convinced she was behind it, all of it, including todays' calendar mishap. Like you said, she has an agenda."

"I wish I could say I'm glad that you've come around to my side, but I can't sweetheart. This isn't one of the times I wanted to be right. She's definitely up to something and she's coming for our girl."

"Yes, she is. I just wish Zsasha could see it like we do."

"I know sweetie, I know."

* * * * *

"Hey Z, you're home earlier than I expected. What have you and your girls been up to?"

"I was out with Ellie. We did a bit of shopping in Crystal City."

"Oh really? You don't usually hang out in that area."

"You're right, that's not my usual stomping ground but I wanted to do something different."

"What you mean is you didn't want to be seen hanging with the enemy. Isn't that it?"

"If it was, is ain't no more."

"Really, how so?"

"Those bitches ran right into us. I couldn't say shit."

"How did they react to that?" Simon snickered.

"Pissed the fuck off!"

"Well, can you blame them?"

"Yes, I can. They don't like Ellie and they're over-reacting, making too big a deal about the auction."

"Well, if that's how you feel, then why not talk to them about it before the whole thing gets blown out of proportion."

"Yeah, well we're supposed to meet up at the gym tomorrow or something."

"And there's your chance. Excuse me sweetheart, that's my cell."

Simon took his phone call on the opposite side of the room, speaking briefly while Zsasha checked her calendar. For a minute, she allowed her mind to contemplate what might have happened with the two events that disappeared from her calendar. That minute was cut short when one of the maids-in-training entered the room. Ms. Honey was standing in the doorway observing her trainee.

"Ms. Zsasha, Mr. Simon, dinner is ready. Where would you like it served?"

"Our private dining room will be fine. Thank you." Zsasha replied.

"As you wish."

As Ms. Honey and her trainee moved on to do whatever they needed to do next, Simon was just ending his call.

"Was that the new maid?"

"Yes, I think her name is Anya, I could be wrong."

"What did she want?"

"About dinner. It'll be served in our private dining room. Who was that on the phone?"

"That was John Lee getting back to me. I wanted to make sure he would be available over the next few days to help me secure the remaining pieces from our last showing still at the gallery."

"That makes sense."

"Right. I want to make certain everything is where it's supposed to be before we head to the Catskills. No need to have valuable art on loan in our possession if we don't have a business need for it."

"You think of everything, don't you sweetheart?"

"Well you didn't marry me for my good looks!"

"You're right, it was definitely something else." Zsasha smiled.

Simon kissed his wife and together they made their way to the private dining room for dinner.

Chapter 25

"Good morning love." Rick said softly as he heard J'Nae come out of the bathroom.

"Good morning." She replied, planting a kiss on his head.

"You're up early for a Sunday, and with a purpose."

"Yeah. Meeting the girls at the gym so we can work some things out."

"Really? Angry sex wasn't enough for you last night? You still have unresolved issues?"

"What? What are you talking about?"

"Hm, the way you pounced on me last night and again this morning...I would think you'd worked out all of your issues on me." Rick grinned.

"Oh, my goodness, I'm so embarrassed." J'Nae confessed as she sat down on the side of the bed.

"Don't be. It was my pleasure to meet the other side of you, the one I knew you had and kept hidden deep down inside."

"Is that right?"

"That's right. You just saved me the trouble of having to pull it out of you by going in my box."

"Your box?"

"You know what I'm talking about. My tool kit."

"Uh hm. The one you keep threatening to use?"

"Exactly. I had planned to bust it out a while back when you didn't do what I asked you to do, remember that?"

"Yes, I do...kind of. I think you wanted me to call you daddy, was that it?"

"No, it was not. You were supposed to text me when you arrived at your girls' house and then again when you were leaving. It was late and it was raining, remember now?"

"Vaguely, so why are you bringing that up now?"

"Just to let you know I hadn't forgotten that you're due a punishment."

"Really now? All the extra effort I put in last night didn't offset that?"

"I'm afraid not sweetie, it doesn't work like that."

"So how does it work then?"

"I'll let you know when I'm ready to let you know. Just be aware, when I tell you to do something, which won't be very often, it is for your own good and I expect you to do it. Otherwise, there will be consequences for disobedience."

"Consequences, huh? Will it be painful?"

"Yes, it will be physically painful, but it won't hurt."

"What?"

"That's all I'm saying for now but know that you got it coming and I'll decide when you're going to get it."

"Alrighty then, freak boy. Have it your way."

"Oh, I will, little lady, I will."

"You're beginning to sound more than a little freaky."

"Don't go getting scared now. With all of that you did last night and this morning, I know you're ready for it."

"Stop it.!"

"I will, then I won't, then I will again."

"Whatever."

"I'm serious. You'll learn to do what I ask of you, besides, you let Pandora out the box all on your own. You can't put her back in now."

"We'll see. I gotta run."

"Okay love."

"We'll talk later."

"Or not."   Rick smiled.   You could still see the look of satisfaction on his face as she left the room. Shaking her head from side to side, she went outside and got in her car. She was barely out of the driveway when her phone rang. It was Rona.

"Hey what's up?"

"Hey hon. Are you on your way?" Rona asked.

"Yeah, I'm just leaving Rick's house, why?"

"Slight change of plans. We're going to meet at the juice bar next to the gym. I'm still feeling jet lagged and Vonne ain't feeling it either. Something about her and Lee staying up real late."

"Don't tell me they were fighting again."

"Nope, quite the opposite."

"Is that right?"

"That's the way it sounded to me, but you can ask her yourself in a minute. Although you probably won't have to wait long, you know she can't hold water."

"You're right about that."

"And she wears her emotions on her face. You'll have your confirmation the minute you make eye contact."

"You're a mess, you know that."

"Uh hm, but you know I speak the truth. I was right about Ellie, wasn't I?"

"Well, I have to admit, I'm beginning to come over to your side, just a bit."

"Seriously, you're not totally convinced at this point?"

"I don't know. I mean at the end of the day, nothing bad actually happened."

"Come again."

"Okay, it's like this. Yes, there was an overbooking of two very important events, right?"

"Go on."

"Well both events occurred when they were supposed to, and neither was negatively impacted by whatever force may or may not have intervened."

"Says who?"

"The reviews. I've followed up online with the top media outlets and read all comments and reviews posted online."

"Well, where is all this at? I want to read it for myself."

"No problem. You can start at the NBCC's website. If you still need confirmation, then you can go to Ahsasz website or google The Silent Charity Auction hosted by Zsasha and Simon Stewart. I created both of those websites, you know. If you don't want to do that, I can just text you the URL and you can view them that way if you prefer."

"No need for all of that, consider it done. I'm pulling it up now."

Once inside, J'Nae could see Vonne and Rona seated at a table in front of the
window. Both looked as though they needed a bit more sleep and J'Nae shared her
thoughts the moment she was at the table.

"Dang! You weren't kidding. You both look like you could use a few more hours of sleep."

"We know." Rona replied. "That's why we changed plans this morning."

"Ain't nobody feeling perky today. Lee and I were up celebrating and what not. I didn't get enough sleep and drank too much wine."

"It's cool. And you were right Rona, it didn't take five minutes."

Vonne looked back and forth at her two friends trying to figure out the joke. She knew it was about her but not sure what it was. Truthfully, she was too tired to care.

"By the way, did either of you let Zsasha know about the change?" J'Nae asked.

"I didn't." Rona replied. "I really didn't think it was necessary."

"Me either." Vonne chimed in. "When was the last time you've known for Zsasha to go to the gym, other than the one she has at home?"

"Yeah, and that's why we're sitting up front by the window. We'll be able to see when she arrives."

"Okay, whatever." J'Nae shrugged. "On another note, is everybody still onboard for our trip? It's getting rather close to go time."

"We are. Lee and I finalized everything with the management teams last night, so we're all set."

"That's good. What about you, Rona?"

"Ah, remember, I'm the one who booked everything so of course I'm going. By the way, you should all receive an email with more information by the end of business day tomorrow.

Including the amount of reimbursement per couple, meal selections and a list of things to do in the area, for those who want to venture out."

"Sounds like you got everything taken care of."

"I do. I'm pretty good at delegating and the few good staff members I keep close to the vest know what to do and how to do it."

"What about Zsasha, did she get in on any of the planning?"

"That would be a negative. The last thing we need is little Miss Ellie getting involved. She might have our asses staying in a cave instead of a cabin. Y'all know I don't trust her."

"We *knooooow!*" Vonne declared. "So J'Nae, how are things moving along with Rick? You two lovebirds seem pretty solid, and quite happy with yourselves. Anything you want to share?"

"Since you asked, I would definitely say we're getting closer, for sure, yeah."

"And..."

"And he's amazing. I'm honestly looking forward to our relationship progressing. I don't even think about the age difference anymore and I know he doesn't either."

"How so?"

"Well, if you must know, the reason why he's not driving up with me is because he needs to stop in and check on his mother."

"Oh. Is everything okay? Does he have a reason to be concerned?"

"No, nothing out of the ordinary. He hasn't had a recent visit with her lately and thought it would be a good time to visit and maybe tell her about me."

"Wow! I guess things are getting serious with you too."

"Honestly, I think I'm falling for him."

"Really? So, you guys haven't said the 'L' word yet, either of you?"

"No, not yet exactly. We might say 'hey love' or something like that but neither of us have come right out and said, 'I love you'."

"Well make sure you don't say it first. I taught you better than that." Zsasha commanded.

Everyone looked up in surprise at Zsasha's sudden presence as she appeared out of nowhere.

"Where did you come from?" Rona asked. "I didn't see you pull up."

"That's because you weren't paying attention, none of you heffa's were."

"Be that as it may, yo ass is late!" Rona stated.

"No the hell I ain't. I started not to come at all because I know y'all fucking with me."

"You think?" J'Nae uttered.

"Yes, I do. Y'all know I don't do gyms. Not even the one I custom built at my house."

"So, what did you show up for?" Vonne asked.

"Because I felt bad about yesterday."

"For blowing us off for something you yourself scheduled or for blowing us off for her?"

"Yeah, for that, all that."

"Well, what happened? Why did you do it?"

"Real talk, it wasn't intentional. I forgot about our plans."

"You mean the plans you made."

"Yes Rona, the plans I made. Really, I just forgot."

"And how did that happen? It was on your calendar, remember?" Vonne reiterated.

"I do, I just hadn't looked at it in a day or two. I knew the two major events this month had come and gone and really, I just kind of checked out for a minute. I didn't even have my phone on. Really, that's all it was, I promise, it wasn't personal."

"But you can imagine how we felt not by you blowing us off but seeing you with her." Vonne explained.

"Yeah, that was hurtful." J'Nae assured. "So how is it that you are okay with her after what happened at the auction? I don't get it."

"Neither do I." Rona added. "Unless it happened differently from what they told me, the only way I see you breaking bread with her is if you're breaking it over her head. This just isn't like you, so if you have something to share, now's the time."

"It was an unintentional mistake, nothing more and nothing less."

"You believe that Z?" Rona snapped back.

"Yes, I do. Besides, no one outside of us witnessed what happened and furthermore, the bitch can do whatever she wants with it. She owns it now."

"We know all of that, Zsasha."

"So then, what's the problem?"

"I don't like how that shit went down." Rona advised.

"Me either." Vonne agreed. It just seems shady, that's all."

"I'm sorry y'all feel that way."

"What about all the shit she said to convince you to sell it to her. She blatantly lied and that's not cool." J'Nae determined.

"All she had to do was give you the courtesy of letting you know she was going to auction it off." Vonne added. "She knew that painting was personal to you and at the very least, you deserved the courtesy of knowing what she was planning to do with it beforehand."

"Yea, it seemed a bit intentional if you ask me." J'Nae agreed.

"Well, I didn't and y'all gonna have to get over it. Nothing bad came of it so we're all good."

"Yeah, okay. Whatever you say, Zsasha."

"But I do want to make it up to you guys for flaking on you yesterday."

"And how are you planning to do that?"

"Here's a check to cover the cost of our trip, for everybody."

"For real?"

"Hell yeah, and I've also made arrangements for Ms. Honey to join us. She'll arrive the day before us and take care of all the shopping and prepare our meals."

"Is that right?" Vonne asked.

"You mean, is that it?" Rona interrupted. "Is that the best you got? Shoot, we all know you got a shit load of money. We got money too."

"Hold on girlfriend. Ain't none of us broke, but by no means do we have Zsasha King money, cumulative or otherwise. It just doesn't add up." J'Nae announced.

"And when did you have time to do all of this and how did you get the total cost?" Rona inquired. "None of my staff informed me of this change and everything that happens in my office goes through me."

"Well not everything, girlfriend." Zsasha revealed. "I have a great deal of influence in this town, you know me."

"All I know is somebody's going to be in the unemployment line tomorrow, you wait and see." Rona smirked.

"Girl let it go. If it makes you feel any better, your assistant gave me a really hard time about it and that's the truth. Yes, I have Ahsasz money, we all know that, but it doesn't mean this gesture isn't from the heart."

"You're right." J'Nae acknowledged.

"I'll just wait and see if y'all stories match up, then I'll go from there." Rona advised.

"So, we're good?"

"Oh, we're good but I still don't trust her. I don't trust Ellie Porter at all."

"Understood."

Chapter 26

R ick arrived at J'Nae's house a short time before she was due to leave for the Catskills. He had wrapped up work a bit early so he could check out her car and ensure it was safe to drive.

"Your car looks fine. All the fluids are at the appropriate levels and the air pressure on your tires are exactly where they're supposed to be." Rick said as he walked through the living room to the master bedroom.

"You didn't have to do all that. I told you I just had my car serviced not too long ago."

"I didn't want to take any chances. Besides, it's hard to get a signal once you get up in those mountains and those roads can get tricky if you're not used to driving on them."

"You're so sweet, thanks babe. I appreciate you looking out for me." J'Nae said as she blew her lover a kiss.

"That's it? That's how you're gonna thank me? After all I've done? All the time and sweat I put into making sure everything is copesthetic? Really? That's the best you got?"

"I've got plenty, but you're just gonna have to wait until you make it to the cabin to get it."

"Seriously, you're gonna make me wait to taste your love? Sorry, no can do."

J'Nae walked up to her lover and into his waiting embrace. "You want some of this baby?

Rick instinctively tightened his grip around her waist. "You know I do." He replied.

Rick tried pulling her in towards him, but his actions were thwarted when J'Nae took control and him in towards her as she took steps backwards until she was up against the dresser in her bedroom.

"Well come and get it."

Responding to her invitation, Rick presses tightly against her as she welcomed him by opening her legs. Snug and in her warm embrace he began kissing her gently while running his hand inside her blouse. Just then his cell phone began to ring. Looking at the caller ID for a hot second, he placed the phone face down on the dresser to silence the interruption and return his attention back to J'Nae. He caressed her shoulders tightly pulling her in a bit more closely while at the same time rubbing her breast with a gentle yet invigorating touch. With his left hand, he unbuttoned the top two buttons of her blouse so he could gain better access to her hardening nipples. As he licked her nipples he tugged on them ever so gently, causing a shutter to run through her body. He made his way down her stomach, pulling her blouse out from where it had been tucked in. She could feel his erection pressing against her groin which automatically caused her to push up her skirt, so it was up around her waist. The open passage was a clear signal for Rick to insert one finger than two inside her moist and throbbing pussy, causing a moan louder than the one a moment before. He began massaging and groping her pussy, fingers in and fingers out until it got wetter and wetter with each touch of his hand. Kissing and sucking gently on the inside of her thigh, his tongue gently brushed across her clit, as if to tease her on purpose. Her grip on his left shoulder tightened as her excitement increased. Masterfully he began a gentle thumb rub on her clit with a circular motion, alternating with salacious licking. The sensation caused her clit to swell slightly and increased her sensitivity to his touch. J'Nae leaned forward a bit, placing her hands around the side of his face and head, gently pulling him towards her, initiating a kiss. It was passionate and deliberate and excited her even more.

"I need you, baby. I need to feel you right now." She whispered.

Rick obliged by lifting her off the dresser and positioning her to receive him. Neither of them realized in doing so, his cell phone was pushed backwards and fell behind the dresser. Placing her on the bed they quickly pulled off what remained of their clothes. Eager to jump back in, Rick placed his right knee in between her legs to separate them a bit more so he could have more room to work. He returned to the magnificent task of licking and sucking all her juice that flowed.   When he finally penetrated her saturated and throbbing pussy, the thrusts were quick and aggressive.   Her grip on his dick was tight and controlled and she held and released, held and released in rhythm with his stroke. Within minutes they climaxed together. Collapsing next to each other on the bed they both took a minute to catch their breath.

"Okay, you're officially ready to go now." Rick said, smiling.

"I'm not sure I want to leave."

"I'll be joining you before you know it. Don't worry. Besides, I can't be away from you for long."

"Me either baby."

Shortly thereafter, J'Nae had showered and changed into casual attire and stood with Rick next to her car, anxiously waiting for the others to arrive. The plan was for everyone to meet at J'Nae's house because it was most easily accessible to the interstate. Just moments ago, Rona had phoned to say she was making a last-minute stop at the local food mart to pick up some nuts and healthy snacks for the 6-hour road trip. Vonne and Lee were riding up with Zsasha and Simon while Rona decided to ride with J'Nae. She could keep her company and catch up with girl talk since Rick wouldn't be joining them until later.

Getting out of her car, Rona reached out to J'Nae and Rick and waved them over towards her for assistance.

"Hey guys. You two are certainly looking very cozy with one another. Where's everybody else?"

"They're not here yet. Zsasha and Simon are picking up Vonne and Lee so there could be any number of reasons why there's a delay."

"Well, we don't know for sure if there's an issue with Vonne and Lee so let's not speak it into existence. I'm sure they'll be here shortly."

"Hey Rona, nice to see you again." Rick said as he approached. "Here, let me help you with your bags."

"Dang, are you sure you packed enough clothes? We'll barely be gone a week."

"You know me. I have to be prepared for any situation that might present itself."

"Or anyone who might present themselves!"

"Whatchu said girl, whatchu said. You ain't never lied!"

"Well don't hurt yourself, sista."

"Hell, where's the fun in that!" Rona replied more as a statement than a question. "My days of playing it safe and low key are a thing of the past."

"So what, are you trying to take a play out of Zsasha's playbook? That's where you at now?"

"Girl, no. In fact, that's a hell no! Now I'm not judging anybody or anything, so if *you* like it, I love it…. for you…not necessarily for me. Even I draw the line somewhere."

"I thought you weren't judging?"

"I'm not. If that works for her or anybody else, go- for it. By all means, do whatever makes you happy."

"I feel you."

"It's just not my cup of tea, that's all I'm trying to say."

"I get it."

"Here they come now."

Zsasha and Simon pulled up in the Cadillac Escalade usually reserved for the residential staff members to run errands around town. No way was Simon going to drive one of their high-end SUV's in the Catskills. Vonne and Lee were tucked tightly in the driver side corner of the rear passenger seat. They seemed to be quite cozy and unaware the car had just come to a stop. Rolling down the passenger side front window Zsasha greeting Rona, J'Nae and Rick, hardly able to contain her excitement.

"Wassup…y'all ready to roll out?"

"We've been ready, just hanging out waiting on you guys." Rona Said.

J'Nae gave Rona a quick eyeball check for perpetrating an early arrival just before she tapped on the rear window to get Vonne and Lee's attention.

"Hey, what's going on back there? Y'all can't take a minute to be cordial? What's up?"

"Vonne got her own thing going on. They've been like that ever since we picked them up. Don't pay them no mind. Based on what's been going on in that household, they need to be doing exactly what they are doing right now. Let' em be." Zsasha stated. "So Rona, you got everything you wanted when you stopped, right? J'Nae, you all gassed up and ready to roll?"

"We're ready. I just need to say goodbye to Rick then I'm good to go."

"Oh yeah, I forgot he wouldn't be joining us until later."

"Yeah, he wants to stop and see his mom on the way up."

"Alright then, y'all wrap it up so we can get moving."

J'Nae walked over to her car where Rick was holding the driver side door open for her to get in making it easy for her to walk into his waiting arms. She felt a tug on her heart looking at what she was leaving behind.

"I hate that I have to get in this car, leaving you behind."

"I hate that you have to make this drive without me."

Kissing gently in between their exchange of words, momentarily, it looked as if it was a real good-bye."

"Girl come on. He'll catch up with us before you have a chance to miss him. Now get in the car and let's go." Rona said.

"Don't forget to lock up sweetie."

"I won't. I'll drop the key through the doggie door. And why do you have a doggie door? You don't have any pets?"

"Kids, pets, grew up, moved out. You're up to speed. Now can we get going?" Rona interrupted.

J'Nae got in her car and like a gentleman, Rick closed her door.

"Y'all be safe and call me when you've made it there."

"Alright sweetie. See you soon."

"Yes, you will." Rick said as he planted a kiss on her forehead. "I love you."

Rick turned and walked away from the car not waiting for a response. J'Nae, not sure she heard him right, just let her eyes follow him as he walked towards the house. She pulled off slowly, not saying a word aloud although her mind was replaying the last words he spoke.

"He just told you he loved you." Rona said with surprise. "I didn't realize things had gotten that serious with you two."

J'Nae still didn't speak. She sat there just following the rest of her friends.

"J'Nae, did you hear what I just said?" Rona asked. "Better yet, did you hear what he said?"

"Ah, yeah, yeah. He said he loved me. No big deal, right?"

"Well that depends, sweetie. Was that the first time he said it?"

"Ah, yeah, yeah. That was definitely the first time he said what he said."

"He said he loved you." Rona reiterated. "I guess you weren't expecting that?" Rona questioned. J'Nae didn't quite know how to respond so she said nothing.

"So how do you feel about him?" Rona asked. "Inquiring minds want to know."

"I don't know, I mean he's a young guy."

"He's a grown man with grown man responsibilities. He's got an awesome job and he's fine as fuck and very much into you."

"Yeah, yeah, that's all true."

"So, what's the problem?"

"Who said there is one?"

"Um, your mouth might not have been talking but your face is telling its own story. This can't come as a complete surprise, right. I mean, you guys have been spending a great deal of time together these past few months. He's seen more of you than any of us."

"Well, we do enjoy each other's company and he has a knack for making me forget all about our age difference."

"Honey, that was the easy part. Just look at yourself. You barely look 40. No one would think that you're 48, no one."

"You think?"

"I know, and you should too. Rick is living proof of that! That man had his eye on you for quite some time before you gave him the time of day. He never gave up because he knew what he wanted and when he saw it, he went after it. In my opinion, looking at the two of you together, you both look age appropriate.   That younger man, older woman thing may describe the two of you on a technical basis but visually, not a chance. And truthfully, I don't think he would care either way. In fact, we all kind of knew he had some real feelings for you. I mean we knew this was more than just a friend with benefits type thing. We thought you did too."

"I guess I had an idea, kind of, sort of, but I didn't want to be presumptuous. My issues with our age difference wouldn't allow me to admit to myself how I really feel."

"And exactly how is that J'Nae?"

"I think I love him too."

"You think?"

"I do...I love him."

"So, what are you going to do about it?"

"I don't know...sleep on it for right now."

"Not right now I hope."

"No silly, I'm driving. I just mean that I won't make any decisions until I've had time to process it all."

"Well okay, if that's what you want to do."

"I think that's best."

"If you say so, I got you."

J'Nae and Rona continued to ride for a while without much conversation. Both were contemplating the recent revelations about Rick's feelings toward J'Nae and hers as well. Rona knew her girl had been thrown for a loop, but she seemed to be keeping it together, at least for now, for the road trip up.

* * * * *

Back at J'Nae's house, Rick spent the next few hours straightening up the garage where he had been working then showering and changing clothes for his trip to see his mother on his way to the Catskills. She had long since moved out of Prince George County where he grew up, leaving that dreadful neighborhood and the high crime rate behind. She remarried a few years after Rick finished high school and started a new life. What was now referred to as the family home was a far cry from what they had before.

It was just a few hours away and a straight drive to Carney, Maryland, the suburb where Rick's mother and stepfather now lived. He locked up the house and tossed her spare key through the doggie door on the side of the house. Getting directly on the highway, Rick decided not to stop at the station and check in. He needed this time to himself so he could relax and unwind. Especially since he'd been dealing with a nagging headache on and off for the past few weeks that was getting harder and harder to cover up or get rid of. He thought it best to arrive before dark so he wouldn't have to deal with the headlights and high beams some random idiot behind him would almost certainly have on.

He had only been on the road for 30 minutes when he decided to call and check in with his mother. It was then that he realized he didn't have his cell phone with him. He didn't immediately know where he'd last had it, so he began mentally retracing his steps. It wasn't long before he remembered laying it face down on the dresser to silence it while with J'Nae. He briefly considered turning back to get it but just as quickly as that thought entered his mind, he dismissed it. He knew he was too far gone to head back now and the traffic he would run into would push his arrival time back significantly. And he wanted to arrive at a decent hour which would be anytime suitable for his mother to cook his favorite meal, if she hadn't already done so. He would just have to pick up another phone in the morning.

Rona was almost asleep in the passenger seat when her cell phone rang. It was Zsasha.

"Hey, y'all doing alright over there? Y'all need Lee to drive a bit for you?"

"J'Nae, Zsasha wants to know if you need Lee to drive for a while?"

"No, I'm good. We're almost there anyway." J'Nae answered.

Turning her attention back to the phone, Rona relayed the message back to Zsasha.

"So, what kind of place did you get us, lady realtor?"

"You're asking me that now, we're almost there."

"Yeah, I'm asking now. I'm just making conversation. You forget I know you. Your taste is more extravagant than mine, so I know whatever it is, it's on point."

"So, what are you worried about it for? Just relax and be pleasantly surprised. I got this. So, what are you guys up to?"

"Well whitegirl is asleep. I knew her bougie ass wouldn't be good company for this long ass ride. Lee and Simon are in a deep conversation about wildlife or something. Going back and forth about lions, tigers and bears. Something stupid that don't have nothing to do with nothing. They're really getting on my nerves."

"Well it won't be much longer now. We should be there in just under an hour."

"Bump dat. I wanna switch cars and ride with you bitches. Tell ole girl to pull over so I can jump in."

"Zsasha says to pull over so she can jump in and ride with us."

"Tell her no. I'm not stopping. She will just have to put up with them for a little bit longer."

"Did you hear that, Zsasha?"

"Yeah, I heard her." Zsasha said, sounding perturbed then mumbled under her breath, "bitches."

Hanging up the phone, Rona and J'Nae just looked at each other and smiled.

"She does this every time we go anywhere." J'Nae said.

"Yeah, she does, but usually you let her have her way."

"Well not this time. She's dealing with the newly empowered and more confident version of myself I call J'Nae 2.0."

"Is that right?"

"That's right!"

"You go girl!"

Chapter 27

Arriving at the cabin, the girls hurry inside to check out the layout of the land. It was a six-bedroom cabin with 4 bedrooms upstairs and 2 on the main floor. The floor plan was open, and the kitchen was up to date with the top-of-the-line appliances. Although stainless steel and granite accented the kitchen, a wood table and chairs still inspired a country look and feel throughout the cabin. Downstairs was a fully finished basement equipped with an 8-foot slate pool table, a dart board, a billiard table, a movie room with an entertainment system, all surrounded by a plaid covered sofa, a loveseat and a few reclining chairs. Out back was an open and uncovered hot tub ready for anyone willing to be exposed to the elements and anything else that might creep up. The girls loved it.

"Well Rona, you really out did yourself with this one." J'Nae said. "What is this, about 4000 square feet?"

"That's pretty damn close, girlfriend. You might have to come work for me."

"Didn't you two bitches try that before?" Zsasha asked matter-of-factly?

"Ah, yes they did." Vonne confirmed.

"Who asked you." Rona added, more as a statement then a question. "That was a long time ago. Besides, I was just giving her props on her skillful eye, that's all. J'Nae has a job and a damn good one!"

"Yes, I do, but I'm not making Rona Wright money, that's for sure."

"Like you need it." Zsasha remarked. "I know you're still sitting on at least one of the nest eggs Julian left you. I don't even know why you work at all."

"Hold up. I know you ain't talking about wealth and stacking cash, not with all you got going on with the art gallery and the down low club." Rona revealed.

"You mean the clubs. That's right bitches, Simon has been working on setting up a second club. We're expanding. I didn't mention it because, well, y'all ain't supposed to know about the first one. But yeah, we got that kind of money, hell we all do. That's no surprise."

"Clubs? What kind of club? Vonne asked trying to sound innocent.

"Girl, stop tripping. Ain't no need to play it off. I know all you bitches know about *Ahsasz Down Under*."

"Well, yeah, I've known for a long time." Said Vonne as she took steps towards the front door. "What's taking Lee and Simon so long with the luggage? I'll just see if they need help." Vonne replied as she escaped to avoid that conversation.

"You know I've always known." Rona declared. "I've even been there a few times."

"Yes, I know, and I've been aware of how Vonne came to know about *Ahsasz Down Under*."

"I know, but what about J'Nae? She's not looking like this is news to her either."

"That's on me...bitch caught me slippin. I left the door from my office to the club open and she just happened to be in my office snooping around."

"So, what difference does it make? We're your girls. We don't judge."

"I ain't worried about you bitches judging me. I just don't want y'all horny asses hanging out there and disrupting the flow of my money. I better not see none of y'all down there, understand? None of you bitches!"

"I kind of recall you saying something about inviting us at some point, remember?"

"Yes, I did, but I never said when."

"Why not let us come to the one coming up? Rumor has it The Summer Charade is just a few months away. Isn't that what you call it? It sounds like fun to me." J'Nae said with enthusiasm.

"J'Nae honey, I love you but you ain't ready for this, trust me. And no, the mid-season Masquerade Ball we like to call The Charade of Summer."

"Close enough, so what do you say? Can we -

"Girlfriend, I said no, and I mean it! It's not for you."

"That's what you said about Rick when you found out his age. Now look at us."

"No sweetie, that's what *you said* about Rick. At least until you got sprung!"

J'Nae didn't say anything but the grin on her face said it all. It didn't take long for Zsasha to pick up on the fact that J'Nae had a secret.

"What? What's going on? What did I miss?" Zsasha inquired. "Why are you looking like that J'Nae?"

"I think she's just reacting to what you said about being sprung, that's all." Rona revealed.

"Yeah, that's it." J'Nae said, smiling ear to ear. "Sprung."

"Girl you might as well spill. We already know you can't hold water. And if we didn't know before, we know now. So, go on, tell her."

"Tell her what?" Vonne asked as she reentered the living room.

"I don't know." Zsasha said. "But it's got something to do with Rick."

"That Rick is kind of feeling me, that's all." J'Nae perpetrated.

"Bump that...He told her he loved her right before we left."

"Damn girl." Vonne sounded surprised. "I didn't know it was going down like that!"

"I did." Zsasha said. "Don't forget, I knew this freak back in the day. She might have y'all fooled but I see right through that veil of innocence and it ain't what you think."

"I'm serious. I heard it myself. He said I love you and kissed her goodbye."

"Wow, really?   I guess I didn't think it had gotten that serious." Vonne declared.

"That's understandable, you've been preoccupied with your own family drama. God knows your sister is more than a distraction for you. How is Lee handling all of that?" Rona wondered.

"He hasn't said too much lately. Maybe she won't be an issue anymore, maybe I got through to him and her."

"Well, she'd be an issue for me. You don't ever let another woman live in the home you share with your husband. Inviting a woman in is just asking for trouble, sister or not." Zsasha said. "I thought I taught you better than that."

"It's funny that you say that Zsasha, especially with your chosen lifestyle. How is that any different?" Vonne asked.

"That's easy. They don't live with us. They are there by invitation only and for a predetermined period of time. Simon and I are on the same page when it comes to all that. We have rules of engagement we live by.   Protecting the primary relationship is essential for people like us. That's understood from the start and it's the only way this lifestyle works, no exceptions."

"So, you're confident he'll never cheat on you, even with all the temptation he encounters?"

"What would be the point? If there's something or someone one of us wants, we just simply discuss it with one another."

"So, it's that simple? Simon can have any woman he desires by just letting you know about it first?"

"No, that's not what I'm said. It's always a joint venture and neither one of us can indulge in solo encounters...ever. That's one of the foundational rules."

"So, what if he desires a woman that's outside the lifestyle? What do you do then?" Vonne asked.

"He'd be shit-out-of-luck. And if it were me, I would be too."

"So, you just trust that he will respect the rules after all the years of having intimate relations with countless other women?"

"I see you don't have a full understanding of the lifestyle, sweetie. It's not like we entertain others every day or every week. It really doesn't happen as often as you think. And there's a methodology behind it all anyway. If anything, it's designed to eliminate infidelity, not promote it."

"Yeah, but only if you play fair."

"True, it is about trust, for sure. But isn't it always about trust? Any married person has a choice to cheat or be faithful. There are enticements everywhere you go no matter who you are or how you and your mate get down. It really isn't any different than a traditional marriage except for the rules of engagement or terms and conditions, whatever you want to call it. We agree to this, you agree to that..."

"Exactly. That's what you and Simon have agreed to, and it works for you. Lee and I are okay with Kiera staying with us temporarily. She's my sister and there's nothing she has to offer up that Lee doesn't already have with me. The principles are the same. Just a different set of rules of engagement."

"Except for the fact that your sister has an agenda. She's jealous of you and what you have and she's out to get her share of it. Mark my words, you'd better not sleep on a bitch."

"Don't worry about my situation, it's under control and so is his dick."

"Alright ladies, that's enough." Rona interrupted. "We're all friends here, no need to throw daggers at each other. This weekend is all about chillaxin and kicking back; embracing love, not hate."

"How about a light snack? Rick packed a few things so we would have something to snack on. I'll just run out to the car and grab the cooler."

"I'm sure the guys took brought it in already and Ms. Honey already prepared dinner for us this evening. We just need to heat it up when we're ready to eat."

"Ms. Honey? Oh, right, I forgot." J'Nae admitted.

"Yes sweetie. She arrived yesterday so she could stock the kitchen and make sure everything was ready for us. She'll be here the entire time."

"Wow Zsasha, you and Rona really thought of everything. Thank you."

"You should know by now I don't do anything halfway, sister girl or Rona either."

"I do."

Vonne was unresponsive and completely oblivious to the conversation the girls were having. Her mind was preoccupied with thoughts of Kiera and her husband she just couldn't shake. She had a tad bit uncomfortable about the situation for a while now, but her pride wouldn't let her admit it. At least not to the girls. Having this time away from home and her sister would help her and her husband reconnect and put things back in perspective. She knew she wouldn't be able to hide her doubts for long and hopefully after this trip she wouldn't have too.

* * * * *

"Hi mom. I'm calling through the car service. How are you?" Rick asked his mother.

"Son, is that you?"

"Yes mom, it's me. I left my phone behind and didn't realize it until I was on the road."

"Oh, okay. I didn't recognize the number, so I was hesitant to answer. You know you shouldn't be traveling without a phone, it's not smart or safe."

"Sorry mom, it's fine. I can make calls from the car service for now and I'll just pick up a new phone in the morning. How's Walter doing? Is he treating you right?"

"Yes, yes, we're fine. How have you been feeling lately? The last time we spoke you said you've been having headaches again and more frequently. Are you sure you're up for this trip?"

"Yeah mom, I'm fine, no need to worry but I do want to talk to you about a few things, you know, about dad and how things went down. Are you up for that?"

"Of course, son. I've been concerned about you and the headaches you've been having. Are you experiencing any other symptoms?"

"Let's just wait until I get there, we can talk about it then."

"Are you okay, sweetheart?"

"I'm fine, mom, I had a headache earlier today, that's all. But it's gone now. It's not the first and won't be the last. I just want to talk with you about dad and get a sense of a few things, you know, how it was for him and stuff. Plus, I met someone special, and I'd like you to meet her."

"Really now. She must be pretty special if you want me to meet her."

"She is mom, she is. I've never met anyone like her. Her name is J'Nae and she's…. Ugh…ahh….ma…ma…ahh…"

"Hello? Hello? Are you still their sweetie? Hello…….."

The call was abruptly cut off and any attempts she made to reconnect with her son were unsuccessful.

Chapter 28

I'm heading up to the main cabin to use the phone to call Rick." J'Nae said as she headed for the front door.

"Wait up a second." Vonne replied. "I'll go with you."

"Yeah, that's a good idea. It's dark outside and neither of you need to be out alone." Lee acknowledged.

"Hold up, I'll drive." Simon said.

"Oh no, that's alright. We girls got it." J'Nae rebutted. "It's just a short trip. We'll be back in no time."

"Well dinner will be ready when you do. Zsasha added."

"Yeah, so don't be long. You know how I feel about Ms. Honey's cooking." Rona revealed. "This here is about to get real serious real soon."

"Already know." J'Nae replied. "We'll be back in a few minutes. He's probably at his mom's house by now, chilling with the family. I just want to leave him a quick message letting him know we made it okay."

"Alright then, hurry back." Said Rona.

Vonne and J'Nae walked outside and hopped in her vehicle.

"We're driving up? I thought for sure you'd want to walk it out." Vonne stated.

"You heard what Rona said, she's ready to eat."

"Yeah, but it's really nice out here tonight. I guess I wanted a minute alone to ask you how you really feel about Rick and what he said. It ain't nothing to take lightly, that's for sure."

"Trust me, I'm not. But I'm not blowing things up either. I mean, is it real? Is he for real? I don't know. Like, I care for him a great deal, I know that, but do I love him? Do I really love him?"

"Ah, yeah, that's the million-dollar question. But whatever your answer, whatever you decide, just make sure it's what you feel and not what others expect or want you to feel. You know I spent the better part of my life living it to please others."

"Vonne sweetie, I hate to burst your bubble, but you still do. All you do for your sister and your husbands narrow behind too.... You can't get away from it, girlfriend. It's just part of who you are."

"Well, maybe so, we'll see, but you, you have to be sure. And don't let anyone's timetable put pressure on you. I can already tell you Rona's gonna ride your ass about it and Zsasha's gonna downplay the whole relationship."

"You're right, more or less."

"I'm right, girl, trust me."

"I didn't realize you were so intuitive."

"I'm not. I just know our girls better than any of y'all think."

"So, what, you've been playing stupid or something?"

"No, not at all. I mean, I know Zsasha calls me whitegirl behind my back."

"You know about that!"

"Oh hell yeah! She's been doing it since we first met."

"And you never said anything?"

"Why bother? She doesn't mean anything by it, other than the obvious. It's just her way."

"Yeah, it is. It's because she loves you, I know you know that, right?"

"Absolutely. Like I said, it's just her way."

"Well damn, does she talk about all of us like that, with nicknames and shit?"

"Nah, not y'all. At least not with me. But don't forget, Zsasha and I have some history, you know. I know y'all met in college and everything, but it wasn't long after graduation when her and I met during an unfortunate situation."

"Yeah, that's what I heard but I don't know much of the details."

"And you won't learn about them from me either."

"Why not?"

"Because that's a conversation for another time besides it's not just my story to tell. Don't you have a call to make?"

"Oh, yeah. Be right back."

J'Nae heads inside the main cabin to use their guest landline phone to call Rick. Glancing at her watch, she realizes it's close to 9:00 pm and he should have arrived at his moms' house by now. Dialing his cell phone, she doesn't get an answer, so she leaves a message.

"Hey sweetie, sorry I missed you. Hope everything is good with your family. And you were right about cell phone coverage in this area so I'm calling from the landline at the main cabin. We all arrived safe and sound to a wonderful meal Ms. Honey prepared for us. I miss you so much, I really do. I can't wait until you get here…" Momentarily, J'Nae contemplated ending the call with 'I love you too' but realized she would be immature saying it for the first time on voicemail and not face to face like he did. "By sweetie. I'll call you in the morning. Have a good night."

Later, back at the cabin, dinner was outstanding as usual. Ms. Honey had prepared a hearty country meal. She never disappoints, no matter the occasion. She had even gone as far as to unpack everyone's luggage as the group sat down to dinner, dessert, and conversation.

* * * * *

"Good morning ladies." Vonne said with excitement in her voice as she walked into the kitchen. Rona and Zsasha were already seated at the breakfast table having coffee.

"Well good morning sunshine. What's got you in such a good mood so early in the morning?" Rona asked.

"You know what it is." Zsasha commented. "Lee was looking and acting the same way when his happy ass came and woke up me and Simon this morning."

Vonne was grinning ear to ear.

"Dang, girl, it must have really been a while for you, huh?" Rona asked.

"No, not really, but we had some catching up to do." Vonne said proudly.

"Well don't hurt yourself, we'll be here a few days, so you have plenty of time to do just that." Zsasha added.

"You got that right." Vonne replied. "Where's J'Nae? Is she still asleep?"

"No, she went to the main lodge to use the phone to check her voicemail." Rona replied.

"Yeah, I'm sure she's waiting on a call back from Rick. It sucks that we can't get any service up here. It's got to be driving her crazy, you know...the way they left things..."

"Girl, I don't know what all the fuss is about. That young boy ain't talking bout nothing. I wouldn't even react to it until he put some action behind it. You know what I mean, Rona?"

"I hear what you're saying Zsasha, I just don't agree. That young man as you put it was diligent in his pursuit of our girl. We all saw it and on more than one occasion. Could he be for real? Absolutely. I think, anyway. He was halfway between smitten bordering on stalker before she broke him off. So, yeah, I think he is for real. I believe he believes he's in love." Rona declared.

"And why not." Vonne stated assuredly. "That's our girl and she is loveable. She's sweet, sincere, open minded and virtuous. Any man would be lucky to have her."

"Yeah, all that's true, for sure. I'm just not ready to jump on Rick's love boat just yet. I'm looking at the big picture, where this can realistically go for her. I don't want to see our girl get hurt her first time out the gate." Zsasha explained.

"Her first time out the gate?" Vonne inquired.

"Yeah. Her first time potentially having any real feelings for a man since Julian. When he died unexpectedly, we all saw what it did to her and how long it took her to get past it."

"I feel you, Zsasha." Rona agreed. "Julian was the love of her life and for years she never considered dating again. Not until her kids were grown and married and totally on their own."

"And even then, I had to set her up on a partially blind date just to get her the slightest bit motivated." Vonne recalled.

"Look Zsasha, I get why you're not onboard with this Rick thing just yet. But J'Nae has grown from that fragile and timid young woman she was back when Julian passed. We all know life is full of risk. We take chances every day with everything and everyone we hold dear. We never know what the next moment will bring us. We simply have no control over that. We can only control how it impacts our lives going forward. If we live in fear of the what ifs, then we're not really living at all, we're just reacting. And what kind of life is that for anyone?".

Zsasha didn't have time to answer Rona's question before there was a knock at the front door. Vonne, seemingly the only one that could pull away from the conversation, got up to answer it.

"Good morning. My name is Charlie and I'll be your driver and escort for the next two days. I'll be back in 90 minutes to pick you up and take you to the main lodge where you'll meet your group activities coordinator."

"Okay Charlie." Vonne, feeling like this would be a great way to break up the intensity at the breakfast table, decided to introduce Charlie while he was at the front door.

"Hey everybody, this is Charlie." Vonne all but shouted. "He's our driver and will be back to pick us up in an hour and a half to meet with our activities coordinator."

There was no response from either Zsasha or Rona, just a confused look on both of their faces. Vonne turned her attention back towards the front door.

"We'll be ready. Thank you."

"Thank you, mam. And be sure to have on comfortable footwear with support. You'll do a bit of walking."

"Good to know. See you in a bit." Vonne closed the door and returned to the breakfast area. "Did y'all hear anything I said?"

"Yeah, shoes, walking, pick up in an hour or so. Did I miss anything?" J'Nae asked while walking into the breakfast area.

"Where did you come from, J'Nae?" Vonne asked.

"I came in through the back. I wanted to look around the property, it's beautiful out here."

"Yes, it is." Rona confirmed. "Were you able to get through to Rick?"

"No, I didn't, and he hadn't left me a message either."

"Well, I'm sure he knows you arrived safely, otherwise he'd be blowing up your phone." Rona replied.

"He's probably just tied up with his family." J'Nae uttered, purposely trying not to show too much concern.

"Probably so." Zsasha replied. "Now let's eat."

The ladies joined the men who were already seated at the table ready to eat the breakfast feast Ms. Honey prepared for the group. The conversation was light as they discussed the scheduled events for the day. Immediately following breakfast, everyone retreated to their rooms to change and prepare for their outing, then gathered at the front door where their driver was waiting to lead them on their way.

A few hours later, Charlie returned the group and their activities coordinator back to the main lodge. Just about everybody was feeling the effects of the extended walking tour they had just experienced. Some more than others.

"I sure worked up an appetite, how about anyone else?" Rona asked.

"Sure, I could eat." J'Nae replied.

"Yeah, me too. Lee honey, are you feeling lunch right about now?"

"Well Simon and I were planning on doing some light fishing this afternoon." Lee replied. "If that's okay with you, sweetie?" Vonne blew her husband a kiss signaling her approval.

"Y'all about to make me sick with all this lovey dovey." Zsasha said.

"Stop hating." Vonne replied. "Let's head into town for lunch, maybe do a little window shopping."

"Yeah, let's check out this town and see what it has to offer." Rona added.

"Sounds like a plan to me." J'Nae confirmed.

Lee and Simon retrieved the fishing gear they packed in the van before leaving the cabin. Charlie, the driver/group tour guide, had already mapped out a nearby location where Lee and Simon could fish. After providing them with a map and detailed instructions, Charlie escorted the girls to the van to begin their afternoon.

"So, ladies, where to first? Do you want to have lunch and then shop or shop and then eat?"

302

Vonne was the first one to answer.

"It doesn't matter to me, what y'all want to do first?"

"Did y'all not pick up on what he said." Zsasha asked. You could hear the change in her voice as well as see the shift in her demeanor and attitude. "Uh uh little boy. You slick trying to throw some shade on us sisters."

J'Nae and Rona turned towards each other in sync and in harmony. "What's she talking about?"

"See, y'all little thirsty heffa's too busy looking at his pretty white ass and not paying attention to what he's saying." Zsasha declared.

"White. I'm not white. I'm Italian and Portuguese, mam. I am not white."

"Why are you in your feelings, Zsasha? What exactly did he say?"

"He said *Lunch and then shop or shop and then eat*. What are you trying to say Charlie? How come we can't shop and then lunch, huh?"

"Girl, you know you're tripping, for real Zsasha, you're tripping."

"No, no, Madame, let me explain. See, if you eat now, after your exhilarating walking tour, and shop later, you'll be lunching. However, Madam, if you shop first, you will return depleted and exhausted and then eat like scavengers."

Rona and J'Nae fell out laughing.

"He's right, you know." J'Nae agreed. "If we wait until later, we'll overeat and won't be any good for the rest of the day."

Zsasha twisted her lips and mumbled something under her breath.

"What honey, what was that Zsasha?" Rona teased. "Did I just hear you say something? He's right and you're wrong? Come on now, we want to be clear we're all on the same page, girlfriend."

J'Nae and Rona could hardly keep it together, while watching their girl squirm.

"It's been a minute since I've seen you tongue tied." Vonne said intent on sounding facetious. "I wasn't even sure it was possible."

Zsasha rolled her eyes while allowing the girls to have their fun at her expense just as Charlie pulled over and parked the van.

"Here we are ladies. Our three restaurants are right here in this general area and a variety of shops are also within walking distance. You should find everything clearly marked on your maps or you can ask a local for assistance. I will be back to pick you up at this spot at the time you pre-selected, however if you choose to leave prior to that, I will be parked at the taxi station 2 blocks up the road on the left. It's also on the map. Enjoy ladies."

The ladies exited the vehicle and began their journey of discovery. Three hours later, they were back at the cabin where they would remain for the rest of the day.

* * * * *

"OMG! This feels amazing." J'Nae admitted. "I think I want to stay in here all night until I fall asleep."

"Girl please. I know your butt ain't soar. The three of you heffa's work out all the time. That little bit of walking shouldn't have phased you one bit." Zsasha observed.

"I'm good." Vonne remarked.

"Yeah, piece of cake." Rona said nonchalantly.

"These days, I get most of my exercise outside the gym with my own trainer, in a personal and private setting." J'Nae shared.

"So Rick's working it out, huh?" Rona teased.

"Yes, he is." J'Nae bragged while pouring another glass of wine. "And quite well I might add."

"It's about damn time you and Vonne got your groove back. Rona and I have been holding it down for a minute." Zsasha said, looking over at her partner in crime. "Speaking of holding it down, why are you flying solo on this trip? That's not like you."

"I'm here on vacation, like the rest of y'all. I needed a break, and this felt like the right time and place to take one. What's wrong with that?" Rona replied.

"I shouldn't have to say this sista girl, but usually, especially when it comes to people like you, no, fuck that, when it comes to you, a vacation or getaway typically involves some dick and some dollars, and not just any dick, sophisticated, highly educated and very wealthy dick. Yo ass never travels alone. What gives?"

"Yeah Rona." Vonne added. "What's up with that?"

"Like I said, I just needed a break."

"I don't get it. What's the point of a getaway if a man ain't there wearing you out?"

"Well I guess that depends on what you're trying to get away from!" Rona confessed.

"Damn girl, for real! You finally got tired of Ricardo whisking you away, from here to there and everywhere?"

"Well, yes and no. Ricardo is great, when we're together or should I say when he has time for me. Most of the trips we take are an extension of some business he needs to handle. More often than not, business usually has him tied up, considerably."

"Really. How come you never said anything?" J'Nae asked.

"Because I was content sight-seeing and shopping at his expense, for a while anyway. At first it wasn't a big deal spending my days alone, I had some much needed me time. He usually made it back in time for dinner or whatever but eventually it grew from being an infrequent occurrence to an unacceptable standard, and then I got bored."

"Okay, then what happened?" J'Nae questioned in between sips.

"I found another way to entertain myself."

"Let me guess, you started seeing someone else." Zsasha speculated.

"Well, yeah, I did."

"So, I don't get it." Vonne admitted.

"Me either." J'Nae slurred.

"I still don't see the problem." Zsasha conveyed. "You guys are not in an exclusive relationship, right?"

"No, we're not."

"So, if it's not that you're seeing someone else, then it must be who you're seeing, right?" Zsasha continued.

"Well, kind of, sort of, but not the way you think."

"Girlfriend, just spill it." Vonne commanded.

"Yeah, spill it. Who is this dirtbag disrupting your flow?" J'Nae inquired slowly slurring her words.

"His name is *Jon-Paul,* and he works with Ricardo. Sometimes Ricardo would have him fill in when he couldn't make dinner or whatever plans we had for the evening so I wouldn't be alone. That's how we became acquainted. Soon we discovered we had a lot in common, sharing interest in a variety of things. Lately, he's been working very closely with Ricardo, and I don't know if that's a happy coincidence or a strategic move on his part."

"Playing in your own backyard...that's not like you." Zsasha commented.

"You're right. Although having more than one toy has never been the issue, playing with them in the same playground has always been on my 'Not To Do List'."

"Do they know about each other?" Vonne asked.

"Jon-Paul knows about Ricardo of course, but Ricardo is completely in the dark about Jon-Paul."

"Aren't you worried about Jon-Paul telling Ricardo?"

"Not if he wants to keep his job. He knows what his role is and so do I."

"I feel you. I mean, not that Simon and I keep any secrets from each other and y'all know what we do, what we've always done. But what you might not know is how much work it takes. We're only in a relationship with each other. All that extra shit is just that, extra shit. When we want it, if we want it and how we want it. I can imagine keeping more than one man happy requires discipline, hard work and prioritization. I give you your props on that, sista girl."

"You still don't get it, Zsasha. Or maybe you just forgot who I am. Since my divorce and my commitment to making myself happy, you ain't never known for me to have any trouble satisfying a man or men. For the most part I was dating two at the same time, anyway. Y'all know how I roll. In fact, the last time I flew solo for any real period of time, it was by choice and I was married, you feel me?"

"So, if they're not wearing you out, then what's the problem? Why do you need a break?" Vonne questioned.

"It's not about being physically tired, it's more of a mental thing. They have very different tastes, you know. And since Jon Paul works with Ricardo, If I'm around one, I'm around the other because they often travel together on business. For the most part I'm with Ricardo, our trips are about us spending time together unless he's working late, that's when he sends Jon-Paul to escort me for whatever we have planned for the evening. That's how it all started."

"I still don't get it." Zsasha declared.

J'Nae was preoccupied refilling her wine glass with the bottle on the bar adjacent to the hot tub. She could hear what was being said but most of it didn't register.

"Oh my gosh! Y'all are killing me! Zsasha, you of all people should know what I'm talking about."

"You lost me, girlfriend, you lost me." Zsasha shared.

"Ditto." Vonne reiterated.

"I needed a break because it quickly became unmanageable." Rona looked around at the dumbfounded looks that were still present on Zsasha and Vonne's faces. "What one wanted versus the other..." Still Zsasha and Vonne looked confused. "Are y'all with me?"

Vonne shook her head indicating she was still at a loss.

"You got me with this one, Rona." Zsasha confessed.

"I guess I'll just have to spell it out for you. Ricardo likes his pussy steamed clean fresh and Jon Paul likes his two days dirty."

"Ah, hell." Vonne uttered in a loud voice. Zsasha immediately burst out laughing, like it was the best joke ever told.

"Two days dirty? How in the hell are you supposed to manage that, seeing that all three of you are somewhat together at the same times?"

"Well, now you see my dilemma. Every time I hooked up with Jon Paul, I had to put Ricardo off the night before and find an excuse to be unavailable the next evening, or vice versa, y'all get it, right?"

"Got it!" Vonne declared.

"Wow! You mean to tell me you didn't wash that monkey for 48 hours? I don't believe it!" Zsasha taunted.

"It was more like 36 hours or so...fuck! Who am I kidding! By the time I got up with Jon Paul, it would be about 48 hours, for sure."

"Nasty ass!" Zsasha added.

"Hell, I've been called worse, Zsasha and you have too."

"Damn girl, I can't believe this coming from you." Vonne replied. "As prissy as you are, didn't you feel dirty and uncomfortable?"

"The first time I served it up that way, I did, I really did, but that didn't last long. After he did all he did with it dirty, it didn't even matter. I couldn't help myself. Dude ate like it was the last supper...and after that, it never crossed my mind again. Actually, I was happy to do it. Boyfriend doing some new shit."

"Really now..."

"Yes girl, yes and I must admit, tasting my own juice in its purest and most natural form was intoxicating. I love it!"

"So, you *can* teach an old dog new tricks, huh..." Vonne laughed.

"Y'all can laugh all you want but one of y'all better get your girl." Rona determined.

Zsasha and Vonne looked over at J'Nae who appeared to be almost passed out at the far end of the hot tub slightly hunched over. Zsasha realizing her party was over, got up and out and quickly dried off.

"We can't do nothing with that heffa. Stay with her and I'll send Lee and Simon out here to carry her ass inside."

Zsasha retreated to the basement area of the cabin where Simon and Lee were shooting pool.

"I hate to bust up what is obviously a good time, but we need you guys to carry J'Nae's passed out ass out of the hot tub and take her to her room."

"J'Nae?" Simon asked. "What the hell happened?"

"Damn, girlfriend got herself twisted already. That's not like her." Lee remarked.

"No, it's not. Apparently physical exertion, wine and hot tubbing don't mix well, even in this weather."

"Baby, I know she's your girl and all, but I prefer to keep my distance for her." Simon revealed. "Weren't y'all watching her? You know she's vulnerable right now."

"Yeah, and that's your girl, y'all supposed to have her back." Lee mumbled.

"I don't know how we missed it. She didn't have that much to drink. I know she's stressed and worried about Rick but still, she didn't drink any more than we did. I don't get it."

"Rick, huh, and where is he? Ain't, he supposed to be here by now?" Lee asked.

"He's not due to arrive until tomorrow but J'Nae hasn't been able to make contact with him since we arrived."

"Well maybe that's the reason why she got wasted. Ever thought of that, sweetie?"

"Truthfully, no, and don't have time to think about it now. Can y'all please go get her and carry her upstairs? Thank you, and I'll be right up to change her clothes."

"We got it, we got it." Lee said, taking initiative to head outside.

"Just make sure you're in her room *before* we get there." Simon said to his wife.

"Already on my way, boo. Thank you."

Zsasha headed upstairs to make her way to the bedroom occupied by her friend, noticing a bottle of muscle relaxers on the night table. If she had taken any of them after our outing, it would explain how quickly she became intoxicated.

"Okay, where do you want her?" Lee asked as he and Simon carried a barely conscious and dripping wet J'Nae into the bedroom.

"Over there, over there. Put her in the chair. I'll need to dry her off and put her in some dry clothing." Zsasha responded.

"That's my que." Simon stated as he happily marched out of the bedroom with Lee following close behind.

309

Zsasha turned to survey the wet pile of mess slumped before her just as Rona and Vonne entered the room.

"We thought you might need some help getting her into bed." Vonne speculated.

"Yeah, and based on her track record, that's no easy task, up until now!" Rona commented, causing laughter among the group.

"Y'all crazy. Grab those grandma pajamas laid across her suitcase then help me pull this wet suit off her."

The moment the girls stood her up attempting to remove her swimsuit, they thought better of it as J'Nae began to moan and respond to the touch of their hands.

"Rick, baby...ahh...Rick."

Just as quickly as her mumbling started, it was over. Laying her wet body across the bed, the girls were able to slide off her swimsuit, dry her off then pull on her pajamas. They managed to tuck her in just as she mumbled a few more words.

"Dang." Rona said. "Even when she's drunk as hell her mind is on that man."

"He must have done a number on her." Vonne added.

"Come on, y'all." Zsasha said heading for the door. "Our job here is done."

"Yep, and so is she!" Rona blurted as they walked out the room.

Zsasha just shook her head as she headed downstairs in search of Simon and Lee. Rona said her goodnights and trailed off to her room while Vonne followed Zsasha.

Chapter 29

The next day J'Nae woke to an empty cabin. The sun was out, and the silence surrounded her as she sat up in bed. Scratching her head, she looked around the room for her cell phone so she could see the time of day. Realizing it was late afternoon, she sprung up from the bed and threw on a jogging suit that had been laid out for the zipline excursion planned for that day. Her attempt to walk swiftly down the hall to the stairs was thwarted by the toll last night's activities had taken on her body. She moved as best she could down the hallway then pausing at the top of the stairs. She heard faint voices as she began her descent, then realized it was the tv.

"Good afternoon, Ms. J'Nae. How are you feeling?"

"Like I got hit by a truck...twice. Where's everybody at?"

"The zipline tour was scheduled for today. We tried to wake you, but you said you wanted to sleep in."

"I did, really?"

"Yes, sweetie. You were still drunk and said you needed to sleep it off before Rick arrived."

"Oh, okay. I wonder why he didn't wake me up when he got here?"

"He hasn't arrived yet, sweetie. Maybe you should give him a call."

"I will. Can you drive me to the main lodge? The cell phone reception out here is terrible."

"Of course I can. I'll just leave a note for the others in case they come back while we're out."

"Great. Thank you, Ms. Honey."

J'Nae hurriedly put on a jacket and grabbed a pair of boots she found near the front door. She struggled for a minute, not realizing they weren't hers. All she could think about was Rick. He should have been here by now and that worried her, on top of the fact that she hadn't been able to make contact with him since they left home.

"Okay, all set. Are you okay, sweetie?" Ms. Honey asked.

"Yeah, yeah, I'm fine. Let's just go."

311

The two ladies got in the sports utility vehicle parked out front and drove to the main cabin in silence. Ms. Honey could tell J'Nae was worried about her friend, so small talk and chit chat would not work as a distraction. She decided to just let her be, for now.

"Oh my goodness!" Vonne exclaimed, walking inside the cabin with the others. "That was so much fun!"

"Yes, it was. That was my first time ever on a zipline." Rona admitted. "What about you two?"

"It was a first for me also." Vonne replied.

"No, it wasn't. We did this several years ago, back when we were dating." Lee recalled. "How could you not remember that?"

"Easy, more than likely I was stoned out of my mind."

"Probably so baby, probably so."

"Best believe, it was my first and last time." Zsasha announced. "Y'all heffas are gonna be sore as hell in the morning. My ass is already chafed and irritated from the harness and those straps tight as fuck all around my girlie parts."

"Shouldn't you be used to that sort of thing by now?" Vonne joked.

"Yeah, I thought swings and harnesses were right up your alley." Rona teased with laughter.

"Y'all bitches think you're funny. Swings in my house or not, just wait. We'll see who's laughing tomorrow."

"We're not trying to be funny, at least I'm not." Rona replied.

"Remember, I've seen the place you call *Ahsasz Down Under*, so I have a pretty good idea of the things you've been exposed to."

"Like I said, y'all don't know nothing. Just because I have some freaky ass shit at the club don't necessarily mean I go that route."

"Motha fucka please!" Vonne declared. "Everybody knows you're a freak, Zsasha! That cat ain't *never* been in the bag! Not as long as I've known you!"

"Dang Z!" Rona exclaimed. "She called you straight out, *girlfriend*."

"The hell you say!" Zsasha replied.

"Give it up, sista girl." Rona commanded. "She got you on this one and she even used your own catch phrase to do it!"

"Whatever...bitches!"

"Damn, I could hear y'all outside as I was pulling up to the cabin. What's going on here?" J'Nae asked, obviously perplexed by the conversation.

"We're just teasing Zsasha, like we do." Rona replied. "Where are you coming from?"

"Ms. Honey drove me to the main lodge so I could call Rick again, then we picked up a few things at the country store. She's bringing them in now."

"Damn, you just gonna leave her hanging like that...all on her own?" Simon asked as he entered the room.

"My bad...I guess I just rushed in hoping Rick had made it."

"Wasn't he supposed to be here today around noon-ish?" Lee asked, coming up from the lower level.

"That was the plan."

"Well maybe he's just stuck in traffic or something. These hills aren't easy to navigate if you're not in the right vehicle." Rona added.

"I suppose it could be that." J'Nae said. "But I haven't been able to make contact with him since we left to come up here. The cell service up here sucks."

"What cell service?" Rona jokes. "I haven't received a call, text, notification or email from my office yet and that's unusual."

"Rick is a grown man and fully capable of taking care of himself." Lee stated. "There's no reason to get yourself worked up. Just relax, J'Nae. He's only a couple hours late. Any number of things could have held him up."

"Yeah sweetie, I'm sure he'll be here soon." Rona replied.

"Well maybe I'm overreacting."

"Probably so J'Nae, probably so." Vonne agreed. "Don't be surprised if you wake up in the morning with him right beside you."

"You're right, I'm sure he'll be here soon."

"Cool, now can we eat!" Simon remarked.

Dinner was pretty much uneventful. Ms. Honey delighted everyone with a fiery batch of her famous white chicken chili she'd spent most of the afternoon preparing. Lee and Simon spent an hour or so packing their gear for a hunting trip they signed up for which was scheduled to depart at the butt crack of dawn. The girls helped Ms. Honey wash dishes, clean up the kitchen and pack up what was left of the chili before sitting down to relax.

"So, what now?" J'Nae asked.

"I'm ready for a drink." Ms. Honey stated. "Since you ladies were nice enough to help me square away the kitchen this evening, all my work is done."

"Well it's just us girls." Vonne shouted. "Ms. Honey, name your poison."

"Well ladies, there's two pitchers of margaritas I made earlier, but beware, I added my own special ingredient that's sure to put even the most seasoned drinkers on their ass! Check the fridge but drink at your own risk." she instructed.

"Suki, suki, now." Rona commented. "There's a side of you I don't see very often."

"This is just the tip of the iceberg darling, so less talking and more drinking."

"That's what I'm talking about." Rona announced. "I'll get the pitcher and glasses. Zsasha, play some funky music and J'Nae, grab the rest of the tequila over there on the shelf, and some shot glasses too. We're about to get lit!"

The ladies made their way to the sitting area by the fireplace and continued to enjoy the freshly made margaritas along with some chips, homemade salsa and fresh guacamole dip compliments of none other than Ms. Honey. They were so engrossed in entertaining each other, drinking, dancing and acting silly they didn't notice Simon enter the kitchen stocking a tray with snacks, two bowls of Ms. Honey's white chicken chili and a bottle of scotch for the men to enjoy downstairs.

"Are we eating first or drinking?" Simon asked. "There's a microwave right over there to warm the chili."

"Both. I'll get the ice; you warm the chili." Lee replied. "So what do you make of dude not showing up today? If he was gonna cancel, he should've called her or sent her a message or something. He could've even left word at the main lodge if he couldn't get through."

"Yeah, but if he texted, emailed or left a voice message from a place where he had good service---"

"You mean like from home?"

"What I mean is he would have no way of knowing she didn't receive it. But I still think he's coming. He probably just got held up or something." Simon reiterated.

"Shit, if he's coming, he'd better come on. Charlie mentioned it's supposed to snow late in the morning, and lover boy doesn't drive an SUV."

"I know. He's still sporting a sedan, top of the line of course, but a sedan nonetheless."

"You know he's supposed to go hunting with us in the morning. What if he doesn't show? Are we still going without him?" Lee asked.

"I don't see why not. We booked a time slot which I'm pretty sure we can't change now. I don't think he'll be to upset about it though. He's here for J'Nae, not us."

"True, true."

"You wanna get a quick game of 9-ball in before it gets too late? We've gotta get up early."

"Yeah okay, but I'm breaking." Lee asserted.

"Suit yourself, I'm still gonna whoop that ass!"

"We'll see."

When the guys made their way upstairs after several games of intense 9-ball, the women were on their third pitcher of margaritas and the party had mellowed out considerably. They were seated around the fireplace in their pajamas and slippers with a few Afghans shared between them. As Simon and Lee moved closer to the sista circle, the conversation between the girls became clear.

"Well if you bitches are gonna ask real deep dark secrets, we might as well turn it into a game." Zsasha suggested.

315

"What did you have in mind?" Rona asked.

"Truth or Dare." Zsasha replied.

At that precise moment, Simon and Lee made an abrupt turn and were now heading upstairs. Intentionally making their exit known, they waved goodnight over their shoulders while loudly saying good night. It was sure to be a conversation they didn't want to hear or be a part of. It was of no surprise to either of them their words and actions didn't draw a response. They knew when the girls were in their sista circle, nothing else mattered.

"Truth or Dare, huh? That sounds like a lot of fun if you play with the right people...count me out ladies." Ms. Honey announced. "I'm going to bed."

"Oh, Ms. Honey, tapping out so soon, are we?" Vonne teased.

"Oh yeah, for sure. While you'll be hungover and sleeping in, recuperating from my special 'Honey Margarita', I'll be doing what I do. And I don't want to be tired while I'm doing it, so goodnight."

The four ladies said goodnight and shared wishes for a good night's sleep as Ms. Honey left the circle and headed to her room.

"Okay, who goes first?" "J'Nae asked

"Whoever has the least amount in their glass goes first." Vonne ruled. "And the question is directed to the person on their left. So who has the least amount in their glass?"

"That would be me." Rona acknowledged.

"Alright, J'Nae, this is for you. Truth or Dare?"

"Truth."

"Okay, what's your truth? When was the last time you sucked a dick, a big dick, little dicks don't count?"

"Uhm, let's see...that would have been the day we drove up here, nosy."

"Oh, so you're getting it in like that, huh." Rona questioned, smiling ear to ear.

"No wonder his ass is sprung!" Vonne exclaimed. "I bet you do it hands free, don't you... little freaky ass."

"I taught my girl well, and don't y'all ever forget it!" Zsasha declared.

"Okay, okay, my turn. This is for you Vonne." J'Nae said as she turned her entire body to face her unsuspecting friend. "Truth or Dare?"

"Truth."

"Okay, what's your truth? Reveal a secret you know about one of us in this circle that you're not supposed to know and how you came to know it."

"Hold up, wait a minute now." Zsasha interrupted. "When you choose truth, it's supposed to be *your* truth, not someone else's. You can't reveal somebody else's secret, it ain't yours to tell."

"Lightened up little lady, it's just a game. We're all friends here." J'Nae affirmed, slightly slurring her speech.

"Uhm, I agree with Zsasha." Rona stated without hesitation. "It has to be their truth, not someone else's."

"Alright, fine." J'Nae stammered. "Majority rules! I'll try again."

"Not so fast honey bunny. You know the rules of this game, we've played it before, so you forfeit your turn." Rona decided. "And don't try it again, with your drunk ass."

"I'm not drunk because I'm still drinking." J'Nae replied.

"Whatever. Who's turn is it now, Zsasha's or Vonne's?"

"It's Vonne's turn because I went last, and my question was to her."

"Alrighty then, Vonne you're up."

"Okay, Zsasha, this is for you."

"Bring it on."

"Truth or Dare?"

"You know damn well I'm gonna say dare."

"Yes, I do. So here's your dare. Dare you to kiss one of us in the circle, deeply and with tongue for 15 seconds right now."

"Piece of cake." Zsasha grinned and nodded. She made her way over to J'Nae who had almost checked out. Grabbing her by the back of her neck, she swiftly pulled her in close. She took only a moment using her tongue to part J'Nae's lips and kissed her deeply and passionately for all to see. Although caught off guard, it took only a few seconds for J'Nae to respond with equal intensity. Once time was up, Zsasha pulled away."

"Wow, that was intense." Vonne revealed. "I wasn't sure you'd do it and J'Nae would have been the last person I would have thought you'd kiss, especially like that."

"Really? I don't know why. That was easy, super easy. It's not like it was the first time." Zsasha revealed.

"Wow! That's a truth and a dare!" Vonne acknowledged.

"That's it, that's it, I'm done!" Rona yelled. "This is too much, way too much. Some of this shit is better left in the dark."

Zsasha looked over towards J'Nae with a look of satisfaction on her face.

"What do you think, love? It's not too much, right? Like you said, it's just a game."

Zsasha continued to laugh and take pleasure in the point she purposely made. Vonne was right there with her, grinning and snickering and not at all surprised by the revelation. J'Nae's face was unreadable. Either she looked like she didn't care very much, or she was too drunk for it to register. But one thing was for certain, Rona did not look pleased. The girls ending the game, said their goodnights and turned in for the evening.

Despite the late night and the heavy drinking, J'Nae woke up just after 8:00 in the morning. She was heartbroken and extremely concerned realizing Rick wasn't asleep next to her. Getting up, she didn't bother to shower before dressing but did manage to brush her teeth before heading downstairs. Lost in her own thoughts, she barely acknowledged Ms. Honey or the savory smell emanating from the kitchen. She simply grabbed her coat, keys and cell phone and left the cabin.

Once inside her vehicle, she started her car, plugged in her charger, and once again tried to retrieve messages. There were none. She felt heat blowing from her vents right away that told her someone had either used her car or started it for her knowing she would be taking this short trip first thing in the morning. She didn't disappoint.

Like all the other times she tried to make contact, again she was unsuccessful. Driving back to the cabin, her mind was swirling. She realized she knew nothing deeply personal about his life and those he was connected to. Other than chef Alex and she didn't even know her last name.

Once back at the cabin, J'Nae walked around aimlessly with no specific purpose or direction, obviously distracted by Rick's unexplained absence. Rona, Vonne and Zsasha were all in the kitchen having coffee while deep in their thoughts about their friend. They struggled to find words of comfort to put her mind at ease but there just weren't any.

"I think I'm gonna pack up my things and head back home. Rona, can you ride back with Zsasha and Vonne or maybe leave with Ms. Honey? I'm sure one of them has room for you."

"I suppose we could work it out sweetie, but I don't think it's a good idea for you to leave out today." Rona said.

"She's right." Zsasha insisted. "If you want to leave, we'll all go. But we should wait until later to do so. Driving down these mountains is a different trip from driving up when it's snowing, and it's already started."

"No, you should stay. All of you should stay and enjoy yourselves. I just can't. I won't be able to relax until I hear from Rick and figure out what's going on."

"Girlfriend, we got you. We all came together, therefore we're all leaving together." Vonne inserted.

"Yeah, we ain't gonna leave you hanging no matter what." Rona reiterated.

"I'm sure Rick is fine and there's a simple explanation for why his ass ain't here, so I'm gonna give him a pass, this time, but anything not on point after this, I'm coming for that ass." Zsasha assured.

"I second that." Vonne said. "But for right now, we can't do much of anything until Simon and Lee get back from their hunting trip."

"Since we can't reach them on their cell phones I'll drive up to the main lodge." Rona offered. "I'm sure the staff can get in touch with their tour guides. They must have walkie talkies or some source of communication in case of emergency."

319

"While you do that, we'll start packing up. And be careful out there, it's snowing, and the roads can be very slippery." Zsasha conveyed.

Once Rona returned from the main cabin, everyone continued to follow Zsasha's lead, packing up their personal belongings as well as any remaining food and alcohol purchased for their trip. Two hours later, mostly everything was packed and by the door ready to be loaded up. They each had a small overnight bag they could grab in case they had to stay another night.

"Hey, y'all see what time it is?" Vonne asked.

"Never mind the time, are you paying attention to the snow that's been coming down steadily for the last few hours?" Rona inquired.

"Yeah, it's coming down pretty good out there." Zsasha confirmed. "Isn't it about time for Simon and Lee to be getting back?"

"According to the ranger, they should be back at the main cabin any time now. They're supposed to call us when they arrive, so we'll have a better idea when they'll walk through the door."

"Good, because girlfriend is falling apart over there." Vonne warned. "She's been pacing back and forth for over an hour now. We need to come up with something to distract her from all of this."

"Sweetheart, I believe we're way past that now. Aren't you worried about Rick?" Rona asked.

"Yes, I am." Vonne answered speaking in a low voice. "We all are."

Rona paused for a moment as if in deep thought.

"Zsasha, Vonne, come over here for a minute." Rona whispered signaling to follow her stepping further from J'Nae.

"What's up, Rona?" Zsasha asked.

"Look y'all, I wasn't being completely honest before."

"What are you talking about?" Vonne asked.

"The truth is I have received some emails and text messages since we've been here. They've been significantly delayed, and

I can't determine when they showed up, but they've made it through."

"Wow, I had no idea.   Simon and I have our phones completely shut off.   We haven't wanted to check emails or messages."

"Does she know you've been receiving communication?" Vonne asked.

"No, and we're not going to tell her, either."

"I agree." I think that's best for now. But maybe you should shut your phone and tablet completely off, so she doesn't hear or see anything come through on your devices. If you think it's bad now, just wait. Something like that would trigger a complete meltdown." Zsasha explained.

"You're right. I'll take care of it."

Rona didn't waste any time in putting action behind her words. The last thing J'Nae needed was to hear notifications coming through on her cell phone or tablet. As she made her way through the living room, she heard the guys come in through the front door of the cabin.

"Oh hey, you guys made it back." Rona acknowledged as Vonne and Zsasha greeted their husbands.

"Yeah, we did, but it was rough." Simon replied.

"I thought the tour guide was going to have you call us when you got to the main lodge?" Zsasha questioned.

"That was the plan sweetie, but the roads were getting worse by the minute, so we didn't want to waste the time."

"That makes sense." His wife agreed.

"Yeah, but the tour guide radioed the main lodge and spoke to the park ranger. He was supposed to come by in person and update you guys about the change of plans. They said he was in the area. Didn't he do that?"

"No, he didn't." Zsasha replied. "But it's all good. Y'all made it back safe and sound, that's all that matters."

"So what's with our luggage packed up by the door? We're not scheduled to leave for a couple more days." Lee asked.

"Sweetheart, J'Nae is dead set on leaving today. We were just waiting for you guys to return so we could head out. She's beside herself worried about Rick; we all are."

"I'm not surprised." Simon interrupted. "Unfortunately, the snowfall has caused some issues including an avalanche or two which has blocked travel on a few roads, specifically the one down the mountain leading to the main roads."

"Are you shitting me, Simon?"

"Nope, not at all Z. As of right now, nobody is going anywhere tonight, at least not until the roads are cleared and reopened."

"How long is that going to take?" Zsasha asked.

"I don't know for sure, but this sort of thing happens up here all the time so I would think they have things in place to deal with these issues." Simon stated. "But the way I see it, it could take several hours, maybe more, depending on the temperature and how much snow we get."

"Let's hope it clears up soon, I can't imagine how she'll handle being stuck up here much longer." Vonne noted.

"Well then I suppose y'all need to break the news to your girl." Lee determined. "And sooner rather than later."

"She's not going to be happy." Rona shared. "She's already having a hard time with all of this."

"I'm sorry to hear that." Lee added.

"Yeah, me too." Vonne agreed

Rona shook her head in disbelief at the unfortunate circumstances they found themselves in. Gearing up for what was ahead, she asked Simon and Lee to quietly go up to their rooms, change or do whatever but not to join them for at least twenty or thirty minutes or so allowing them time to talk to J'Nae about the situation. As they guys put their marching orders into action, Rona followed directly behind them and continued to her room to shut off her cell phone and tablet before rejoining the girls in the theater room two floors down.

When she entered the theater room, she noticed the girls were watching the comedy channel with some unknown comedian on the mike. She refilled her glass of wine, cut off the TV and sat down next to J'Nae and repeated the information

322

Simon and Lee shared moments ago. She fully expected J'Nae to have somewhat of a fit but surprisingly she didn't yell, scream, or fall apart. Calmly, J'Nae revealed she already had in her mind the weather would complicate her plans a bit but was hopeful it would work itself out.

"Can I get you anything, J'Nae?" Zsasha asked. "Something to eat maybe or a glass of wine?"

"I'm not hungry but a glass of pinot would be nice."

"You got it sweetie; I'll be right back." Zsasha assured.

"Don't get up." Vonne called out. "I got it; I'm getting a refill myself. What about you, Zsasha, can I top you off?"

"No, not right now, maybe later."

Vonne dispensed the wine refills then sat down rejoining her friends. With no one knowing quite what to say, a hush came over the room which made everyone feel more anxious and uncomfortable than before.

"I think I'll just finish this in my room and turn in. There's no point in sitting up all night. If we can't get out, he can't get in."

"Here, let me go with you so I can tuck you in." Zsasha offered.

"No, that's okay. I'd rather be alone right now."

"Are you sure?"

"Yes, I am. I'll be alright."

"Okay, but I'm going to check on you before I go to bed."

"We all are." Vonne asserted.

"I appreciate you guys, really I do. I can't imagine going through this without you."

"That'll never happen, J'Nae." Rona promised. "We will always be here for you, for each other, no matter what."

"Count on it." Vonne confirmed. "Now go on up to your room and get some rest."

"And I promise to wake you and let you know of any updates, okay girl? I'll make sure Simon checks in with the park ranger every couple of hours, don't worry."

"I love you guys."

"We love you too." Zsasha replied.

"Goodnight, y'all."

"Night J'Nae."

"Night sweetie."

Shortly after J'Nae retreated to her room, Simon and Lee came downstairs, entered the theater room, and joined the girls. Right away both men picked up on the intense vibe that hung over the room that under any other circumstance would cause them to tread lightly. In this instance, their desire to know J'Nae's state of mind was crucial. Simon was the first one to speak.

"How did she take the news, Z?"

"I'm not sure sweetie."

"What do you mean? Did she freak out or what?"

"No Simon, she didn't."

"I'm surprised. I was certain she would have lost it."

"If she didn't, that's a good thing, man." Lee commented. "What do you think, Vonne?"

"I'm with Zsasha. I don't know what to make of it just yet."

"Me either." Rona added. "What I find troubling is the fact that she didn't freak out."

"That's what I'm saying y'all, that's what I'm saying." Zsasha reiterated.

"Baby, that's your girl and you've known her longer than any of us."

"Right, I have, all the way back since college. And this just isn't like her under circumstances like this. She's always overreacting about shit. But let's face it, something is definitely up. He could've called the main number from anywhere and left a message at the main lodge. That's a landline phone they have up there and if we can use it to call out, then he could've used it to call in, so yeah, I'm worried, I'm worried for sure, no doubt, but she doesn't need to know that."

"You know what, I never even thought about it like that." Vonne said, sounding surprised.

"I didn't either, not until Rona revealed her secret; that some of her communications were coming through."

"Yeah, but J'Nae was going to the main lodge to call him once or twice a day. Why didn't she realize that, especially since she

324

was able to leave messages on his voicemail?" Vonne questioned.

"I don't know sweetie, probably for the same reason none of us did, we just thought he was late due to traffic or something or was close enough where he didn't have any reception and just wasn't getting her messages."

"It's all jacked up." Vonne determined.

"So, what's our next move?" Rona asked.

"It's late. Simon and I are going touch base with the park ranger, update y'all if necessary, then go to bed. Hopefully, we'll be able to pull out before noon."

"Let's hope." Rona replied.

The call to the ranger didn't reveal any new information so Zsasha and Simon headed upstairs to turn in. Being true to her word, she stopped by J'Nae's room and without going inside could clearly hear her snoring. Deciding there was no reason to wake her up she joined her husband who was already naked and in bed.

* * * * *

Late the next morning, J'Nae awakens to the smell of warm cinnamon buns and hot coffee on a tray being delivered by her girl Zsasha. Still feeling a bit groggy, she instinctively turned away from the intrusion as she felt the need to stay in bed and sleep. But a few seconds the fog cleared, and she was immediately reminded of the events leading up to that moment.

"Good morning love, did you sleep well?"

"Um, I slept hard and yes, I don't recall waking up at all last night. Thanks for the coffee, you can keep the cinnamon roll."

"You need to put something on your stomach. You'll feel better."

"So, what's going on with the weather? Are the roads clear for travel?"

"Well, it continued to snow all night long, but it was somewhat light."

"Does that mean we can head out?"

"I'm afraid not, at least not just yet. The ranger is aware of our need to leave asap, and he promised to let us know personally when we can head out. But for right now, we're still snowed in."

"I thought you said it was a light snow?"

"It was, but honey twelve or so hours of continuous snow, even light snow, is a hindrance in the mountains with these temperatures. There's nothing up here to melt it away."

"I guess. So what now, we just sit here?"

"Pretty much."

"Uhm."

"Well, we knew you'd want to try and call Rick again but for now there's no travel even to the main lodge. So we set it up with the reception to do a 3-way call whenever you're ready."

"That's sweet but it's not necessary."

"What do you mean? Am I missing something?"

J'Nae, sipping on her coffee, took her time to put her words together before she responded to her friend. She didn't want it to seem like she'd been keeping anything from her.

"J'Nae, what is it? You can tell me."

"Zsasha, the last two or three times I called him, I couldn't leave a message."

"Why not? Weren't you able to get through?"

"Yeah, I got through."

"So what happened? I don't understand."

"His voicemail was full, full of unanswered and undeleted messages."

"Okay, well sometimes that sort of thing happens. It happened to me a time or two. In fact, it was one of you heffa's that had to tell me about it. It's not like my phone is going to let me know."

"I know, but with everything else, I just have a bad feeling."

"Nonsense, we ain't fixing to focus on that. I'm sure there's a reasonable explanation for this. He was on his way to see his mother, right?"

"Yeah, he was, so?"

"Maybe he got caught up on some family stuff. You never know."

"Yeah but..."

"No buts. We're gonna go downstairs, get you some lunch--"

"Lunch?"

"Yes love, you missed breakfast. Didn't you get the hint?"

"Oh, no, not really."

"Well, get it in gear and come on down. Ms. Honey made something special just for you."

"Okay. Give me twenty minutes to shower and dress."

"Okay sweetie. See you in a bit."

J'Nae didn't get up right away. She remained in the same spot while mentally going over recent events and the conversation she'd just had with Zsasha. She did her best to keep her feelings in check but dreaded the thought of doing it all day long. Mentally, emotional, and physically consumed with worry, she knew her only escape was sleep.

Despite her mental exhaustion, she approached her friends who were all gathered around the table for lunch. Rona announced her arrival.

"Here she is. You're just in time for lunch."

"So, I see." J'Nae responded, taking a moment to look out the window. "Wow, it really did come down a bit overnight. I can see why we're delayed."

"Come sit here next to me." Vonne suggested. "Ms. Honey prepared something special for you, but we don't know exactly what it is."

"I do." J'Nae bragged. "I'd know that smell anywhere."

"Let us in on the secret." Rona insisted.

J'Nae took one look at Ms. Honey and knew she'd better not open her mouth. It wasn't the first time Ms. Honey prepared this dish and her recipe smells and tastes just like her mom's.

"I think not, but I'm confident you'll be pleasantly surprised."

"Whatever, can we eat now, I'm starving!"

"You, Rona, I can't remember the last time I saw you put away some food. This must be a first."

"Ah, yeah girlfriend, been sitting here working up an appetite waiting on your funky but to show up." Rona replied.

Zsasha burst out laughing like a fool. Everyone looked at her because she was obviously the only one in on the joke.

"What the hell is so funny?" Vonne asked.

"Choice of words, choice of words." Zsasha grinned.

"Huh?" J'Nae asked.

"Sista girl, I'm just gonna put it out there. I know for a fact your ass did not shower when you got up. You weren't up there long enough to throw no water anywhere but on your face!"

"Zsasha!" J'Nae exclaimed.

"Girl don't get mad at me. I didn't call you out, she did. She called you funky. Hell, I wasn't gonna say anything at all. But damn, maybe you bypassed that task one too many times these past few days."

"Y'all know y'all ass's foul, right?"

"Well apparently so are you!" Vonne teased.

Everybody laughed at J'Nae's expense while Ms. Honey was bringing the food to the table. J'Nae knew Zsasha was right, but she would never admit it.

"Um, smells so good." Lee remarked.

"It does, but what is this mystery meat you got going on over here, Ms. Honey?" Vonne asked. "I don't recognize this."

"It's pepper steak." J'Nae revealed. "It was my favorite dish growing up. Ms. Honey's recipe tastes just like my moms, and it's delicious!"

"Don't you feel special." Lee remarked.

"I do."

Ms. Honey delivered a few ice-cold bottles of beer to the table, along with a bottle of Moscato and a few non-alcoholic beverages."

"Hey where's the hard stuff, Ms. Honey?" Lee asked.

"No liquor, you never know when we'll get the okay to leave." she replied.

"Good looking out."

Lunch wrapped up around 2:00 and the blackmanitis set in. Lee and Simon retreated to the game room while the ladies got comfortable in the theater room. Rona played a random movie on Netflix while everyone reclined in their seats.

"Is this Roots? Girl, you know how long this movie is?" Zsasha asked.

"Yeah, it'll help pass the time."

"I suppose it would if we were conscious and aware of what time it was. Look around, both of them bitches are asleep."

"After that meal, can you blame them?"

"No, not really."

"Quit your bitchin and enjoy the flick."

"Seriously? This is Roots. Nobody gets any enjoyment out of this. We're all traumatized enough so can you turn to something else please? Nothing depressing, we got enough of that around us right now."

"Whatever, but no lovey-dovey crap."

"Okay fine, just find something else."

"How about the Wiz, with Stephanie Mills?"

"Yeah, okay whatever."

"Cool."

Chapter 30

After a two-day delay due to the weather, the roads were finally cleared for travel. The ride down the mountain was slow and steady as they carefully made their way. J'Nae, Rona and Zsasha were all passengers while Vonne drove J'Nae's car. Simon and Lee rode together.

J'Nae was more than anxious to get home or at least to a place with regular cell phone reception. Not having heard a word from Rick in all this time exceeded general concern and looked a whole lot like *wtf happened*.

Silence was the only sound heard during the long drive down the mountain. No one knew what to say to J'Nae or even what to think. But they were all in agreement about one thing and that was something just ain't right and they had good reason to be concerned.

"I just don't get it; I just can't make sense out of it." J'Nae blurted. "Something must be wrong. I should have heard something from him by now, even if the cell reception was poor. He still could have left a voice message on my phone, a text or an email. Something so I would know he's okay."

"Well, I wouldn't jump to any conclusions just yet. Since we weren't near any cell towers our phones also didn't update. So, any messages probably won't come through until we connect with one. That will allow our phones to update the time, date, news highlights, text messages and voicemails." Rona assured.

"Yeah, she's right, you'll see." Vonne confirmed. "Soon you'll have a hundred messages from him telling you he loves you. Then you'll feel stupid for worrying like you are."

"I agree." Rona reiterated. "Rick is a big boy and can take care of himself. He may be young, but he's a grown man. I'm sure he's fine."

"Yup. A full, grown man." Zsasha said smoothly. "A fine man. With all the things a full-grown fine ass man has."

"Girlfriend, is your ass drooling or what? And did you just cock your head to the side and let your eyes roll back in your head when you said that? That's her man all the way. You know she's got it bad for dude." Rona stated firmly.

"So, you caught that, huh?" Zsasha replied. "Oops. My mind just got away from me for a minute. Chalk it up to temporary insanity, my bad."

Zsasha tried hard not to let her true feelings show. The truth of the matter was she was more than worried about Rick. Giving J'Nae and Rick a hard time was just a ruse. Secretly, she quite liked the young man and thought he was just what her girl needed in her life. It had been way too long, and she is more than deserving of a good, strong viral man. And it doesn't hurt that he's younger.

The girls continued to reassure J'Nae that everything was fine and thanks again to another muscle relaxer with a red wine chaser she fell off to sleep. Time seemed to pass slowly, and the chatter was at a minimum. All were thinking the same thing and none of them wanted to voice their concerns out loud. Two and a half hours into their journey the silence was cut short by the ringing of Zsasha's phone.

"Oh, wow, we got service now. Hey baby, what's up?" Zsasha asked.

"Baby, it's not good and I need you not to react to what I'm about to say. Just act like everything is fine. Tell Vonne we are pulling off at the next exit to check one of the tires or something."

Zsasha did as she was instructed. J'Nae, reacting to the ringing cell phone, promptly reached for hers and dialed Rick's number. Again, it went straight to voicemail.

"So, you want to get off at the next exit and check it?" She responded.

"It's Rick, baby. He died. We don't know how it happened or when but he's dead. That's why he never made it to the cabin. He's dead and it's all over the radio."

Zsasha's heart sank for her girlfriend. This can't be happening, not to J'Nae... not again.

332

"Baby, keep it together. Pull off at this exit so you can tell her what's going on. And make sure you don't turn on the radio. I'm sure you don't want your girl to find out like that."

Zsasha hesitated for a moment, but instinct kicked in and she was right back on point.

"Damn, didn't y'all check the tires before we got on the road?"

"That's my girl."

"Whatever."

If the girls were paying attention, they would have noticed her comment ending the call lacked the fiery edge that was usually present when she was annoyed, especially with her husband. If they caught it, they didn't let on.

"Vonne girl, we need to pull off the next exit behind guys. They need to check the tire or something, okay?"

"Yeah, sure." Vonne replied. "They probably just need to put some air in it or something."

"Yeah, probably so."

With her last statement, Vonne glanced in her rearview mirror at Zsasha, having picked up on the tone of her voice. Rona, who was also seated in the backseat next to Zsasha watched her demeanor change as well. She felt more than a bit uneasy, but something told her to let it go, at least for now.

The guys pulled off the next exit and turned into the first place they saw which was a country store. They both exited the vehicle watching the ladies pull in directly behind them. Vonne cut the engine off taking the keys with her and immediately got out of the vehicle to join her husband who stood anxiously by the passenger side door in front of them.

"I thought you said they needed to put some air in one of the tires or something. Why are we parked over here away from the pump?" J'Nae asked, looking confused.

Neither of the ladies said anything. Zsasha took a deep breath peering out the passenger side window. She could tell from the look on Vonne's face that Lee and Simon had broken the news to her. And if she could tell, J'Nae could too.

"What's going on?" J'Nae asked again.

Rona grew concerned but remained still and silent as she looked toward Zsasha for answers. But she got none, not right away. Zsasha, who always had something to say, was truly at a loss for words. She knew she had to say something as her continued silence wasn't an option. She could stall no more. She needed to tell her girl what was going on and she needed to tell her now.

"Alright, y'all. What the hell is going on? Why ain't nobody saying anything?" J'Nae demanded.

Zsasha looked over at Rona in search of magical words of comfort. But Rona had no idea of the news Zsasha was about to share. She only knew it was serious. Very serious, but nothing more. Getting out of the back seat, Zsasha got in the driver's seat to be next to her friend. J'Nae looked over at her and knew it was not good.

"J'Nae, baby," Zsasha said, sighing and with hesitation.

"What? Talk to me. Say something."

"Sweetheart, it's Rick. He's gone."

"What do you mean, he's gone?"

"Rick is gone, sweetheart, he died."

"What are you talking about, he died. Where are you getting this from?"

"Simon and Lee heard it on the radio just a few miles back. Because he's a radio personality, it's pretty big news."

J'Nae let her head fall slightly and into Zsasha's arms. As she sighed and closed her eyes, you could see the tears begin to flow.

"I can't believe this is happening. I knew something was wrong when I didn't hear from him. What happened? Do you know what happened?

"No sweetie. We don't have any details as of yet. They just heard the news on the radio and didn't want you to find out that way. I'm so sorry sweetie."

Rona sat quietly taking it all in. She leaned forward putting her arm partially around J'Nae.

"Oh sweetie, I'm so sorry. I'm here for you."

"We're here for you. All of us are here for you."

"Whatever you need J'Nae, we're here."

J'Nae could hear everything Rona and Zsasha said but could not completely wrap her head around it. She was in denial and disbelief at the news her girl had shared with her. She turned to the satellite radio in hopes of hearing his voice. As if for some unforeseen reason he suddenly had to work and couldn't reach her. She was hoping it was a bad dream or a mistake. However, those thoughts were short-lived. Within the next few minutes of airtime, it was confirmed. Rick Moss was gone. Her lover was no more. She continued to cry and moan as if excruciating pain, which she was.

"Sweetie let's sit in the backseat. Rona can ride up front with Vonne. Come on, sweetie."

Zsasha and J'Nae got out of the front seats while Rona got out of the back. Vonne said a few words to the guys and rejoined the girls in the car.

"Honey, are you okay?" Vonne asked. "I'm so sorry for you. I know you cared for him very much."

"Can we just go? I need answers, answers I can't get sitting here listening to the radio."

"Yes, of course sweetheart. We can leave now."

There had been constant mention of Rick's passing all over the numerous stations in and around the Maryland, Virginia and DC area. Disk jockeys were sharing the personal memories and encounters with Rick and the condolences were coming in non-stop. DJs at his home station were thanking their listeners for the cards, flowers and prayers sent in for his family and friends. No specific information had been announced regarding his arrangements however his station did announce a weekend tribute to Rick Moss consisting of highlights from various blooper reels, celebrity clips and interviews of him with special guests on the show, all to be rebroadcast in remembrance of one of their own.

J'Nae continued to sit quietly while listening for any relevant information on the radio. She heard none. At least not much more than what she had already been told.

"When did this happen? Does anyone know when he passed?" She asked.

"I'm afraid not sweetie." Zsasha replied. "But I can make some calls and see what I can find out. Are you okay with that?"

"Please. I need to know what's what. It's not like any of his friends or family will reach out to me. I never met any of them and most likely, they don't know of my existence."

Rona, who sat quietly in the front passenger seat, sighed at the remark her friend just made. She was hurt and saddened for her friend and didn't really know how to help her. Zsasha, on the other hand, had a slew of associates and contacts. Some of which were people of power and influence and of course of considerable wealth. It took her less than ten minutes to gather most of the relevant information J'Nae was looking for.

"J'Nae, one of my contacts at the Chronicle said he was being laid to rest this afternoon."

"What! This afternoon! How can that be?"

"Calm down sweetie."

"I don't understand, Zsasha. Why so soon? How can this be happening today?"

"From what I was told, he died the same day we left while driving north on I695. He was probably on his way to see his mother at the time."

J'Nae broke down in tears again.

"I don't get it. Rick's a good driver. What did they say happened?"

"Sweetie, I don't have all the details, just that there was some sort of a low impact traffic incident on the interstate. That's all the information she had; that and he is being laid to rest in Parkville, Maryland."

"Parkville...that's not far from where his mother and stepfather live. It's a small town in northeast Maryland."

"Have you been there?" Vonne asked.

"No, I haven't. But we need to head there now."

"Of course, anything you need." Vonne replied. "Zsasha, can you call Simon and Lee and let them know where we're headed?"

"Already on it."

336

The girls drove the next few hours with little conversation. No one knew quite what to say in this situation and the radio didn't provide many more relevant updates. Following the information Zsasha's contact provided led the group to Moreland Memorial Park Cemetery.

It was after 3 o'clock when they arrived. The girls drove around the property looking for a gathering of what could be Rick's family laying him to rest but didn't find a group of people anywhere on site. Eventually Vonne stopped when she saw a casket next to a gravesite with two workers nearby. They all exited the vehicle just as it appeared the workers were just about to lower the casket in the grave. Rona and Vonne lead the charge while Zsasha hung back to support J'Nae. She was depleted and emotionally drained.

"Excuse me. We're looking for burial services for Rick Moss. Can you direct us to the burial site? He was to be laid to rest this afternoon."

"Yes." Vonne added. "It probably would have been a very large group of people. The deceased was a well-known radio personality, Rick Moss."

"Oh, oh yes." The undertaker uttered with a heavy accent. "His service ended about 30 minutes ago, right over there."

Vonne signaled to Zsasha and J'Nae to follow her over to the designated spot. J'Nae could barely walk by this time and placed most of her weight on her friend. The caretaker walked alongside Vonne to make sure they went to the right plot.

"Ma'am, your friend looks very upset."

"She is. He was her boyfriend, and no one called her about all of this. We just found out on the radio a few hours ago."

"I understand. Officially his services ended a while ago and everyone has left, but please take all the time you need to say goodbye to your friend."

"I thank you for that."

"No problem, ma'am."

Vonne met up with the girls as they made it to the casket which was still above ground.

"I can't see him?"

"J'Nae, honey, I'm so sorry. I wish there was something I could do."

Talking through her tears, J'Nae was able to mutter a few words as she knelt down and placed her hands on the casket.

"Why Lord? Why is this happening, again? Why? Why?"

Zsasha, taking charge of the situation, immediately knelt beside her.

"Sweetie, we don't know why God does what he does, and when he chooses to do it. Some things are out of our control and beyond our understanding."

"It just doesn't make any sense. We were just together a few days ago. He seemed fine, Zsasha, he seemed fine!" J'Nae screamed with passion as well as frustration in her voice. "What am I supposed to do now, Z?"

Zsasha embraced her firmly.

"It's gonna be okay, sweetie, it's just gonna take time."

Rona and Vonne had been silent up until this point but couldn't hold back any longer.

"Sweetheart, all you can do is take it one day at a time. And we're all here for you." Rona confirmed.

"Yes, we are all here for you baby, you're not alone. We'll go through this together. We're your girls and we got your back." Vonne assured.

"And we all know how you felt about him." Rona added. "As difficult- "

"No, you didn't. None of y'all knew how I felt about him. And he didn't either. He told me he loved me right before we left, and I hesitated. I more than hesitated. I dropped the ball. He died not knowing how I really felt about him, and I will never forgive myself for that!"

J'Nae continued to sob as she tightened her embrace with his casket. Shaking her head in disbelief she continued speaking her feelings.

"I love you, Rick. I do love you. I don't know why I flaked when you told me you loved me. I guess I was scared and afraid of what it meant for us."

Her pain, regret and sorrow were clearly overwhelming her as she reached upward and threw her arms and upper body onto the casket.

"I'm so sorry I didn't tell you when I had the chance. I'm so sorry baby."

Zsasha, who was now a few feet behind her, got up to move beside her friend.

"He knows sweetie. You have to trust and believe he knew what was in your heart."

"But why baby, why now? Why did you leave me?"

Zsasha again embraced her friend. She wanted so much to have the answers J'Nae was looking for but knew nothing she could say would ease her pain. Knowing her past, there was no doubt J'Nae had a tough road ahead of her, but it was a road she would not travel alone.

"Sweetheart, it was his time. He didn't want to leave you sweetie. It was just his time."

J'Nae continued to sob while her emotions soared and surrounded her mind, body and soul. She was flooded with memories of their last conversation, their last kiss, and the last time they made love. It all came crashing down on her and she was lost underneath a multitude of emotions.

"What am I supposed to do now?"

"Whatever you decide, J'Nae, we're right here for you." Vonne assured.

"No matter what you need, I got you." Zsasha said.

"We got you." Rona confirmed. "We're all here for you."

The girls continued with their kind words, warmth, and support as best they could. Zsasha was closer to J'Nae than Rona and Vonne had been and had known her the longest. But they are all very much aware of how devastating this could be for her since it wasn't the first time she's dealt with the loss of a man. They saw how losing Julian impacted her life and the number of years she shut down and closed the door to relations with men. And although she had been married to Julian for several years before he died, her relationship with Rick would still have a significant impact on her mentally and emotionally.

339

"I need him to know how I feel. I need him to know that I love him too."

"Baby, I'm sure your feelings for Rick were conveyed to him in everything that you did together. I'm sure he knows."

Continuing to sob, J'Nae could hardly speak through the tears.

"I wish I had told him how I feel. I wish I had said it back when he said it to me. Now I'll never get the chance to tell him just how much he meant to me."

"I know sweetheart. But you can't focus on that right now. Take this time, take some time to focus on and reflect on Rick and his own uniqueness, his kind heart and generosity. Believe it or not, it will help.

They all stood silently in support of J'Nae as she continued to cry softly. Shaking her head in denial, J'Nae's attempted to get up and stand with her friends. She was unsuccessful as she struggled to regain her composure. She instinctively dropped back down to her knees, not ready to let go of her lover.

"Rick baby, Rick. What happened boo. Why didn't you call me? I could have helped you. I could have been there for you. What about the promise you made that you would never leave me? What about that? What am I supposed to do now, Rick? What? What? Just tell me."

Feeling completely overwhelmed and exhausted, J'Nae collapsed completely to the ground, her sobbing was barely a whisper as she lay next to the casket that held the body of her lover. All the while keeping one hand on the casket.

"Zsasha, we need to get her." Simon said gently touching his wife on her shoulder. "We need to get her home. There's nothing more for her here."

Simon walked up to J'Nae, wrapped his arms around her and whispered in her ear it's time to go home. J'Nae remained incoherent as Lee and Simon scooped her up and carried her to the car. The others followed behind in silence. No one knew what else to say and soon after driving out of the cemetery they stopped trying.

The drive home was quiet and uneventful. J'Nae, fully exhausted, had cried herself to sleep.

Chapter 31

Several months later...

The private dinner invite from Magda and Milo was just what Ellie wanted and needed. She successfully convinced Magda to limit the guest list to only 3 couples, knowing Zsasha and Simon would be her first choice. And since they were all such good friends, it didn't look the least bit suspicious. What it would do, is give Adam the forum to get more intimately involved with Zsasha, as well as Ellie with Simon. They were all friends. But the magic of the evening was cultivated by the intentional late arrival Ellie and Adam planned, making sure to catch Zsasha and Simon by surprise.

Ellie, dressed in a midnight blue Oscar De La Renta dress with matching shoes, paused at the foot of the stairs to the main entrance of the mansion. Adam was just a few steps behind her, looking dashing in his Tom Ford tuxedo, courtesy of Ellie.

"Are you ready, darling?" she asked. "You know what you're supposed to do tonight, right? Are you up for the challenge?"

"I am. I'm more than looking forward to this." Adam confirmed.

"Well don't be too damn happy about it. Remember this is a job and part of a much bigger plan, got it?"

"I got it." Adam replied.

"Good."

"Incidentally, do you think Simon told Zsasha about running into you in New York?"

"Nope, not at all. If he had, Zsasha would have said something to me about it. And the fact that he's keeping secrets from her, just makes my job easier in the long run."

Adam extended his arm to Ellie.

"Well then, shall we?"

Ellie, glowing in all her splendor, replied "Yes, we shall."

As they entered the main sitting area while following behind the butler, Ellie could see Zsasha and Simon having cocktails with Magda and Milo. Zsasha looked marvelous in her solid black leopard print form fitting dress specially made to match the Tom Ford leopard-flock dinner jacket her husband was wearing. Neither of them was aware of the latest arrival.

"Magda, please pardon our late arrival, traffic was a nightmare." Ellie said.

"I'm sure it was unavoidable." Magda replied as she leaned in to exchange cheek to cheek kisses.

"You look splendid this evening." Ellie remarked. "And your home is divine!"

"Thank you, darling. It's been in our family for many years. Please, join us for a cocktail. Dinner will be served shortly."

"Absolutely, thank you." Turning her attention towards Zsasha. "Zsasha, you look ravishing this evening as well. I feel like I'm a bit underdressed."

Zsasha didn't look the least bit uneasy by Ellie and Adam's arrival. Instead, she seemed quite pleased and found it somewhat entertaining that her new young friends wanted to be in the company of people more than a few years older.

"Nonsense, you look lovely, both of you do. But I didn't know you were invited. We've spent time together recently, but you didn't mention it."

"I didn't? I was sure I had. It must have slipped my mind with everything going on, you know."

"Yes, I'm sure that was it." Zsasha replied.

Seconds later, two servers approached the group carrying fresh cocktails. Ellie reached for two glasses of champagne offering one to her friend.

"Zsasha, another for you?" Ellie asked.

"No, not now thank you, maybe after dinner. I must say you two are looking kind of cute tonight."

"Is that right? Well maybe later we can see where the cuteness leads us." Ellie replied.

"Come again?" Zsasha frowned. While she looked puzzled by Ellie's comment, her thoughts were interrupted by the butler announcing dinner was now being served in the main dining room.

It began with a clear fish broth with diced tomatoes and parsley, followed by a small mixed green Mediterranean salad. The main course featured pork tenderloin drizzled with a mushroom gravy, newt potatoes and freshly steamed asparagus. Although the meal was heavy, the conversation throughout dinner remained light.

"My dear Simon, are we still on target to finalize our building purchase as planned or have you encountered any additional delays?" Milo asked as the staff cleared the table.

"My dear friend, I would prefer not to discuss business at dinner or while in the presence of mixed company."

"My apologies my friend, we can discuss later." Milo added.

"Ladies, shall we retire to the parlor for dessert and coffee?" Magda suggested. "I'm sure the men will retreat to the cigar room."

"You can keep the desert, sweetheart I don't need it and coffee...girl act like you know me and what I like." Zsasha teased.

Before she could utter another word, one of the butlers was trailing right behind her with her signature cocktail.

"Now that's better, let's chat."

"Well I just want to say how nice of you and Milo to have us all over this evening, Magda." Ellie interrupted.

"It's been delightful." Magda replied. "We should do this more often, yeah?"

"Absolutely. I find pleasure in intimate settings such as this." Ellie confessed. "So, tell me, do your plans for this evening include a shared experience, one where we all come together, a bit more intimately?"

"I beg your pardon." Magda replied, just as her cell phone buzzed on the table next to her. Instinctively, she decided to seize the opportunity her buzzing phone provided her to avoid the upcoming conversation. Directing her attention to Zsasha, "Darling, I'm going to let you handle that. Excuse me for a moment."

Zsasha knew exactly why Magda chose to leave the conversation at that point, making it obvious she wanted her to

343

fill in the blanks. Even though this wasn't her house or her dinner party, she knew it was personal; about her, Simon and the club.

She had a pretty good feeling that Ellie had planned all this out but she wasn't sure of Magda's involvement, but she should be present either way. Nonetheless, Zsasha chose to address the situation she was thrust into. She and Ellie had become closer over the past several months and on some level filled the void J'Nae left in her life. She considered her a friend, young and a bit clingy, but nonetheless a friend.

"Did I say something wrong, Zsasha?"

"Well, it's not a matter of right or wrong but..."

"Well, what is it then? I've made it no secret what my interests are."

"Slow your roll, Ellie."

"So?"

"Look here little girl, I just don't think you are really ready for all this."

"I am...we are."

"Well for starters, there are rules to this lifestyle, different rules, depending on who you are and your involvement and most importantly, the nature of the primary relationship."

"I don't understand."

"I know you don't, that's the problem. See, from where you are, you see a bunch of fun-loving people getting together to have sex with one another, openly and freely, whenever you want and with whomever you want."

"Well yeah, something like that."

"Well, it's not that simple. For starters, as far as *Ahsasz Down Under*, an active member has to vouch for you just to put you in front of us for consideration. You can't just roll up on a sista and get in. There's a deep dive background check and investigation..."

"I know all of that and so do you. It's already been done."

"I know. But there are rules that have to be followed for the safety and privacy concerns of all members, not just you."

"I know about that too."

"Look, indulging in the lifestyle and joining *Ahsasz Down Under* are two very different and separate things. I know people that swing that don't know about the club or know and are not members, for any number of reasons. You just can't make assumptions because this one swings or that one goes both ways or that anyone in the lifestyle is open to discussing their business in mixed company. Did you and Magda discuss going down this path?"

"No."

"There you have it."

"My bad."

"And as far as the club, there's a lot more to it. You see, aside from the personal rules between the two parties in the primary relationship, there are other rules as well. For starters privacy is of the utmost importance. Our clientele consists of highly respected, well-established people from various professional backgrounds, some of which are in the public eye. General membership does not give you access to every member and or all things Ahsasz...it's more complicated than that. New members start with access level 1 and work their way up over time. This is necessary for existing members to remain anonymous and receive the privacy they pay very well for."

"I don't have any problems with that."

"However, you came here tonight with the illusion that the six of us would partake in sexual activity, didn't you?"

"Well, on some level, yeah, maybe."

"That'll never happen. You should know that as the owners and founders of *Ahsasz Down Under*, Simon and I do not engage in swinger activities with any of our members, past or present. It presents a serious conflict of interest."

"I was completely unaware."

"Yes, you were."

"It's just that I'm really surprised to hear that. I happen to know for a fact that you and Simon engage in swinger activity with Magda and Milo. It's no secret. And why are you talking to me like that, all uppity and whatnot. You don't sound like yourself."

"Well that's because this isn't a friend-to-friend conversation. This is about business, and this is how I discuss business. And furthermore, Magda and Milo aren't members of *Ahsasz Down Under*, they're investors. That's an entirely different relationship with its own set of rules and regulations, none of which I am going to discuss with you."

"I see, but are we okay?"

"Yeah, we're fine. But next time come to me one on one so you don't embarrass yourself like you did tonight."

"I will."

At that moment, Magda re-entered the room acting as if she hadn't heard the entire conversation between her new friend and her old one, but she had.

"Are you ladies ready for a nightcap?"

"Yes, I am sweetie, then I'm afraid I'll need to wrap up for the evening."

"I'm good, Magda, thank you." Ellie responded.

"Well what did you think I meant when I said 'nightcap'?"

"Oh damn, you're putting a sista out, huh?"

"I'm afraid Milo and I have other business to attend to this evening."

"Well thank you for having us over. You've been a delightful host."

"We'll have to do this again sometime soon."

With that, Zsasha finished her drink and she and Ellie met Simon and Adam in the foyer where they gathered their coats, said goodnight and headed home for the evening.

During the drive home, Zsasha mumbled a few words about Ellie under her breath just as Simon was calling Milo. He ended up being on the phone the entire drive home discussing details of the new club they were opening in New York City with Magda and Milo as investors. It wasn't until they were safely home and upstairs in their bedroom that the call ended, and Simon turned his attention back to his wife, picking up on the comment she made a short time ago.

"You know, I was pretty surprised with what you said about your girl on the way home." Simon remarked.

"Oh, so you heard me then?"

"Yes, I did, and I must say I didn't see that coming."

"Really?" Zsasha inquired. "I don't know why not. Wasn't it you that said you needed to keep your eye on her and that you thought she had an agenda?"

"Eye on her, yes, agenda, no, must have been one of the girls."

"You're right, Rona did say that."

"Yeah, but that was a long time ago. She's proven herself to be genuine and good natured. She definitely had your back and came through for you at the auction, remember?"

"Of course I do, but she's still trying to get us in the sack, mainly you. I told you she was sweet on you, or did you forget that?

"I must have. With everything that's been going on these past few months you've been preoccupied. I've been focused on the new venture and haven't thought much about her."

"What do you mean preoccupied? I'm on point. What exactly are you talking about, boo?"

"Zsasha please! You know you've been worried about J'Nae. And I know you well enough to know that your silence is not golden! And no, you have not been as involved with the planning aspects of the Masquerade Ball, not like usual. Thank goodness we have Ms. Honey and good help." Simon chuckled.

"You need to quit. I handle all my business, no matter what's going on around me. Otherwise, we wouldn't have all this! And just so you know, everything is taken care of. We are good to go!"

"True, true but you haven't been involved with the setup of the new club at all. and let us not forget your name is tied to it just like mine."

"I know that, but if you feel that way, why am I just hearing about this now?"

"Because I love you and I support you. And you don't have to tell me what's going on or if you need help for me to step in and take on more. This is a partnership, and I got your back."

"As you always have, and I've got yours too. I guess I just can't see where I've slipped up."

"It's all good, babe. It's just usually, you're much more involved than you've been lately. You're just distracted, you'll pull it together. And if you don't, I got you."

"Yeah, well we'll see." Zsasha snickered.

"What!"

"Boo, you know as well as I do, shit can get tricky."

"Babe, why do you do that? Why take it there, especially in light of our situation, one that's worked for us all these years. You know I love you."

"I know you do, and I love you too. I also know shit happens."

"Not here, not with us. The only shit happening here is the shit we want to happen. I can't even believe we're having this conversation, after all this time."

"Oh, so you can fuck with me, but I can't fuck with you?" Zsasha laughed. "You know it ain't going down like that."

Zsasha began to make her way towards her husband who was standing in front of the full-length mirrors along the right-side wall in his walk-in closet.

"What can I do now, boo, to help with the new club?" Zsasha asked as she turned toward her almost naked husband.

"Well, I could use your design skills to come up with a logo."

"I thought you outsourced that task."

"I did but I wasn't happy with anything they came up with. Do you think you might have some time over the next 2 or 3 weeks to come up with something...if you're up to it?"

"You must have forgotten who you're talking to. I'm always up for it...can't say that about you now can I." Zsasha giggled. "And by the way, Ellie and Adam will be joining us as our private guests at the ball. I think they need a bit of exposure to the lifestyle they seem so eager to become a part of."

"Well, okay, if that's what you want to do, I'm on board."

"But there's one catch..."

"What's that?"

"We've got to make it a bit more interesting for them, more so than with any ordinary client."

348

"I didn't think we had any of those, baby."

"You know what I'm talking about, boo. I just want to spice it up a bit...put temptation right in their face and see how they react."

"I don't know if that's a good idea. They're young and you've said a hundred times they ain't ready for this." Simon laughed.

"Maybe, maybe not. I just want to see where this goes. Like I said, she's sweet on you, and I want to see what she's up to."

"Trying to use me as bait, is that it?"

"Don't worry boo, we won't break any of our rules for newbies or otherwise, we'll just expand on them a bit, nothing serious."

"Alright fine, but the fallout is on you, all of it."

"I got this boo."

"Fine, now can we go to bed?"

"Yes, baby. Goodnight."

"Goodnight, Z."

Simon laid down on his side of the bed wondering how all of this was going to play out. After choosing not to divulge his recent yet random run-ins with Ellie during his last few trips to New York, add that to Zsasha's unexpected invite and game play, Simon suddenly became weary about his decision. How Ellie managed to be in New York, in the same general area and at the same time had to be a mere coincidence. No one knew about the New York business venture outside of the four partners so it couldn't have been planned. It had to be a happy coincidence. Making peace with his decision he saw no reason to add to her plate which was already full.

* * * * *

"Hey Zsasha!"

"Hey Ellie, how are you?"

"I'm good, I'm good. So glad you reached out to invite me to lunch today. I hesitated to call you after the dinner party. Felt as though we were a bit disconnected, and I wasn't quite sure where your head was at."

"My bad. I've had a lot going on lately, trying to get a handle on a few things. I should've hollered at you a bit sooner."

"No worries sista girl, I'm just sorry to hear that you've had some issues to deal with, but I must confess, I am a bit relieved that our disconnect wasn't a result of anything I said or did at dinner that night."

"Oh don't get it twisted little girl, you were all the way out of line, without a doubt. You and I already discussed what was appropriate and what wasn't and yet you still managed to go there."

"Oh, my goodness, I'm so embarrassed. I'm so sorry."

"Motha fucker please! Sorry...no you're not! Like so many others before you, you want what you want, and you thought you saw an opening to get it. You thought things might be a little different for you because of our relationship."

"I really didn't mean to cross the line with you. I respect our personal and professional relationship, Zsasha. Please accept my apology."

"I'll think about it, but it's not just me you need to apologize to. You were a guest of Magda and Milo's, not mine and you were in their home. That's who you should be reaching out to first and foremost, understand?"

"Yes, I do. I will make a point of taking care of that today."

"Cool.... Because real talk, we all know what's up."

"Huh?"

"Where you're coming from; why you said the things you said and acted the way you did. You forgot what I told you when we first met. I ain't new to this, I'm true to this. I've seen it all before and so have they. So quit acting like you ain't know what the hell you were doing."

Ellie was speechless, not prepared for Zsasha to call her out and be on point with it. Even though she knew Zsasha was spot on, for the most part, she had no intention of letting her know that no matter what. She pretended to be shocked by Zsasha and caught off guard, but the truth was this was the reaction she was counting on but kept that piece of information to herself.

"So, since you're so interested and intrigued by *Ahsasz Down Under*, consider yourself invited to this season's Masquerade Ball as our personal guests."

"Seriously?"

"Yes, and that invitation extends to Adam as well, but only Adam, no one else."

"Really! I don't know what to say, Zsasha."

"Don't seem so surprised. You went through the same personal examination as anyone else, Adam too. Aside from your obvious desire to sleep with my husband, isn't this exactly what you wanted?"

"Well, I wasn't sure if it was ever going to happen. It took a bit longer than I anticipated."

"That's true. Adam wasn't as easy to vet as you were, but it all worked out. Just know that you are solely and completely personally and financially responsible for him and all things pertaining to him. So plan to attend and be prepared for a night you'll never forget."

"I can hardly wait!"

"Good. I'm glad you're excited."

"Isn't the ball in a few days?"

"Yes, it is, and?"

"Ah, nothing, it's all good, we'll make it work."

"Of course you will, and you'll do good to remember what I said; we approved him through our VIP membership program which is based largely on you and your membership."

"I got it; I understand completely. Thank you Zsasha."

"Although he will be required to sign the same privacy agreements and such, in the event of a breach of any kind, you both will be liable and potentially open to be sued by other members if they are in any way damaged by your breach, or his."

"That's fine, I'm good with that. I trust him completely."

"There's a great deal of forms both of you need to sign, waivers and such, confidentiality agreements, dos and don'ts, you know, our standard code of conduct agreement, what's acceptable behavior and such, you get the idea, right?""

"Absolutely. We can take care of that first thing tomorrow." Ellie exclaimed.

"Actually, I have everything right here. You just need to have your signatures notarized and back to me before the ball. Let's check in with each other tomorrow and see what time works for both of us."

"No problem, I can make myself available whenever it's good for you."

"And the membership fee for Adam will need to be paid at that time also. It's the same amount you paid for yourself."

"I can write you a check right now."

"Let's just take care of everything at the same time. That will give each of you time to read over the details so you're fully aware of what you're signing, cool?"

"Yes, yes!"

"And also, sweetie, there's one more thing."

"Whatever it is, I'm cool with it."

"Good. And I'm sure you'll understand my request."

"Okay, what is it?"

"Because of the nature of my business I have private relationships with individuals attached to my business as well as my finances. With that said, I prefer no I require you to have your signatures notarized at Prestige Bank and Trust, the branch on Main Street. It's a privacy thing, you understand, right?"

"Consider it done. Anyone in particular I should ask for?"

"Actually, yes there is. Please ask for Delilah Sampson. She will take care of you from there. Just make sure both of you are present, have proper state identification with you and you must sign everything in her presence. She will give you two sets of copies of everything you sign, one for me and one for yourself. Then text me when you're done so we can set up a time to meet up."

"Thank you, Zsasha. I'm so excited for the opportunity to explore the lifestyle and in the environment you offer to do so. I feel safe and protected, we both do."

"I'm glad to hear that." Zsasha acknowledges. "We pride ourselves on safety, privacy and discretion."

"Good to know."

"However, since we're cutting it a bit close, I may or may not have time to take the two of you through the official orientation process, at least not before the ball."

"Orientation? I don't recall you mentioning that before. Is it going to impact our experience at the ball?"

"No, it won't impact your experience at the ball, but it might impact your expectations, especially if you don't read everything word for word before you sign. Like anything else, it's a process."

The look on Ellie's face was a mix of confusion, contemplation and uncertainty.

"Not to worry, everything will be fine. Worst case scenario, I'll take you through a modified version of it at the ball, in fact, let's plan for that." Zsasha assured.

"Truthfully, I thought I'd messed things up so badly at Magda's dinner party that I had blown any chance of ever getting in."

"Well, you came close, sista girl, but you've come through for me a time or two so. . . I reconsidered."

"I can't tell you how much I appreciate you doing that."

"Well I appreciate you too. And in case I hadn't mentioned it before, the Silent Charity Auction we held on your ship--"

"It's a yacht Zsasha, a yacht, not a ship."

"Whatever, that big ass boat of yours, it was a tremendous success! I've gotten so much positive feedback from the board that I don't know how I'm going to top that next year!"

"You can use it again, next year or anytime you want."

"I'm gonna remember you said that. But seriously, just think a bit about what you say around mixed company next time, whether you're with Magda and Milo or anyone you come in contact with through Ahsasz or *Ahsasz Down Under*. Everybody ain't as open about their lifestyle choices as you might think, and you don't want to be in violation of the privacy agreement. There's a pretty hefty financial penalty if you do and possibly legal ramifications. Safety, privacy and discretion, understand?"

"Yes, I do."

"Good, so tomorrow you and Adam are going to Prestige Bank and Trust and Trust to see Delilah Sampson and you'll check in with me when that's all done, right?"

"Absolutely, sounds great!" Ellie exclaimed.

"Good."

"We'll talk later."

"For sure sweetie, bye now."

"Bye Zsasha."

With that, Ellie left the restaurant noticeably excited. She was feeling very pleased with herself and her progress and couldn't wait to share the news with her partner in crime.

Chapter 32

Vonne was happy to sleep in a bit longer today so she could spend a little more time with the girls in preparation for the ball. She'd received a late-night invite via text message from Rona inviting them both over for afternoon tea which is code for day drinking which they liked to do in preparation for a night out. But since the ball was still a day away, today's 'tea' was just something to do since Rona had taken the day off. For Vonne, it was all the more reason to sleep in.

The preparation involved in opening a new store requires a time commitment that often clashes with her personal life or what would normally be considered her free time. But like any other aspect of her business, it's an investment. That concept kept her motivated time and time again. *Time yields money, she thought to herself, or is it money yields time?* Either one is true given the right circumstances and conditions coupled with one's perspective of course, and Vonne being the woman she is planned to benefit either way.

Now feeling well rested, she began to reconsider the late-night invitation. It would be nice to meet up at Rona's house, a place they rarely visit. But she only intended to take a few extra hours off in the morning before jumping back into her daily routine. She decided to check her calendar to see if she could squeeze out a bit more time for herself so she could hang with the girls for a bit.

Walking through the formal living room to the office, Vonne noticed her husband's cell phone on the desk next to his ninja container filled with contents that appeared to have been sitting for at least an hour or two. It looked as if he hadn't touched it at all. It wasn't like Lee to leave his one and only daily attempt at clean and healthy living untouched and at room temperature. Yuck. He wasn't religious about much, but he was religious about juicing. Every morning, he started his day juicing and maybe a run despite the fact that everything he put in his body, thereafter, totally counteracted any benefit juicing might have provided.

Figuring he'd just stepped away; she ignored his wastefulness and began to flip through a stack of files so she could see what she might be able to put off for a while. That's when she heard his cell phone ping. She saw his phone on the desk when she first walked in, yet it didn't register right away. She was focused and, on a mission, to see how much work she could put off until later, so she didn't pay it any attention until it pinged for a second time.

Glancing down at the phone she could see a notification across the screen. It was a text message. She froze immediately, recognizing the sender's name and number that appeared across the screen. It was all too familiar and at the moment, confusing. It was Kiera's name and number on the phone followed by the start of the message. Wondering why her sister was texting her husband she didn't hesitate to open the message. The message read: *Did you find the store keys??? Where are you? Vonne's gonna kill me if I don't open up on time…*

Instinctively Vonne relaxed a bit, feeling regretful for her temporary lapse in judgement that allowed her mind to become suspicious of her husband and her sister. Lee was a lot of things but even he knew better than that. But as her thumb touched the screen again, it opened up to the home screen and like any curiously suspicious wife she never once considered putting it down. Before she realized what her fingers were doing, she had accessed the messaging function, narrowing in on her sister's message and her message thread. What she saw was overwhelming to say the least. She read one message after the other noting dates and times. It didn't take a full 5 minutes before she was able to get a good feel of the content and context of the shared messages between her husband and her sister. With phone in hand, she left the house.

* * * * *

"Hey, you two, sorry I'm late. I had some issues come up and I lost track of time." Vonne announced as Rona escorted her into the formal living area. "Y'all know how it is."

With that statement, Rona and Vonne casually looked over at Zsasha, neither of them made any attempt to hide their mutual and obvious reference directed at her.

"At some point you heffa's got to get over all that. Sometimes people just make mistakes, double book or just forget to put shit on their calendar."

"Whatever girlfriend." Vonne replied. "And can a sista get a glass of wine? I've had a rough start today."

"Had yo ass been on time, you would've had a glass waiting for you." Zsasha teased.

Rona shook her head and sighed while Vonne retrieved a wine glass for herself.

"I didn't think you were coming so I put it away."

"Like I said, a rough start to my day and Zsasha, the only reason why we're at Rona's house is because you're still getting the gallery together for the ball so cut it out." Vonne stated firmly.

"You're in a mood. What's going on girlfriend?" Rona asked. "Are you that busy at work these days?"

"Y'all ain't gonna believe this shit!"

Neither Rona nor Zsasha had any doubt Vonne had another issue with Kiera. It was becoming sort of a routine thing.

"Somebody want to tell me why my husband and my sister have been texting each other back and forth?"

"Texting, what's the big deal?" Rona asked. "All of you live in the same house and pretty much work together right, so what's the problem?"

"The problem is that most of the messages have nothing to do with work." Vonne replied.

"So, what exactly are you saying, sista girl?" Zsasha asked.

"OMG! I can't even get my thoughts together enough to verbalize what I read."

"Well damn, is it that bad?" Rona asked.

"Little girl, you know I don't want to say it, but I'm gonna say the shit anyway. I told you about having another bitch move in your house being around your man. Sista or no sista, some bitches are fucked up like that."

357

"Yeah, you warned me, and I chose not to listen."

"True dat, but don't beat yourself up about it. You genuinely wanted to trust her and help her out. We all get that, girlfriend." Zsasha responded.

"But tell us what happened. What's the nature of the messages?" Rona inquired.

Vonne reached in her pocket and retrieved Lee's cell phone and slammed it down on the table in front of her.

"Here, see for yourself!"

Zsasha picked up the phone without hesitation, anxious to read what the two had been up to.

"So, Vonne, what are you prepared to do about this situation?" Rona asked.

"Ask her." Vonne replied, pointing towards Zsasha who continued to scroll through the phone. "Zsasha, what do you think?"

"I think the bitch needs her ass beat, that's what I think."

"For real girl, it's like that?" Rona asked.

"Hell Yeah. All this texting and flirting is way across the line."

"Zsasha, let me see the phone." Rona insisted.

Rona took her time reading through the text messages including the date and time they were sent. Some of them were directly related to work and work issues but others were not. She noticed a few other details that Vonne and Zsasha may have overlooked.

"I don't know Vonne, what I see here is very one sided."

"How so?" Vonne asked.

"Well, if you look at the time and date, you can determine that Kiera initiated just about every conversation. She was definitely the one flirting and I don't see anything inappropriate with Lee's replies and I can't see where he just all of a sudden reached out to her either."

"So, you think I'm overreacting?"

"I didn't say that. I would have a talk with Kiera, for sure."

"You mean another talk." Zsasha snickered.

"Maybe, yeah, but I just don't see where Lee did anything wrong. You all live in the same house and she's working in your stores plus he helps out every now and then, so he was probably just being polite, that's what I think."

"I guess it's possible." Zsasha reconsidered. "But you still need to deal with ol'girl. She's out of line."

"That's old news." Rona reflected.

"So, for now, it is what it is." Vonne acknowledged. "Anyway, who picked this wine?"

"J'Nae did, awhile back." Zsasha replied. "It's one of her new faves. I believe it was something Rick introduced her to."

"Speaking of J'Nae, have either one of y'all heard anything from her lately?" Vonne asked. "She's been visiting her daughter for quite a while now."

Rona was the first to respond.

"She sent out a group email a while back. That's the last communication I received."

"Same here. I ain't heard nothing from that heffa. She didn't even acknowledge our 49th birthday and we've been celebrating our birthdays together for years."

"Awe, you're missing our girl?" Vonne observed.

"Well I'm certain she won't forget about the next one, the big 5-0. Didn't you guys send out your *Save The Date* notices like ten years ago or something." Rona jokes.

"Whatever bitch, and it wasn't ten years ago, it was like two."

"Sounds to me like you're in your feelings, Zsasha."

Zsasha was hurt by J'Nae's absence and lack of communication but had no intention of letting it be known. No matter what was going on in the sista circle, Zsasha had to be Zsasha; never showing weakness or emotion. It was what everyone expected and relied on. It was always her job to show strength and courage and most importantly downplay situations that would cause the others to overreact.

"She's probably just enjoying time with her daughter and grandkids." Rona added. "But I am a bit concerned with everything that happened and all the time that's passed, it's a bit much. She could reach out to one of us, so we'll know she's alright."

"I agree." Zsasha stated. "Even though she's with family she could holla at a bitch, but real talk, I'm sure she's fine. Aiden or Taizja would have reached out to one of us by now if there was a real problem."

At that moment, Zsasha's phone began to ring. It was Simon calling from the landline at the gallery.

'Hey sweetie, what's up?"

"Not too much, I was just wondering if you had some time today to meet up at the gallery. Magda and Milo want to see the final details we put in place for the masquerade ball beforehand and I thought it'd be a good idea for us to walk them through it together."

"They're sure taking this partnership seriously aren't they." Zsasha jokes. "Do they realize what a silent partnership is? We should've known they weren't going to be quiet for long."

"True, true, they're probably just happy to have something to do other than sail through life on family money."

"Maybe, maybe not, but do you want to meet at the gallery or at the house? You see, if we meet at the gallery and go over details, we'll have to do a show and tell, live and in living color."

"Oh so what, you worried about them wanting to get their freak on?"

"Oh no, not that. It's just that if you want them to continue to be all up in everything, then let's meet at the gallery, otherwise put a little distance between them and anything to do with Ahsasz, up or down. They're only partners in the new venture, not everything else."

"Okay then. I'll text you shortly and let you know what's up. Love you baby."

"Love you too, boo."

"Bye."

"So what's all that about? Ellie getting a bit too involved in your business?" Vonne suggested.

"No, it's not that. In fact, it's nothing to do with her. We're cool and all but we ain't like that."

"Oh okay. So what's up?" Vonne asked.

"Well, right now, outside of me and Simon and you bitches, Magda and Milo are the only ones that know anything about the new business venture and that's only because they partnered with us."

"Does this have anything to do with the new club you guys are setting up in New York?" Rona asked.

"How did you know about that?" Zsasha frowned.

"I didn't really, I just guessed." Rona announced.

"Girl, I can't believe you!" Zsasha declared. "That information is not public."

"I get it, it's just that Simon has taken a few business trips to New York over the last few months, and I know y'all don't have anything going on there, so I just put two and two together."

"Wow. I don't know what to say." Zsasha confessed.

"I just figured it's either old business or new business and there's no old business in New York."

"True, but you have to keep this information to yourself. You can't tell anyone at all Rona, or you either Vonne, you can't even tell your husband. I mean it. Until everything is finalized and official, not a word about it."

"Of course." Vonne confirmed.

"Sure, *we* won't say anything but what about your girl, Ellie? If I could figure out what's going on, she probably can too."

"You think?"

"Absolutely, especially because she's all up in your gallery business. I'm sure she's just as aware of Simon's recent trips as we all are. And isn't she friends with Magda and Milo? As I recall, they were a bit more vocal and transparent than you and Simon. At least that was my impression of them initially."

"That was a long time ago and they know better now. We kind of cut 'em loose for several years for that reason."

"Wasn't that around the time you guys first opened the art gallery?" Vonne asked.

"Yeah, around that time they were a bit too open for our taste, so we just needed to ease them out of our inner circle. Business is business and bullshit is bullshit. Y'all know how we do." Zsasha stated.

361

"I always thought there was a little more to it than that." Vonne revealed. "I thought maybe she was crushin on you a bit."

"Who, Magda?"

"Yeah, her."

"Maybe a little, I don't really remember, it was a long time ago." Zsasha said. "But it's all good now. We're friends and now business partners, that's it and that's all."

"Cool, cool." Vonne replied as she watched Zsasha stand up and slide her clutch under her arm.

"What's up, are you heading out?" Rona inquired.

"Yeah, I've got to meet up with--"

"We heard already!" Vonne exclaimed. "You don't have to tell us again."

"No, I don't, but I will tell you this, up close and personal, that information I shared better stay within our sista circle, got it?"

"We got it girl, *now bye.*"

Both the girls could hear the sassiness in Vonne's voice. Rona was eager to cut in before Zsasha had a chance to even think about taking it to another level.

"Come on Zsasha." Rona instructed. "Let me walk you out."

"Okay, cool." Zsasha agreed as she followed Rona to the front door. "Listen, I know whitegirl has a lot on her mind these days, but she better not forget what I said. I'm serious, Rona. That can't get out right now."

"Zsasha, I doubt she's even thinking about your business ventures right now. Did you forget she's opening a new boutique plus all the family drama in her household? She ain't got time to be thinking about you and yours."

"I hope that's the case."

"Real talk, you're worried about the wrong one."

"What do you mean?"

"I mean Ellie. That girl has finagled her way all up in your life and in your business too. You know I don't trust her, and I've told you before I think she has an agenda."

"I don't know what it could be." Zsasha replied. "Even Simon ain't concerned about her anymore and he wasn't feeling her from day one."

"All I'm saying is just be careful. Most times people won't see a snake in the grass until it bites."

"I feel you girl, trust me, I ain't sleeping on her or anybody else. I got this."

"Alright, but don't say I didn't warn you."

"Now you're tripping Rona, really. I gotta go. You two are still coming to the ball, right?".

"Wouldn't miss it."

"Alrighty then, I'll see you then."

"Bye and drive safely."

Rona returned to her lingering guest in the sitting room. You could tell Vonne had a lot on her mind but choose not to open up about it for whatever reason. She said her goodbyes and headed out shortly after Zsasha.

While Zsasha drove toward the interstate, she took a quick peek at her phone and saw there weren't any missed calls or messages from Simon. Not knowing exactly where they were to meet, she decided to call him instead of getting on the interstate and heading in the wrong direction. Her call went straight to voicemail meaning he was probably on the phone.

"I know what I said, and I meant every word of it, but we have to do things a certain way, there's a lot at stake. This affects more than just me and you. People we love could get hurt."

"I know Si, but you gave me your word. You promised we wouldn't have to stay completely in the shadows, that you would have a place for us to be us."

"I will and you know I'm working on it. But I can only spend so much time in New York without creating suspicion. Zsasha is a very smart woman."

"You think? Because you'd figure by now, she'd know about you; that she'd know about us. Living this way, pretending day in and day out after all these years is driving me crazy. I don't know how much longer I can do this."

363

"Hold tight baby, it won't be long, I promise. Trust me, it will all be worth it in the end. But right now, I gotta go. She just called and it went to voicemail. We're supposed to be meeting up right about now, so I'll have to call you later."

"I love you Si."

"I love you too."

Simon took a moment to gather himself and refocus his mind before calling his wife back. He didn't want the anxiety he was feeling from being pressured to do what he wanted to do, what he needed to do to impact his disposition while talking to his wife. Before he had a chance to reach out to her, she was calling him back.

"Hey boo, what happened? I thought you were gonna text me back and let me know where to meet you guys?"

"My bad, baby. Something was going on with Magda, so Milo called to cancel, and we ended up discussing everything on the phone."

"Well that worked out even better. So where are you right now?"

"About fifteen minutes from the house, what about you?"

"Just leaving Rona's."

"Are you coming straight home?"

"Hmm, probably not. I need to try and meet up with Ellie right quick and make sure all the paperwork is signed. I just texted her to meet me at the gallery. I promise it won't take long."

"Sweetheart, she's always available for you and it will take as much time as you need and allow her to have. You know what it is."

"I do?"

"Looks to me like it's the Magda situation all over again. She's definitely sweet on you."

"You think, because the way I see it, she's sweet on yo ass!"

"Nah, that ain't it baby, that ain't it at all. But in any event, call or text me when you're heading home. And don't be out too late, we both need to rest up before the ball. You know how exhausting it can be for us, sometimes." Simon snickered.

"Not this time, boo. This time it's strictly business, entirely by the book. And did you forget the girls will be there?"

"No, I didn't, but they don't have pass keys, do they?"

"Only Rona but she's mostly an observer. I doubt Vonne or J'Nae will ever hold pass keys. They ain't about that life."

"Hmm." Simon contemplated his wife's words.

"Even though they know what it is, they ain't ready for all that."

"Alright then, it looks like you've got everything under control, so if you're not worried, I'm not worried."

"I got it. Now I've got to go. I'll text you and let you know what's up and when I'm heading home."

"Okay baby. See you soon."

"Bye boo."

Zsasha ended her phone call with Simon just as she arrived at the gallery. She could see Ellie had already arrived and was waiting patiently at the front entrance. Zsasha exited her car and greeted her new friend while unlocking the door to the gallery, allowing them to enter.

"Thanks for coming out to meet up with me really quick. I know it's getting late."

"Not a problem. I'm surprised you have any free time right before the ball. Shouldn't you be preoccupied tying up loose ends?"

"No, not really. Our masquerade ball is a yearly event which we've held many times now and also one we host mid-season."

"I see. So, are you excited?"

"Well that's one of the things I wanted to ask you, it being your first time and all."

"I'm over the moon and Adam is too! We still can't believe you invited us."

"Isn't this what you both wanted? You asked, you applied, and you signed up. You'll get the same privileges as anyone else just joining. Did you bring everything with you?"

"Yes, I have it all here."

"Wonderful. Did you have any questions about anything covered in your packet?"

365

"No, not at all. Everything was pretty well defined and easy to understand."

"Well then, I guess I'll see the two of you at the ball."

"Count on it. Good night Zsasha."

"Good night."

Zsasha took a quick moment to glance over the contracts and the check before locking them in her office. It was her intention to head home and get a good night's sleep so she could be on point and look ravishing as the queen of the ball.

Chapter 33

Pulling slightly past the valet area the young couple exited the vehicle leaving their personal driver behind. Walking hand in hand towards the main entrance to Ahsasz, excitement began to build for young Ellie and Adam as the temptation of the unknown and unexpected grew as they approached. At the door they gave their individual names as well as the verbal passcode Zsasha had given them for entry.

"Well darling, are you ready?" Ellie asked. "Are you really ready?"

"I am, love. Let's do this." Adam replied.

The two of them walked through the main entrance making sure to stay within the velvet rope walkway leading to the focus point in the center of the gallery.

"Oh wow!" Ellie remarked. "They certainly rearranged things, wouldn't you say?"

"You would know better than me, sweetheart. You spend a lot more time here than I do."

"You're right, but that's about to change, isn't it?"

"Yes, it is."

The two shared a smile standing just a short distance from where the velvet ropes ended and remained motionless while taking it all in. The focus point in the center of the gallery were two large bronze statues consisting of a man and a woman sitting on the ground with their legs folded underneath them both facing away from one another. There was a large heart mounted and supported on their backs representing love equally shared between a man and a woman. Looking around the gallery, they could see various statues and sculptures, some of a sexual nature and others just various shapes. They encountered two professionally dressed staff members, one male and the other female, both of which were heading in their direction, and both appeared anxious to greet them.

"Good evening, Madame Ellie, Sir Adam. I am Gerome and this is Eve."

Both Ellie and Adam nodded in acknowledgement not knowing what else to say.

"As distinguished guests we would like to extend to you our personal services for the duration of your stay this evening."

"Thank you. We accept your gracious offer of hospitality and are excited to allow you to guide our endeavors."

While the look on Adam's face did not match up with Ellies remarks, he thought it best to follow her lead as this was her show.

"Please allow me to place a bracelet on each of you. If for any reason you require assistance, have questions of any kind, or would like a guided tour, simply place your thumb over the emblem on your bracelet and gently press down, until you feel a slight tingle or vibration."

"Wonderful." Ellie remarked.

"And you'll be able to find us no matter where we are?" Adam asked.

"We'll be able to find whichever one of you signaled for us. It's very possible that you two may not be together the entire evening. Our job is to make sure that you have everything you need for the most optimum experience here at Ahsasz."

"Excellent. Thank you both so much."

"It's our pleasure. Take some time to walk around and enjoy!"

Doing what they were told, Ellie and Adam walked around what was once the gallery floor. In addition to the sculptures and statues placed throughout the gallery there were also movable walls creating enclaves, some with and some without leather seating. Although there weren't any doors to the enclaves, they were positioned in such a way to provide the allure of privacy.

There were still several paintings creatively displayed throughout the gallery but with a great deal less than normal. They were both amazed at the transformation that had taken place, so much so they didn't notice Zsasha approaching until they were face to face with each other.

"Ellie, Adam, so glad you both could make it. You look stunning Ellie."

"Thank you, Zsasha. I must say, the changes you've made, the layout...unbelievable. It doesn't look like the same place, at all."

"Well that's the point. So, you've already met with Gerome and Eve, is that right?"

"Yes, we have. They were delightful, very personable."

"The best of the best." Zsasha added. "You're in good hands."

"That's lovely, however I assumed we'd be in your hands, yours and um Simons, as your guests, of course."

"Relax girlfriend. Right now, you're free to mingle and have a few drinks. We'll come get you later. In the meantime, if you need anything just reach out to Gerome or Eve and wear your Masque, it adds to the mystery and intrigue of the ball."

"Of course." Adam replied. "Again, thank you for the invite."

"Don't mention it."

Ellie and Adam watched Zsasha as she walked away towards a small crowd gathering near an enclave towards the rear of the gallery. Even with their Masques on she recognized Rona and Vonne with whom she assumed were their partners.

"Hey Vonne, hey Rona...wasn't sure if you guys were gonna make it. You're just getting here, right?"

"Yes, Zsasha and it's entirely my fault." Vonne confessed. "I would have been on time if not for my sister and her shenanigans."

"I'm not the least bit surprised." Zsasha revealed. "I told you to get that heffa out of your house."

"Yes, you did Zsasha."

"What was it about this time?"

"Oh, she was methodical about it, slow and steady."

"Really? You make it sound so clandestine." Rona disclosed.

"It kind of was. She started off moaning and groaning about us not spending time together outside of work."

"Seriously?"

"Yes ma'am. She said our relationship would never improve unless we started spending time together and getting to know one another as mature adults, that we needed to let go of the past and focus on moving forward."

"That doesn't sound like Kiera."

"No, it doesn't. But it sounds a lot like something Lee would say, especially to her."

"You need to talk to your husband."

"Yes, I do, and I will, but she took it a bit further."

"How so?" Zsasha asked.

"Can you believe she wanted an invite?"

The look on Zsasha's face changes drastically.

"An invite to what?"

"Your masquerade ball, of course."

"Fuck outta here!"

"Really, I couldn't believe it myself."

"How did she even know about it?" Rona asked.

"It's not a secret, not the ball anyway."

"I guess not. So that was her issue tonight, huh? That's why y'all were late?" Rona asked.

"For the most part, yeah. I'm just thankful Lee was upstairs getting dressed when all that was going on. Otherwise, it probably would have blown up into a big thing...another big thing."

"Well look, regardless of the issues your sister has created, she ain't here right now. And from where I'm standing, Lee has been sitting over there with a drink in his hand acting like he's sulking for a minute now, so baby girl, get over there and get your man. Did you forget where you're at?" Zsasha asked.

"What? Huh?" Vonne asked.

"You obviously got over the issue with the texting so go for it. It doesn't matter where or how he works up an appetite just as long as he comes home to eat. You feel me?"

"Actually, I do, sista girl and I'm horny as hell too! Good looking out Z, good looking out."

"I got you girl. Even though I give you a hard time, I love you and I have a special treat for you and your husband. In a few minutes, Gerome will be giving you guys a special pass key along with some instructions. Trust me girlfriend, just go with it."

"Oh! Okay, cool." Vonne replied, completely redirecting her focus. "I got this."

"I know you do, sweetie, I know you do."

Both Rona and Zsasha watched as Vonne joined her husband in his temporary hideout with Gerome trailing at her heels. Once there, he presented a bottle of champagne and a pair of flutes on a crystal serving tray which he set down on the table in front of them. After pouring each of them a drink, he placed a metallic like card on the table in front of them, purposely pushing it closer to Vonne then placed a bracelet on each of their left wrists.

"This card will grant you access to our Peek-A-Boo Hideaway. If and when you are ready to use it simply activate your bracelet. One of us will escort you."

Vonne and Lee looked both stunned yet excited at the prospect. Gerome hadn't made it ten feet in the opposite direction before Vonne activated her bracelet. Gerome smiled looking over his shoulder and quickly made an about face.

As always, Zsasha and Simon consistently made their way throughout the gallery keeping a watchful eye on everyone and everything and checking in with their invited guests. Over the past hour or so, they'd noticed several members discreetly making their way towards the rear of the gallery which provided secure passage to *Ahsasz Down Under*. Because the nature of their business was so very private, Zsasha and Simon made it a point to connect and interact with the newbies no less than three times during the course of the ball so that the declining crowd wouldn't arouse suspicion. If you didn't know any better, you would assume those heading to the rear of the gallery were heading outside to the parking garage.

While Gerome was the first to respond to Vonne's 9-1-1 request, Eve showed up right behind him. He abruptly took command of the situation and directed Eve's attention towards

371

Rona and her date. It was at Zsasha's request simply because she knew the last thing Lee needed was another beautiful and sexy woman leading him anywhere. Those two have enough problems.

On the other hand, Ellie had her head in the game and was nowhere near as caught up as Vonne or Adam whose mind was completely preoccupied with the unlimited possibilities surrounding him. She knew she had to stay on point, and she knew she had to snap Adam back to reality and it didn't take her long to do so.

Moments later Zsasha and Simon joined the two just as they were quietly discussing their options.

"Hey, so what do you guys think? Are you having a good time?"

"Absolutely." Adam replied. She could almost see his mouth watering.

"It's a unique experience. I'm looking forward to opening more doors and embracing a more in-depth exploration."

"That's why we're here. Simon and I will be your guides. Shall we?"

Simon and Zsasha led the way towards the rear of the gallery where the private elevator is located.

"I had no idea." Ellie remarked.

"You weren't supposed to." Simon declared.

"So, this is how we'll enter *Ahsasz Down Under*?"

"Sometimes, but not always. We'll explain all of that once you have full access. Right now, you're considered newbies and have a probationary period. Did you read the paperwork?"

"Yes, I did. I'm aware."

"Good."

The elevator doors opened to a dimly lit area with the sweet scent of white strawberries and mint. A slight smoky mist filled the air as Simon and Zsasha led the way. Less than a minute later they were greeted with a familiar face. It was Ms. Honey, immaculately dressed for the event. Her attire was provocative yet sexy in a subtle way while age appropriate.

"Welcome Ellie, Adam. Allow me to introduce you to *Ahsasz Down Under*. I'm here to answer any questions you may have; however, my main goal is to provide you with a memorable and fascinating experience."

"This is amazing." Ellie announced. "I've never seen anything like this."

"Before we proceed, I'll need to exchange your bracelets."

"Alright." Ellie replied as she and Adam replaced their bracelets with the ones Ms. Honey held in her hands.

"Right this way."

As expected, Ellie and Adam took the lead. Just a few feet away, they were exposed to a large area also dimly lit with targeting lighting in a few select areas. One of which appeared to be a bar that went from one end of the room all the way down to the other. But it wasn't like a typical bar. It had no seating. Among the highlighted areas were a couple of cages all of which were occupied by one or two individuals engaging in erotic dancing. Throughout the room most individuals were wearing masks and a costume of some sort making it almost impossible to distinguish members from staff unless you were already familiar with the environment.

"Since this is the annual Masquerade Ball, this area is restricted from explicit activity and is utilized for general gathering. The specific themed rooms which vary from time to time will house all activities requiring physical contact."

"It's a lot to take in."

"Yes, it is." Ms. Honey confirmed. "Why don't I get us some drinks. What would the two of you like?"

"Champagne." Ellie replied.

"Scotch on the rocks, for me."

With that, Ms. Honey disappeared to fill their drink order. Ellie and Adam were so elated with their newfound surroundings; so much so they were completely unaware of the intense conversation going on behind them between Zsasha and Simon. Moments later Zsasha turned towards the two and excused herself for a moment explaining she had a bit of unexpected business to attend to.

373

"I'm placing you in Simon's hand. Ms. Honey will also be here to assist you. I'll catch up with you guys later."

Ms. Honey, unaware of Ellie's desire to get Simon alone, took Adam by the hand and led him away.

"Why don't you come with me. I have a few things to show you that might be of interest. Simon will take care of Ellie for now."

Adam nodded and allowed himself to be led away. At the same time, Ellie was excited at what she thought was an unforeseen opportunity that just fell in her lap. Things seemed to be going in her favor and she was ready to plant yet another seed.

"Is she right? Are you going to take care of me, Simon?"

Simon heard every bit of the seductiveness in her voice but chose to act as though he didn't. He wasn't about to let her know how much she affected him or how much he was secretly attracted to her. He had to ignore any intimate thoughts he was having and focus on the professional relationship.

"I am. You are my guest, our guests this evening and I will make certain you are more than pleased with your experience."

"That sounds a lot like everything I've been wanting."

"Not so fast sweetheart, this is your first visit to *Ahsasz Down Under* and you must complete your probationary period."

"And how long is that?"

"That depends on a few things, but ultimately, it's at our discretion. But I promise, it won't be anything unreasonable."

"I trust you; now shall we proceed?"

"Yes of course. Follow me."

Ellie did as she was instructed, following Simon through what seemed like a maze or sorts. Stopping in front of an area that appeared to be tucked away in a corner. It had a solid pink door with an image of a cat in white lights.

"You'll notice none of the areas have names, just lighted images indicating the theme. We call this *'Purrrfect Pleasure'*. It's for girls only and not available for viewing by others."

"Interesting."

"I thought it would be right up your alley. Of course, if at any time, in any of our themed settings, you are open to being watched, we have a few options for that as well."

"Is that right?"

"Yes, it is."

"I had no idea how in-depth, how specific the setup would be. Very distinguished."

"We pride ourselves on that. It's part of the package. It's what we built this business on."

"I see."

"We aimed to provide an outlet for whatever your fantasy or kink may be, just as long as it's legal."

"Of course." Ellie chucked.

"I should point out that not everyone can access this room. Obviously, it's for females only and they are the only ones that know how to gain access."

"So, I could access this room right now if I wanted?" Ellie inquired.

"Uhm, no. I'm afraid not. You haven't been authorized to access this room as of yet, but don't worry, it's coming."

"Then tell me this, as probie's, do Adam and I have access to anything tonight?"

"Yes, you do. And we'll get to that in a bit. But right now, I have a few more areas I need you to see."

"Lead the way."

As Simon led Ellie to her next adventure, he checked his company device tracker and saw that Ms. Honey and Adam had just left 3's Company and were heading towards their current location as scheduled.

"We call this room Trespasshers. It's designed for women and men that want to explore a rape fantasy while still maintaining some degree of control. It's one of the few rooms that allows exterior viewing from various points within this section. You will find a few semi-private nooks and crannies tucked away here and there but for the most part you'll always be in view of others."

"Wow! I'm outdone. The level of detail and management of the activities is overwhelming. I had no idea."

"Zsasha and I are well aware of that. But you wanted in, right?"

"Yes, I did."

"Let's continue." Simon asserted. "As with all activities, especially select themed areas, there are specific rules that must be followed for anyone seeking entry to that area. This room is not open to all members."

"I'm ready, let's go."

Simon chose to ignore her blatant sexual advance and continued with his explanations.

"Prior to entering the room, you are required to select a thin metal bracelet with a symbol representing the type of experience you're open to. They are lightweight and small in nature and the symbols lightly glow in the dark, making it visible so that others can identify who's a match and who's not. Members must scan their bracelet and enter their personal access code to gain entry."

Looking at the bracelet options being guarded by a tall muscular security officer, Ellie didn't hesitate to reach past the unknown guard, grab a bracelet then immediately turn towards Simon.

"So what exactly does this one mean?"

"Well, my dear, the bracelet you're holding bears an X symbol which indicates you are open to all forms of individual one on one front side sexual activity, whether it be male or female."

"Go on."

"If your bracelet bears an O symbol, your back door is open as well as your front, also for individual male or female activity."

"It's sounding more and more interesting." Ellie revealed as she returned the bracelet to its original place then quickly retrieved the bracelet they hadn't yet discussed. "What about this one? What secrets does this unlock for the wearer?"

"Ah, the infinity symbol, yes, this one is different."

"How so?"

"Well, entering the room with this bracelet means you are open to all possibilities, not just individual male or female activity but gang related activity as well."

"Like I said, I'm ready, are you?"

Ignoring her innuendos once again, Simon continued with information about Trespasshers even though it was completely spelled out in her packet.

"Of course, access to the room comes with a universal safe word all are required to adhere to."

Simon felt like he'd lost her attention for a brief moment.

"Ellie, are you still with me?"

"Yes, I am. Please continue."

"Trespasshers was set up so no one could enter the room by accident. With secured access in place, if you're in the room, you're there because you want to be, plain and simple."

"Of course." Ellie confirmed.

Once again Simon checked his personal device which was tracking Ms. Honey and Adam's location. He could see their current location but couldn't determine why they were delayed. He was anxious to put some distance between him and Ellie as her sexually aggressive behavior towards him had him rattled. He had already lied to his wife a few times by not telling her about Ellie showing up in New York, he was beginning to regret agreeing to this mental rouse his wife cooked up which put him in this difficult and uncomfortable situation. With her incessant teasing and flirtation, he became totally discombobulated that he blurted out a question he should have never asked.

"Tell me Ellie, looking at this right now, the savage nature of it all, the dominance and control one has over the other, how does it make you feel?"

"Simon, my panties have been wet since the elevator ride down." Ellie confessed as she stepped out of her panties snatching them up with her right hand then slowly rubbing them across his face. "Is there anything you can do about that?" she asked, tucking them in his inside jacket pocket.

"You don't play fair, Ellie. I've told you multiple times Zsasha and I don't mix business with pleasure. Ever. It's how we manage to keep our marriage and our business thriving. We have rules in place, rules that we live by."

"Rules are meant to be broken, baby."

Simon, in all his years of sexual trysts, innuendos and cunning personalities he encountered as part of the lifestyle, stood there speechless, not at all prepared for what he had just heard, was silently reeling from what she had just done. Had it not been for Zsasha's perfectly timed arrival, there's no telling what she would have said or done next.

"So how is it going?"

"Great. We're right on schedule. Looks like Adam and Ms. Honey just arrived on the north side. We're just about to join them."

"Cool. Maybe she can finish up so you can meet me in my office?"

"I don't see why not. Give me fifteen minutes and I'll be there."

With that, Zsasha left, presumably towards her office. Ellie followed Simon around the viewing area of Trespasshers where they met up with Ms. Honey and Adam.

"Hey." Adam said while embracing and kissing Ellie. "This is beyond my wildest dreams, baby."

"Mine too." Ellie responded.

"You both have access to the Peek-A-Boo Shelter, which is a themed room setup for voyeurism, but if you prefer, you can go to a private room instead."

"Sounds good to me." Adam replied.

"You can go in and out at any time if you decide you want to spend some time watching others. When you're in your private room you can stay as long as the club is open, and no one will disturb you. You'll find drinks waiting for you at the private bar in your room as well as a few things you may or may not want or need. For this evening, either Gerome or Eve will be outside your door in the event you want or need anything we haven't provided."

"We'll start with the private room first, if that's okay."

"That's fine. Remember, either Gerome or Eve will be right outside your door, if you need anything." Simon explained.

"And where will you be Simon?" Ellie asked.

"Zsasha and I have other guests to attend to and you probably won't see us again this evening."

"Well then, I should thank you again for a wonderful evening. It has been a very exciting and entertaining experience."

"I'm glad to hear that. Ms. Honey will take over from here. Adam, Ellie, good night."

"Goodnight."

Simon heads back towards the private elevator that only staff members have access to. He didn't want to be caught with Ellie's panties in his possession, so he made his way to his office as quickly as he could. Closing the door behind him he sat down behind his desk. He pulled the panties from his inside jacket pocket and turned to toss them in a small trash can next to his desk. He hesitated for a moment thinking about what he was about to do. Realizing he couldn't just drop them inconspicuously in his trash can for Ms. Honey to see when she cleaned the offices, he needed to dispose of them properly.

His first mistake was bringing them to his office to discard instead of discarding them in the club. Anyone could have been the culprit and if he was careful to avoid the cameras, no one would have had a clue. He tucked them back inside his inside jacket pocket intending to get right up but he didn't. He remained seated, feeling compelled to to be still and listen to the inner voice he'd been trying to ignore. He grabbed the panties from inside his jacket and held them to his nose, taking in a long deep breath. Having surrendered to his weakness, fully embracing the scent, her scent which he secretly craved yet eluded him all this time, allowed his mind to wander into the 'what if' realm. Fascinating thoughts danced throughout his mind for several minutes before he was interrupted by the sound of his wife's voice over the intercom.

"Hey, is everything alright? I thought you were coming this way?"

"I am. I just had to handle something really quick. I'm heading to you now."

"Okay boo, see you in a minute."

Chapter 34

A week after the masquerade ball, the girls have been radio-silent for the most part. Most of their gatherings are usually hosted by Zsasha and almost always at the gallery when wine is involved. However pre-scheduled or random meetups in the early morning hours were typically at The Coffee House next door.

Unlike Rona who was off doing typical Rona stuff, Vonne had been feeling the need for girl time for a few days now but wanted to give Zsasha some space. Afterall, she had put so much time, effort and energy into planning and bringing the ball to life, not to mention being the host, it just didn't feel right to disturb her.

With Simon in New York, Zsasha finally had some well-deserved down time to herself. But as Vonne continued to reflect on recent events with her sister, her inner turmoil got harder and harder to ignore. Soon, her dilemma got the best of her and without further hesitation she sent out a group text message in hopes of getting a response. She got two.

Both Rona and Zsasha agreed to meet up, however Zsasha didn't feel like going anywhere, especially Ahsasz. So they agreed to hang out at Zsasha's house, something they didn't do often enough but was an easy sell to just about anyone.

At Rona's request, Vonne drove to her house, parked her car and rode shotgun, allowing Rona to steer the car and the conversation as well. The two of them on a journey without one or both of the others was something Vonne found unusual yet surprisingly delightful. Vonne and Rona didn't have a decades long history of hurt, pain or emotional baggage to bond over. They were tight, yes but only came together through their mutual association with Zsasha.

Most of the time when the girls meet up, it's typically in the DC area at Ahsasz and they drive in separately, each coming from a slightly different direction. But today, Rona had a plan and driving in with Vonne would give her the time she needed to set it up and execute it. When they arrived, they were greeted by one of her housekeepers who led them to the wine room where Zsasha was waiting.

"Hey, hey." Zsasha said with excitement. "Wassuppp! How y'all doing?"

"Fine, fine." Vonne replied.

"I'm good. You seem to be in a cheerful mood."

"I am girl, I'm good, definitely up for company, I just didn't feel like putting myself

together and leaving the house and I definitely didn't want to go to the gallery to hang out, I've had enough of that place for a while."

"I get, for sure. You've worked so hard these past several weeks, you have earned some much-needed time off and time away from Ahsasz."

"True, true."

"So how long will the gallery be closed?"

"Not as long as I'd like. We have a few events scheduled right around the holidays and of course our annual Christmas Drive & Open House. That's when we have everything on display."

"Everything?"

"Everything that didn't sell at an exhibit with each piece dedicated to a specific charity or organization."

"Sounds like you're gonna be busy again real soon."

"No, not really, not like I was planning the Masquerade Ball. It's always a bigger event than the Summer Charade and there's always something on the books around Thanksgiving. And as far as the Christmas Open House, girl, I can put that together in my sleep."

"I don't doubt it, not one bit. You've done it enough times." Vonne recalled.

"That's true, but J'Nae usually helps me decorate around Christmas."

"Oh yeah, I forgot about that. So what's the latest word? Anyone heard from her yet?"

"Not me." Rona replied.

"Me neither."

"It seems like she communicated with us more during the months she was laid up in the bed grieving. Once she left to spend time with her daughter, she became more and more distant, at least that's what I'm thinking." Rona revealed.

"I agree." Zsasha said. "I think it's a bit strange that we only get updates and communication through email and the occasional text messages. I even left a message with her daughter a while back to have her call me and still haven't heard anything back."

"Well personally, I was a bit surprised earlier on." Vonne confessed.
"After spending all that time in bed with the occasional visit to grief
counseling, she suddenly jumps out of bed and starts attending the support group on a regular basis, like we'd been suggesting all along."

"Are you're surprised she finally got up and took our advice?" Rona asked.

"No, not at all." Vonne replied. "It's just the way it all happened. She was barely going to counseling at first then suddenly she began going more frequently and after a while, she abruptly left to stay with her daughter, that's what surprises me."

"So how long has it actually been since Rick passed?" Zsasha asked.

"It's going on nine, ten months give or take." Rona answered.

"Damn, her grieving period lasted longer than the relationship." Zsasha concluded. "Something's up with that."

"I agree, even with her history of dealing with sudden loss, there's something more going on here." Rona advised.

"So what can we do? If anything was wrong, really wrong, I'm sure Taizja or Aiden would reach out to us so it's not that." Vonne replied.

"No, it's not that, but it's something." Zsasha acknowledged.

"So what do y'all want to do?" Vonne inquired.

"For starters, I'm going to go by her house and talk with her neighbors, see if the mail is being picked up or forwarded, if the yard is being maintained and just check things out."

"I think that's a good idea, a starting point anyway."

"I should be able to swing by in the next day or two."

"Cool. Be sure to let us know what you find out, even if it's not much." Zsasha requested. "In a minute, I'm starting to worry about her ass."

"I know, me too. I'll touch base with you as soon as I see what's up, both of you." Rona confirmed.

"Sounds like a plan." Vonne confirmed.

Both Vonne and Rona grabbed their belongings and stood up as if to leave.

"Thanks for having us over, girlfriend."

"Yeah, I appreciate you looking out for me. I really needed to get out of my headspace. You ready, Rona?"

"Wait a minute, hold up, bitches! I finally invite y'all scary asses to my private yet elite masquerade ball, the most coveted event of the season, this year and every other year and neither one of you bitches got shit to say about it? What's up with that?"

Both Rona and Vonne looked directly at each other and locked eyes for about 5 seconds then simultaneously turned toward Zsasha, each exhibiting the same look on their faces which resembled one of Zsasha's unique facial expressions that always accompanied her infamous catch phrase. And in case she couldn't read their facial expressions, they both blurted out the one thing they've been longing to throw right back in her face.

"Motha Fucka, please!" they hollered simultaneously.

Since both Rona and Vonne had been on the receiving end of Zsasha's notorious phrase many, many times, they were all too happy to return the favor and knew this would be the perfect opportunity to do so. However, since Rona knew Vonne would break character prematurely, she had a plan. Without giving Zsasha a chance to rebound, respond, or regroup from the shock, Rona followed up with a quickness, totally catching her girl off guard...*again*.

"How is it that you can fix your mouth to ask us about an experience, our experience, personal, intimate and private that according to you requires, no demands discretion at all times. If I answered that, if we answered that, we'd be making ourselves vulnerable and your business at risk, maybe even opening ourselves up for being sued. Isn't that right, Zsasha?"

Vonne had cracked a smile a few moments prematurely, but Rona didn't let up.

"Girl, I have heard you go on and on about client privacy, discretion, etcetera, etcetera, etcetera for some time now. I've known about *Ahsasz Down Under* a lot longer than Vonne or J'Nae. And I know you are well aware that I also have to deal with a certain level of discretion in my line of work. I can't believe you thought we'd come in here all googly eyed running our mouths about what we said or what saw or did, who was with who and all that. Nice try, girlfriend, but...what is it again, Vonne - Motha Fucka, please!"

"Damn! Y'all bitches been waiting to say that shit for a long time, haven't you?"

"Uh, yeah." Vonne replied, purposely avoiding the side eye she could feel Rona was giving her.

"You know you had it coming." Rona reinforced. "Ain't no way I was passing that up."

"Whatever bitches. I just wanted to know if y'all had a good time, that's all."

"Lee and I found it quite stimulating." Vonne confessed. "Very much so."

"I'm sure y'all did. Probably didn't even make it home before -"

"You're right, we didn't"

"Cool. That's how it's supposed to be, sista girl."

"And it was, it was!" Vonne exploded.

"Dang girl, you act like you haven't had any for a while." Rona observed.

"Right again. Y'all know we've been going through it for a while now, and Rona I took your advice better yet your interpretation of those text messages and didn't let them spoil our night."

"Good, I'm glad. Maybe you guys aren't as out of sync as you thought." Zsasha suggested.

"Unfortunately, that's yet to be determined. Whatever magic overcame us that night was good, hell it was great, but it was also gone by morning."

"I'm so, so, sorry, sweetie. Things will get better soon." Rona advised.

"Yeah, they will, just as soon as you get that bitch out of your house, things will go back to normal."

Vonne couldn't fix her mouth to say anything. She knew in her heart of hearts Zsasha was right.

"Well look, it's been real, but I really do need to go. Zsasha, do you need us to help clean up or anything?"

"Seriously...you know I got people for that, right?"

"Yes, I do...what was I thinking!" Rona jokes.

"You guys rode together, right?"

"Yeah, we did." Rona answered.

"We needed time to plan our attack."

"Damn! Y'all heffa's got me, for sure."

'Yes, we did." Vonne agreed.

"What are you about to do with the rest of this evening?" Rona asked.

"I don't know. I was gonna have John Lee go by the gallery and retrieve some paperwork Simon's gonna need in the morning. But I think I'll go instead. It'll give me something to do for the next hour or two."

"This late, really?" Rona questioned.

"Yeah, I'll be alright."

"Okay, but since it's late I'm implementing the phone tree. I'm gonna need you to call or text me when you leave the gallery and again when you make it home."

"Not just her, me too Zsasha."

"I can do that, no problem. So, which one of you bitches is coming back by to tuck me in? I think it's your turn Rona."

"I'm serious, Zsasha. Call or text. Don't forget."

"I won't. Goodnight, y'all. Be safe."

"You too."

"Remember, phone tree." Rona reiterated.

"Aight, now by."

* * * * *

By the time Vonne retrieved her car, chatted a bit more with Rona then made her way home, she was feeling the full effects of the wine she had that evening. On the plus side, she didn't feel any of the stress and anxiety she'd been feeling earlier in the day. She felt good.

Entering the house through the exterior garage door, Vonne walked through the laundry area which led to the kitchen, noticing leftovers still on the stove. Opening the skillet and pots she took a whiff at what prepared food awaited her. Seconds later, her attention was averted to the voices she heard not so far away. Vonne grabbed a dinner roll that had been left on the counter as she allowed herself to be guided towards the voices which slowly became familiar.   It was Kiera and Lee in conversation. It seemed to be coming from the winter sunroom where the indoor swim-spa was located. Vonne walked toward them, now fully aware of the participants in the conversation. A conversation which seemed enthusiastic and jovial.   For the obvious reason, Vonne paused just short of the entrance way to the indoor swim-spa, not allowing Kiera and Lee to become aware of her presence.   But she could clearly hear their conversation.

"I'm serious! There is no legitimate reason for you not to begin dating. At least not one that you've shared with me." Lee said as he came up for air.

"My thoughts exactly...nothing that I've shared with you so far." Kiera responded with enthusiasm.

Lee pulled himself out of the warm water onto the side of the swim-spa. He felt the conversation take on a more serious tone and he wanted to give Kiera his full attention.

"Baby girl, everybody has a past. And the older we get, the more colorful it becomes, at least for most of us anyway...those that want to keep it one hundred."

387

"Yeah, but----"

"Yeah, but nothing. You need to stop listening to what everybody else says about you. Most of 'em are haters anyway. If they can't say something bad, they won't say anything at all. You gotta get to the point where what they say, think or feel about you and your worth is irrelevant. You gotta stop caring so much. No matter who you are, hell, Jesus himself was hated and distrusted by many. And he proved himself 1000 times over, yet they still hung him. Shit, you can't please nobody no more and you can't live for anyone other than yourself."

Jumping back in the swim-spa, Lee swam to the far end and back again while his words resonated with Kiera.

"You know, that was deep. I heard everything you said, and just for the record, you made a pretty strong argument. One that I can't ignore."

Lee, now stepping out of the swim-spa, grabbed a towel to dry off. Although the luxury towel could easily have covered his body, there was no hiding the smile on his face at her compliment.

"I know what I'm talking about, despite what people will have you believe. Sure, you made some mistakes in the past, who hasn't. But you're straight, you're good people. You just need to trust yourself a little more. Venture out and do something a little different than in the past. You'll be alright, I'm sure of it."

Kiera smiled as Lee left and headed towards the main kitchen, stopping when he saw his wife a few feet away.

"Hey baby, I didn't hear you come in."

"I just got in a minute ago."

"Did you eat yet? There're some leftovers on the stove. I could make you a plate."

"Sure, thanks sweetie. Will you bring it upstairs?"

"I sure will boo. You go on up and take your shoes off and get comfortable. I'll be right up. Glass of wine with that?"

"That sounds really nice."

"You got it babe."

Vonne retreated up the staircase just moments after Kiera retreated to her room. She was tired and wanted this day to end but she made a mental note of what she just observed. Shortly thereafter, Lee entered the master suite carrying a small plate of pasta and vegetables and two glasses of red wine. They didn't speak, instead they locked eyes and smiled.

After setting her plate and glass of wine on the table next to her, he grabbed the remote control and turned on some music. As the smooth and relaxing sounds of Luther Vandross filled the room, he began massaging her feet as she relaxed in the chaise lounge nibbling at the small plate of food be prepared for her.

"I know you don't like to eat anything heavy this late, so I didn't give you much but make sure you eat everything on your plate. You need replenishment so you can sleep well and function properly in the morning."

Damn, Vonne thought to herself. Any other time this treatment would be on point but tonight, tonight she was just too damn tired. Ten minutes into her dinner and foot massage, she was out, fast asleep in the chaise lounge. Totally unaware that Lee didn't hesitate to retrieve his wine glass and stroll back downstairs.

* * * * *

As promised, Rona arrived at J'Nae's house the next day to look around and check things out before reporting back to her friends. Missing coffee and wine with the girls, no big deal but ignoring phone calls, text messages and emails, well that's another story.

As she walked up to the front door nothing appeared to be out of place. There wasn't any mail piled up like you would expect if someone was away from home for a while and her lawn and landscaping looked as it should. Her car wasn't visible, but she usually kept it secure in the garage, so it didn't really mean much. Nothing seemed at all out of place. Taking a moment to peer in the front windows did not bear any fruit. After a few minutes more, she retrieved the hidden key J'Nae kept on the backside of the mailbox which was affixed to the front of the house. Letting herself in, right away she heard a bit of soft music coming from upstairs. There were several lit candles placed around the living room in various places including every few steps along the staircase.

"What the hell?" Rona muttered as she took full stock of the rooms in her immediate view.   Before she could pull it all together, a voice, a singing voice was approaching from the kitchen.   Instinctively, she flicked on the lights just as a large figure approached.   She naturally took a defensive stance and aimed her pocket size pepper spray at the unknown individual who was equally caught by surprise.

"Ahhhhhh!"

"Ahhhhhh!"

Both screamed, suddenly becoming aware of each other's presence.

"Who the hell are you?" Rona shouted.

"I could ask you the same thing?"

"Where's J'Nae?   J'Nae!   J'Nae!   Are you alright?" Rona shouted.

J'Nae ran quickly down the stairs in response to the sudden commotion.

"Rona, what are you doing here?"

"Well damn.   I could ask you the same question, but the answer is obvious.   Who the hell is this?" she asked, pointing to the man in the bathrobe.

"Um, well, that's Wes, Wesley Hill.   He's a friend of mine."

"Really now?" Rona said sarcastically.

"Look, let's just all have a seat.   Everything's fine Rona, I promise."

"J'Nae, I'm going to get dressed.   This robe is a bit too short for sitting.   Be down in a minute."

J'Nae grabs Rona by the arm and hurries her to the living room.

"Girlfriend, what the fuck?   Is this why you've been missing in action for the past all this time?"

"Well, I've been a bit busy."

"I can see that but what's with the cloak and dagger bullshit? We've been really worried about you.   You've been ignoring our calls, not returning text messages or emails, what gives? Why didn't you let us know you were back?"

"Like I said, I've been kind of busy. Work has been brutal."

"I bet."

"No, really. I've been going in early quite a bit."

"And then there's this." Rona smirked.

"Yeah, yeah, then there's this."

"So how long has this been going on?"

"We met in grief counseling, before I left to visit Taizja."

"And you didn't feel you could share that with us? I don't understand."

J'Nae sighed and took a deep breath as she took a seat on the couch.

"Here, come sit." She said to her friend.

"I didn't know how to tell you. I didn't know how to tell anyone."

"Well, I could think of several ways, some of which you've used before. I don't get it."

"Well, Rona, I was a little bit..."

"A little bit what?"

"Y'all are a bit...."

"A bit what?"

"He doesn't really know much about..."

"What J'Nae, just say it."

"Well, I was a little bit embarrassed."

"Embarrassed? Embarrassed about what? Is he broke or something, maybe in between jobs?"

"No, nothing like that."

"Well then what is it?"

"I just didn't know how you all would react to me moving on so quickly, you know, after Rick died."

"Oh sweetie. We would never judge you like that. We want you to be happy. Life is short."

"Really, you mean that?"

"Yes, I do. And although I can't officially speak for Zsasha or Vonne, I'm pretty sure they'd agree with me that you've waited long enough. I know how deeply you cared for the man, but he wasn't your husband. There's no set amount of time that you have to grieve before you can move on with your life."

"I know what you're saying is right, but Zsasha can be harsh at times and kind of judgmental, you know that."

"Yes, but not about something like this. She loves you like a little sister, we all do, and we've always supported you getting back out there, after Julian died. Damn girl, you can't give your life to a dead man, not again."

"Stop it, Rona."

"No, I'm serious. You cut yourself off for years when Julian died. It was the kids and us, that's it. You shut down emotionally and we were forced to watch you go from mourning Julian to mourning your life and we promised we'd never allow that to happen again. Girl we love you. You need to do you. Make yourself happy. Besides, it's been how long since Rick died?"

"Not quite a year."

"Well sweetie, that's long enough. Y'all's relationship didn't last that long, so you're good."

"I never thought about it like that."

"Stop being so hard on yourself. Let whatshisface do that."

"You're silly."

"No, I'm not. Ain't nobody judging you like that. We want you to be happy."

"I am. Wes makes me happy, really happy. He's my soulmate."

"Say what? Never mind. We'll leave that discussion for another time. Sorry for the interruption, but check in every now and then, you know."

"I will, Rona, I promise. I'll meet up with you guys soon, very soon."

"I'm holding you to that. And what am I supposed to tell them? They know I was planning to stop by here today."

"Whatever you feel you need to. I'll have to face them eventually so tell them whatever you want. I'll deal with it later when I see everybody."

"How about tomorrow morning, for coffee? They miss you, seriously, it will all be fine."

"You think?"

"I know. We just want you to be happy, that's it and if you're happy with whatshisface?"

"Wes."

"Wes, then we're happy for you."

"Well, okay."

"Now go on and get back to your business. I'll see myself out."

"Thanks sweetie. I love you." reaching to embrace her friend tightly.

"I love you too, J'Nae, but you have warned me. I don't want none of that."

"Bye girl!"

"Bye."

Chapter 35

The next morning Rona was the first one to arrive at The Coffee House. She had sent out the necessary invites the night before but didn't stay up to see who responded nor did she take the time to read through her messages that morning. She really didn't want to know or even think about the highly emotional conversation she knew was coming her way. Just as she sat down, she saw Zsasha coming in.

"Hey Z, how are you?" Rona asked.

"I'm good, you?"

"I'm straight. Wasn't sure you were going to make it this morning. It was kind of last minute when I reached out last night. No need to call the waitress, she's our regular and I already ordered for you. It'll be here in a minute."

"It's all good, so what's up? What's going on?"

"With me, not a whole lot. What's up with you? How's your friend, *Ellie*?"

"Yeah, that's right, friend. She's alright, for a youngster."

"I'm glad you pointed out the age difference. What gives? I'm a bit surprised to see you getting so chummy with someone so much younger than you. What's that about?" Rona inquired.

"Nothing, really. I guess I find her to be in need of a big sister type, someone nurturing, mature and experienced."

"Nurturing, big sister type? And you think that's you, huh?" Rona laughed.

"I'm serious. There's something about her that makes me want to just take her under my wing and guide her, you know, do things with her, share things with her, teach her about...life in general...you know, shit like that."

"So, what you really mean is to teach her about the lifestyle, am I right or wrong?"

"No, not really, in fact I'd prefer it if she didn't have an interest in that at all or my husband. I just feel drawn to her. I don't know how else to explain it, I just feel like it fits, we fit; that we're supposed to be friends."

"I don't get it girlfriend and I'm not going to pretend to understand. Just be careful." Rona advised. "We've already had one that flew the nest which we didn't see coming and Vonne...don't get it twisted. She's on overload. You've known her much longer than I have but I can clearly see whatever she's got going on in her life that stressing her is way worse than she lets on. I promise you. She's never this quiet or out of touch. Think about it, she requires too much attention, period. And when she doesn't it's because she's got some real deep shit going on and instead of turning to us for support, she goes inside herself and shuts down, hiding from us the best she can. I don't know why you can't see it. I can."

"Maybe Simon was right. Just before the masquerade ball he basically accused me of slipping. Passing off a lot of my responsibilities to Ms. Honey and other staff members. He said I was too preoccupied with J'Nae and her absence and all of her issues Rick's death drudged up. Maybe he was right, and I just didn't see it, either that or you're overreacting. Only time will tell."

"Well, not just time, I'm going to tell."

"What are you talking about?"

"I'm going to tell...you. I was hoping she'd be here to tell you herself, but she's left me no choice. It's not something I can keep to myself, especially now."

"Just spill it."

"It's J'Nae. Did you know she was back?"

"Ah, no. Did you?"

"Of course not. I only found out by accident when I stopped by to check things out at her house. Apparently, she's been back for a while now."

"What?"

"Yes, mam and she's not alone. She's been seeing someone for several months now."

"The hell you say."

"Seriously, I walked in on them during an intimate encounter and if I hadn't, I'm not sure when she would have let us know she'd returned."

"When the hell did this shit happen?"

"From what I gathered, they met during the grief counseling sessions she attended for a few months before she left to visit her daughter and they connected sometime later via social media or something. From what I understand, they've pretty much been dating ever since."

"So, what's with the secrecy? Why didn't she say anything to us?"

"Because she thought we would judge her harshly for moving on so quickly."

"You mean she thought I would judge her harshly."

"Well to be honest, yeah, that's what she said, for the most part but she was concerned about how all of us would react, not just you."

"So, when did you talk to her?"

"When I stopped over to check on the house like we discussed. And after letting myself in, I inadvertently interrupted a private liaison between her and her new beau, Wes."

"Wes?"

"Yep. Wes. And that's all I know."

"Well, we're gonna have to pin her ass down and get the 411 on all of this. And maybe she can explain herself to us. I was really worried about her wellbeing."

"I know, I was too."

"I can't believe this shit. All this time we've been worried about her trifling ass, and this is how she treats us, ah hell no. I got some words for her ass."

"Well as it happens, you'll have the opportunity to share that with her now. Here she comes."

"Really?"

"Yep."

"That's wassup."

One of Zsasha's talents is her ability to turn it on or off at will. She could be sweet then sour at the drop of a hat. No one ever really knew what was truly going through her mind at any given moment and she liked it that way.

"Well look what the polecat dragged in." Zsasha smirked.

"Hey Zsasha, Hey Rona." J'Nae said as she greeted both friends with a kiss and a deep bear hug. "How have you guys been? I've missed you."

"We've missed you too. Where have you been hiding?" Rona asked.

"Girl please! You know I know you already told her about the other day."

"Huh? What?"

"Girl cut it out. One thing I know for sure is that there are no secrets among our sista circle. Can't none of y'all hold water."

"You're right. And in all fairness, I told you I was going to tell her, Vonne too."

"Where is Vonne? Is she on her way?"

"Excuse me, you can't just show up like this, say a few words and think we're all good. I just can't get over the fact that you dropped our asses like hot potatoes. Seriously, you've been here all this time? And didn't say shit to nobody? I know you know I'm not letting that shit slide, not for a minute. What's up with that?" Zsasha demanded.

Before J'Nae had a chance to respond, Rona changed the direction of the conversation. Although she felt some kind of way about J'Nae's handling of the situation, she couldn't ignore her history dealing with love and loss.

"So, tell us about him? What's he like? Where did you guys meet?"

"His name is Wesley Hill, Wes for short. He's a 54-year-old retired officer of the Judge Advocate General's Corps. with the U.S. Army. He's a widow of 18 years and has no children."

"Judge Advocate General's Corps., sounds impressive." Said Rona.

"Keep going girl." Zsasha persisted.

"Well, we met in passing at the counseling center, you know, the one you both begged me to go to for grief counseling."

"I remember, and?" Zsasha moaned.

398

"Well, we went out for coffee once or twice at a spot around the corner from the counseling center. Sometime later I left to visit my daughter and not long after I arrived, he reached out to me to see how I was doing since I hadn't shown up at the counseling center in a while. I had only been at Taizja's for a short while when he reached out to me on social media, you know, through that dating app y'all set up for me."

"Yeah, I remember that too, and?"

"We just started communicating. We were both grieving a sudden and devastating loss of someone close and at the same time. We kind of bonded over our shared grief. After we developed a personal interest in one another, we decided to make it a priority to not focus on our shared grief so that it wouldn't be the sole thing we had in common or the foundation of our relationship. After a while, we stopped talking about it altogether."

"Alright, that all sounds well and good but what's with the secrecy?"

J'Nae glanced over at Rona in an attempt to read her expression before she blurted out a lie she could potentially get caught in. Rona could see J'Nae was reluctant to tell the truth so she made a move that would force her to do so.

"You might as well tell her, J'Nae. You know I already did."

Taking a deep breath and pausing to choose her words, J'Nae spoke her truth.

"I didn't say anything because I knew you would judge me, all of you."

"Uhm, that's not exactly what you said the other day J'Nae." Rona added.

"That's because I didn't want to hurt your feelings Rona, but I should've told you the truth like I'm telling you now, both of you."

"Unbelievable!"

"I'm sorry. It all happened so fast, and it was completely unexpected. I believed every last one of y'all would've had a problem with it."

399

"But why? Why would it be an issue for us, any of us? I don't get it?"

"Because it happened so soon after Rick died."

"It's not like the man was your husband and y'all had built a life together over the years. From what we saw, your mourning period lasted longer than the time he was in your life."

"Stop it, Zsasha." Rona insisted.

"I'm serious! We're your girls and we always got your back. Besides, we've been telling you for years to dust off that cookie."

"I did, with Rick." J'Nae admitted.

"Yeah, but that was the only relationship you've had in how many years now?" Zsasha asked.

"That's pretty much it, since Julian died, right?" Rona insinuated.

"Yeah, it was. So y'all don't see my behavior as ho-ish at all?"

"Hell no! In fact, you couldn't be a ho even if you tried." Zsasha declared.

"Yeah, I'm gonna have to agree with Zsasha on that one. Girlfriend, you just don't have it in you, not even an ounce."

"Does he know about Rick?"

"He knows that I lost someone I'd been seeing for a while, but he doesn't know any of the details. I didn't see any point in rehashing all of that. At the meetings, we had a bit of anonymity. We only shared our first names and the first names of our loved ones. At the time, he had his own loss to deal with, you know."

"That was probably for the best. There's no reason to dwell on the past, especially if this is a serious affair. Is it, J'Nae? Is it a serious affair?"

"Yes, it is. We are connected in a way I've never felt before."

"Not with anyone?"

"No, not anyone. And yes, Julian was the love of my life, and no one can ever replace him or even come close to what we shared with one another. But Wes, he's different. He has a calmness about him. Coupled with confidence and self-assuredness, I find it extremely intoxicating. He's committed and dedicated to me and when we're together, I feel safe, secure and loved."

"Wow! Sounds like you're in pretty deep." Zsasha declared.

"Yeah, I am. And he takes care of me, all of me. He knows my heart and he gets it. We are becoming one in the same."

"Sounds like a prince."

"So, when can we meet him?" Zsasha asked.

"Soon. I'll talk with him, and we'll plan something soon, I promise."

"Cool. Now that that's out of the way, does anybody know what's up with Whitegirl?"

"Obviously not me, but what's going on?" J'Nae asked.

"I haven't heard much from her either. Maybe somebody should check on her."

"Whatever's going on, I'm sure it has something to do with her crazy ass sista. I told her..."

"We all did, but y'all know how she is. She's too trusting, always looking to give people the benefit of the doubt."

"Yeah, especially when it comes to family." J'Nae confirmed.

"I think we should pay her a visit, a group visit. Let her know we're here for her if she needs us, no matter what she's going through."

"I'm in." Zsasha said without hesitation. "When y'all wanna roll up on her?"

"We ain't rolling up on her, we're just concerned friends checking in, that's all."

"Rona...always the voice of reason." J'Nae uttered.

"Whatever, I'd rather just roll up on a sista, 3 maybe 4 deep."

"Who's the 4th one, Z?" J'Nae inquired.

"Girl, you ask too many questions."

"Zsasha, you need to quit, for real." Rona replied.

"I'm just saying. So, y'all wanna do this tonight, right?" Zsasha asked eagerly.

"Yeah, let's do it tonight. I want to see her." J'Nae replied.

"I'm sure she wants to see you too, but no, I think that's jumping the gun a bit." Rona explained. "Here's my suggestion, Zsasha, how about you send out a group text like you usually do for girls' night out. We'll meet at the gallery and if she shows up, cool. But if we don't hear from her within the first hour, then it's on. We'll show up in full force. Y'all okay with that plan?"

"You got it girl." Zsasha agreed. "And when it's time to roll out and we *will* have to roll out, mark my words, we'll all ride over together. Y'all cool with that?"

"I'm fine with that." J'Nae said.

"Me too."

"Just make sure y'all heffa's got on fighting clothes, preferably all black and don't forget to grease-up your cheeks. Y'all know what it is."

"Now you're just being ridiculous, Zsasha!" J'Nae insisted.

"No I ain't. If Kiera is anything like Vonne, oh it's on."

"That's true." Rona confirmed. "Vonne will be the first one to throw a punch."

"Hell yeah. That's what I like about whitegirl. She's got that hit first-ask questions later mentality. When it comes down to it...whitegirl is hardcore, when she wants to be."

"For all we know, everything is fine and she's just busy with the new store."

"We'll know soon enough." J'Nae added.

"For sure. I'll send out the group text and we'll go from there. Everybody on board?"

"That's fine."

"Fine by me."

"Alrighty then, see y'all later.

* * * * *

Early the next morning, Rona and Zsasha bumped into each other at The Coffee House like they do several times a week. Rona was in a rush to meet with a client and Zsasha was a bit preoccupied. She didn't hear from Simon last night before bed and she had become a bit concerned.

"Hey Zsasha!"

"Hey Rona, how are you?"

"I'm good. I didn't get that text about meeting up tonight. Did you forget?"

"It slipped my mind for a minute, but I'll send it out as soon as I get in my office."

"Cool. So everything is still on track then, right?"

"For sure. You'll have it in twenty minutes or so."

"Awesome, gotta run."

Taking her coffee to go, and her troubles, she headed next door to the gallery. Once inside, she noted that John Lee was taking in a delivery that apparently arrived a bit sooner than expected.

"Be careful with that. You should have called me when the delivery arrived early." Zsasha explained. "This shipment wasn't due to arrive until tomorrow. This increases our liability."

"Sorry Ms. Zsasha but Simon texted me yesterday evening letting me know the first half of the shipment would be arriving this morning. The Second half will be here tomorrow as scheduled."

"My bad, John Lee. You'll have to excuse me. I didn't sleep very well last night and I'm kind of in a fog. I didn't even notice the delivery truck unloading right in front of me when I walked over to The Coffee House."

"No worries, Ms. Zsasha, it's all good."

Zsasha entered her office just in time to answer her ringing phone.

"Hey sweetie, how are you? I missed you last night."

"I missed you too. It was pretty late when we wrapped up and I didn't want to wake you up."

"I wish you had. Will you be home tonight or tomorrow? A few things have happened that I want to catch you up on."

"Is everything alright, what's going on?"

"Everything's fine. Just want to know when you'll be home. Can you make it back tonight?"

"If I can, it'll be late but don't count on it. I'll just have to see how things wrap up today. Worst case scenario, I'll see you first thing in the morning."

"Okay, maybe I'll just reach out to Ellie, grab dinner or something. I haven't seen much of her since the ball."

"Really, hmm. Well look, I'll check in with you later and let you know where things stand, okay love?"

"Okay boo. Talk to you soon."

"Bye."

Simon ended the phone call and laid his cell phone face down on the table in front of him.

"Was that Zsasha?" Ellie asked.

"Yes, it was Zsasha, my *wife*."

"How's she doing? I haven't had a chance to catch up with her since the ball."

"I wonder why that is." Simon snickered.

"I've just been busy with this and that, you know how it is."

"Really? Because you seem to have time to run into me here in New York every chance you get."

"Strictly coincidental."

"If you say so."

"Are you complaining?"

"No, not at all. I'm just curious about your motives. I thought we agreed the last time was the last time?"

"I'm just being friendly, nothing more, nothing less."

"If you say so. Right now, I've got business to attend to. Take care of yourself, Ellie."

"You do the same."

Simon retreated to his hotel suite and sat down for a few minutes in deep thought. It was time for him to go. He needed to be home with his wife, but his schedule wouldn't allow it, not today anyway. Feeling a bit anxious, he left the hotel and headed for his morning meeting.

Chapter 36

I t seems like you and Vonne have been getting along better
here lately." Lee observed.

"We have and I owe you a big thank you for having my back
when I left the store keys home. Vonne would have killed me
for not opening on time."

"Yeah, well, I think she's too hard on you sometimes."

"You'd better not let her hear you say that. She'd raise all
kinds of hell, for sure!"

"Well then, we'll just keep that between us. Can I get you
more wine?"

"Yes, please, and thank you." Kiera replied.

Lee walked over to the bar and grabbed the already open
bottle of wine and refilled both glasses. Sitting the bottle down
in front of them he returned to his seat.

"This is really nice Lee, sitting here like this, by the fireplace.
It's very relaxing."

"I find relaxation good for the soul. Worry and stress serve
no purpose and a complete waste of energy."

"You're quite the philosopher, aren't you?" Kiera said in a coy
kind of voice.

"Not really. I'm just very observant of others and in control
of my emotions. I have time to be. I consider myself to be
results driven and by that, I mean everything I do has a specific
purpose for a predetermined outcome I want to achieve."

"Is that right?"

"Yes, it is. You'd be surprised what one can achieve if you
know what it is you want and have a specific plan to achieve it.
And it's not about working hard, it's about working smart."

"How so, I mean, you don't work."

"For the most part my work is already done. I'm, let's say,
enjoying the fruits of my labor. Vonne didn't wake up one
morning with all this. She had help."

"I see."

"I'm glad you do." Lee replied.

"Are you ready to eat?" Kiera asked.

"Yes, I am."

"Alrighty then. Seafood pasta coming right up!"

Kiera headed to the kitchen to place some garlic bread in the oven to toast while she set the table for the two of them.

"Need any help?" a voice said from the other room.

"Sure. Can you take the salad out to the table and our drinks?"

"No problem." Lee responded.

Kiera followed behind Lee with two plates of seafood pasta, one in each hand.

"Here, let me help you with that." Lee said, taking both plates out of her hands.

"Why thank you kind sir." Kiera said in a deep southern voice. "I'll be right back with the bread."

When Kiera returned, she found Lee refilling the not yet empty wine glasses for a second time.

"I think that'll be my last glass for the evening." Kiera remarked.

"Nonsense. Enjoy yourself. Everything looks delicious. Let's eat!"

The two dinner companions took their respective seats and began the meal Kiera graciously prepared. After taking a piece of garlic bread, Lee passed the bread plate to Kiera and started chatting.

"So, Kiera, just how involved has Vonne allowed you to get at The Boutique's? Have you met any of the independent designers she works with or her personal buyers? Are you involved in the buying process at all?"

"Well unfortunately not. Vonne and I have had problems that go back for years, and she has every reason to have trust issues when it comes to me."

"Yes, but you've changed. We can all see that."

"But look at how I showed up here. That had to hurt her business or whatever she was trying to accomplish that night. There were a lot of important people at the house that night. All of which saw my drunk and unscheduled arrival."

"True, true but nobody's perfect and we all make mistakes. You're not that same person anymore."

"I know, but I need to show her I can consistently do better. And I haven't done that. She doesn't like me to drink because she feels I can't control it."

"Are you an alcoholic, I mean, what's your deal?"

"Short version, I was in rehab but for something else, well, some other things. Drinking was never my issue, and I didn't do that much of it. After my last stint in rehab, I was good for a while, a good while even when things got tough, I stuck it out. I didn't relapse or use again, but I began dibbling and dabbling and eventually found myself close to climbing back into that dark hole. That's when I left and came here, sort of."

"Sort of?"

"Yeah, I mean, I'm leaving some stuff out but that's the gist of it."

"So, is that when y'all started having problems and couldn't get along?"

"Good God no! Our issues started back before we knew what issues were. I never really understood why she seemed to hate me so much. I mean, we were never close, but I think she just didn't want to share her father with me. I think she just wanted him all to herself."

"So that's the lie you're telling these days?" Vonne asked.

"Hey baby, I didn't hear you come in." Lee stated as he stood up from the table.

"I guess not, with y'all all the way over here. What's all this about?"

"Nothing." Kiera declared. "I just threw together a quick dinner because I thought you were meeting up with the girls tonight."

"I bet you did."

"Vonne, it's not like that." Kiera insisted.

"Looks like it to me. I come home to find the two of y'all having what looks like a cozy dinner and on top of that, I hear you lying to my husband about our past."

"Vonne honey, really, it's not what you think. Kiera was just telling me what she thought was problematic between you two back in the day. That old stuff shouldn't even matter now anyway."

"Well it does. Some wounds never heal. And what's with this little private intimate dinner? Where's my plate?"

"I'm sorry, sis. I only made enough for two because I thought you'd be out with the girls tonight. I can make more, it'll just take a few minutes."

"Don't bother. You two enjoy the rest of your damn dinner!"

With that, Vonne retreated upstairs to the master bedroom. Perturbed, upset and somewhat disgusted, she undressed and jumped in the shower hoping the hot water and steam would wash away her anger and resentment.

* * * * *

Simon could see Ellie just a few doors down, obviously heading in his direction. Once she was upon him, she paused for a minute as the two of them locked eyes as if speaking an unspoken language only they shared. But Simon wasn't having it, at least not right now. He returned his attention to John Lee who was helping him unload a delivery.

"So, are we all set for the showcase?" Simon asked.

"Yeah, everything's here. We just need to stage it, put everything in its place."

"Cool. Just remember what we discussed."

"I got it, I got it." John Lee replied.

"Okay, we'll touch base later on."

Simon entered the gallery leaving Ellis standing by the entrance. She discreetly slipped her phone into her jacket pocket and entered shortly behind him. She could see him and Zsasha directing staff members to position and reposition items throughout the display area while John Lee continued unloading other items from the truck.

"Hey, what's going on? Are you guys moving or something?"

"Or something." Replied Simon, making a point not to make eye contact with the young woman he secretly spent time with in New York.

Ellie could tell Simon was in a mood, so she chose to ignore his obvious rudeness.

"Okay, so Zsasha, I just stopped by, thought maybe we could grab brunch, but you look busy."

"Brunch? Hell yeah. Sista worked up an appetite being all he-mannish and shit."

"You've been here less than ninety minutes telling everybody else what to do, Zsasha, so what are you talking about?" Simon exclaimed.

"Zsasha looked back at her husband with an I don't give a fuck look on her face.

"Whatever. Give me ten minutes Ellie, I'll be right back."

"Oh, Okay, I can come back if I need to."

"Don't be silly. Just hang out in my office. I'll be ready in a minute."

"Well, okay I guess."

Zsasha did a quick look around the gallery as she began walking towards her office.

"Look, I'm gonna leave this to you capable men to work out. One of y'all knuckleheads keep moving what I put down anyway...*Simon*."

"I told you before we got started we didn't need you."

"Yeah, but I like things a certain way. I have an entire concept and layout in my mind. You should know that about me by now."

"I do, baby I do but I got this." Simon replied.

"Well then, let it do what it do. I'll be back."

With that, Zsasha disappeared into her office to freshen up and change. She always kept attire for all occasions in the closet of her office suite. Whatever the occasion, she was sure to have matching handbags, footwear and jewelry to compliment whatever she put together.

Ellie hung back for a bit in an effort to get a read on Simon. He pretended not to notice her continued presence however she was a go-getter. She had no qualms about going after what she wanted, and Simon was no exception.

"When did you get back from your business trip, Simon?" Ellie asked.

"What?" Simon replied, purposely trying not to engage or encourage her.

"I was just wondering when you returned from your trip and how things went."

"I'm good." Simon replied as he turned his attention away from Ellie then towards John Lee. "How much more is there on the truck? I wasn't expecting a shipment quite this size."

John Lee was no stranger to the game. He knew full well that Simon directed him to receive the first part of the shipment the day before. Whatever game he was playing, John Lee knew the rules and went along with it. His response was on point.

"Not much more at all, Mr. Stewart. Just a few pieces we can easily carry in ourselves. I think I vaguely remember Ms. Zsasha mentioning something about last minute additions to the showcase, at the artist's request of course."

"I'm sure she would have mentioned that to me if that were the case."

"Actually Mr. Stewart, with your return being delayed, Ms. Zsasha passed that information off to me. I didn't see any reason to bother you with the updates while you were out of town and I assumed she would have conveyed that information to you herself. My apologies, Mr. Stewart."

"It's all good, John Lee. No harm, no foul."

Walking back into the main gallery area, Zsasha did not pick up on the temperature of the room or the tap dance she almost witnessed. Simon and John Lee were doing the same thing now as they were when she stepped out. Ellie appeared to be nothing more than an observer.

"I'm ready sweetie, let's roll."

With that, Zsasha and Ellie headed out for an extended brunch to include a deluxe mani-pedi, a hydra-facial and a hot stone massage, not to mention a heart healthy lunch.

* * * * *

That evening, Zsasha was standing outside the gallery when J'Nae and Rona parked their cars and walked up.

"Hey Zsasha." J'Nae greeted.

"Hm." Zsasha snickered. You could tell she was still a bit perturbed with J'Nae and her situation.

"Hey Z, what's up?" Rona asked. "Aren't we going inside?"

Zsasha didn't respond right away which was unlike her to hold back or bite her tongue. But J'Nae intervened primarily because she thought Zsasha's attitude was directed at her.

"So, did anybody hear from Vonne today? From what I can tell she didn't respond to the group text." J'Nae asked.

"I haven't heard anything, and I've been tied up with indecisive clients all day and I didn't take time out to reach out to her. What about you, Zsasha?"

"Who me, no, nothing, which is fine by me. I like the element of surprise in situations like this."

"So you really think something might jump off, huh?" J'Nae asked.

"Oh yeah. This was a bad situation from the start and y'all know as well as I do that it's not going to end well. Y'all ready to roll?" Zsasha asked.

"Right now?" Rona asked. "I thought we were going to give her an hour or so before we did anything?"

"That was the plan, but I feel like we need to go now. Who's driving?"

"You really want to do this right now?" J'Nae asked.

"Do you remember the last time she was in The Coffee House?" Zsasha recalled. "What did she look like?"

"A hot mess."

"Okay then. It might not be tonight, or even in the next few weeks, but mark my word, it's going down at Vonne's house, sooner or later. And right now, I'm seeing the signs."

"I believe it. This situation with her sister, whatever it involves, is wearing her down." Rona added. "That plus the stress of opening more than one store at a time...too much."

"Yeah, that too. Whitegirl got a lot on her plate, no doubt."

"She does, she really does."

"So y'all ready or what?" Zsasha asked.

"Let's do it." Rona replied. "I'll drive."

After piling into Rona's car, the girls made the fifteen-minute drive to Vonne's house from the gallery. Rona pulled her car into the circular driveway in front of Vonne's elaborate house. The three of them exited the car and proceeded to the front door.

"Y'all hear that?" Zsasha asked.

Rona and J'Nae looked at each other somewhat surprised.

"See I told y'all it was going down. Go ahead and knock on the door."

There was no immediate answer and the voices continued to rise. Vonne's voice was clearly recognizable. She was yelling at the top of her lungs, but the voices seemed to be moving further away from the main entrance.

"Look, y'all prissy asses move back. Let me knock." Zsasha insisted.

A few moments later Vonne answered the door.

"What are y'all doing here?"

"Hey Vonne, we just came by to check on you. Is everything alright?" Rona asked.

"I don't even know how to answer that. J'Nae, oh my goodness. When did you get back?"

"That's a question for another day." Zsasha declared. "What's going on with you? We could hear you when we first pulled up."

Vonne just shook her head from side to side, not able to form the words to answer her question.

"Maybe you need to get out of the house for a while." J'Nae suggested.

"Was that Lee you were arguing with?" Rona asked.

"Yeah, it was."

"He didn't hit you, did he?"

"Zsasha, you know that fool ain't crazy. He knows better."

"Well, why not come with us for a while, then. We can go back to the gallery, have a bit of wine and you can unwind, tell us what's going on."

"You know what Z, that sounds good. Anywhere is better than here." Vonne replied. "Let's go!"

The ladies all piled into Rona's car and headed back to Ahsasz. They were only in the car a good minute and barely had time for the questions to begin before Zsasha's phone rang. It was Ellie Porter.

"Hello, Ellie?"

"Zsasha, where are you? I'm here at the gallery but I can't get in."

"Oh, right, my bad. We were gonna discuss the possibility of displaying some of your work in the gallery."

"Yeah, that's right. Is everything okay?"

"Well, not really. Something came up with one of my girls and we're going to be hanging out at the gallery. Can we do this tomorrow?"

"Well, I kind of set aside some time tonight."

"I'm sorry. It's just that my girl is going through something, and we need the gallery to ourselves, for privacy, you understand, right?"

"So, you're headed there now?"

"Yes, we all are."

"Well, okay."

"My bad, for real. I'll try my best to work around your schedule tomorrow or whenever you have time. If that doesn't work, we'll look at doing this at another time."

"Oh, no, that won't be necessary. Do what you gotta do and will link up tomorrow sometime."

"Are you sure?"

"Absolutely, it's all good. We gotta do what we gotta do for our friends."

"Okay cool. Good looking out."

"Bye Zsasha, I'll see you tomorrow." But Zsasha didn't respond. She had already hung up the phone and returned her attention back to her girls.

"Everything okay?" Vonne asked.

'Yeah, it's all good."

"What did she want?" Rona asked sarcastically.

413

"We were supposed to meet up tonight. We were planning to discuss the possibility of displaying some of her photography in the gallery."

"Oh really, so what else can she do, carve pumpkin heads with her pinky nail?"

"Stop tripping. I know y'all don't like her." Zsasha confessed.

"It's not that." J'Nae replied.

"Yes, it is." Rona said flatly.

"We just think she has an angle of some sort. She doesn't seem genuine." J'Nae continued.

"Well, we have a lot in common. Like me, she studied art in college and has dabbled a bit in photography."

"Well, is she any good at it?" Rona asked while getting out of the car.

"That's what tonight was about." Zsasha explained as she unlocked the gallery doors. "She had several black and white still photos she'd taken that were on display on her yacht. Most of them had been taken down in preparation for the auction but I'd seen some of them when Simon and I cruised with her. But I appreciate y'all looking out for a sista, however I got this. It's all good, really."

"It better be." Vonne bolstered. "I'm already in fighting mode so it won't take much more for me to hand down an ass whoopin...in fact, I could spar with that heffa right now. It would be like a much-needed stress reliever." Vonne said as she danced around like she was boxing. "I'll beat dat ass! Skinny bitch!"

"All right now, let's get you seated. You need a drink right quick so you can calm down. You're taking this way too seriously Vonne." J'Nae declared.

"Vonne, yes she is but Zsasha, not serious enough." Rona replied. "You can't be caught sleeping on a sista?"

"Hell, I don't ever sleep on a mother fucka, not ever and I'm not sleeping on Ellie. She's harmless and besides, y'all know my name, where I'm from, and how we get down in my hood, shit. But seriously, we didn't come here to talk about the Ellie drama y'all got going on in your head. This is about baby girl and what she's got going on right now."

Vonne jumped up like she was still in fighting mode and turned her energy towards Zsasha.

"Oh, so that's my name now...Baby girl? That's what you're calling me these days, heffa?"

"Motha fucka please! I know you ain't trying to step to me!"

"What, you scared, Z?"

"Never scared, baby girl, never scared."

"Alright then, let's go."

"You don't want none of this." Zsasha shrugged.

"Come on, bitch, get up. Let's go!"

Zsasha just shook her head side to side. "For real though, I know, that you know, I will snap yo pretty white ass like a twig."

"Probably so, probably so." Vonne replied with her excitement beginning to dwindle.

"So then sit your silly ass down and quit playing with me for you get hurt."

Vonne did just as she was told and moments later, they all joked and laughed at the absurdness of it all. With Zsasha being one and a half times her size, Vonne was no match for her, and she knew it. But her timeout was brief. She wanted to have a bit more fun with it and again decided to push the envelope.

"Where's the wine at, bitches?" Vonne shouted, barely able to contain herself as the hardcore tone of her voice was followed by her own laughs and giggles.

"Oh, you really feeling yourself tonight, ain't you?" Zsasha asked. "You lucky I'm feeling sympathetic enough to give your silly ass a pass but watch yourself baby girl. Fuck around and you might be the one to catch a beat down... real talk. Everybody's got limits, don't push it."

Taking a glass of freshly poured wine Rona took upon herself to pour, J'Nae felt the need to add her two cents in. "There will be no ass beating tonight...here at Ahsasz or anywhere else...at least not among us."

"I'll drink to that!" Rona added.

"Damn, y'all twisted for real." Zsasha revealed. "Did y'all smoke something on the way over here or while I was on the phone? I mean really, what's up? We got J'Nae sounding like Rona, being the voice of reason, Rona acting like she's tough, something Vonne does all the time and Vonne thinking she's Billy Bad Ass like me. Maybe you bitches shouldn't be drinking at all tonight. Seems like y'all already fucked up, twisted and confused!"

"Okay, *J'Nae!* Always trying to take things down a notch." Rona said following suit.

"I know, right." Zsasha laughed. "Must be a full fucking moon tonight or something."

"I don't know about a full moon, but Jupiter is in Ur-anus!" Vonne laughed.

"No, not since the late nineties, sweetie!" Zsasha recalled.

"You freak!" Vonne yelled.

"Takes one to know one."

"Can't lie about that." Vonne admitted.

"I bet you've been waiting your entire adult life to tell that astronomy joke, haven't you Vonne?" Rona asked.

"Yeah, pretty much. Don't you think it's funny?" Vonne asked.

"I think it was funny, once upon a time and also true...for that heffa!" Rona remarked.

"Whatever bitches." Zsasha jokes.

"So, do you have anything stronger in house? I mean this wine is great but I'm kind of beyond wine right now."

"Yes, you are and yes, I do. We're always fully stocked here. What would you like, sista girl? Your wish is my command!"

"Well let's see...I'm tired of tall, dark and handsome...I don't really have a taste for that right now. How about something light, bright, and damn near white."

"I can make that happen. Give me a minute, I'll be right back." Zsasha retreated to her office and emerged with a large bottle of Don Ramon Silver Swarovski Limited Edition Tequila and placed the bottle on the table.

"Damn, girl, you don't mess around." Vonne stated.

"Ain't nobody got time for that!" Zsasha snapped, shrugging her shoulders and moving her neck side to side while she spoke.

"So Vonne, are you feeling like sharing now?" J'Nae asked.

"Yeah, we're all very concerned about you." Rona reiterated.

"I don't even know where to begin. It seems like Lee and I are arguing more and more these days and it usually has something to do with Kiera."

"Kiera? Why are you and your husband arguing about your sister? Does he want her gone, too?" Zsasha questioned.

"On the contrary, he thinks I'm too hard on her and anytime she and I have a disagreement, he takes her side, and that usually starts a whole new argument between us."

"Wow, really?" J'Nae sounded surprised at her revelation.

"Yes, really."

"Vonne, I know you've been trying to help your sister and everything, but now it's causing a problem in your marriage. Don't you think it's time to ask her to leave?" Rona asked.

"And go where?" Vonne snapped back. "She ain't got no money."

"What about what you've been paying her? She's been working for you long enough to have put some money up." Rona rebutted. "I'm sure you're paying her well and somehow she finagled her way into a really nice car."

"I am paying her and it's more than she deserves but I don't know what she's doing with it. Maybe she's sending money back to help her dad out. But financially, she's in no shape to live on her own."

"Back to the real issue, your husband. I like his nerve, taking her side over yours." Rona stated.

"It's a little bit more than that." Vonne confessed. "Remember when Lee left his phone in my office, and I saw they've been texting each other for a while?"

"Texting each other...what exactly do you mean?" J'Nae inquired.

"Yeah, I remember. After you calmed down and took time to really review the messages, the time, and date, you determined your sister was the culprit and that Lee was just politely responding and was in no way encouraging her or being inappropriate."

"That's right. See, those earlier messages were mostly about work issues and any time Kiera tried to go slightly beyond that, Lee didn't take the bait. That's how it all started but from what I've seen lately, it's strictly social now. They talk and text more with each other than either of them does with me. And truthfully, I don't think I like my sister having that kind of relationship with my husband."

"And you shouldn't." Zsasha said. "Have you confronted Lee about it?"

"Yeah, that's what we were arguing about when y'all showed up. He says he's just trying to be a friend to her and encourage her to value herself more in hopes of building her self-confidence."

"Well, okay, I can see that, sort of." J'Nae explained. "However, if you feel his behavior has crossed the line in any way, you need to trust your instincts. You know your husband and your sister better than any of us."

"I do, but he says it's totally innocent and I'm tripping. Of course, he followed it up by reminding me that he didn't want her here to begin with but since I took her in, I should follow through on my obligation."

"Not if it's upsetting you and causing marital distress." J'Nae clarified.

"I'm beyond stressed, but maybe I'm overreacting. Lee might do some stupid shit from time to time, but he knows what side his bread is buttered on."

"Are you sure about that?" Zsasha asked. "Because I know niggas. And niggas do nigga shit, every last one of them. You need to put an end to this threesome you've been living, sooner rather than later."

"Dang, Zsasha, did you have to put it like that?" J'Nae asked.

"Why not? When have you ever known for me to bite my tongue, especially about something as serious as this. These words might sting a bit right now but the alternative down the road is a whole lot worse, trust me."

418

"You're right Z, you're absolutely right." Vonne agreed.

"So, what did your sister have to say about the situation?" Rona asked.

"Not a whole lot. She's been at the boutique all day and couldn't really discuss it over the phone with customers all around. She should be home by now."

"You plan on addressing this tonight?" Rona inquired.

"Nah, I'm going to wait until morning while Lee is out for his morning run, then we're gonna sit down and discuss a few things."

"Well, it sounds like you got a plan laid out and you know what you have to do." J'Nae concluded.

"For sure. I already have people coming in early to cover for both of us in the morning so there won't be any excuses."

"I can swing by in the morning for moral support or just to monitor the situation. I remember how you stepped up for me back in the day, so I got you, just say the word."

"Thanks Z but I think I can handle it at this point."

"Cool, just keep us posted, you know, in case anything jumps off, I got you!" Zsasha confirmed.

"We got you!" Rona and J'Nae chimed in.

"I know y'all do and I appreciate that. Now, let's get going. I need to look over the books tonight if I'm gonna take a few hours off in the morning to holla at my sister. Who's driving me back?"

"I can't." Zsasha replied. "I have a few loose ends to tie up here myself. John Lee left a bit of a mess earlier today I need to take care of so one of y'all can drop her off, right?"

"I can." J'Nae said. "It'll give us a little time for some one on one."

"Great."

"Look y'all, I really appreciate you coming through to check on me. It means a lot."

"Girl you know we got you. You're one of us. We ain't gonna let nobody hurt you, not even that nigga. And anything you're going through, we're going through together. Got it?"

"Got it. Zsasha, Rona, holla at y'all later. You ready J'Nae?"

419

"Hold on, I'm walking out with y'all." Rona insisted.

"Y'all be careful out there. I won't be long, I promise."

"We will and since you're hanging here for a bit let's do the phone tree tonight, ok ladies?" Rona suggested.

"Yeah, let's do that." Zsasha agreed.

"Cool and lock up behind us." Rona ordered.

"I'm right behind you, thirty minutes or less, I promise."

"Okay, goodnight."

"Bye Zsasha. Again, thanks for looking out for me."

"Always, I'll text y'all when I'm leaving and again when I get home."

Zsasha closed the door and put the lock on as she watched her friends drive away. She turned and looked at wine and liquor classes on the table and the trash bags left behind filled with remnants from the recent delivery. She just couldn't understand why John Lee would take out all the trash except for 2 bags left by the back entrance.

There's always a ton of packing material when shipments this size come in. Some of the material was reusable but most was not. In any event John Lee or one of the other staff members always took care of this sort of thing. Obviously, it had been overlooked. But since she was cleaning up after the spontaneous girl's night that just ended, it really wasn't a big deal. Besides, it had happened before.

First, she gathered the used wine and liquor glasses, washed them and put them away for next time, then stored her 'Special Occasion' bottle of Tequila in her office. While there, she took a minute to see if there was any trash in her office that had also been missed. There was none. Everything was tidy and in place, so she proceeded to the back door to dispose of the 2 trash bags left behind.

Walking out the rear entrance that also doubled as the main entrance to *Ahsasz Down Under,* Zsasha took a quick look around as she always did. She almost always parked in the alley mostly out of convenience. Grabbing a bag in each hand she proceeded towards the dumpster while realizing the bags were loosely tied and close to coming apart. She dropped both bags to the ground taking a moment to tie each of them properly. The last thing she needed were other tenants complaining about various pieces of Styrofoam all over the alley. Once both bags were properly tied, she tossed one in the dumpster then the other and was abruptly caught off guard as someone was instantly upon her.

Instinctively she wanted to turn around and see what or who was behind her but the moment she tried to move someone grabbed her midsection while forcibly pressing a hard object against her back. It felt like a gun.

"Don't move!" the voice behind her said. "Don't scream and I won't kill you."

"What do you want?" Zsasha demanded with her voice trembling in fear. "I don't have any money!"

"I don't want your money, sweet cheeks." The voice replied as he tightened his grip on her as if to appear more demanding. Yet seconds later, he loosened his hold on her with his left hand and immediately pressed up against her pinning her to the dumpster. "I'm here for you. You're what I want and what I must have."

His right hand began to explore the front of her body, going lower and lower eventually reaching downward then quickly up under her skirt. Zsasha tensed up, frantically looking around for help or a possible escape route. She found neither one. Surely someone was still in the building or at least within earshot distance even at this hour. Before she knew it, her stockings were ripped across her backside exposing her bare ass.

Instinctively, her mind went back to a time much like this one. She was in college extremely intoxicated and vulnerable, something she vowed she'd never be again. She recalled the unfortunate turn of events on that fateful college night and was certain she was in the midst of a real live recreation of that traumatic event. But help had arrived. She heard footsteps then a voice approaching screaming at the individual then chasing him off down the alley.

"Miss, miss, are you alright?"

"Oh, yes. Thank you, thank you so much. He had a gun and was gonna rape me!"

421

"Are you okay ma'am?"

"I will be, in a minute."

"I'm gonna call 911." Just after reaching for his phone, the rescuer looked up, recognizing the woman in distress. "Zsasha? Zsasha, Is that you?"

Zsasha took a minute to look more closely at the face of the man who had just saved her from being raped. After looking closely, it didn't take her any time at all to recognize her hero.

"Adam? Is that you?"

"Yes, it's me, Adam, Ellie's friend."

"Oh boy am I glad to see you! What are you doing here this time of night?"

"I was supposed to pick up Ellie. Where is she, inside?"

"No, I'm afraid not."

"I thought the two of you were scheduled to work on something tonight?"

"That's right. We were supposed to meet here but something came up and I had to cancel at the last minute."

"I should really call the cops."

"No, don't bother. I'm sure he's long gone by now anyway. Besides, he didn't hurt me, just scared me a bit."

"Well, it looked like he was about to..."

"I know what he thought he was about to do but he didn't. So, let's just leave it at that, shall we? I didn't see his face anyway so I wouldn't be able to identify him anyway. I don't even know if he was black or white so what's the point?"

"If you're sure, then I won't."

"I am. And I'm thankful you showed up when you did. I appreciate that, Adam. I'm usually on point 24/7. I don't know what happened just now, but I owe you a huge debt."

"Nonsense. You don't owe me anything. I'm just happy I was here in time to intervene. Are you about to lock up for the night?"

"Yes, I'm done!" Zsasha chuckled.

"Alright then, let me walk you to your car."

"Normally, I would say no, it's not necessary, but this time, yes, definitely a yes. Let me go inside and grab my things then we can go. I'm parked just over there. Just give me a minute."

The two chatted as Zsasha gathered her belongings, locked up the gallery and was escorted to her car. Zsasha had found Adam to be quite likeable and well spoken. He had made a lasting impression on her and she was more than impressed with the young man.

The next morning, Zsasha was awakened by an early cell phone call but didn't manage to answer it before the call was routed to voicemail. Taking a moment to shake off the morning haze, her mind was flooded with memories of last night's unfortunate events. Once she gathered herself and her thoughts, she saw the missed call was from Rona and quickly dialed her back.

"Zsasha, are you still in bed?" Rona asked.

"Yeah, I slept in today, had a rough night. What's up?"

"What's up is that you didn't do the phone tree last night. I'm just checking to make sure you're straight."

"Well actually, something kinda did happen after you all left."

"What are you talking about? Are you alright?"

"I'm fine but while I was taking the trash to the dumpster out back some guy ran up on me and attacked me."

"What? Are you okay? Did he hurt you?"

"Naw girl, I'm good."

"So what exactly happened?"

"Long story short, some idiot grabbed me while I was taking out the trash and pinned me up against the dumpster."

"For real?"

"Yeah. I felt what I thought was a gun in my back, but I don't know now."

"What was it then?"

"I'm not sure. The next thing I know his hand is pushing up my skirt, ripping my pantyhose off so he could feel me up. That's when I knew things were about to get ugly."

"My goodness, Zsasha! Are you alright? Where was Simon?"

423

"I'm fine I said, and Simone was at home. It just so happened that Adam showed up just in the nick of time. He was supposed to pick up Ellie. Remember I was planning on meeting up with her but forgot about it when we decided to go by Vonne's?"

"Oh, yeah, I vaguely remember she called while we were in the car heading to your spot."

"Yeah, she must have forgotten to cancel with him."

"Well things happen for a reason, and it all worked out in the end, right?"

"Oh yeah, I'm straight...I'm good."

"But still Zsasha, you had to be scared. You can't tell me that ordeal didn't impact you."

"Of course it did, but it all happened so fast that I didn't realize what was going on or how scared I really was until after Adam chased him off."

"Guuurrrrl, it was a good thing he showed up when he did, you were lucky. Ain't no telling what would have happened if he hadn't shown up when he did."

"Well, I have a pretty good idea of what he wanted...that motha fucka was gonna rape me!"

"You think?"

"I'm certain of it. I felt his hand under my skirt and like I said, he ripped my stockings and stuck his hand up my skirt."

"Damn girlfriend, I'm so sorry you had to go through all that."

"Yeah, me too, but this morning I can look back and see the irony of it all."

"Irony? What do you mean?"

"You don't see it, huh?"

"No, I don't."

"For real, girl?"

"No, really, I don't. I just see the danger of it all."

"Look, how ironic is it to get sexually assaulted right outside your own sex club!"

"Girl you stupid. I can't believe you went there."

"I'm serious! Potentially, there could have been plenty of people willing to freely give it away just beyond the back door, not last night but you know what I'm saying. He must not have done his research before he took action."

"Maybe, maybe not. But most often, at least nine times out of ten, rape is a crime of opportunity."

"Yeah, but still...easy sex was just a few feet away for all he knew."

"Sweetheart, rape isn't about sex, it's about power."

"So, you're the expert now, huh?"

"Well, let's just say over the years I've had more than one reason to delve into what drives certain individuals to commit certain crimes."

"More so than me?"

"I'm just saying, this isn't something you should take likely, seriously. And you need to report this to the police and get yourself some counseling. This was a traumatic event even if you don't see it right now, it is. And if you don't deal with it head on, ain't no telling how it will manifest itself in your life down the road."

"That's not necessary, seriously, I'm good."

"Are you shitting me?"

"No, not at all. I just don't see a reason to blow it out of proportion. Nothing happened and I'm fine."

"Well keep telling yourself that or whatever lie you feel you need to convince yourself to buy your own bullshit. But let the record show I object to your handling of this situation."

"Noted. Now can I go, I've got a few things I need to take care of this morning."

"Yeah, me too. I have an open house to prepare for. But don't get it twisted, this is one of those things I'll share with Vonne and J'Nae, regardless of what you're talking about."

"Bye girl."

"Bye."

Chapter 37

Almost a week passed before the girls were all together again in part because most of them had a lot going on within their family units. On some level, they were all distracted. Rona was more than concerned with Zsasha's experience and knew more than likely she hadn't shared that ordeal with anyone. On top of that, Vonne had already been going through a lot at home and J'Nae's secretive ass couldn't be trusted to divulge damn near anything. She decided to send out an early morning urgent text requesting each of them to be present at The Coffee House by 7:45 am.

J'Nae woke up to the sound of her cell phone pinging but chose to reach over to the warm hard body that was snuggled up beside her.

"Good morning baby." Wes said.

"Good morning. I'm sorry, did my cell phone wake you up? I forgot to turn it on silent last night."

"It's all good. It's about time to get up anyway."

"Do we have to? Why can't we stay like this all day? I love it when we're in our love bubble."

"I do too, baby, but we need to handle our business, some of which is moving the rest of my stuff in and taking what we don't need to the storage unit."

"Moving the rest of your stuff in...I definitely like the sound of that!"

"Me too." Wes said and confirmed with a kiss. "Have you told the girls yet?"

"No, I haven't. Not quite sure how I want to go about it."

"Just tell them. They already know we've been seeing each other, right?"

"Yes, they do, but seeing each other and living together are two different things. I haven't even told Taizja and Aiden yet."

"The kids will be fine with it. They know we've been dating for a while, and they've met me. If they were against it, they would have said something by now. They just want to see you happy. You are happy, right?"

"Yes, I am happy. You make me happy, Mr. Wesley Hill."

"Good, because I'm happy and I feel like the luckiest man on earth. So don't worry about the kids, they will be fine. You did more than most would have as far as honoring your late husband."

"Thank you for saying that and you're right, the kids are fine with us being together but the girls, that's another story."

"They'll come around as well. They love you and want to see you happy."

"So they've said, but I feel like it's a thing, you know, like an elephant in the room that no one wants to address. I just want to make sure they understand that just because they're just now finding out about us doesn't mean this is a new thing."

"Honey, you're worrying about it too much. Everything will be fine. They've always supported you and your decisions, why would it be any different now?"

"I know and you're right, I'm stressing myself unnecessarily. I'll just plan a get together or something here at the house and just casually ease them into our plans."

"I think that's a great idea considering how we handled things up to this point. And the sooner, the better. Since we already got busted by Rona, I think we should take a more aggressive approach and hit me with everything at once."

"I don't know babe, you don't know them like I do. Even though they seem to be okay with us, they do feel slighted about all the secrecy. Telling them about us dating all this time is one thing but telling them about our plans is next level."

"I know it seems like a lot to take in but in my experience it's best to just rip the band aid off quickly. It'll sting for a minute but once they get past the initial shock, then it's done. We won't have to do this again. Everything will be out in the open. No more tip toeing around. Isn't that what you want?"

"Yes, it is."

"So it's time. It's time to let them know how we feel about each other and share our plans. They need to know I'm in your life for good."

"Yes, they do."

"Well alrighty then. So how soon do you think we should do this?"

"How about a week from this Saturday? I can ask Ms. Honey to cater for us. She's a really good cook. You'll love her."

"I'm sure I will."

"I'll just have to reach out to her and see if she's available. If not, she has a backup she works with regularly."

"So then, what do you want me to do to help pull this off at the spur of the moment?"

"Uhm...you could get some fresh flowers from my florist. Just give them my name and tell them you want my dinner party order. They'll take care of the rest."

"So what, you have a standing order at your local florist?"

"Yes, I do, more than one."

"Why does that not surprise me?" Wes responded, shaking his head in disbelief.

"Quit it. I can't help it if I'm organized like that!"

"I wouldn't describe your behavior as organized, more like obsessive, maybe a bit controlling."

"Oh my goodness, you did not just say that!"

"Yeah, yeah I did, and you know you are."

"*Obsessive*...Me?"

"Yes, you."

"How dare you! You just wait, wait until I get my hands on you."

"Well put your cell phone down and get your hands on me now."

"Sorry, no can do. Emergency with the girls. I need to meet them at The Coffee House asap. It says to be prepared to be there for about an hour, no excuses."

"Well you better get moving."

"I got this."

"Uhm, don't you need to be showering right now?"

429

"Yes, I do, smarty pants." J'Nae replied walking towards the bathroom. "And make the bed!"

"I will, I will, but don't get used to this." Wes chuckled.

Shortly thereafter, J'Nae arrived at The Coffee House intent on grabbing a coffee with the girls for what she thought was a quick impromptu meetup. To her surprise everyone was there and looked quite serious. Intrigued, she took her regular seat and signaled for the waitress to come over with her usual coffee order.

"Good morning." J'Nae said. "I see everybody's here. What's up? What did I miss?"

"You didn't miss anything...*today*. We actually just got here ourselves." Rona replied.

"So what's going on? An emergency meeting on such short notice, something's up."

"Well lately, everyone's been a bit busy juggling their lives and obligations and so on that we haven't really been in touch with each other as much as we usually do, and I thought this would be a good time to check in and see what's going on in each other's lives." Rona explained. "Sometimes we tend to get caught up in our own issues and either forget we are part of a sisterhood where we rely on each other. Sometimes we may want to keep certain things to ourselves for whatever reason instead of reaching out and sharing with each other and utilizing the support system that's been in place for what seems like forever. We get busy with life and before you know it, we're not confiding in each other when change occurs or when significant events happen in our lives."

"Funny that you mentioned that. I was just discussing that very same thing with Wes this morning."

"That's great J'Nae, however that's an example of the disconnect I'm talking about; what 've been feeling, what we've all been feeling. It's part of the reason why we're all here right now."

"Wes? Really?"

"Part of the reason, J'Nae, *part*." Rona reiterated.

"Yeah girl." Zsasha chimed in. "I think we all have a little something we want or need to share with the group, so we all know what's been going on with each other. You know, for support or whatever."

"I'll start." Rona decided. "Vonne, you have been going through a lot lately with your family, so, so much. The situation with Lee and Kiera has been weighing you down and we all see it and what it's doing to you. We're all concerned about you and want you to know that we're in your corner. We're here for you, no matter what."

"Rona, I appreciate that, so much. All of you. Your support means the world to me and yes, I've been going through it with those two on a regular basis for a while now but that's old news. You all did a welfare check on me not too long ago so something else must be going on, so what's up? This last-minute urgent text requesting our presence this morning wasn't called due to my situation. What's the real reason why we're all here? Somebody enlighten me."

"Zsasha, why don't you go ahead and start." Rona requested.

Taking a long sip from her coffee and a very deep breath, Zsasha paused as she processed Rona's request. She looked at everyone at the table, one at a time before she opened her mouth. She knew it wasn't going to be an easy conversation, but it was definitely one that needed to be had. No way Rona would keep this one to herself.... *bitch*.

"Okay, well last week while I was closing up after you all left, I went out back to take out the trash that Simon and John Lee left behind. While I was out by the dumpster a man came out of nowhere, grabbed me and pinned me to the dumpster and ripped off my stockings so he could get under my skirt."

"Oh, my goodness, Zsasha, are you okay?" Vonne asked.

"I am sweetie. Luckily Adam showed up acting like a lightweight gangster and chased the dude off."

"I can't believe this happened, what about your security system? I thought you guys updated it a while back. How could this happen?" J'Nae asked.

"Girlfriend, anything's possible nowadays. We live in a world where a lot of people have lost their fucking minds. There're all kinds of crazy around every corner and most of the time you don't even see it coming."

"But are you okay, I mean for real? Did he..." J'Nae inquired.

"No, he didn't rape me, but I believe he was about to, especially after he ripped my stockings off and had his hand in my crotch. He whispered some bullshit just as Adam showed up."

"Oh my goodness, girl. What did Simon have to say about all of this?" J'Nae asked.

"Nothing, I didn't tell him. I saw no reason to. The guy was as scared as I was. He was a young punk probably high on drugs and didn't really know what he was doing. Trust me, he won't be back."

"How can you be so sure?" Vonne asked.

"I can't believe you didn't tell Simon!" J'Nae proclaimed.

"Me either. He needs to know what happened to you at the club, Zsasha." Rona stated. "He's your husband. You spend a great deal of time there without him."

"Well, I disagree. We've been planning to upgrade our security system again and I'll make sure that happens sooner rather than later. And I won't take the trash out late at night by myself ever again."

"So why did you do it then?" Vonne asked. "This happened shortly after we'd left, right?"

"Yeah, it did. I don't usually take the trash out at all, y'all know I have people for that type of thing. But I almost always park in the back and use the rear entrance. We have camera's covering that door, but they don't expand to cover the alley way. A decision made a while back for member privacy concerns and such."

"So what now? How are you going to prevent this from happening again?" J'Nae asked.

"I just told you. I appreciate y'all being concerned and all, looking out for a sista and all that, but I got this. I'm not even tripping. Really, it's kind of funny when you think about it. I almost got raped behind my own sex club!"

"Seriously Zsasha, you're going there!"

"I'm just saying, with this lifestyle comes certain risks, sometimes you attract the wrong type of individuals. No harm done. It's all good, I promise. I'm taking precautions so nothing like that will ever happen again."

"I hope not." Vonne responded. "But I do think you should tell Simon about it. He'll be furious with you if he finds out any other way."

"He won't. Y'all know the sista code, so forget about it. I'm good. Now J'Nae, we haven't heard from you yet. How about you give us an update about what's been going on in your life."

Momentarily, J'Nae's face went from that of a concerned friend to one of a deer caught in the headlights. She hesitated for a while longer but still didn't open her mouth.

"Well, spit it out girl." Vonne said. We all know what you've been up to lately."

"Yeah, you've been M.I.A. for more than a minute." Rona confirmed. What's up, sista girl? We know it has something to do with that new guy you've been seeing."

"Well, actually it does, but I promise you, it's not what you think."

Bolstering her way into the conversation, Zsasha didn't hesitate to live up to J'Nae's initial concerns about sharing her news. Zsasha and J'Nae had been friends since college and always had each other's backs, but Zsasha could also be judgmental at times and not always tasteful about it.

"I think you've been screwing around with this random motha fucka and been too ashamed to tell us about it." Zsasha declared.

The hesitation and reluctancy had disappeared. She wasn't about to let anybody, even her girls come for her man. She came full force with her response.

"Well, first of all, Wes is not some random motha fucka that I've been screwing around with. Yes, we've been dating for some time now and it's getting serious. Actually, I should say it is serious."

"So, why have you been so secretive about it?" Zsasha asked. "Are you ashamed of him for some reason?"

"I am absolutely not ashamed of Wes in any way! Truth be told, we're in love! In fact, he's already moved in with me and we are planning to spend the rest of our lives together."

"Well damn girl, you got all this going on and kept it from us?"

"Yeah J'Nae, don't you think it looks a little suspect to us? We're your best friends and you chose not to share it with any of us. How are we supposed to feel about that?" Vonne asked.

"I understand, really, I do but I had my reasons for keeping it to myself initially. After a while, it just got easy and eventually time just got away from me and I got comfortable. I simply didn't want anything to disrupt the love bubble we'd created for ourselves."

"Love bubble?" Vonne asked.

"Yes, our love bubble. It's when we block out the entire world and focus 100% on each other. We talk, we share, and it becomes some of our most intimate and treasured time spent together."

"Wow, that sounds amazing. You must really love him, J'Nae."

"I do Vonne, and we're planning our future together."

"So then, why the secrecy?"

"Well, Zsasha...you're my girl and all but you gotta know you are often judgmental and pretty hard on a sista. I didn't think you would approve. I didn't think any of you would approve."

"Approve of what, him, the kind of man he is, what?"

"No, nothing like that. He's truly wonderful."

"Then what?" Zsasha stammered.

J'Nae hesitated, not quite sure how to convey her feelings without being hurtful. She looked over to Rona for assistance. Rona did not disappoint.

"Well, she felt we would have issues with the speed in which she moved on. That was her primary reason for being secretive."

"Is that true, J'Nae?" Zsasha asked.

"Yes, it is."

"So how is it that Rona knows how you feel and Zsasha and I don't?" Vonne stammered.

"Well let me answer that." Rona interrupted. "I walked in on them the night I stopped by to check on the house. After knocking and not getting an answer, I let myself in with the hide-a-key and well, the rest is self-explanatory."

"So, you've known about the seriousness of their relationship all this time?"

"No Zsasha, I didn't. J'Nae never shared anything like that with me. But I will say I had my suspicions. Afterall, we are talking about J'Nae. She ain't just shacking up with somebody for the hell of it."

"That's right. Y'all know I ain't that chick!"

"Yeah sista, we do. But that's a lot to keep to yourself. And now you say y'all planning to build a life together. Just when did all of this happen? How long has this been going on? Where did you guys meet? Does he have any kids? When do we get to meet this Wes?"

Zsasha kept the questions coming without pausing for a moment to give J'Nae a chance to respond. She was obviously hurt and caught up in her feelings of being shut out from what she was learning was a significant part of J'Nae life.

"Well, that's actually part of the news I was hoping to share today."

"Do tell, girlfriend."

"Well, we've been talking about having a small dinner party, just a few close friends...something intimate and private. Sort of like a coming out party but coming out only to those closest to us."

"I can see that." Rona acknowledged.

"Great. We had the idea of hosting it at the house a week from this Saturday evening."

"You guys don't waste any time, do you?" Zsasha snickered.

"Well, if I learned anything this past year it's that time is the most precious commodity there is, next to life of course and none of us know how much of it we have left."

435

"True dat, true dat." Zsasha concurred.

"I don't want to waste any of it, especially when you know what you have is real, that it's right."

"Sounds like things are very serious between you two."

"They are Vonne, and I can't wait for you all to meet him."

"Well, I don't know about these heffa's but count me in. I'll be the one carrying the third degree in my hand and he's gonna get it."

"I wouldn't expect anything less from you, Zsasha. I appreciate you having my back and all."

"Always, you're my girl."

After wrapping up the conversation and morning out some details about the dinner party, the ladies took their unfinished coffee to go and went on with their day. They had a lot to contemplate between Vonne's issues, Zsasha's assault and J'Nae and her news about Wes. Rona was the only one that hadn't revealed anything traumatic or out of the ordinary, at least not yet.

* * * * *

The next morning felt like any other day. Vonne was up a bit earlier than usual. As planned, she had staff members opening two locations of The Boutique so she could have some leisurely time with Kiera for a talk that was long overdue. So as not to come off abrasive or harsh, Vonne took the time to prepare a light and healthy breakfast they could share to ease into their discussion. It was long overdue and having peace in her home was a necessity.

"Good morning."

"Hey, good morning Kiera. I made breakfast, help yourself."

"Really, that's a nice surprise." Kiera replied. "Thanks."

"I'll join you. It'll give us a chance to talk."

"I feel an ambush coming. What is it this time?"

"Cut it out. I'm not going to let you make me out to be a villain just because I want to discuss a few things with you. By the way, what's all that you brought down with you?"

"Some stuff I want to drop off at the dry cleaners early enough to get it back today."

"Oh, well I can drop it off for you. You've been using Charlie's, right?"

"Yes, I have."

"Okay. I'll drop it off on my way out this morning."

"Are you sure?" Kiera asked. "I don't want to take you out of your way."

"No, I've got it. I have a few things to pick up anyway."

"Okay, cool."

Kiera began to eat some of the sliced fruit and yogurt on her small plate.

"Is that all you want?"

"Yeah, for starters. So what did you want to talk to me about?"

"Well, let's see…. boundaries, yeah, that's the best way I can put it. I think there are some boundaries that you're crossing that make me uncomfortable, here, in my home."

"I don't understand. Can you be a bit more specific?"

"Yes, I can. For starters, I don't like you texting my husband and being overly sociable with him."

"Seriously? Lee is just like a friend. We're just being friendly with one another, that's all."

"Sweetheart, my husband is your brother-in-law. He is **not** your friend. And other than in an emergency, there is no reason why you two should be texting each other about your day and so on. It's highly inappropriate."

"I don't know what the big deal is. I barely know anybody here and you're always out with The Girls. I'm almost always by myself. It's not like you invite me for wine and cheese at the gallery and you spend a lot of time there, really."

"That may be true but it's not the point. You need to go out and make your own friends and stop looking towards mine and my husband to fill whatever void you may have in your life. It's just not right Kiera, private dinners by the fireplace or on the patio with my husband, no honey, that's my job, not yours. You don't need to be doing anything with Lee, you understand?"

"Yeah, I got it."

"I'm serious Kiera. We've had a few other issues, but this is next level."

"It's not all on me, you know."

"I do so trust and believe I'm already on it. Lee is a generous person, and this would not be the first time his generosity and stupidity created issues. So no, I'm not putting all this on you, but remember, you're a guest in my home. Respect is a minimum. And if you can't do that, we'll have to look at modifying this arrangement. Helping you is not supposed to hurt me, in any way."

"I'm sorry, sis. I really didn't think it was an issue but it's cool. I understand and I promise I'll do better."

"I hope so, because you're getting pretty good running your store and I would hate to have to replace you."

"I appreciate you saying that Vonne."

"I mean it. I admit, I didn't think it was a good fit at first, but you have proven me wrong."

"Thanks sis."

"So, I'm gonna grab up this stuff to drop off at Charlie's, can you put the leftovers away?"

"Absolutely. I love you sis."

"I love you too, Kiera."

With that, Vonne gathered the garment bag and walked out of the kitchen to the garage where her car was parked. She tossed the garment bag over the passenger seat and headed on her way to Charlie's. She was relieved with the result of her talk with Kiera and somewhat surprised it didn't go south. There had been so much tension building up between them recently that it was almost predetermined to end badly. Nonetheless she felt Kiera really heard her this time and understood her issues. Parking her car, she grabbed the garment bag and headed inside.

"Good morning, Charlie."

"Good afternoon Ms. Vonne. How are you?"

"I'm good. You know I never get tired of saying that."

"I know, angel. And I never get tired of hearing that." Charlie confessed. "I've got you all setup right over here."

"That's great. Can you put all of this on my account?"

"Absolutely. And I was able to get the stain out of your silk blouse."

"My silk blouse? I don't recall giving you a silk blouse to clean, but it's been almost a week since I've been here. I guess I just forgot."

"No Ms. Vonne, your sister dropped it off two days ago, the light blue charmeuse blouse. Here, take a look."

As Vonne was looking over the contents of the items she was picking up, she was caught off guard once again, realizing that some of the items she was picking up had been dropped off by Kiera which prompted her to look through the garment bag she was dropping off now. And of course, some of the items were hers. Not only was she dropping off and picking up her own clothes she hadn't worn recently, she knew her sister had been borrowing her clothes without asking. Some of which cost more than what average Americans make in one week. How dare she!

"Well thank you Charlie. I'll just be taking these home and I'm sure I'll see you soon."

"Yes, you will and thank you, Ms. Vonne. Have a good day."

"Bye Charlie."

Furious and steaming, Vonne carried her items to the car with a stride that was quick and purposeful. With every step her anger grew beyond the step before. It's never going to end, she thought to herself. I give her ass an inch and she'll take a fucking mile. All she had to do was ask. I would have let her borrow just about anything in my closet...well probably not but damn, this bitch is going through my things and just taking what she wants when she wants it. I'm not putting up with that, especially not in my own house.

She decided to head home and have another conversation with Lee. But when she arrived, the house was completely empty. She could tell he had returned from his morning exercise routine because his dirty jogging clothes were laid out in the laundry room. She could also see that he had a bite to eat, and his car was gone.

Heading back to her car she called her husband to see where he was, but she didn't get an answer. She drove for a bit contemplating her next move. Kiera was closing up that night, so she knew it would be a while before she would make it home. However, this was too much. Vonne felt that it just couldn't wait until late in the evening. She decided to make arrangements to cover for them both, which would give Vonne time to deal with her sister. She just couldn't wait until later in the evening when they'd both be at home.

Meanwhile, Zsasha arrived at the gallery shortly before another truck showed up to make a delivery. It contained new and updated staging equipment she and Simon ordered to accommodate some of the larger, out-of-the-ordinary sculptures the younger, new age artists often created. Simon was otherwise occupied with some sort of business, so Zsasha had to handle it on her own.

It was still early enough in the day whereas the sun hadn't completely gone down, so she had no issues being outside with the delivery men overseeing the items carried inside. She'd done it before many times however this was the first time she'd been alone at the gallery since the attack.

"Here, let me get the door for you." Zsasha said as the driver and his assistant began unloading large well packed containers from the rear of the truck.

"We usually deliver to the rear entrance, but someone called and requested we deliver to the front entrance today."

"That's correct. That was me." Zsasha replied.

"Just let us know where you want us to set the items down, ma'am. Most of these are extremely heavy."

"I can help you with that." A voice replied.

Startled, Zsasha swung around, a bit surprised by yet another random voice. It was Adam.

"Adam, hey. What are you doing here?"

"I just stopped by to check on you and make sure you weren't alone and doing what you're obviously doing by yourself."

"You didn't have to do that."

"I know I didn't have to, but I wanted to. I hadn't seen or heard from you since that night, and I wanted to make sure you were okay and being taken care of. I was hoping you changed your mind and told your husband what happened, and he'd be here handling this sort of thing, and yet... here you are."

"Well, that's more my fault than his."

"Oh really...how so?"

"It's simple. I never told him about the other night."

"Really now...well why not?"

"I didn't want to."

"I don't understand. Do you think he would blame you for what happened or something?"

"No, nothing like that."

"Well then, what is it?"

"I just didn't tell him, alright. He's got a lot on his plate. Just let it go."

"Maybe I will, maybe I won't. But under no circumstance should you be out here alone taking deliveries in the rear or in the front, even if it's still daytime. What happened the other night was serious, very serious and could have been a lot worse. Don't you get that?"

"Yes, I do, but there's nothing much I can do about it now, is there?"

"Wrong answer. There are several things you can do about it. Number 1, quit coming out here alone late at night, regardless of the circumstance. Number 2, hire staff to deal with this sort of thing, preferably a big, strong, scary looking black man and I'm not trying to be racist either. But big, strong, black men are really intimidating, to scrawny little white boys like myself and that guy was a scrawny little white boy."

"You got jokes."

"Yes, I do, and number 3, improve your scheduling."

"What exactly do you mean?"

"I mean, schedule deliveries to arrive during the day or even better yet, during a specific 2-4-hour window that you determine. Have staff onsite to deal with the deliveries and unpacking, then delegate how you want things staged, better

441

yet, map it out. Realize the power you have. These up-and-coming artists are willing to do more than you realize to get their artwork in a gallery like yours."

"Is that right?"

"Definitely. From what I see, you're still running the place like it's a step above a startup. It's not like you guys are hurting for money or anything. Use some of that massive fortune you and Simon have accumulated to make managing your business easier on yourselves. Trust me, it's possible. And for all you know, freeing up your time may end up yielding greater returns for the gallery as you become more available to seek out new talent or maybe spending time creating your own works of art. I know you have it in you. You're an amazing artist."

"Wow Adam, you're smarter than you look."

"Hmm, Is that a compliment?"

"For sure. You just might be onto something."

"Well thank you, Ms. Zsasha. And please feel free to pick my brain or ask for whatever assistance you may need. I would be more than happy to help you in any way I can."

"That's awesome, Adam. I just may have to take you up on that. More than a few things have fallen through the cracks, and it might be a good idea to have someone else dedicated to managing certain things. It would definitely make my life easier."

"Well just let me know how I can help you make that happen. I have a few contacts in the area that might be able to assist you in finding just what you need."

"That sounds great, but I don't think it's necessary."

"Beg your pardon, ma'am."

"I think I've already found just what I need."

"Really?"

"Yes, really."

"Ok cool. But if that's the case, why haven't you already put the plan into action?"

"I'm working on it right now."

"So then where is this solution? Who or what is it you think is the solution to your problems?"

"You."

"Me?"

"Yes, you. Don't act so surprised."

"I don't understand."

"Sure you do.   The entire time you were critiquing my business needs, you were purposely highlighting the ones that best fit your skillset."

"That's not true, at least not entirely."

"There you go...let the truth surface, you'll feel better in the end."

"I didn't come here with an agenda, Ms. Zsasha. I came here completely out of concern for you."

"No doubt, but there's more, am I right?"

"Well I care very deeply for Ellie, and she seems to be growing fonder of you the more time you two spend together. So, when she's happy, I'm happy."

"So smart yet so young...but it's more than that. I can see your potential.   You're smart, dedicated and full of top-of-the-line ideas about many of the issues Simon and I have had for some time. I would be lucky to have you in my corner. You've already proven your value in more ways than one and I feel as though I can trust you."

"Really? Wow. So exactly what did you have in mind?"

"I was thinking of something like 'Operations Manager'. What do you think about that?"

"Operations Manager? That sounds vague and general."

"Okay, what title do you feel would reflect the job you'd be doing, based on what I've shared with you so far?"

"Well, how does the Director of Procurement and Special Projects sound? That matches up a tad bit better with what you need handled, don't you think?"

"How about Manager instead of Director? This is my shit. I'm the only one directing anything around here!"

"I could work with that."

"Cool!"

"When would you like me to start?"

"How about I run some numbers tomorrow and if you're cool with what I come up with, you can start a day or two after that. I've already got a background check on you from your application to Ahsasz so we're good on that level. But you must be able to separate Ahsasz from *Ahsasz Down Under*. Now that you're an employee, you cannot discuss or share information or access with family, friends or Joe the Plumber especially anything about the club. You can't even confirm its existence. Is that understood?"

"I can do that."

"Alrighty then, and for now, don't mention our potential arrangement to Simon or any of the staff, cool?"

"Cool...but I can share it with Ellie, right?"

"Yeah, but that's it until I tell you otherwise, got it?"

"Got it."

"And she needs to keep it to herself as well."

"No problem."

"I guess I'll holla at you tomorrow."

"Sure, but I'm still staying until you leave."

"That's fine, I'm on my way out but just so you know, I'm not about to add personal security to your job description." Zsasha laughed.

"Of course not. I provide those services free of charge. But only for a select few." Adam smiled.

"I guess I got lucky twice in one night."

"Want to go for three?"

"You already know the answer to that." Zsasha said matter of factly. She knew it was coming, she just didn't know when. "Let me grab my bag and we can lock up and get out of here."

"Okay cool. I'll wait for you by the door."

Zsasha headed towards home surprised by the feeling of relief that was suddenly upon her. Not realizing how distressed she was, she was more than happy with the final outcome of the events that evening. Adam had come to her rescue once already, maybe he would do it again. Freeing up time for her and Simon to spend together would reignite their marriage.

Even with the unprecedented marital arrangement, things can still become stale.

Adam left the gallery feeling quite accomplished with himself. He managed to save Zsasha from an assault and score a job shortly thereafter. Things were moving along better than expected and he couldn't wait to share his news with Ellie. He decided to call her.

"Hey Adam, where are you?"

"I'm just leaving the gallery, heading your way."

"So how did things go with Zsasha?"

"Better than expected. I found my opening."

"Wonderful, can't wait to hear all about it!"

* * * * *

A short while later when Zsasha arrives at home, surprised yet relieved to find Simon still out and about and not answering his phone. She had no idea what she was going to tell him or if she was going to tell him and appreciated that she didn't have to think about it right away. All she wanted to do was shower and relax and distract herself with the TV. Her only companions were a bottle of Chateau Rieussec, a small fruit and vegetable plate and the television remote control. She was only twenty minutes into her me time before her cell phone rang. It was J'Nae.

"Hey J'Nae, how are you?"

"I'm good, how about you?"

"Fine, just at home chilling, enjoying some me time. What are you up to?"

"Not a whole lot. Just wanted to update you since we decided to push back our dinner party a little bit."

"I think that's a good idea, especially with everything going on with everybody."

"True, true. I admit, it would have been a bit rushed, plus Ms. Honey wasn't available that day and since I bragged on her so much to Wes, it was kind of a deal breaker."

"Well I'll be sure to thank Ms. Honey for being busy... with me." Zsasha laughed.

"So, did you guys decide on another day or what? You just gonna show up at the gallery on girls' night witcha new nigga on your arm...wassup?"

"Never that. Our sista circle is sacred. The only outside influences allowed are wine and liquor."

"Don't forget about the occasional blunt."

"What?"

"Never mind. So when and where is it?"

"Just a week later. Don't worry, you'll get an invite."

"An invite? You'd better be checking with me first if you plan on having Ms. Honey cooking or serving. You know she works for me, right?"

"Yes, Zsasha, I know. She said her schedule was wide open that day, which is why I'm reaching out to you now, so if you have anything not yet on the books that may require her services, find somebody else."

"Girl, it's all good. I have other people that can fill in for her if I was to suddenly need her for some reason so yes, she's yours for the entire day Saturday. Better yet, I'll make sure she's available to you from noon on Friday till the party wraps up. How does that sound?"

"That sounds wonderful. In fact, after we discuss some menu options and serving staff, there won't be much left for me to do. Floral arrangements, maybe but not much else."

"You can thank me later."

"Thank you Zsasha! I love you. I appreciate your sacrifice, and of course I'll pay her nicely."

"I know you will sweetie, it's not necessary but I'm sure she'll appreciate it. So how many guests are you expecting?"

"Let's see, aside from the four of us and our partners, I haven't finalized anyone else. And remember, this is basically just to introduce him to my girls. That's the agenda."

"I see, so you're keeping it on the small side, huh?"

"Yep, that's the plan. Oh, and I also plan to invite Kiera. I might even have a date for her."

"Seriously? How does Vonne feel about that?"

"I'm sure she'll be okay with it. Despite their issues, she wants to make an effort to include Kiera in some things, every now and then."

"She told you that?"

"Yes, she did. If she's not okay with it, she'll have the opportunity to let me know."

"Cool. And it is your house and your dinner party so, have it your way."

"That too, but I definitely don't want to do anything to make any of my girls uncomfortable. I'm just, you know…"

"Yeah, we all know J'Nae. You're just being you."

"Who else can I be?"

"Nobody but you sweetie, nobody but you. But look, I'm about ready to call it an early night for once. Lee's still out and I ain't waiting up for his ass either. So I'll holla tomorrow then, cool?"

"For sure. Sleep well Zsasha."

"I will, you too, sweety. Good night."

"Good night."

At the same time Zsasha and J'Nae's night was coming to an end, Vonne's evening was about to explode. After spending a few hours at the boutique she was currently working out of, she was able to find someone to come in and close up at the last minute. She didn't want to give Kiera the heads up about her visit, so she postponed her visit to just before closing time. She definitely wanted to catch her by surprise and after all the customers were gone however, like many of her plans of late, that didn't happen. By the time traffic allowed her to make it to the Arlington store, Kiera was long gone. At that point, Vonne decided to pick up some takeout and head home for the night. Maybe she'll have the opportunity to get her ass in check sometime later in the evening.

Chapter 38

Vonne arrived home to find Kiera in the kitchen grabbing a beer from the cooler. When she parked her car, she noticed Lee was still not at home which gave her the opportunity to have a private, uninterrupted talk with her sister...again.

"Hey Vonne, thanks for sending Brina over to help me close up. After giving me a late start today, you really didn't have to do that." Kiera confessed.

"I had a reason for that, sister."

"What's up?"

"You want to explain to me why you were having some of my clothes dry cleaned...clothes I haven't worn in quite some time?"

"Um, yeah."

"Don't um yeah me. What are you doing wearing my clothes? I never said you could go through my stuff and borrow whatever you want, whenever you want. You're taking way too many liberties, sista and it's got to stop!"

Kiera frowned at the unexpected issue at hand.

"I didn't think you'd mind, you have so much stuff, I didn't think you'd miss it."

"That's not the point. I allowed you to stay here in my home and I even gave you a job. Maybe I've done too much for you and you're getting too comfortable around here."

"It's not like that Vonne, really. I didn't think it would be a problem. It won't happen again."

"Oh it's a problem alright."

"I'm sorry. I didn't mean to do anything to upset you. I really didn't think you'd mind, owning your own boutiques and all."

"That's not the point. Any reasonable adult would know to ask before they help themselves to someone's personal belongings, clothes or otherwise."

"You're right, I should've asked first. My bad, sis. It won't happen again."

With that, Kiera turned and left the kitchen and went upstairs to her bedroom. She plopped down on her bed, and mumbled, "What a bitch!" But she wasn't quiet enough for Lee, who was just coming down the hallway past her bedroom and overheard her remark.

"Hey, so who's the bitch?" Lee asked, sticking his head in the doorway.

"You heard that?"

"Yes, I did."

"Well forget I said it."

"Too late, what's going on?"

"Vonne is upset because I borrowed some of her clothes without asking."

"So why didn't you just ask her?"

"Have you seen her closet? Of course you have. I just wanted to look nice while I'm working at the shop, so I borrowed some old stuff, the stuff she hasn't worn since I've been here. God knows I can't afford anything off those racks, so I improvised."

"Yes, you did." Lee laughed.

"What's so funny?"

"Don't sweat it, it'll work itself out."

"Ya think?"

"Yeah, I do."

Lee moved on his way leaving Kiera alone in her room with her thoughts. He made his way downstairs to find Vonne coming in the kitchen unpacking some takeout food she purchased on her way home.

"Is that dinner?" He asked.

"Yeah, I ordered from Caroline's and picked it up on my way home."

"This late? I'm surprised they had anything available for you. They usually close kind of early."

"Did you eat already?"

"No."

"So then what the hell is the problem?"

"What? Lee questioned.

"Never mind. Are you gonna eat?"

450

Lee sucked his teeth dissin her obvious attitude and replied with a simple and polite no. He made his way to the office and closed the door for privacy. He sat at the desk and grabbed a stash phone he had hidden underneath the desk. A moment later he was dialing a number, one that he doesn't keep in his primary cell phone.

"Hello?"

"Hey Sam, it's Lee. How are you?"

"Hey stranger, I'm good, how are you?"

"I'm good, I'm good. Listen, I need a favor from you."

"What can I do for you?"

"You know Vonne has her sister Kiera working in the Arlington store, right?"

"Yeah, I do. What's up?"

"I need you to put together a small wardrobe of work clothes for Kiera from your location and put it on my personal account."

"No problem, I know her size. Should I include accessories with that?"

"Ehh, better hold off on the jewelry and handbags for now. Kiera just needs a little help dressing more professionally. She's the first person a customer sees once they enter the store and I want her to represent us and make us look good. And it'll make her feel better, more confident."

"You don't have to explain anything to me. I got you."

"I know, just trying to help a family member out."

"Of course. Do you want me to have it delivered to the house?"

"No, I'll pick it up myself. Can you have it ready the day after tomorrow, say around 6 pm?"

"I sure can."

"Thanks Sam, and as always, keep this between you and me."

"No problem."

"Cool, cool. I appreciate you."

"No doubt."

When he returned to the kitchen, his wife had left the takeout food on the counter and was nowhere to be found. He made himself a plate and got comfortable by the fireplace and tuned in to ESPN. Several hours later he was still in the same spot.

* * * * *

Zsasha was awakened in the morning to find Simon kissing her forehead repeatedly while saying goodbye. Seizing the opportunity to avoid updating him on recent relevant events, she offered him nothing more than a return kiss and a few well wishes while he went off to do whatever it was, he was going off to do in New York. Not only did she not tell him about the attack Adam thwarted that night at the gallery, but he still had no idea the result of that fiasco led to Zsasha giving Adam a full-time job. She figured she'd get around to it eventually.

Unlike most mornings when Zsasha would grab a coffee at The Coffee House on her way to the gallery, today waking up feeling refreshed, she decided to do some work from home. She didn't have much on her agenda other than putting together some figures and finalizing an offer for Adam. She could do that from just about anywhere and well, there's no place like home. Getting on her phone to get the day started, she reached out to her new hire.

"Good morning, Adam, how are you?"

"I'm well. How are you?"

"Well rested and refreshed. Can you be at my house at 10:00 am this morning? I want to finalize your offer and get you started on a few things."

"Not a problem. I'll just need your address and I'll be on my way shortly."

"Great, I'll text you the info. See you soon."

After Zsasha provides him with the relevant details, she heads downstairs to grab a bite to eat before his arrival. An hour or so later his arrival is announced by a member of her staff and the two of them take their meeting in her personal study.

"Good morning, Adam."

"Good morning, Ms. Zsasha. Or should I call you Mrs. Stewart?" Adam nervously inquired.

"I prefer not to be called by my married name. It kinda feels like a property declaration of sorts, and well you know..."

452

"Say no more, I got it."

"Good. I'm glad you could make it over on such short notice. I thought it was a good time for us to iron out some details and get the ball rolling."

"Great, excellent. Will your husband be joining us for this meeting?" he asked, although he was well aware of Simon's last-minute trip to New York earlier that day.

"Actually no, he won't."

"I see."

"Actually, I'm sure you do. With all that's been going on here and in New York, I haven't actually had the opportunity to tell him about hiring you but I'm sure he'll be pleased."

"I hope so. It's my goal to relieve the two of you from some of the day-to-day responsibilities you both have been dealing with. I aim to lessen the time the two of you spend at the gallery handling some of the functional duties associated with your business."

"Sounds good to me." Zsasha replied.

"Anything I can do to make your lives easier and less stressful."

"Well I'm glad to see that we're on the same page and off to a good start."

"Me too."

"In the spirit of that, I have a few things to give you to get you started, explain a few things and see if you have any questions right now."

Adam nodded as Zsasha handed him a large envelope that contained some printed material along with a set of keys and a personal swipe card. He took a moment to review what was in the package paying close attention to the written details and instructions. Zsasha, being the woman she is, didn't wait for him to ask any questions before she began explaining the items, how they should be used, some instructions and her personal expectations.

"You have your own keys and swipe card which gives you access to the gallery as well as to your office. You also have access to our storage areas where we store artwork not currently being displayed. You'll have to learn our inventory system which you'll update as you move items to and from storage and how to properly secure them. You must use the alarm code to set and deactivate the alarm every time you enter or exit the gallery whenever it's closed for business. If the alarm goes off and the deactivation code is not entered within 90 seconds the police will be dispatched. And just so you know, false alarms cost money so be sure not to let that happen."

"Sounds good." Adam remarked.

"Cool, there's more. You also have login information for your computer which you'll find in your office. Do not change the password. I need to be able to access your computer if you are unavailable for one reason or another. Don't share your keys, access card, or passwords with anyone and never allow anyone access to the gallery including Ellie. I may or may not provide you with a company cell phone on which you can and will be tracked and monitored so if I give it to you, don't abuse it. We will know."

"Well, you've been very thorough so far."

"Always, no matter what. And of course, your offer letter and compensation package is enclosed. I will need you to sign and return to me as soon as possible if you accept my offer."

"I accept."

"Really, so fast?"

"Yes. I know a good opportunity when I see one and this is it."

"Cool. So how soon can you start?"

"I can start right now."

"My kind of man!"

"So, is there anything you need me to take care of right now?"

"Yes, I want you to go to the gallery and get your computer and office setup the way you like it and check your computer login information and swipe card. I want to make certain you're fully functional tomorrow morning. You should have an email waiting for you granting access to view my calendar and get familiar with what we have coming up and then we'll touch base when I arrive. How does that sound?"

"Sounds great. Again, I appreciate this opportunity. I'm very excited."

"Well off you go. I won't be at the gallery at all today so once you have your space setup like you want, go ahead and lock up when you leave. And memorized the alarm code. You will need it as soon as you enter to shut off the alarm and again when you leave to activate it. There's a map of the main floor showing you were everything is, including your office. Got it?"

"Yes, thank you."

"Okay then. Welcome and I'll see you later."

As if she had been listening to the entire conversation, Ms. Honey appeared and escorted Adam to the front door where his car awaited. He barely made it a mile down the road before he called Ellie with an update.

"Hey Adam, how did it go?"

"It went great, in fact, it couldn't have gone better. She gave me keys to the gallery, my own swipe card, almost everything."

"Awesome. That'll make things a little easier for us, won't it?"

"Yes, it will. Did you get the text I sent you? I wasn't sure if you had their home address or not."

"Yeah, I got it, but I probably won't need it."

"Why is that?"

"I'm thinking now that you have access to the gallery, it might be a more plausible place for everything, you know...less hassle, especially since you have access now."

"I can see that; I can see that."

"Good. Glad we're on the same page. Are you heading home now?"

"No, I'm going by the gallery to get my computer and office setup for tomorrow. What about you? What are you doing and when do you plan to be home?"

"I'm just keeping my eyes on Simon for right now or at least someone else is keeping their eyes on him for me at the moment. Just want to make sure I make the same flight back."

"Looks like you got everything under control."

"You know me."

"I guess I'll get with you when you get back."

"Yes, you will. See you later, Adam."
"Bye."

Chapter 39

J'Nae, having finalized her dinner party planning decided to stop by The Boutique and invite Vonne personally. She also wanted to feel her out hoping she'd be open to Kiera attending as well. She knew they have been having some issues but thought a group outing making Kiera feel more included might ease some of the tension between the trio. Not sure how all of this would go over with Vonne, she entered the shop with a sense of purpose and confidence, kind of like I'm in charge and I'm not taking no for an answer.

"Hey Vonne! How are you?"

"J'Nae, hey. What are you doing here?"

"I wanted to talk to you and since it's been a good while since I've been in any of your boutiques I thought, maybe I'll just come see you in person. Everything looks great in here. How are things going?"

"It's all good, girl. You look great and …. happy!"

"I am. Wes is a wonderful man. He's strong, supportive and the type of man that will carry your load without having to be asked. You'll see once you get to know him better."

"And when will that be, sweetheart? Have you rescheduled already?"

"Yes, we have."

"You may have been secretly spending time getting to know one another these past several months but we're all just hearing about it, so excuse me for being eager to check his ass out!"

"Relax Vonne 2.0, that's why I'm here."

J'Nae handed her girlfriend a personal dinner invitation. It had a candid yet intimate photo of her and Wes, up close and personal which reflected their obvious love towards one another that anyone could clearly see right away. Vonne looked at it and immediately smiled and felt the love it portrayed. On the reverse side were the details including date and time as well as the location of the event which of course was her home.

"Wow, I see you went all out."

"Not really. I made these myself. They look good, don't they."

"For sure. I would've never guessed you did these yourself. You've got talent!"

"Maybe, maybe not. But what I do have, now that I'm back at work is access to all kinds of software and technology that just wasn't available or hadn't been developed back in the day. I'm learning a lot."

"I see. And of course, I'll be there. We'll be there. Despite what issues Lee and I have right now, I'm sure he'll have no problem showing up if for no other reason than to check dude out. We got you."

"I knew I could count on you." J'Nae replied.

Taking a moment to regain the nerve she had when she first arrived, J'Nae contemplated whether or not it was a good idea to discuss inviting Kiera to the dinner party. But as luck would sometimes have it, that decision was made for her. Kiera approached the duo having come from the storeroom.

"Hey J'Nae. How are you? Haven't seen you in a while."

"Oh, Kiera! Hi. I didn't realize you were here."

"She was just on her way out." Kiera announced.

"I thought you worked at a different location. How have you been?"

"Obviously not as good as you from what I just heard. Dinner party for you and your new beau. Sounds great. I can't wait to meet him."

Before Vonne could open her mouth to object or advise her half-sister that she wasn't invited, J'Nae seized the opportunity to benefit from the unforeseen yet favorable circumstance that allowed her to get the result she wanted without the blame or the drama had it been her idea.

"Of course you can, Kiera. You can even bring a plus one. I have another invitation in my purse, let me grab it."

J'Nae purposely avoided direct eye contact with Vonne as she was sure her facial expression revealed surprise and utter disbelief of what had just occurred. Even though it was her own party, and she could invite anyone she wanted to, she really didn't want to alienate her bestie. However, this way, if it ever came up, she could always say that she just didn't want to be rude. Vonne would never be the wiser.

"Wow J'Nae, these invites are lovely. Thank you."

"You're welcome."

"I hardly know anyone here; I don't know who to bring."

J'Nae seized another opportunity to walk through an opening that came out of nowhere.

"Maybe Lee has a single friend or two that he could maybe set you up with. Isn't that right, Vonne?"

"Oh yeah, sure. He has a few single buddies I can think of off the top of my head. I'll be sure to make that happen." Vonne declared. "It's time for you to meet men and make your own friends while you're here. I think it's a great idea."

"Awesome. I'm looking forward to seeing you both there. I've got to run so I can drop off invitations to Zsasha and Rona before it gets too late."

"Well thanks for coming by girlfriend. And let me know if you need help with any last-minute details."

"I think I've got it covered but thanks. See you later sweetie."

"Bye J'Nae."

* * * * *

Lee was sitting by the fireplace with his boy, Carl when Vonne called.

"Hey, I just wanted to remind you I'll be doing some check-ins this evening, so I'll be getting in pretty late. Think you can fend for yourself tonight?"

"Yeah, babe. I got it. I knew you had plans, so Carl and I are grabbing a bite in a minute. You want me to bring you something back, we'll probably get wings."

"Wings do sound good but no, I'll grab something while I'm out."

"Okay then, see you later."

"Wow dude, that sure sounded easy. I thought Vonne was up on you a lot harder than that."

"Man, she usually is, but lately she's gotten so busy with the new stores and everything and of course there's the girls, we hardly run into each other."

"And how's that working out for you?" Carl inquired.

"It works for me just great. I avoid the tension that seems to always show up when she's here."

"Y'all having problems, dawg?"

"Man, it ain't nothing." Lee replied.

"Well then come on, let's go. Nigga hungry as a hostage."

"Hold up, bruh, I'm waiting for her sister to come home, which should have been 30 minutes ago."

"Word. You trying to hook up nigga up?"

"Nah, bruh, it ain't like that. I just need to talk to her about something before we head out. I think that's her now."

Lee got up and walked towards the kitchen where he thought he'd heard Kiera come in. He was correct.

"Hey Kiera, I thought I heard you come in. How was your day?"

"It was fine."

"Good."

"Listen Lee, about what you overheard me say yesterday----"

"Forget about it. For real, pretend it never happened."

"Really?" Kiera asked.

"Yes, really. Now go to your room."

"What? Is that some sort of next day punishment or something?"

"No, silly. I left something for you in your closet. Hope you don't mind me going into your room. I really had no choice."

"Okay."

While Kiera went upstairs to her room to see what was going on, wondering what on earth he could have left in her closet, Lee rejoined his friend Carl whom he found halfway between where they'd been sitting and the kitchen.

"Man, she's hot. Is that your sister-in-law?"

"Yeah man, that's Kiera."

"Damn, that whole family is fine."

"Yeah, she's cute."

"Cute, okay. How can you stand living in the house with all that up in here?"

"Man, chill out. That's my wife's sister."

"Right, but don't act like you ain't never thought about it. Remember, I know you."

"Whatever Carl."

"So, what was that all about? What did you send her to her room?"

"Were you eavesdropping, dude?"

"Not on purpose?"

"Whatever, man."

Moments later, Kiera reappeared and trotted into the room where Lee and Karl were chilling.

"Oh my goodness, Lee, where did all that stuff come from?" Kiera said, bouncing down on the sofa. "What did you do?"

"Just a little gift from the family."

"What? Are you serious?"

"Yes, I am. You had a valid point yesterday about how you dressed while working in the stores. It is a reflection on us and since you've been there a while now, everybody knows you're family. Besides, you deserve it, for all your hard work."

"Oh wow, I can't believe it!" Vonne exclaimed, but she couldn't shake the burning question taking center stage in her mind.

"Does Vonne know about this?" she asked.

"No, not yet, I did this all on my own. I didn't like how things went down the other day. Y'all are sisters and family is everything."

"I'm not sure she's gonna feel the same way about it."

"Don't worry about that. I'll take care of it." Lee insisted.

"I don't know what to say..."

"How about thank you?"

"I can do better than that." She declared as she nearly pounced toward him with open arms and a big tight bear hug showing all of her appreciation.

"Okay, okay, Kiera. It's all good. Wear them in good health."

461

"I will. Thank you so much."

"You're welcome. Carl, let's roll out."

"Hold up bruh, aren't you going to introduce me?"

"Oh, yeah, of course. Carl, this is Kiera, my sister-in-law. Kiera, my man Carl."

"Nice to meet you, Carl."

"The pleasure is all mine, Kiera."

"Okay, are we good? Can we head out now?"

"Yeah man, I'm right behind you, partner."

The two men left the house to do whatever men do. Kiera was beyond thrilled and hurried back to her room to try on her new clothes.

* * * * *

The next night Kiera worked late closing at Vonne's location giving her sister an early night off to meet with the girls. Just as she was walking the last customer out and preparing to lock up for the night, Lee appeared mysteriously from around the corner.

"It's not too late to check inventory, is it?" Lee smirked as he walked past Kiera and turned back to lock the doors.

"Not at all, boss man." She replied.

Lee took a few steps and looked around the shop as if he was scoping it out. He let his dangling backpack slip off his left shoulder and allowed it to touch the floor while still holding the strap by his right hand.

"Real talk...to what do I owe the pleasure of your surprise visit and how did you know I'd be here? Are you checking up on me?"

"Do I need to?" Lee grinned.

"Well, if you did, it's a little late to start now, don't you think." Kiera smiled.

"You got jokes!" he replied.

"And you got secrets. So, tell me, what's the real reason you're here? What's on your mind?"

"I've wanted to see how you like everything and if they fit now that you had a chance to try some of it on."

"Actually, I haven't tried very much on yet."

"Is that why you're not wearing any of it today"

"No, not at all. You just gave me so many things that I want to take the time to go through everything and see what's what. Really, it's all good. It's better than good."

"Cool, because I've been thinking about everything that's been going on at the house between you and your sister and I feel like she's been way too hard on you. I mean your family is dysfunctional to say the least and yeah, both of you have issues, but I do think she is over the top with some of her expectations. Every once in a while, we all need a break, we all need a moment to chill and relax and indulge in things that make us happy without fear of being judged."

"So, that's why you're here, to give me a break?"

"Yeah, something like that."

"So, what are you talking about? You gonna cover for me and give me a few days off or something...what?"

"Uhm, no, not what I had in mind."

"So, what then, what's up? It's getting late and I still have to close the register and balance the receipts for today."

"Oh, I'll help you with that. But first, I want you to relax a bit and let go of some of that stress and tension that's been building for a while now."

"Is that right?"

"Yeah, that's right."

"So, how am I supposed to do that here tonight with you?"

"Is anybody else here?"

"No, just us."

"Cool. How about we start by following me to the back office where we can enjoy a drink."

"A drink? What? Unless you're open to sharing the month-old strawberry slim fast I left in the fridge, I ain't got nothing for you."

"Kiera, you underestimate me. I came prepared. All you gotta do is find something for use to drink out of, unless you're comfortable taking it straight to the head."

"What, nah, those days are behind me. I'll find something in the kitchen, give me a sec."

"Cool, and while you're at it...never mind."

"What? What else do you need?"

"Ice, you got some ice in that kitchen?"

"As a matter of fact, I do."

"Cool. But like I said, I'm here to check inventory, so meet me in the back office."

"Okay, be right there."

"And make sure the door is locked."

"Will do!"

Lee walked in the office looking around for a solid yet hard and dry surface. He settled on the top of the desk and cleared an area large enough for all their drinks and stuff. There were two chairs in the office, one seated behind the desk and the other stashed away in the corner. He rearranged the chairs, so they were both on the front side of the desk and facing one another. Reaching into his bag, he retrieved a bottle of Hennessy Paradis and a few other items he placed on the desk. Moments later Kiera entered the office with two paper cups half filled with ice. Lee had his back towards her as she entered the room. She stopped short of the open seat just a few feet away from him.

"This is the best I could do on short notice." She boasted. "I hope you're okay with this."

"It's fine, Kiera. I wanted to do something nice for you. You've been so stressed lately, you need a break. I hope you're okay with this."

Turning around to meet her eyes where she stood, Lee revealed a surprise she didn't see coming.

"Is that what I think it is?"

"Yep. The best blow in town."

"I didn't see that coming."

"Relax. Here, do a line."

"Kiera hesitated for a brief moment, but quickly picked up the straw and snorted a line he had made just for her."

"Damn, that's some good shit." she uttered while snorting.

"Like I said, they best blow in town. Here, have another."

Kiera didn't disappoint. She snorted the second line harder than she did the first and didn't have any regrettable feelings about it. Although she had been working on cleaning up her life since she arrived, meetings and 12-step programs were never part of her process.

"So, what made you go and do this? And how did you know I'd be cool with it?"

"I just knew." he replied as he snorted two lines he'd made for himself. "And of course, Vonne's been bitching about you and your issues for years. Anything unfavorable in your past, and I do mean anything, she pretty much made public knowledge every chance she could."

"Damn, that's fucked up."

"Don't sweat it. The same people that know about your past, are the same people that know about hers."

"Really?" Kiera asked, snorting another line.

"Really. Don't get me wrong, I love my wife but her ass ain't squeaky clean. She did some of the same shit you did. That's why I feel the way I do about how she's treating you. If you repeat what I'm about to say, I'll deny it, but her ass was a hot mess when I met her. Trust me, if you knew what I know, you two would have an entirely different relationship right about now."

"For real?"

"Hell yeah!"

"So why are you telling me this?"

"Like I said, I think she's being too hard on you."

Feeling a bit relieved that Lee seemed to understand her dilemma, she snorted another line of cocaine, then another and another, taking turns with Lee until it was all gone.

Chapter 40

Hey love, where are you heading off to?" Wes asked.
"Ah, the girls and I decided to meet up at the gallery
this evening for some girl talk...just want to catch up and have
some one-on-one time before the dinner party."

"Well, I thought we'd spend the evening together."

"We will sweetie. It just won't be all night. Besides, It's just
some wine and cheese and conversation. You wanna come?"

"I think I'll pass."

"Okay fine but wait up for me. I promise I won't be very late.
I need my beauty rest so I can look good for the party tomorrow
night."

"Honey, you always look good, no matter what."

"See that right there, that's why you're getting it."

"Is that why, really?"

"Yessir, that's why. Now give me a kiss. See you later, love."

"I'll be right here."

"Yeah, you will."

Twenty minutes later, J'Nae parks her car on the street right
in front of the gallery and makes her way inside.

"Well look who's the last one to arrive and this is in your
honor, too. What's that about?" Rona snickered.

"I wanted to make an entrance."

"Well you did that." Vonne confirmed.

"Yeah girl, wassup?" Zsasha asked. "You got everything
situated and under control for dinner tomorrow night?"

"I do, thank you. So what's been going on with you all lately?
I know I've been a little busy, maybe a bit checked out which is
why I wanted us to get together tonight before the dinner party."

"Oh you've definitely been checked out and for a few months
I might add."

"Zsasha, are you going to ever get past my absence?" J'Nae
asked.

"Oh sure, maybe when I'm convinced he's worth it, leaving your girls hanging and all."

"That really wasn't my intent. I just needed to take care of myself and that's what I did."

"It's all good, J'Nae. Zsasha's just messing with you." Rona revealed. "Ignore her."

"Easier said than done. So Vonne, how are things with you and yours?"

"Same shit over here. Lee's been coming home a bit late a few nights but I'm so tired of the drama, I don't even ask where he's been."

"Sorry to hear that. I was hoping things would get a little better between the three of y'all."

"I suppose that's why you invited Kiera to your dinner party tomorrow night, huh?"

"You invited her sister-wife?" Zsasha asked. "Seriously? I can't wait to see how that hot mess plays out."

"I think everything will be fine once Kiera begins to feel included."

"Why? She's already included in more than she should be." Zsasha stated. "If I said it once, I said it a hundred times. That threesome y'all been living is gonna create all kinds of problems for you, real problems, worse than the ones you got now. Never let another bitch move up in your house, not even family. At least not for an extended period of time. Two weeks at the most and that's only if they're closely related."

"Yeah, well that was last season's cover story, what's new? What's on the front page of this week's edition?" Rona snickered.

"I'm serious. Vonne, you've been asking for trouble for some time now."

"There's not much I can do about it now. She's here and not going anywhere, at least not in the foreseeable future."

"Uh huh." Zsasha acknowledged.

"Can we just change the subject please? And of course, more wine, thank you."

"You ladies can stay and drink as much wine as you would like but I need my beauty rest for tomorrow."

"Wes gave you a curfew, huh?" Zsasha teased.

"Something like that." J'Nae laughed. "But really, I have an early day tomorrow, so I need an early night."

"It's all good. We'll see you tomorrow night love and take these two bitches with you when you leave. I'm tired of them and their shit."

"I ain't got no shit going on, so you must be talking about Vonne." Rona remarked.

"I guess today just ain't your day Rona, now bye-bye."

"Daammm...she just put a bitch out." Vonne commented.

"You still here?"

"Come on girl. Let's get away from this hateful hussy. You know she ain't right."

"We know but does she know..." Vonne jokes. "We'll see your evil ass tomorrow Zsasha, and don't be late."

"Wouldn't dream of it, now bye bitches."

Rona and Vonne walked to the vehicles which were parked out front, one behind the other. Vonne waited for Rona to pull off first before she headed on her way. Not sure of what may be brewing at home, she decided to take the scenic route just to kill off a bit of time.

* * * * *

The next morning began with sunshine, blue skies and a slightly higher than average temperature. J'Nae awoke to the freshly brewed aroma of her favorite Italian coffee Wes was kind enough to make. Her walk downstairs and towards the kitchen wasn't like her walk most other days. Each step was filled with joy and excitement of this much anticipated day, yet she felt like she was floating on air.

"Morning love."

"Good morning." J'Nae said as she stepped in to kiss her lover. "Thank you for making coffee. I have a lot to do today and I'm really going to need it."

"I know love. It's my job to know what you want and what you need before you want or need it. If I don't, then I'm not doing my job."

"Well no need to worry about that. You do everything well and I do mean everything...always on point, boo."

"Alright now. If you keep talking to me like that, you might not leave the house until noon."

"As tempting as that sounds, we just can't have that."

"I know sweetie. So look, you enjoy your coffee while I go grab a shower. I have a few last-minute things I need to take care of today as well."

"Okay boo." J'Nae replied while sipping her coffee. "Were you able to get confirmation from any of your people?"

"Only one. My best friend Maurice. He promised to show up."

"Great."

"But I'm still working on Bailey. We've been friends since we were in the Corps."

"Good, I'm glad to hear that. While I'm officially introducing you to my clan, I want you to do the same."

"I will. But if not tonight, then another time."

The two love birds kissed again then Wesley went on to shower. J'Nae continued to sip her coffee while checking her day planner for anything she might have missed. It appeared she had everything under control.

Kiera left the house a bit earlier than usual hoping to avoid direct contact with her sister. She'd been trying to shake off the guilt that flooded over her the moment she woke up but then decided it best to avoid any potential run ins that might reveal the events of the night before. Snorting cocaine can have certain tell-tale signs especially for those with a long-term history of using.

Going into work early was her best plan of action to keep her out of the line of fire, Vonne's line of fire. So much so, she was no longer perturbed with not only having to work today but having to work right up to the start of J'Nae's dinner party. Of course, it would be too gracious of Vonne to ask someone to cover for a couple of hours so she could go home and get pretty for the party. Oh no, Vonne wasn't feeling generous in the least. But it didn't matter. Kiera didn't miss a beat. With her tumultuous childhood and parental instability, she learned that the ability to adapt to ever changing circumstances was a necessary survival skill she had to master.

Stopping to get a latte to go, she saw a somewhat familiar face off in the distance. She didn't automatically recognize the gentleman, so she continued moving her way through the line to place her order when there was a slight tap on her shoulder. She turned to her left and to her surprise it was Carl. Lee's friend she met at the house.

"Carl, right?"

"Right. Lee's friend. We met a few nights ago. Kiera, right?"

"Yes. How are you?"

"I'm good, I'm good." Carl said. "I'd ask you how you're doing but I can look at you and tell you're fine...absolutely...without a doubt."

"Thank you."

Kiera, not in any way new to the game, knew when and how to bat her lashes acknowledging she was receptive to his obvious flirtation. At the same time, she took a closer look at his head-to-toe swag while they were face to face with the sunlight beaming through the window dancing on his mocha brown skin.

"What brings you to this part of town? It's kind of out of the way from the house just to get coffee."

"Ah, yes, it is. I work in one of Vonne's boutiques a few doors down."

"Right, right. Lee mentioned you were managing one of their stores."

"I try."

"So listen, would you be interested in going out with me, maybe dinner and some drinks?"

"Actually, that's a good idea. Are you free this evening at 6:30?"

"Oh, um, yeah, I can be. Did you have something specific in mind?"

"Actually, I do. I need a date for J'Nae's dinner party this evening. You know J'Nae, right?"

"Yes, I do."

"You probably know the whole gang."

"I've encountered them a few times. Vonne is pretty tight with her girls."

"She is. So Carl, can you pick me up here at 6:30 tonight?"

"I can and I will."

"Cool. I'm looking forward to it. Here's my number in case anything comes up."

"Bet. See you tonight, Kiera."

"It's a date, Carl."

As Carl left the coffee shop and Kiera retrieved her drink, the new couple was all smiles as they went on their respective ways. Kiera was excited to have finally connected with someone even if it was one of Lee's friends. Having something personal to do and look forward to, fueled her day as well as her attitude and even improved upon her customer service. Luckily, she toted more than one of her new outfits in her car so she could pick something more appropriate for a woman on a date as opposed to a third wheel. This was going to be a good night.

Chapter 41

Taking a survey of the room, J'Nae could see that almost everyone who was invited had arrived. The small yet intimate crowd seemed self-sufficient as everyone mingled and moved about with ease. J'Nae was about to ask everyone to join her in the dining room when the doorbell rang. Answering the door for whom she knew to be the only guest not present was Kiera, and she was not alone.

"Hi Kiera, thanks for coming and again, welcome to my home."

"Thanks for inviting me J'Nae. This is Carl, my date."

"Hello Carl."

"J'Nae, good to see you again. You look well."

"And you do as well. Please, come in, have a drink and make yourselves comfortable."

"Thanks, J'Nae and you did say a plus one, right?"

"Absolutely. I find it more enjoyable when everyone is paired off, but it'll work either way." J'Nae replied at the same time one of her male servers approached. "He'll take your drink order and bring it to you once you're seated."

"Cool."

"We were just about to begin serving. Why don't you two follow me and I'll show you where you'll be sitting."

"Great, thank you."

Kiera and Carl followed J'Nae into the formal dining room where a large extended table was set up to accommodate the guest. Everyone else was just beginning to take their seats. A tall, slender bi-racial woman began placing appetizers on the table while a young man visited each guest with a red and white bottle of wine in tow, asking for their preference as well as any requested drink orders guests had made.

"Wow J'Nae, you really went all out for this occasion." Rona stated. "To what do we owe the pleasure of this event?"

"We'll get to that a little bit later."

"Oh, so you're gonna make us wait, sista girl?" Zsasha asked.

"It's not like we don't already know why we're here." Rona interjected.

"What gives?"

Taking his cue from the conversation and the look on J'Nae's face, Wes positioned himself next to J'Nae and took her hand in his. In unison they turned to face each other and whispered back and forth for a brief moment, then turned their attention back to their guests.

"Please everyone take your seat." J'Nae announced as she glanced around the room barely able to contain herself. "Thank you all so much for coming to share in my celebration. I'm sure you all know that Wes and I have been dating for quite a while now and have decided to move forward with our relationship."

"I know this chick did not have a party to tell us they're shacking up." Zsasha mumbled softly under her breath.

"Wes, my dear sweet Wes has asked me to marry him, and I accepted."

"Oh Damn, sista girl, I didn't see that coming. Congratulations." Zsasha exclaimed in excitement as she rose to her feet.

"Congratulations, girlfriend." Rona blurted as she jumped out of her seat and rushed to give J'Nae and Wes a hug. "I had no idea things had gotten this serious. I'm so happy for you both."

"Thanks Rona. I appreciate that. I wasn't sure how you girls were going to take the news."

Most of the guests were up and out of their seats rushing to congratulate the couple on their announcement. Vonne was angrily slinging back her third drink while Rona and Zsasha rushed over to congratulate their friend.

"Girl, how many times have I told you to stop worrying about what other people think of you and to make yourself happy." Zsasha reflected.

"Too many to count."

"Great then, so you know this is long overdue! I can't believe it, I'm so happy, so very happy for you."

"Thanks sweetie."

"So tell us, how do the kids feel about the news?" Rona asked.

"We've discussed it with them a few days ago and they're both on board. They couldn't be happier."

"That's great, J'Nae. If anyone deserves happiness, it's you."

"Thanks for your support, Rona. I am happy, very, very happy."

Just then, Wes approached and dragged J'Nae away so some of his guests could convey their congratulations and well wishes.

"Zsasha, let me talk to you for a minute."

Rona casually led Zsasha a few more feet away from the happy couple where they were still visible to the crowd but far enough from J'Nae and Wes where they could talk privately and not be overheard.

"Zsasha, do you see what I see?"

"Oh yeah, for sure. Whitegirl got some shit going on over there but today ain't her day."

"I'm sure she's aware of that. It's probably the reason why she looks the way she does."

"Yeah that, plus she's throwing em' back like it's a 1980's party. Whatever she's got going on, she's gonna have to fall back."

"I agree, Zsasha, but damn, do you see her face? The way she's looking right now, I don't see that happening."

"Me either."

"And look at Lee. He doesn't look much better." Rona added. "Maybe you should say something to her, pull her aside, maybe take her to the kitchen. That way she can holla at you, give her a chance to at least get it off her chest, privately and without disrupting J'Nae's celebration. Because right now, what I'm seeing, she looks like she's ready to blow."

"She does, doesn't she. I'm guessing it's got something to do with Kiera or Lee, maybe both. Y'all bitches know how I feel about that threesome shit they got going on. I told her that shit was going to cause problems and whatever it is, I'm sure Lee's ass is knee deep up in it."

"Probably so, and by the way, who's that guy with Kiera?" Rona asked. "How did she get a date?"

"Oh, that's Carl. He's a friend of Lee's. You've met him before, don't you remember?"

"No, not really Zsasha."

"Yeah, that's one of Lee's boys from back in the day. They used to run together pretty hard back when Lee was still playing college ball. I think Carl played too, maybe or was somehow connected to the team."

"If you say so, I don't remember his face."

"It has been a while, maybe some years in fact."

"I wonder how he ended up here and with her."

"I have a few ideas, one of which might explain the look on Lee's face but I'm really hoping I'm wrong about that."

"Really? What's on your mind? Care to elaborate?"

"Girlfriend, you can't figure it out yourself?"

"Well, the only way Kiera could have met Carl is through Lee, right?"

"Yeah, continue."

"And Vonne is almost always upset with Kiera about one thing or another but that doesn't really explain why Lee has an issue or where it stems from."

"Rona, think about it for a minute. Think about Lee's history and one of the many reasons why we've always felt he wasn't good for our girl."

"You think he's fucking with Kiera and mad about his friend swooping in?"

"I don't know about the fucking part but yeah, that's exactly what I think has Lee pissed off. He's jealous."

"That would explain the tension I'm sensing as well as the mean mug on his face." Rona explained.

"How so?" J'Nae asked as she approached the huddle between Rona and Zsasha.

"Nothing sweetie, we were just making an observation." Rona reiterated. "I'm so happy for you, we're so happy for you."

"Quit trying to change the subject, Rona. Just because I haven't commented on it doesn't mean I'm not aware of the trouble brewing at the other end of the table."

"We are talking about Lee, and we all know his track record ain't shit." Zsasha admitted.

"Yeah, but that's Vonne's husband and because we love her, we put up with him."

"Yeah, okay J'Nae, but I would keep my eye on him especially with that one, if you know what I mean." Zsasha revealed. "If it's not already too late."

"By that one, you mean Kiera?" J'Nae inquired.

"I absolutely mean Kiera. I don't trust her, and you shouldn't either."

"Well, she may not be trustworthy, but I think Lee knows better than that by now anyway."

"Only time will tell." Rona added.

"You're right, but right now let's take our seats. Dinner is about to be served."

"Those of us that got up from the table." Zsasha mumbled as she returned to her seat, rejoining her husband. Five minutes later, dinner was served.

The meal consisted of grilled lemon pepper salmon over top of a bed of orange cilantro rice paired with bacon wrapped asparagus. It went over very well. With dessert, there was general conversation amongst most of the guests with the focus on how, when and where the two lovebirds met. Everyone was tuned in to the happy couple, especially those who were familiar with J'Nae's issues with love. However, no matter how much chatter was shared amongst the group it was obvious to a handful of people there was barely a peep from Vonne.

By now she was on her sixth drink and ripe for a toxic dramatic event. Everyone had migrated to the formal sitting area for their final well wishes to the happy couple. Rona, Zsasha and J'Nae took comfort believing the powers that be managed to prevent any Vonne family drama from upending J'Nae's happy occasion.

As the party wrapped up, it wasn't long before everyone was gone except for the girls and their dates, Kiera and Carl and Ms. Honey and a few of the servers that stayed behind to clean up.

Vonne had done pretty well keeping her issues to herself throughout dinner and desert. But as the room emptied, she

477

could see Lee and Carl having a little chat amongst themselves. If you didn't know Lee, you would've thought his smiling face indicated an innocent and friendly conversation between two friends which was exactly what he wanted to portray. But those who knew him well would've known right away that his body language told a different story that didn't match his facial expression.

Kiera was also aware of the tension building between the two men and decided to interrupt their bromance by tugging Carl's arm in her direction indicating she was ready to go. However, Lee responded with a sudden gesture reaching out to pull her back in then quickly thought better of it and tried his best to play it off. If the room was full of strangers, he might have been able to pull it off somewhat. But what he couldn't do was fool his wife and without hesitation, Vonne began approaching the trio with a purpose and intent that would have put even the strongest and most confident individuals on notice. It was obvious, she was about to handle some business.

As it happens, Kiera was positioned in a way that she could see her sister coming towards them and was pretty sure it was about to go down. In a last-ditch effort to divert what she knew would be an explosive encounter, she stepped away from the three-ring circus moving towards her sister intending to cut her off at the path. She was somewhat successful.

"Hey sis, we're about ready to go?" Kiera stated. "Are you alright?"

"Really Kiera? You have to ask??? No, I'm not alright. I'm sick of you and your bullshit."

"What are you talking about Vonne?"

"You can play dumb if you want too, I know better."

"Huh?"

"I can't believe you're stupid enough to steal clothes out of my boutique and wear them to a party hosted by one of my best friends and think I wouldn't notice!"

"Steal? I ain't steal nothing from you! What are you talking about, Vonne?"

478

"I'm talking about the dress you're wearing right now! Last season or not, I know you can't afford to buy that outfit or much of anything else in my boutiques. Hell, I know what I'm paying you."

"You're wrong, Vonne. It's not like that."

"It's not like what? Are you denying that you're standing here wearing one of last season's signature dresses from my boutique that you didn't pay for?"

"Yes, I mean no, that's not what I'm saying but can we talk about this later, like at home maybe? You're embarrassing me and you're embarrassing yourself."

"Fuck that shit. Why are you worried about being embarrassed in front of my friends? They all know you ain't shit."

"Vonne, please. Can we talk about this later on?"

"Hell no! Your ungrateful ass ain't getting nothing else from me, not even consideration. Now get your ass up out of here."

Lee had tried hanging back for a while but could tell the conversation had surpassed its boiling point. He walked over to his wife and sister-in-law to try to get things under control.

"Vonne, that's enough. I think you've had too much to drink. We should go home and talk about this later."

"I ain't going nowhere until this motha fucka answers some questions. How this bitch gonna steal from me when I'm already giving her damn there everything. Food, shelter and a job, damn girl, you got me."

"Vonne, you're making a scene that's not going to end well. Let's take this home and we'll talk about it when you've sobered up." Lee stated.

"How the fuck are you defending her? If she's stealing from me, then she's stealing from you too, dumb ass!"

"I ain't stole shit!" Kiera repeated.

"Vonne, let's go." Lee said as he tugged at her arm trying to get her to leave. "We can talk about this later, at home. Now is not the time."

"Yes the fuck it is Lee. I trusted this bitch and she's gonna steal from me? Awe, hell no. And I can't believe you're standing here in my face taking up for her."

By this time, everybody was completely aware of what was going on and not surprised at Vonne's outburst. They all knew something was going on with her throughout the evening but had no specific idea what it was about.

"I'm not taking up for her. This has just gotten way out of proportion, and we need to go home and clear things up."

"Ain't nothing to clear up. Possession is 9/10th of the law and she is obviously in possession of merchandise from my boutique that she did not pay for. That makes her a thieving bitch!" Vonne yelled as she took another step closer to her sister putting them face to face. "If you stole this, I know you stole more." She breathed.

"Again Vonne, I ain't steal nothing from you." Kiera said, looking back and forth at Lee waiting for a sign or signal that he was going to step up, but it never came. "And you need to back up off me a bit or you're about to get your feelings hurt."

"I ain't worried about no feelings, I'm already hurt. I've done so much to try to help you and I can't believe you would do this to me. I should have turned your bitch ass away at the door. You ain't never gonna change Kiera. You're always going to be a lying, thieving ass mother fucker!"

"For the last time sista, I ain't steal nothing from you."

"Lying bitch."

The whole while this argument ensued, Lee was contemplating his next move, all the while sweating bullets as the situation continued to escalate.

"I ain't lying. Yeah, this dress is one of yours from last season, but I didn't steal it."

"Borrowing without permission is the same motha fucking thing."

"Vonne please, let's take this home and deal with it." Kiera said as she looked towards Lee one last time to come to her defense. But he chose to be silent.

"What's the matter Kiera, cat got your tongue?"

"Well, if you must know, it was a gift from your husband, along with several other designer pieces left over from last year or the year before."

"Bitch you're so full of shit. You just can't stop lying."

"I ain't lying, just ask your husband. Let him tell you."

Vonne turned to look at Lee intent on asking him point blank. But there was no need to ask him anything. His answer was written all over his face and his silence told her what she needed to know. The look on her face was priceless. While the color drained, you could see the shock, horror and utter disbelief consume her mentally, physically and emotionally, causing her to immediately go silent. Every emotion and indignation she rightfully felt was completely exposed to everyone still remaining in the room and she knew her sister's words were true.

"Vonne, let's go. Simon and I will drive you home." Zsasha said as she approached Vonne and nudged her towards the door. John Lee can pick up your car tomorrow."

Things had gone south right quick and, in a hurry, but she knew things could easily get worse, especially with whitegirl pissed off to the hilt and liquored up.

"Hold on a minute Z, I need to talk to my husband."

"Vonne please. We can discuss this at home." Lee pleaded.

Vonne turned her attention towards her husband. The look on her face revealed the hurt, pain and a betrayal of trust like no other. But she wanted confirmation. She needed confirmation. She had to have confirmation from him. And as excruciating as it was, she needed to ask him point blank. She needed him to admit to her face what she already knew to be true. Fully convinced of his guilt and absent of any reasonable doubt she asked the question if only to allow him the opportunity to fess up.

"Lee, is she telling the truth?" she asked. "Did you do this?"

"Yea Vonne, I did. I gave her some of last season's clothes from the boutique so she could feel and look like she belonged there in front of **our** clients, selling to **our** clients. I just hadn't had the chance to tell you about it yet."

"You hadn't had the chance? Motha fucka don't we sleep in the same bed every night? All you had to do is roll over and tell me. And the fact that you didn't tell me indicates that something more is going on here."

481

"Baby, it's not like that. I was just trying to help her out, especially after what happened the other day. She needs her own shit to wear if she's going to be representing us in front of our clients."

"I agree with part of that, and I wouldn't necessarily be opposed to the idea. She definitely needs her OWN shit to wear. Maybe, had you come to me with it, we could have worked something out. But the fact that you just took it upon yourself to make a decision like this without talking to me about it first, that's a problem. Especially with all the drama that's been going on lately. You should've known better, in fact, I believe you did, and you just didn't give a fuck."

"That's not true, Vonne. It's not like that."

"Really, because all this texting and private dinners y'all been having says otherwise. I know yo ass and I know her. And I'm telling you, both of y'all need to get the fuck out of my house, tonight!"

"Come on, Vonne. That's your sister we're talking about."

"Really? Because it seems like the two of you have overlooked that very important fact. That's MY sister!"

"Vonne, really...don't you think you're overreacting a bit?" Lee insisted.

"Hell no, and just so we're clear, let me repeat myself. You and that ho need to get the fuck out of my house. You need to find somewhere else to sleep! Tonight!"

With that, Vonne grabbed her purse and took off walking straight through the front door without saying another word. Not that it was necessary to say goodbye, everyone still there heard every bit of what transpired. Zsasha grabbed Simon and followed right behind her but by the time they made it outside she had jumped in her car and drove off.

Everyone at the party was stunned, especially J'Nae and Wes, who had returned from their sudden and unplanned short disappearance just in time to catch the last half of the Vonne, Kiera and Lee show. Things had gone beyond interesting. Simply put, it was a hot mess.

While there was quite a bit of chatter amongst the inner circle of friends that hung back, Carl noticed Kiera slipping outside just minutes after Vonne's dramatic exit. She had been walking at such an intense pace you would've thought she was planning to hop in a car and follow her sister. But that wasn't the case, mainly because she hadn't driven to the party. This gave Carl the opportunity to catch up with his date.

"Hey, slow down. Where are you going?"

"I don't know, just away from here. I'm sure you heard all of that, didn't you?"

"Yeah, I did. I wanted to jump in but it seemed like a family issue and I didn't want to overstep."

"It's all good."

"Well look, why don't you hang out here and I'll go get the car."

"Yeah, and go where? I can't go back to the house, you heard her."

"Everybody heard her."

"Right."

"You're welcome to come over and crash at my house. I'm sure this will blow over tomorrow. Vonne and Lee just have some shit to work out, that's all."

"I appreciate that but no, I don't think that's a good idea."

"That's cool but look, I'll take you wherever you want to go. A friend's house or a hotel room, it's whatever. I brought you here so you're leaving with me."

"How about you drop me off where you picked me up. I can hang out there for a night or two, that will give me some time to figure out my next move."

"You're next move? It's not that serious, trust me. Vonne has always been melodramatic so this ain't nothing new. She'll be alright in a minute or two so don't go making any life changing decisions based on this bullshit. Trust me, it'll work itself out."

"If you say so."

"I do. So do you have an overnight bag, or do you need to run back to the house and get anything?"

"No, I'm good, thanks. I keep a bag in my car."

"Alright then, wait here. I'll get the car and pull up right here and we'll be on our way."

"Thanks Carl."

"It's all good, beautiful."

While Carl is busy driving Kiera back to the boutique, Lee arrives home in spite of the explicit directive his drunk wife demanded as she stormed out of the party. To his surprise, she had arrived home first. Fully aware he was in for a fight, he parked his car in his regular spot and entered the house through the kitchen.

"I thought I told you to find somewhere else to sleep tonight. Are you looking for trouble?"

"Vonne, first of all, you need to put that glass down you're holding on to for dear life. You've already had more to drink than you can handle, and you need to pull yourself together."

"Pull myself together? Motha fucka please! You ain't in no position to tell me shit right now, you dirty ass motha fucka. How are you gonna disrespect me by doing what you did and in front of my friends...oh hell no! You got me fucked up."

"I don't think so sweetie. If you remember, I was against this bullshit from the start, but you insisted."

"So..."

"So my ass. You plead her case and yours too, talking about how rough she had it and shit, how you needed to make amends...and for what, I don't know but that was your argument. How you were willing to overlook her troubling past, her bullshit and whatever other issues she had that you never shared with me and yet you still wanted her to stay, so I got onboard. As your husband I supported you despite the fact I didn't think it was a good idea. But you wanted it and I agreed but only because she was family."

"Hold on, you can try and flip this shit on me if you want to but I'm not having it. What you did and how you did it was wrong, straight up and there's no denying that."

"I admit I could have handled it better. But we wouldn't be here had you not insisted on doing this. And now that she's here and we're helping her out, guess what else, she's helping you.

484

She's helping us both. And let us not forget she came during a time that you needed help. Against my advice you took on the task of opening a few stores at the same time and having her here, working for you has made that manageable. So you're mad I gifted her a wardrobe? Some clothes from the last two seasons, I don't get it, Vonne, I don't get it at all. As far as I'm concerned, I did something you really should have done a long time ago. She's your sister and working in our boutiques at a critical time no less. Everybody knows she's family, that she's your sister. So how do you think it reflects on us, more specifically on you, when she's dressed like she walked straight out of Target and is obviously out of her league? She's the first visual point of contact for anyone who comes into that boutique. We sell high end clothing and what do you think people say or think when she looks out of place? It reflects directly on you, sweetheart and not in a good way. And yeah, I could have and should have told you what I was doing before I did it but that's our issue. That's between me and you, not her. And yeah, she shouldn't have borrowed your clothes without talking to you first, but I totally understand why she did it. Are you aware of how you make her feel, how you make people feel in general? You have this way of seeing yourself apart from everybody else, like you're better than they are. I think you get that from your bougie ass friends. You talk down to people all the time, especially her. You never let up and you never give her a break. She's your sister, so if anyone and I do mean anyone is going to benefit from your out-of-season overpriced clothes that nobody wants, she should be at the top of the list. She should be getting more than anybody else, including those heffa's in your sista circle. Ain't that what you call it?"

"Fuck you, Lee."

"Yeah, that's your drunk ass rebuttal to what you and I both know is the truth. You give your girls all kinds of discounts and back-end deals. Hell, I wouldn't be surprised if none of those bougie ass bitches ever paid for your shit either. I know how you do, that is for those you want to do shit for. And she should be part of that."

485

Vonne sucked her teeth intending to blow him off as she walked upstairs for bed. At this point, she was too drunk to be mad and definitely tired of arguing. She stripped down, jumped into bed and didn't realize she'd slept alone until she woke up the next morning and saw his side of the bed undisturbed.

Chapter 42

J'Nae and Wes began their day recalling the events from the night before. Remarkably neither one of them were terribly upset with Vonne's family drama or her belligerent behavior. They were both quite happy with themselves and upcoming events they were eager to plan.

"Uhm look here baby, I know we were planning to spend the day together but I'm feeling like I need to go check on Vonne. Last night was over the top and she's been having a lot of issues and concerns about Lee and Kiera and I know for a fact she was devastated to find out what he's been up to, especially the way she did. I just feel like I need to go check on her. Do you mind if I skip out for a bit?"

"Of course not." Wes replied, slightly kissing her forehead. "You do what you feel you need to do. I'll be here when you get back."

"Thanks sweetie. I promise I won't be long."

"Okay, love you."

"Love you too."

When J'Nae arrived at Vonne's house she was surprised to see Zsasha and Rona's vehicles already in the driveway. She didn't waste any time getting out and knocking on the door. Rona answered and let her in.

"Hey Rona, did I miss an invite or something?"

"No girl, it wasn't like that at all. We just all got the same idea around the same time. We've only been here about 10 minutes ourselves."

"How is she doing?" J'Nae asked.

"Hey, y'all stop all that whispering over there and come on over here. Zsasha just went to grab a bottle of wine to go with the snacks she brought over. You doing alright, J'Nae?"

"I'm fine. The question is how are you doing?"

"It is what it is." Vonne replied.

"Is Lee here? Did he come back with you last night?"

"No and yes. And before you ask, we got into it pretty good, at least until I got drunk and tired and went to bed."

"You were drunk and tired when you left my house, sweetie."

"Yeah, I was and I'm about to be drunk again...thanks Zsasha. Y'all pour yourself a glass of wine. It's after 12 o'clock so bottoms up."

"Like that's ever been an issue for us, any of us." Zsasha jokes. "Day drinking has become one of our regular pastimes, even for Miss Goody-Two Shoes over here."

"Not sure that's something we should be bragging about." Rona added.

"I ain't bragging one bit, I'm just keeping it real." Zsasha stated in a matter-of-fact tone. "Real bitches don't need no schedule to tell them when they can drink and when they can't."

"Uhm, somebody could've used a schedule last night."

"Never mind that bullshit, Rona. I could have been stone cold sober and would have said the same shit. Y'all know what he did. And that negro tried to flip it and put it on me...said it was my fault."

"He said what?" Zsasha asked.

"Yeah, he said he was doing what I should've done a long time ago. Said she's a reflection on me or us and that I should have made sure she was looking good and wearing our own stuff."

"I guess I could see that." "J'Nae added.

"Yeah, maybe, but even if that's true it doesn't excuse his fucked-up behavior or hers either." Zsasha declared. "Kiera ain't have no business going in Vonne's closet or bedroom for that matter. Looking around, borrowing shit, uh uh, there ain't no excuse for that, none at all."

"It wasn't just on her. Lee did what he did and didn't have the nerve to tell me or talk with me about it first."

"Look here, I don't know what his raggedy ass was thinking but he wasn't thinking about you. You've put up with so much shit from that nigga, I don't know how you continue to do it after all this time. Surely you know you can do better, right?"

"I know shit is looking real crazy right about now and you warned me from the start Z, but we're not there yet."

"Okay, if you say so but keep your eyes open. I don't like the smell of any of this shit, not for a minute."

"I will Zsasha, but now can we talk about something else? J'Nae sweetie, have you guys thought about a date yet?"

"Well since you asked, yes! We want to have our official engagement party at the end of the month."

"So soon?" Zsasha asked.

"Yes, it's what we both want."

"Looks like y'all ain't wasting no time."

"Isn't that exactly what you and Rona have been telling me for a while now?"

"Yeah, but damn girlfriend, we barely know him."

"I said our engagement party, not our wedding. And might I suggest you make an effort to get to know him better over the next several weeks. You'll still have some time after the engagement party and we're not planning the wedding for at least six months."

"Now, hold on a minute J'Nae." Rona interrupted. "Don't you think things are moving a bit fast? How well do you know him?"

"Well enough. We met at the grief center after Rick died. We weren't dating or anything at that time, just being supportive of one another through our shared grief. We kept in touch after that."

"And what about the big 50th birthday party bash you and Zsasha have been planning for a few years? How does that fit into your schedule, or did you forget about that?"

"Of course I didn't forget about that. That date is set in stone, and we can start making plans for that now. Obviously, the wedding date won't clash with our birthday event, but we can do both. We have time."

'That's cool and all J'Nae but let's back up a bit. How big of a part did your shared grief play in your emotional bonding?"

"Trust me Zsasha, he's solid. We're solid. I've actually already started planning the engagement party and have some ideas I want to share with you all about the wedding. I just threw the dinner party to ease you guys into the whole idea of me and Wes. I know it seems like it's sudden and that's my fault. I shouldn't have kept you all in the dark as long as I did or at all. I apologize for that. I should have trusted my girls would've had my back."

"Yes, you should've trusted us." Zsasha agreed.

"We love you and only want what's best for you."

"Thanks Rona, I appreciate that. I appreciate all of you supporting me. And just like I should have trusted all of you, I'm asking you all to trust me. This is real. It's what I want and what I need and I'm happy, I'm really happy!"

"We can tell." Vonne uttered.

"So you finally pulled your head out of that bottle of wine long enough to say something relevant, huh sista-girl? I thought we lost you a bottle back." Zsasha admitted. "You look like you could use a good nap right about now and maybe something to eat."

"Actually, I could. Y'all don't mind wrapping things up, do you?"

"Sweetie, we just came over to check on you and make sure you were alright." J'Nae stated.

"And we can definitely tell you ain't feeling no pain." Zsasha snickered.

"Do you want us to straighten up for you, maybe put the snacks away?"

"No, I'll leave it for later. I might get hungry while I'm laying here napping."

"Alright love, we'll see ourselves out." Rona replied.

"Bye girls."

"Bye."

"Later hun."

"Call us if you need anything, okay."

"Okay J'Nae. See you later."

Once outside, the advisory panel quickly formed as it always did when any one of its members was in trouble. Away from Vonne, they were able to share their true thoughts and concerns and the opportunity to be brutally honest without further traumatizing their friend.

"What do y'all think? Should we be worried?" Rona asked.

"No more than usual." Zsasha replied.

"I just think we should keep a really close eye on her. She's been through a lot of nonsense with him, but this is different, this involves her sister."

"You're right J'Nae, she has, and we should." Zsasha concluded.

"Maybe we can keep her busy with your engagement party. And by the way, let me know the date as soon as possible. I have some travel plans coming up in a few weeks and I want to make sure I'm here for your special occasion."

"Sure thing Rona. I'll text you the details tomorrow. For now, let's just stay in touch with her more often...and each other. Zsasha, you're quiet all of a sudden. Is everything alright?"

"Everything's straight. So we'll talk later ladies."

"Yes, we will. drive safely, J'Nae. "You too, Zsasha."

"Bye now."

"Bye."

Chapter 43

A week into her newly acquired yet humble living arrangements, Kiera was delighted to have been asked out on a second date by Carl who had no interest in the unpleasant accusations hurled at her by her sister. He was determined to make his interest in her known no matter what.

Having gone through the clothing she carried in her go bag or what she'd stashed at the boutique every now and then, it was time she went to the house to gather a few things she needed especially if this living arrangement was going to continue. As she headed out the door of the boutique, she was met by an unexpected yet familiar face. It was Lee and again he had his backpack with him.

"Hey Kiera!"

"Lee, what brings you here?"

"I hadn't seen or heard from you since the other night, and you weren't answering my texts, so I decided to swing by and check on you."

"I'm sure your wife would have a problem with that."

"Nonsense. I'm sure she's been concerned too."

"Whatever man."

"So, can we go inside and talk? The shop's closed so how about it?"

"How about what?"

"We go inside, silly."

"Oh, yeah okay, but just for a bit. I happen to know Vonne is off meeting up with the girls so it's a good time for me to go to the house and grab a few things."

"No doubt." Lee agreed as the two of them walked to the back office where they had hung out before."

"Oh snap! You've turned the office into a studio apartment. You've got a TV setup, what looks like a breakfast nook and a sofa sleeper. All you need now is some family photos and it'll start feeling like home."

"You got jokes today, don't you?" Kiera stated with sarcasm. "Besides, this was the best I could do on short notice."

"I'm sure but you know you can't continue to live like this girl. You need to just come back to the house, Vonne will be fine."

"I don't know about all that."

"I'm telling you, she'll be alright. Now, can you grab some glasses and ice?"

"Word?"

"You know how I roll."

"I do." Kiera replied. "I have a few plastic cups right here and the ice is in the mini fridge just inside the storeroom. Just grab one of the mini trays in the freezer."

"Cool."

While Lee poured the drinks, Kiera began to think back to the last time he showed up unannounced. He definitely didn't come empty handed in fact it was like a snow day in December. Except it wasn't December and the snow had a numbing effect. She wondered if history would repeat itself today.

"I can see the wheels turning in your head. Don't worry, I come bearing gifts."

"Do you now?"

"I do. Do you still have our setup from before?"

"Nope but I can rectify that quite easily."

Kiera took a moment to cut a straw she had stashed in her cup holder and retrieved a mirror from her purse.

"Will this do?"

"Absolutely." Lee confirmed. "Here, why don't you go first."

"Don't mind if I do." she replied as she made herself a line and snorted it. "Damn, that first drain that hits the back of your throat is always the best one."

"For sure." Lee said as made and snorted two lines, taking them back-to-back and straight to the head. His were considerably bigger than the line Kiera made for herself probably because until recently she hadn't done it in quite a while. And she knew enough about cocaine that less really is more.

"So how did you end up bringing Carl as your date to the dinner party?"

"Oh, it was kind of last minute. I ran into him the day of or the day before the dinner party and just asked him. J'Nae said I could bring a plus one, so I did."

"Cool, cool. Carl's a good guy."

"Yeah, he seems like it. In fact, we're going out again this week."

"Oh yeah, okay...okay."

"I'm actually looking forward to it. Your wife said I needed to find my own friends, so this is me finding my own friends."

"I feel you. So what do y'all have planned? Dinner, maybe a movie or something?"

"I think he said something about a dinner cruise on the Potomac."

"That sounds romantic."

"You think? He mentioned dinner, drinks and live music. Just a regular night out to me."

"That just happens to be on a luxury yacht...!"

"Yeah, something like that." Kiera chuckled.

Lee sat back in his seat for a moment processing what he had just heard. He wasn't sure he liked the idea of his friend dating his hot ass sister-in-law. Even on a casual basis. Carl has a history with women, and he's well known for being a player, even at his age now.

"Is something wrong, Lee?"

"Oh no, not at all."

Leaning forward to do another line he was hit with the visual image of Carl fucking Kiera right here in this office. He refreshed their drinks and snorted yet another line hoping to rid his mind of that unpleasant content.

"Here, this one's for you."

"Cool." Kiera replied.

After which, Kiera stuck two of her fingers in her drink then leaned her head all the way back so she could let the liquor on her wet fingers run off into her nostrils. Once she lifted her head forward, she was met with another unexpected surprise. It was Lee. He was face to face with his sister-in-law, close enough they could feel each other's hot liquor breath on their faces.

495

Without hesitation, he leaned in and planted a deep wet kiss on her lips. She returned the passionate kiss while they embraced each other tightly. Then without warning she stood up pulling away from Lee and his embrace.

"What's the matter? Did I get my signals crossed?"

"Uh...I gotta go. I need to get to the house and grab a few things while Vonne's not around. Can you lock up on your way out?"

"Yea, sure but what's the rush?"

"I just need to go. Lock up please. Bye Lee."

With that, Kiera was out the door and behind the wheel of her car. She couldn't pull off fast enough but only drove a few blocks before pulling over to compose herself. She couldn't believe what had just happened. Lee kissed her. Her sister's husband made an unmistakable pass at her and she had no one to talk to about it. Yes, there had always been a little sexual tension around the house, but Lee was always a gentleman. And now this coming out of nowhere, it must have been the drugs. Yeah, that's it. He didn't mean anything by it. He just let the drugs and alcohol get to him, quite quickly it seems.

Kiera decided to write it off as an impulse brought on by the drugs and alcohol they shared pledging that would be the last time they shared that stuff again. Shaking it off, she continued on her way to her sister's house to grab a few things, hoping to avoid running into either one of them at this point.

* * * * *

"So sweetheart, you said Zsasha asked you not to come to the gallery to work this week, huh?" Ellie asked.

"That's right. She still hasn't told Simon she hired me to work in the gallery or anything about the attack in the back alley."

"More deceit. I like it. He's going to be so pissed off when he finds out. It will work in my favor."

"I'm sure it will."

* * * * *

While Kiera was heading to the house, Vonne had arrived at Ahsasz to meet with the girls and to everyone's surprise she was on time.

"Hey Vonne, wasn't sure you were gonna show up let alone be on time."

"Well you're in luck Z. As it turns out I needed something to do away from the house today. Just so happens I'll be doing the same thing here as I was there."

"Is that why I saw you get dropped off by a car service?"

"You are correct. I didn't think it was a good idea for me to drive, you know...I've been sipping all day. Are Rona and J'Nae coming?"

"They both confirmed by text so yeah, them heffas will be here in a minute." Zsasha declared. "Well damn, speak of the devil bitches now."

"Hello to you too, heffa. What's got your panties all tied up and twisted in knots? Somebody hurt your feelings, Zsasha?"

"Hell nah. You know better than that."

"What's up then?" Rona asked.

"We'll get around to that later. Who wants wine and who wants bourbon? I got everything setup over there." Zsasha pointed in the direction opposite of their usual nook. "I had to move things around a bit, felt like I needed a change."

"That's just how I've been feeling lately, like I need a change. And since Kiera's been staying at the shop all week and Lee coming and going as he pleases, I've been thinking about making some moves of my own."

"He's been doing that since he retired, that's nothing new so what else has you feeling this way?"

"You're right Rona, he has but it's different now, somehow. I can't put my finger on it just yet, but it is, I know it is. Something ain't right."

"You know your man." J'Nae acknowledged.

"I do, that's why I know something's up."

"Well, I think I've said enough about fucked up shit that might evolve from your trilogy but right now, I wanna hear about some of the moves you've been thinking about making. What's up?" Zsasha asked.

"I thought we were here to get an update from J'Nae and offer our help. Her engagement party is just around the corner."

497

"Yes, it is, but we wanna hear about this first, don't we Rona, J'Nae?"

"Yes, we do. I can update y'all later. Spill it Vonne." J'Nae demanded.

"For starters, I haven't been at any of the boutiques all week."

"Really?" Rona asked.

"Yes. I've decided to step back a bit, you know, work less, play harder...that sort of thing."

"We get it." Zsasha stated. "And who's gonna manage the stores and deal with your designers and stuff?"

"I have enough staff to handle most of that for me, some of which have been with me from the very beginning and others long enough for me to trust."

"Really, it's that simple?" Rona asked.

"I'll continue to oversee contracts and other executive decisions, but I want to relinquish most of the day-to-day responsibilities and start enjoying the fruits of my labor."

"And you deserve it." Rona acknowledged. "You've been at this for a long time, and we all know you have money to burn so I say why not."

"I agree." J'Nae announced.

"Me too." Zsasha affirmed. "Do you, sweetie, do you. But what about your sister? Will she still be working for you?"

"I haven't made a final decision on that yet but I'm leaning towards **Hell No!**"

"Smart girl." Zsasha assured. "You've done more than enough for her. It's high time she gets her ass out of here."

"Whatchu said girl, whatchu said." Vonne agreed. "So J'Nae luv, where are you at with everything? Since I'm making these changes effective immediately, I have time to help you with the engagement party if you'd like."

"Actually, I hired a party planner a while back, maybe a month or so."

"Did that happen to be during the time you kept us in the dark?"

"Yes Zsasha, it was. But you're not in the dark anymore so let it go already, okay?"

Zsasha threw J'Nae a look letting her know she better tread lightly.

"I gave her a few instructions, shared my color pallet with her and before I knew it, she had everything arranged, including the caterer, the design and setup team and the band. All we have to do is show up."

"Sounds like you've got everything covered." Rona admitted.

"I do, I mean we do. Invitations went out yesterday, so all you guys have to do is respond. Everything else is taken care of."

"What about Taizja and Aiden? Will they be there?" Vonne asked.

"Unfortunately, neither of them will be able to make it. The grandkids have school and Aiden is undertaking some kind of special ops training assignment of sorts. But make no mistake about it, the wedding day will be set at a time when they'll both be available to attend."

"For sure, for sure." Zsasha muttered under her breath. "And how do they feel about all of this? Are they concerned that things are moving along rather quickly?"

"No, not at all. They've known about us for some time now and they've both met Wesley while I was visiting Taizja. Remember, he came out there a few times."

"My bad, I can't imagine why I didn't remember that." Zsasha reflected. "Oh yeah, that's right, we were the ones kept in the dark. We didn't know shit!"

"Zsasha..."

"I suppose they've become quite comfortable with dude, having had so much time to get to know him and all...unlike us."

"I can see you are still bothered by this situation or at least my handling of it but I've apologized more than once, several times in fact. There really isn't anything more I can say or do. However, if you can't forgive me and get past it, I would understand if you chose not to participate in our celebrations of love."

At that moment, Zsasha was about to come back with her notorious catch phrase 'Motha Fucka What', but she took a
499

breath and chose to respond and not react, even though she felt the right to do so. Sometimes it's best to take the high road especially when dealing with someone you truly love.

"Look here sweetie, I am and will always be your girl, no matter what but I'm also gonna be me. Just because I have some issues with how everything went down doesn't mean I don't love and support you. But you gotta understand a few things too; I'm entitled to my feelings, whatever they may be and if you love me like you say, you're just gonna half to accept that and your part in it. I'm going to need some time, real talk. But don't get it twisted, I'm here for you no matter what and will be there for you for each and every occasion celebrating the love the two of you share but give a bitch a minute to process some shit, damn." The girls all chuckled. "I'll get there, sweetie, I'll get there simply because I love you and love conquers all."

"Thank you Zsasha, I love you too and I'm truly sorry for not trusting our sista-hood. Your feelings are legitimate, and I accept my part in it. Just know I wouldn't want to go through with any of this without your support and participation."

"And you got it. And because I love you so much, I will make an effort not to throw my issues up in your face as much as I have been."

"Every fifteen minutes..." Rona mumbled.

"Yeah, yeah, about that..." Vonne added.

"Fuck y'all heffa's. And J'Nae, that's the best I can do, y'all bitches know how I am."

"I know, we all do, and love you for it."

"Great, fine, wonderful! Now can we crack open another bottle of wine, please." Vonne insisted. "I'm thirsty."

"I got you. I got all of you." Zsasha reiterated as she left to retrieve a chilled bottle of wine. She knew it didn't matter whether it was red, white or rose, they just wanted to drink something cold, and didn't care what it was. Afterall, a lot has transpired recently with all of them, some more serious than others. It was definitely time to decompress.

About two hours later, the four friends began preparing to bring the evening to a close. Despite her higher than usual level of intoxication, Vonne managed to call for her car service while the others cleaned up and put things away. Both Zsasha and J'Nae noticed the repetitive notifications on Rona's phone but didn't give it much thought. Shortly thereafter, Vonne was picked up by her car service and safely on her way home and the others left right behind her.

Once Rona made it home, she poured herself a large glass of wine in anticipation for what was next. She walked upstairs to her bedroom suite and disrobed, redressing herself in lounge wear. In the distance she could still hear a series of notifications on her cell phone and continued to let them go unanswered, for a while. Once settled comfortably on her chaise lounge, she checked her phone and was in no way surprised that her ex-husband was the culprit. She knew she had to call him back and did so right then.

"Hey Rona, how are you feeling today?"

"Hey Reggie, I'm good, thanks for asking."

"I know you're still keeping up the pretense and everything even though I don't agree with it, but I wanted to check up on you and see how you're doing."

"Thank you, sweetie, I appreciate that. You haven't said anything to the kids, have you?"

"No, you asked me not to."

"Good. There's nothing to tell until there's something to tell."

"I don't know, maybe you're right. No need to put the cart before the horse besides, I'm sure everything's going to be fine."

"I share your optimism." Rona smiled.

"Have you finalized your appointment and our travel plans yet?"

"Actually, I just did. I was waiting for confirmation on the date of J'Nae's engagement party so I could plan to be here. We'll be leaving early the next day."

"You and your girls, I swear…."

"Oh yeah, after everything J'Nae's been through, I wouldn't miss this for the world."

"I get it."

"So look, here's what I was thinking. Since you'll be flying out with me early the next morning, why not just come to the engagement party as my date. Stay at the house that night which will make it easier for us to leave the next morning. I know you would love to see J'Nae...2.0 as I'm sure she would love to see you too."

"That works for me, it's whatever you need. I'm here for you."

"Cool. Let's plan on doing just that, okay. And the kids don't have to know anything about it or us taking this trip together. They probably won't even notice we're gone at the same time, being so busy and caught up in their own lives."

"I agree. We can video chat with them from anywhere and I can barely lock 'em down on the phone for more than 5 minutes anyway."

"Really, you too...And I thought they all developed some late-stage mommy issues or something. I didn't know what was going on."

"I know you know better than that. Our kids worship you. You were and are the best mother they could've asked for. You know that love."

"I guess so. You weren't that bad either, now that I think about it."

"Oh, it's like that huh?"

"Sure is." Rona laughed.

"Whatever, just email me all the details for the trip so I can square things away at my office. The sooner the better."

"Uhm, Reggie..."

"Yes, love."

"Do you know who I am?"

"Of course I do."

"Check your email sweetheart."

"My bad."

"We'll talk again soon."

"Bye babe."

"By Reggie."

At the same time Rona wrapped up her conversation with Reggie, Vonne's car service had dropped her off at home without incident. Once she made her way inside, she felt the house quiet and undisturbed as if she were home alone. Her current level of intoxication did not deter her from pouring yet another glass of wine, but it had made her unaware of her sister's car which had been partially sticking out of the garage. After a few sips of wine, she realized she was not home alone and began to make her way towards the noise she thought was her husband Lee. She was mistaken.

"I thought I told you to keep yo ho ass out of my house. What the fuck are you doing here?"

"Damn Vonne, It's like that?"

"Yes bitch, it's like that. I tried to look out for you and let you all up in my house and yo ass got way too comfortable. Somehow you got shit twisted and started believing that what was mine was yours and you already know I ain't wit that shit."

"I'm sorry. I just needed to grab some of my stuff."

"You mean to tell me that after all this time you've been posting up in the shop that you didn't just help yourself to clothes, shoes and let us not forget panties because we all know how much you don't like to wear them motha fucka's!"

"Look, I can see you've been drinking, and I didn't come over here to start anything. I just needed some of my personal things, that's all."

"Well little sista, let me enlighten you. You ain't walking out of my house with anything I haven't inspected. I don't trust your bitch ass."

"Then here, go ahead and do your inspection." Kiera conceded while tossing her bag toward Vonne's feet. "I don't have anything to hide. In fact, everything your husband gave me is still upstairs in the closet. I don't want anything of yours that you don't want me to have."

"Really bitch? Does that include my husband? Because I feel like yo ho ass is helping yourself to him as well...bitch."

"Seriously Vonne? You're taking it there? I ain't did shit to or with your husband and I'm sorry that you feel otherwise. The only thing I'm guilty of is picking a bad time to come get my stuff, so right now, I just wanna leave. I didn't come here to upset you or cause any drama so can you just toss my bag back to me, please and I'll be on my way?"

"Like I said, you ain't taking nothing out of my house, now get yo ho ass up outta here before shit really jumps off."

"So I can't have my stuff?"

"Fuck no, you've helped yourself to way too much of my shit. Now for the last time, git gone bitch. Now!"

Kiera did as her sister demanded but wasn't happy about it at all. She drove back to her temporary living arrangement in tears, in part because she was truly hurt by her sister's accusations and also mad as hell for being blamed for inappropriate behavior when Lee was guilty of doing just that.

Fuck Vonne, she's clueless. He was the one who made a pass at me, and I turned him away and now this bitch wants to blame me...nah, fuck that. I learned a long time ago, if I gotta do the time, I may as well do the crime, especially with her ass. Without a moment of hesitation, Kiera reached for her phone and called Lee.

"Hey, where are you right now? What are you doing? Can you get another batch of that shit you had earlier?"

"Just out and about and yeah, I can get more, wassup?"

"Cool. Get more and meet me back at the shop. I'm headed there now."

"Okay. I can be there in 30 minutes, cool?"

"Yeah, just let yourself in, I'll be in the back."

"Alright, bet."

Once Kiera arrived at The Boutique, she was surprised to see Lee had already arrived. His car was parked two blocks down and across the street from the boutique. It was obvious to her he was trying to be incognito, but she was focused and, on a mission, and easily spotted his car right away. Once inside, she made her way directly to the back office without pausing for any reason. Thankful she was able to steal a shower before Vonne became aware of her presence, she entered the office with a purposeful stride, snorted a line of cocaine Lee had laid out for her, chased it with a swig of whatever brown liquor he poured in a cup then made her way to where he stood. Face to face, she

504

didn't hesitate or tremble as she planted a hot, wet sensual tongue kiss on the man she had rejected earlier that day. He pushed back for a moment, barely long enough to look directly into her eyes before ripping off her blouse and restarting the passionate kiss he had pulled away from just moments ago. The rest was history.

Chapter 44

A few days had passed since Zsasha had been in touch with the girls and she found herself feeling a bit anxious. She wasn't sure why or what had brought it on but could sense something was on the horizon, just didn't know what. Unsure of what to do with her feelings she turned her attention back to her work when Simon entered her home office and greeted her with a forehead kiss.

"Hey sweetie, I was looking for you." Simon remarked.

"You were, well I've been right here. Wassup boo?"

"I've got to fly out to New York again. More club business. Some licensing issues that require my presence."

"I thought you took care of all that a while ago?"

"I thought I had but you know how these things go. You think you've taken care of everything and then boom, something else happens then everything goes to shit!"

"Is it that bad?"

"No, not exactly but it is urgent and can't be avoided."

"When will you be leaving?"

"I'll fly out the day after tomorrow and plan on being in New York for a few days."

"Really...what about the engagement party? You can't miss that."

"I promise I won't. Even if I have to fly back just for the day I'll be there."

"Okay because if you're not here, mama won't be happy."

"We gotta keep mama happy, don't we?"

"Yes, we do because if mama's not happy, nobody's happy!"

"Don't I know it." Simon snickered.

"Whatchu said boo, whatchu said."

The lighthearted conversation between Zsasha and Simon was just what she needed to ease the unsettling feelings she's had over the last past day or two. She was even more delighted to see a call coming through from Ellie. They hadn't chatted in a while.

"Hey Zsasha, how are you?"

"Hey girl, I'm good. How are you?"

"Fine, just reaching out, hadn't had the chance to catch up with you in a while. What's been going on?"

"This and that, been here and there...you know just the usual shit. Oh, my girl J'Nae got engaged!"

"Oh yeah, that's so cool. Please congratulate her for me."

"I will for sure, count on it." Zsasha replied. "Wait, hang on a sec."

Zsasha noticed the look on her husband's face just as he glanced down at his phone to review an incoming text message that just came in. It was from Ellie. He found the tone of her message unsettling and was unable to regroup before Zsasha noticed.

"You straight, Simon?" his wife asked.

> *Ellie: I've been thinking about you ever since our time in New York. Are you missing me yet...I'm missing you...*

"Yeah, everything is cool. I'll be in the gym if you need me."

"Okay sweetie."

"Is everything okay, Zsasha?" the voice on the phone asked.

"Oh, yeah, my bad...just talking with Simon. He's heading back to New York soon and he's not happy about it."

"Sorry to hear that."

"It's all good, it's just business."

"Cool. So what do you have going on today? Can I interest you in a bite to eat and a bit of shopping?"

> *Ellie: I know you want me. I can tell by the way you kissed me in New York. No one has to know...we can keep it between us.*

"Maybe another time. I've got a few things I need to take care of today and like I said, Simon is leaving town soon so it's not the best time for me."

> *Simon: Yes, I'm attracted to you, but I never should have kissed you and this can't go any further.*

508

"I understand sweetie. I'll check in with you some other time."

  Ellie: *Don't be like that Simon. Quit lying to yourself, you know you want this...*

"Let's make a point of it. We haven't hung out in a while and I kinda miss spending time with you."

  Simon: *I'm married.*

"So it wasn't all business, huh, between you and me?"

"Of course not and I know you know that by now."

  Ellie: *Like that's ever stopped you before...besides isn't that part of the deal you guys got going on?*

"I was just checking..." Ellie giggled.

"I hope so, I mean you've definitely been there for me, no doubt. And you've helped me out, even saved my ass a time or two with gallery business and such but while doing so we got to know each other a bit and developed a friendship."

  Simon: *It's not that simple, we have rules besides you and Zsasha are friends.*

"I'm glad you consider me a friend, Zsasha. I admire you and all of your accomplishments. You're a talented and strong black woman I can learn a lot from. I look forward to growing our friendship wherever it may lead."

  Ellie: *All the more reason why we should.*

"Me too, sweetie. We'll get together soon."

  Simon: *I can't do this right now...gotta go.*

"Sure thing, Bye Zsasha."

"Bye Ellie."

Simon put his phone down to get on the treadmill but not before deleting the thread of text messages between him and Ellie. He considered blocking her number to put an end to this nonsense before it gets out of hand but on some level, he wasn't ready to cut her off, not completely and not just yet.

Early the next morning, Kiera was awakened by a notification on her cell phone. It was from Lee asking her to call him when she got his message. She didn't hesitate for a minute.

"Hey you, wassup?"

"Hey, just wanting to check on you and see how you're feeling about everything. Any regrets?"

"Uhm, yeah...that we didn't do it sooner."

"Is that right?"

"Pretty much, yeah. Does that surprise you?"

"Not at all."

"Really...because the way I see it, no matter what I did or didn't do, Vonne would've ended up doing exactly what she did, no ifs, ands, or buts about it. Now I just need to figure out my next move. I'm not going back to her house, and I can't continue to live in the back office any more than I can continue to work here. That's just not gonna work for me or her for that matter."

"I was thinking about that too but hold on for a minute. For now, just keep a low profile and I'll have something worked out soon, real soon I promise."

"Something like what?"

"For starters, better accommodations, something more permanent and after we get over that hurdle the rest will fall into place."

"Really, wow. I'm surprised. I can see you gave this some thought."

"Yeah, I have and while I'm fessing up, I should also tell you that I've been feeling this way for a while, quite a while. And I don't think I'm alone in it, am I?"

"No, you're not but...."

"But what? Our marriage has been over for quite some time now, I know it and she know it too. We just got comfortable with our routine and pretty much stayed out of each other's way. This isn't on you so don't stress yourself one bit. This was just the push that I needed to make the moves I've been wanting to make for some time now. You just have to be patient and let me work a few things out so that I get what's mine. That's all I'm asking."

"That's fine, I mean I don't have any expectations from you about anything, anything at all and we don't even know if this is going anywhere or not so for now just do you...do what you gotta do."

"I'm gonna do that for sure but I'm also not gonna leave you hanging, you feel me. I am just as responsible as you if not more. If I really wanted to put the brakes on, I would have handled things differently, several things. This is not on you, remember that."

"I'll try and I appreciate that. However, right now, I need to get ready so I can open the shop on time."

"Okay but check this out, if she comes by there for any reason, text me right away, okay?"

"Do you think she knows anything?"

"About what happened...no, absolutely not, how could she?"

"I don't know, I'm just stressing, I guess."

"Well don't, everything will be fine. But like I said, text me if she shows up at all, okay?"

"Will do, talk to you later."

"Bye Kiera."

"Bye Lee."

Chapter 45

The engagement party was just a few days away when Zsasha decided to plan a personal and private surprise for the girls in honor of J'Nae's big event. With Simon in New York, Zsasha had time to plan a day of indulgence at an out-of-the-way private spa resort tucked away in the hills of Virginia, about an hour from the gallery. The treat came as a surprise and was scheduled for the day before the party and J'Nae was happy to let her maid of honor plan a day of pampering for her and her closest friends.

The girls were all comfortably stretched across a series of massage tables in a private room where they could indulge in all the girl talk they could handle. It was time for J'Nae to dish.

"This is nice, Zsasha. Where did you find this remote spot? It's quite extraordinary and secluded." J'Nae asked.

"It's owned by one of my clients."

"Oh really." Vonne chimed in. "And who might that be?"

"Does it matter?"

"Not really...I just wanted to know who to thank for all this delicious eye candy all over this place. *I could eat!*"

"Vonne, need I remind you that you're a married woman? A woman that already has way too much drama going on in her life."

"No J'Nae, you don't have to remind me of that but you ain't seen nothing yet. There's more to come."

"Girl what are you talking about?" Zsasha asked.

"I already told y'all that I'll be making some changes in my life real soon and some of those changes might involve expanding my circle of friends and acquaintances."

"Just what type of friends are you talking about, the ones that come with benefits?" J'Nae asked.

"Indeed. What other kind is there?" Vonne said rhetorically. "You have to bring something to the table otherwise I have no need for you."

"Sounds like a mission statement to me, but can you live with that? Will you find fulfillment surrounding yourself with people that exist only to please you or provide something for you?" Rona inquired.

"Absolutely."

"Uhm, Vonne dear, we haven't really been here all that long, so did you start drinking before we got here because this doesn't sound like you at all." J'Nae shared.

"You must not have been paying attention the last time we all got together. Meet Vonne 2.0. It's a new day!"

"I guess you're serious about all of this, huh?"

"I am J'Nae."

"And how does your husband feel about all of this?" Zsasha teased.

"I don't know and right now, I don't care much. At the end of the day, he can get on board with it or get out of the way. I'm going to do me from now on."

"I ain't mad at you girl, just be careful. You know how people can be. Things can get complisticated."

"What? Complisticated? What the hell does that mean, Rona?"

"Is that even a word?" J'Nae questioned.

"It means sophisticatedly complex. It's a term often used by bougie bitches like us." Rona explained.

"Speak for yourself, sista girl." Zsasha warned. "Ain't a bougie bone in my body."

"I think you're a lot of things, Zsasha but I'll let you have that one."

"Cool, cool."

"So... J'Nae, how are you feeling? Are you nervous, anxious, scared...what???" Vonne interrogated. "Talk girl."

"Surprisingly, none of the above. I'm happy and excited and I can't wait for us to start our lives together."

"Technically, you already have...since you guys are living together."

"True, true but I don't care. I'm happy. I love Wes and he loves me and that's all that matters."

"I'm happy for both of you, sweetheart."

"We all are."

The girls smiled as they came in close for a group hug before moving on to their next mani-pedi. After getting situated in a circular seating area, the girls all requested refills on their champagne and continued with their conversation.

"Rona, who's your plus one for the engagement party? Anyone we know?" Vonne asked.

"Actually yes, I'm bringing Reggie. He hasn't seen you guys in a long time, and he's asked about you guys a few times."

"Is that right?" Vonne inquired.

"Sure, you know we are in contact periodically and of course he wants to share in J'Nae's happiness, so I thought he'd be perfect to accompany me."

"No doubt, it just comes as a shock." Vonne admitted.

"How so?"

"You haven't mentioned him in forever. I just thought you'd bring Fernando or Alexander." Vonne replied.

"Who?"

"Girl, she means Jon Paul or Ricardo. Vonne you're officially cut off from wine for the rest of the day."

"Like hell I am. I'm doing just what we came here to do, relax and be pampered. Thanks Z, I really needed this."

"You do know this is all about J'Nae, right?"

"Girlfriend, it may have started out that way but I'm going through stuff with my man, and this was just the distraction I needed. And what about you? What's up with that man of yours? Have you told him about Adam and what happened behind the gallery, huh?"

"No, I have not but it's not a big deal. Simon ain't gonna trip about that."

"Then why not tell him?" Rona inquired. "He would want to know about it."

"I just haven't gotten around to it."

"It's not like you to bite your tongue or hold anything back. What's really going on here?"

"It just brought up some old memories that I'd rather not relive so just leave it alone. I took precautions so nothing like that will happen again so let it go."

"I think we should do what she asked." J'Nae reiterated. "She knows what's best for her."

"I do, good looking out J'Nae."

"You got it girl. But will Simon be back from his trip in time for the party tomorrow night?" J'Nae asked. "Wes is really looking forward to getting to know the guys a little better. He really wants to fit in."

"I'm sure he does and yes, Simon will be there, for sure. Damn, I thought I put my phone on silent. Who the hell is that coming through on my phone?"

"Either you didn't put your phone on silent like you thought or it's someone on your breakthrough list."

Zsasha had her manicurist retrieve her phone to see where the call or notification was coming from. She was surprised to see it was her security company and asked her technician to answer and put it on speaker.

"Hello Mrs. Stewart. This is Chad Rudney from Merciless Security."

"Merciless Security!" Vonne snickered.

"Shhh..." Zsasha said, directing her request to her noisy friend. "Yes, this is Mrs. Stewart."

"Mrs. Stewart, we have received three false alarms at your art gallery Ahsasz within the past two hours."

"I haven't received any calls or notifications prior to this."

"After responding and determining it was a false alarm, we reached out to Mr. Stewart first however he was unreachable the last time I called."

"Okay, well did you go by and check things out?"

"Yes, we did, and everything appears to be fine. I can have a technician come out tomorrow and check things out and see why the alarm continues to go off."

"Yeah, I guess but I'll be tied up all day away from the gallery."

"Is there anyone with access that can meet us there?" the caller asked.

"I believe I can work that out." Zsasha replied.

"How does 2:00 pm sound?"

"That works. I'll have my assistant meet you then."

"Great and in the meantime, if there are any more false alarms between now and then, we'll have a car posted overnight."

"Thank you, Mr. Rudney. We'll see you tomorrow."

"What was that all about?" Vonne asked.

"Is everything alright?" J'Nae followed.

"Just a couple of false alarms at the gallery. They'll check out the security system tomorrow. Hopefully they will figure out what the malfunction is and why it keeps going off."

"Maybe somebody broke in?"

"No, it's not that. They responded every time and saw nothing wrong. All doors and windows were secure. I'm sure it's just some kind of system malfunction. Nothing to worry about."

"If you're sure about it."

"I am. Y'all ready to wrap this up?"

"I am." J'Nae replied.

"Me too."

"Vonne, you good? Do you need to call your car service?"

"No ma'am. They're outside waiting on me now."

"Have they been out there all this time?"

"Affirmative."

"Oh you ballin, huh?"

"Like I said, it's all about me."

"You go girl."

The girls all made their way out to their cars, said their goodbyes and headed in the respective directions. Zsasha drove towards the gallery while calling Adam about today's alarming events, Vonne was chauffeured home where she continued to enjoy more wine and Rona went home then reached out to Reggie to firm up their plans for the next few days.

Chapter 46

The next morning began with a clear sky and comfortable temperatures, perfect for a day of celebration. Kiera was slightly awakened by what she thought was someone inside the boutique moving about but quickly dismissed the idea when the alarm didn't sound. When she continued to hear what she was certain was movement she quietly slid out of bed and retrieved a small baseball bat she kept close by. She tiptoed towards the door intending to open it slowly when she was startled that it opened from the other side. Still, she lunged forward with the bat in hand ready to crack whomever upside the head. To her surprise it was Lee.

"Dude, what the fuck! You almost got knocked the hell out!"

"I doubt it, I would've grabbed that little bat and snatched it right out your hand. You never would've made contact baby, not even close."

"You think?"

"I know." Lee said while giving Kiera a kiss. "Good morning."

"Yeah, yeah, yeah, good morning. What are you doing here so early other than trying to scare the shit out of me?"

"I wanted to see you." Lee replied as he continued to kiss and grope Kiera while backing her towards the bed. "Touch you, taste you."

"This early?"

"Yes, this early, before you had a chance to shower."

"Oh, so you're one of them, huh?"

"With you, yeah, I am. Is that a problem?" he asked as his kisses made their way past her breasts, gently running his tongue across her navel then her inner thigh. First the left one then the right.

"No Lee, that's not a problem at all." Kiera moaned...allowing his tongue to continue its journey of discovery until she could taste her early morning nectar on his lips.

* * * * *

Zsasha was so relaxed from her spa retreat with the girls the day before that she ignored all alarms, phone calls and intrusions from her hired help. She pulled herself together once she realized she was nearly an hour behind schedule. Being late for her regular hair stylist wasn't really an issue. Part of what she paid them covered convenience and inconvenience as well. But she definitely had to make certain Adam could meet with the security company in just a few short hours. She needed to reach out to set that up.

"Hey Adam."

"Good morning Ms. Zsasha, how are you?"

"I'm good, I'm good. Am I catching you at a bad time?"

"No, not at all. What can I do for you?"

"I'm sure you know J'Nae's engagement party is tonight, and I'll be tied up all day with last minute details and I'm going to need you to meet the security company at the gallery this afternoon, early this afternoon."

"Sure, no problem. Is everything okay?"

"Yes, but the alarm has been going off repeatedly for no reason and they want to come by and check it out, reset it if they have to."

"Oh, okay. That's no problem at all."

"I appreciate that and I'm sorry about the short notice."

"It's all good. I wasn't doing anything today and you've been paying me for a while without me actually working, so...don't sweat it."

"Okay cool. I'll send you the details in a few minutes."

"That's fine. Should I call you when they wrap up?"

"I'll probably be tied up but yeah, call me and if I can't answer just follow up with a text message to let me know how everything went."

"Absolutely. Enjoy the party."

"I will, thanks Adam, bye."

"Bye Ms. Zsasha."

Zsasha sent the meeting details to Adam as soon as she ended the call. Needing to confirm his return home in time for the party she immediately reached out to her husband who answered right away.

"Hey Z."

"Hey boo. How's it going? Have you wrapped everything up or are you still working?"

"Actually, I'm just gathering my things so I can check out. I promised I'd be back in time, and I meant it."

"Yeah, you did, and you pretty much keep your word, don't you...so should I pick you up at the airport or what?"

"No need. I figured you have a lot to do in preparation for the engagement party, so I have a car service scheduled to pick me up and deliver me at home in time to shower and change for the party. You go ahead and do what I know you need to do, and I'll meet you there."

"Okay boo. Love you."

"Love you too, Z."

Zsasha let out a huge sigh of relief. She has taken care of everything on her to do for everybody else list so she can spend the next few hours focusing on herself.

* * * * *

A few hours later, Kiera is hard at work rearranging items in the store that hadn't received much attention. For the second time that day, she is surprised when Lee shows up at the boutique, this time with one of the associates from another store location.

"Hey you guys, what's up?"

"Laura is going to cover for you for a while so we can take care of a few things."

"Right now?"

"Yes. I only have a small window of opportunity before the engagement party tonight. Did you forget about J'Nae, Vonne's friend?"

"Kind of."

"Yeah, well Vonne and I rsvp'd so I've got to work around that. Which is why we need to leave now."

"Okay. Let me lock up the office and I'll meet you out front."

"Cool. Laura, you worked out of this store before, so you know what to do and where everything is, right?"

"Sure thing, boss. I'll see you guys when you get back."

"Cool. I'm reachable by phone if you need anything."

"Got it."

Kiera followed Lee to his car and got in on the passenger side. All kinds of thoughts were going through her mind, mainly the fact that someone witnessed him scooping her up.

"I don't know what's going on, but do you really think that was a good idea? I mean we played it off and everything, but she has no loyalty to me. She'll tell Vonne even if she doesn't suspect anything."

"She may not be loyal to you, but she is definitely loyal to me, trust me...I hand-picked her for this assignment."

"And what assignment is this...exactly?"

"Assignment 'Bust A Move'!"

"What?"

"Just relax and enjoy the ride, okay. Everything will be fine. I got you."

Kiera decided to play along and stop asking questions. She knew she was in good hands and had nothing much to worry about at the moment. As they drove through the city she sat back and let the smooth sounds of Jazz coming through the stereo put her mind, body and soul at ease. A few minutes later, they pulled up to a high-rise in Tysons Corner where they were met by a valet. As her car door was opened for her, she stepped out with a puzzling look on her face.

"What's this? Why are we here?"

"This is where you live now."

"What?"

"Yes, this is your new spot, our spot."

"Wow, really?"

"Yeah. Didn't I tell you I would take care of it?"

"Yes, you did but I didn't expect it to happen this fast and especially didn't expect it to be a place like this."

"I think you deserve it; we deserve it."

"Wow Lee, I can't believe it!"

"Are you ready to go inside and check it out?"

"Yes, yes, yes!"

"Let's go!" Lee tossed his keys to the valet. "back in thirty."

The two lovers made their way to the elevator, but Kiera was still clueless. She was so busy hugging and kissing Lee that she didn't pay any attention to what floor he selected when they got in. She only stopped kissing him when the elevator stopped, and the doors opened. To her surprise the elevator doors opened up to what was now her living room, their living room.

"Wow Lee, I've never seen anything quite like this before. This is unbelievable!"

"Well get used to it. This is just the beginning."

"This is beautiful. Wait, so anybody can just get on the elevator and walk right in? That doesn't seem safe."

"No sweetie, no one else can access this floor on their own except the two of us. We have this half of the penthouse floor to ourselves, and it comes with our own doorman. And when we have visitors, they must show ID and sign in at the front desk. The doorman will call and ask if we want them sent up or not. It's very safe and secure. And we can change our access code anytime we like."

"This will take some getting used to."

"It's time somebody showed you the finer side of life. You deserve it."

"I don't know what to say."

"Don't say anything. Take a few minutes to look around and then I'll take you to pick up your car so you can go get the rest of your things. By the time you get back, it'll be partially furnished."

"Is it safe to go to the house now? How do you know Vonne's not there?"

"Because I'm tracking her phone and she's at the salon. That's why we needed to move when we did."

"I get it."

"Can I get it?"

"Not now, like you said we need to go. I've seen all I need to see for now. Let's get going while the going is good."

"You're right. Here's your key and your access code. Don't lose it or lay it down. Once you memorize it, destroy this card, got it?"

"Got it."

The two lovers left the penthouse and Lee dropped Kiera back at the boutique to get her car as planned. So elated and overwhelmed with Lee's surprise, she didn't take a minute to go inside and check on Laura or even give it a thought. Had she done so, she would have run into her sister who unexpectedly stopped by to check up on things. But that didn't happen. Kiera headed straight to her sister's house to grab some of her things. Once she pulled up to the house, she called Lee.

"Hey sweetie listen, are you sure Vonne is still at the salon? The party should be starting in a few hours, and I would think she'd be here getting dressed."

"No, she's still at the salon, I'm sure of it. Like I said, I'm tracking her phone and if I know her and the girls, they're probably meeting up somewhere doing their final touches together. Not to worry. Her car's not there, right?"

"No, it's not."

"Okay then. Just run in, grab your things and run out. Just the essentials. We can have the rest of your stuff packed and sent over tomorrow. I know you need more than what you have right now."

"You're right, I do."

"Just keep your phone with you and I'll call you when she's on the move, okay?"

"Okay."

"Now go ahead and do what you gotta do."

"Alright. See you tonight."

"Yes, you will."

* * * * *

After a short delay, Simon sees his limo and driver pulling up then stopping directly in front of him. His driver gets out and walks around to open the passenger door while nodding his head at Simon in acknowledgement. As he enters the back of the limo, he immediately becomes aware that he is not alone. Ellie is seated in the rear of the limo and anxious to greet him.

"Hello Simon, how was your flight?"

"It was fine. What are you doing here, Ellie?"

"You know why I'm here. I'm here because we have some unfinished business, business that you started in New York."

"I did and I---"

"Stop right there. No more excuses. You and I both want the same thing."

"It's not that simple."

"Yes, it is. You're worried about Zsasha for no reason. She doesn't tell you everything."

"We don't keep secrets from each other."

"I know for a fact that's not true."

"Ellie, you're a very beautiful young woman and you can have any man that you want, but...damn, this is hard." He admitted while shaking his head.

"Is it? How about you let me be the judge of that."

Ellie began to massage his groin.

"You were telling the truth. It is hard."

"Ellie, stop." Simon mumbled while making a weak attempt to push her hand away.

Ellie responded by unbuckling his pants so she could unwrap what she craved. Before he could object any further, she'd taken him in her mouth. As the subtle sounds of his pleasure increased, so did her intensity. His hands went from a gentle caress of her head to a firm grip pulling her in closer as the pressure mounted ever so intensely. Then, as quickly as it started, it was over. Simon's release left him slightly flabbergasted and did nothing to diminish his desire for more.

"I've been wanting to do that for a while now, Simon. I don't know why you put up a fight for so long. It's obvious you want me as much as I want you. And judging from your response, I think you want more."

"Maybe, maybe not. I learned a long time ago that just because you can do something doesn't mean that you should."

"I disagree. I think we should do whatever makes us happy in this life. Besides, why put off until tomorrow what you know you want to do today. Time is of the essence."

"You might be right about that. Driver, change of plans. Take us to the gallery."

"Right away, Mr. Stewart."

Chapter 47

Walking inside her home, anyone nearby would hear the intensity of her stride as she entered her kitchen, purse and keys clacking down on the counter with equal amounts of anger.

"Kiera, Kiera! I know you're here. Bring your ass down here right now!"

Vonne waited for a minute but got no reply.

"Kiera! Little girl, I swear, you better not make me ask again. Get your ass down here!"

"I'm coming, I'm coming, damn!"

Kiera made her way down the stairway to the kitchen carrying a couple of bags containing her personal belongings. She placed them on the floor resting against the island in the center of the kitchen then turned toward her sister.

"What Vonne? What are you bitching about now?"

"You know damn well what I'm bitching about. You, Kiera! You and your trifling ass!"

"Who are you calling trifling?"

"I'm calling you trifling, sista girl. How you gonna come in here and disrespect me in my home like you have, when I'm trying to help your ratchet ass. Taking my clothes without asking, stealing merchandise from the store. And by the way, anything you got packed up in those bags, stays here. It's my shit anyway."

"That's my stuff not yours and I'm taking it with me, all of it. Along with anything else of mine that's here."

"Motha Fucka please! If you don't get yo ho ass up outta my house...that's right, I said ho ass. I just came from the store where you and Lee have been posted up. I could smell his scent all over the back office that you've been sleeping in. I know you been fucking my husband and you need to get the fuck outta my house!"

527

"Whatever, bitch." Kiera said under her breath as she turned her back to her sister and reached down for her belongings.

"What did you say?"

"I said whatever, bitch!"

"You're not even gonna deny it, are you?"

"Why should I? You ain't fucking him so what diff--- "

Kapow!

At that precise moment Vonne's right fist had a close encounter with Kiera's left jaw, knocking her backwards into the dual range oven hard enough so that her head bounced off the oven door causing her to be slightly shaken. Before she could regain her composure, Vonne punched her in the face with another right then left hook causing her to stumble to the side before landing on the floor. Vonne, being sober and a force to be reckoned with, took two steps forward then reached down to pull Kiera to her feet.

"Get the fuck off me!" Kiera yelled, pushing Vonne off her.

Kiera was stunned to the point that what she thought was a forceful shove, barely had an impact on her sister but fighter instincts ran in the family and Kiera soon gathered herself together and became a formidable opponent.

She grabbed her sister and slung her across the kitchen island, clearing the counter in the process. Vonne landed on the kitchen floor, but she didn't stay down for long. As she sprung up and took a fighting stance, Kiera hurled a heavy glass vase in her direction that caught the side of Vonne's face and head. She was bleeding and she was pissed. She ran right up to her sister and returned the favor, knocking Kiera flat on her back giving Vonne the opportunity to straddle her and throw punch after punch to her face.

"Fuck you, Vonne, get up off me!"

"That's what you should have said to my husband, bitch. Instead, you're fucking and sucking and doing all kinds of drugs...being all kinds of disrespectful! And doing it in my store...BITCH!"

Kiera shoved Vonne aside and managed to get on her feet.

"Lee doesn't love you!   That's why he's fucking me.   He doesn't want you; nobody wants you, not even daddy.   He thinks you're pathetic and needy as fuck and lack any real talent and Lee's only with you for the ride so yeah, I'm fucking your husband and I'm fucking him good!"

Vonne stood motionless for a split second as Kiera's words sunk in. All the hatred and disgust she believed her father felt towards her began to consume here.   The memories of him belittling her fed the insecurities she thought had long ago been put to rest. She reached for the knife rack behind her, grabbed one and threw it at her sister's face. Instinctively, Kiera raised her forearms to shield her face. However, the knife sliced across her forearm and blood gushed out immediately. But Vonne was on a mission. She grabbed another knife and came straight for Kiera, again. They struggled with the knife, both enduring cuts on their hands, arms, neck and upper torso, none of which slowed down the intensity of the fight. Blood was everywhere; on the kitchen floor, cabinets and countertops yet their rage continued to escalate.   Eventually, Kiera was able to secure a knife leveling the battlefield and they both continued to attack and defend.

As the fight progressed, they tossed and tumbled their way out the kitchen, down the hall, and into the sitting room leaving a trail of blood along the way. By this time, both had lost their grips on the bloody knives and were standing face to face, now with no weapons in hand.

Vonne took a few steps back and stood there, starring at her sister, wondering where the fuck she went wrong trying to help her. Her friends told her she was asking for trouble, but she didn't listen. Instead, she stood up for her sister like family is supposed to. The same way she wished the men in her life would have stood up for her.

Kiera was standing with her back towards the patio doors looking at her sister who was just a few feet away. She took pleasure in the fact that Vonne had tears streaming down her face revealing her obvious pain and hurt. But Kiera didn't care, she didn't care about any of that.

529

"I can see you're hurting right now, I get it, really, I do. But the pain you're feeling right now won't compare to the pain you're gonna feel later tonight when you kiss your husband and taste my pussy on his lips."

Kiera barely got those words out of her mouth before Vonne ran towards her and lunged with enough force to send her flying through the glass patio doors. The shattered glass pierced and cut through her body as she landed on the concrete outdoors. She had lost consciousness momentarily bleeding from head to toe; totally unaware her sister now stood over her battered body.

"I told you not to fuck with me or mine, bitch. Now look at you. You should've listened!"

✳ ✳ ✳ ✳ ✳

The grand ballroom was located on the top floor of The Mirage Hotel; a lavish establishment known for hosting special events for elite clientele. In the foyer stood a frosted acrylic event sign with modern black calligraphy with the announcement *'Celebrating the Engagement of Wesley Hill and J'Nae Carter.'*

Peeking through the door of her private quarters, J'Nae glanced around the ballroom quite pleased with the décor. She had put a lot of planning into this event and took extra care to make sure things were exactly the way she wanted. The lighting was perfectly set to romanticize the evening and enhance any photos that may be taken. This event was sure to be the talk of the town.

The interior was decorated with sheer ceiling drapes that flowed from the center of the ceiling outwards then down all four walls. Flowing along the ceiling and wall drapes were starlight strands providing the perfect romantic ambience for the evening.

The guests' tables were rectangular and seated 6 on each side with a thick crystal-clear chair back and a seat covered in black satin. Each table was exquisitely decorated and covered with a matching black satin tablecloth. The centerpieces resembled a tall clear vase about 16 inches high with silver 2-inch beading around it starting about ¾ of an inch from the top. Inside were an array of black, white, and silver silk rose petals that served to accent the decor. On each side of the centerpiece was a 12-

inch white candle with the same silver beading as the centerpiece. Scattered across each table were silver glitter engagement ring shaped confetti mixed in with lettered confetti with the phrase *IDO.*

The place settings were made up of 9-inch black and white damask dinner plates with a solid black 11-inch plate underneath. At the center of each plate was a white ring box. Inside the ring box was a black ribbon tied in a loop pinned where the ring would normally be. The backdrop was a candid picture of the happy couple looking lovingly at each other which was also in black and white. A lot had gone into the details of decorating for this event and J'Nae could not be more pleased.

Anxious and nervous about the event, she watched as guests arrived to celebrate their engagement. Wes was a good man and had a gentle and kind spirit. He loved everything about J'Nae, her moral values, loyalty and commitment to her loved ones, even her adult children had a place in his heart. He was everything she never knew she wanted in a man and J'Nae felt blessed to have him in her life.

Just about everyone she'd invited had arrived and seemed to be enjoying the cocktails and hors d'oeuvres while meeting and mingling with other guests. Yes, just about everyone had arrived, almost everyone. A few very important people were noticeably absent; Vonne and Wes.

Vonne hadn't been seen or heard from and Wes hadn't shown his face either. She caught a glimpse of Rona and Zsasha coming her way and was more than happy to have them by her side. Better yet, maybe they had some information on Vonne and Wesley's whereabouts.

"Oh my gosh, you look lovely, J'Nae!" Rona announced as she embraced her girl affectionately.

"Yes, absolutely beautiful, my girl! You are glowing from head to toe and happiness is written all over your face!" Zsasha exclaimed.

"Well can you read worry and distress too?" J'Nae asked. "Where the hell is Vonne? Lee, I expected to flake out with everything they have going on but not Vonne...she knows I'm not doing this without her, and Wesley should've been here an hour ago? Have either of you seen or heard from either one of them?" J'Nae inquired.

"Wesley? Oh yeah, you must be stressing." Zsasha noted. "When have you ever called him anything other than Wes?"

Before J'Nae could respond, the door opened, and he appeared; fully dressed and looking as fine as ever in his black tuxedo sporting a fresh line-up. Her stress level dropped to an acceptable standard for the occasion as her VIP was now in the building.

"Sorry I'm late, baby. I had to put out a few fires and time got away from me. Are you ready? They're about to play our song."

"Vonne's not here boo and nobody has heard from her since last night. I'm worried something's wrong. There's no way she would miss this. She knows how important this is to me."

"Not to worry love, she left me a message saying she's having some issues with her family that require her immediate attention, but she'll be arriving as soon as she can. She said to go ahead and start without her, and she would explain it all later when she arrives."

"Really? Why did she call you?"

"Because she didn't want to worry you. She's fine, I promise."

"And Zsasha, where's Simon, he promised to be here also? Did his plane land on time?"

Zsasha had to think fast and come up with a lie that was somewhat believable or at least close to the truth. She knew his plane landed on time and he'd been picked up by his car service but had no idea why he hadn't arrived.

"Yes, his plane landed on time, and he texted to say he's on his way. I'm sure he'll be here soon but we should go ahead and get started. There are other guests to consider."

Reluctantly J'Nae agreed then asked Wes to give her ten minutes with the girls to embrace their sista circle before signaling to the DJ to play their song. He agreed and left the room.

The girls all came together to form a circle while holding hands, intent on encouraging and supporting their friend.

"So, are you ready J'Nae? Are you ready to tell the world how much you love this man and want to build a life with him?" Rona asked.

"I am, I really am. I'm so in love with him. He makes me feel like I'm his only priority. I feel his love and security around me all the time and I couldn't be more connected to him if I tried. Our hearts beat as one."

"Well then, you're ready." Zsasha confirmed with excitement in her voice.

"I am. Let's do this!"

Zsasha and Rona kissed their friend one more time as they left to take their seats. Eric Benet's 'Spend my Life With You' began playing as J'Nae and Wes made their entrance to the grand ballroom. The happy couple stood front and center as the DJ lowered the music then announced them and their engagement to their guests. The clapping and joyful outburst subsided when the music continued at its original volume. They embraced each other and started to dance.

An hour into the celebration, J'Nae was beyond happy despite those who were still not in attendance. Various appetizers had been shared and re-shared around the room to allow time for Vonne, Lee and Simon to arrive but ultimately J'Nae could no longer justify delaying dinner. Enough time had passed, and she had to consider her other guests.

The DJ lowered the music to make the announcement that dinner would be served immediately following the champagne toast. At the same time the servers presented the champagne, Zsasha heard another notification coming through on her phone. She ignored it. Everyone made their way to their seats in anticipation of the warm and loving sentiments the guests would share about the happy couple.

Sitting directly to his left was Wesley's best man, a former military buddy and long-term friend, Shawn Harris whom he often referred to as his brother. He was seated with his girlfriend of several years who was also close to Wesley. Rona and Reggie were both seated next to Zsasha while Simon, Vonne and Lee's seats remained empty.

The first guest to toast the recently engaged couple was Shawn. He made the traditional best-man speech making sure to point out how lucky he was to find someone as lovely as J'Nae. Zsasha made a toast of her own.

"My dear sweet J'Nae, we have known each other for more years than I'll ever admit out loud and have seen each other through some good times and some bad. Through the ups and downs and curveballs life has thrown your way, you made a bold decision to carve a new path for yourself, one that has opened the doors to the love, happiness and the future you deserve. Nothing warms my heart more than to see your light shining brightly again and that's because of Wesley and I thank him for that. As the two of you embark on building a life together, I wish you both nothing but joy and happiness and a lifetime of love. To J'Nae and Wesley!"

The sounds of cheer and glasses clinking together filled the room followed by a bit of chatter amongst the guests. Traditionally the toast to the happy couple comes from the party members as well as family and friends. But this time it would be different. Wesley stood up, took J'Nae by the hand guiding her to stand with him. Looking intently in her eyes, he began his toast to his beautiful fiancée.

"To the most beautiful person I've had the pleasure of knowing, J'Nae Carter. From the moment I met you, I knew you had a kind and gentle spirit and a generous heart that embodies everything unconditional love represents. I prayed that your personal losses would not darken your heart and soul, hoping you would once again be open to true love. I am so thankful and blessed that you found it with me as I have found it with you. Until I met you, I could never in a million years have imagined a life filled with the love and happiness you've brought to it. Every day you openly and generously give your heart and soul to me and those you love. Your trust, understanding, and support only makes me love you that much more and I am overflowing with gratitude every day you continue to love me. The Lord has not blessed me with children of my own, but I take, accept, and promise to love yours as is they were. I only wish my godson Edrick Mosely, a young man I had the pleasure of teaching, educating and mentoring over many years, was here to meet you and share in our complete and total happiness. But God had other plans. He was called home shortly before we met, and I feel his loss every day. A few of you knew Edrick, whom I called Ed, and the relationship we had over the years and how much he meant to me. Life hasn't been the same without him. Edrick Mosely was a talented radio host known to most of you as Rick Moss. And during his short time here on earth, what he added to my life was profound. J'Nae sweetheart, he would have loved you the same way I love you now and for all the same reasons. Thank you for making my life so complete. I love you, J'Nae Carter. To my beautiful wife-to-be!"

Wesley raised his glass expecting J'Nae to do the same. She didn't. She began to shake uncontrollably, looking directly in the eyes of her lover while trying her best to remain calm. But his words re-played in her mind over and over again. The man she wanted to spend the rest of her life with, the man who just confessed his undying and unwavering love to her, stood in anticipation of a response equal in nature. He would be disappointed. Her mind was reeling. Did he just say Rick Moss? *Rick Moss*...My Rick Moss? This can't be.

Shaken and dismayed, J'Nae tried to un-hear his words, but she couldn't; nor could she ignore the obvious. His loss, his godson...her loss, her lover...one in the same? No, it's not possible, it can't be. How could it be? How could they possibly have been mourning the loss of the same man and not know it? Say it ain't so, *say it ain't so!*

J'Nae began frantically looking around the room, searching the familiar and unfamiliar faces for an explanation, an answer, something confirming this was untrue. But as she continued looking through the crowd, she locked in on the girls. Zsasha and Rona's faces revealed her worst fear. That it *was* real; it was true.

Everyone was staring at her now, waiting for a response, a smile or nod, some sort of acknowledgement of Wesley's toast and declaration of love. But she was too overwhelmed with the new information to do anything. Now with her heart pounding and shortness of breath, her eyes raced across the room looking for an exit or a way out. Suddenly dropping her champagne glass, shattering it as it hit the floor, she ran off abruptly as it all became too much for her to bear.

She didn't say a word to Wesley or anyone else. She just bolted, headed straight for her private suite and then out to the balcony for some much-needed fresh air. Trailing right behind her was Zsasha and Rona, ready to support their dear friend in what they considered a devastating and life changing revelation.

* * * * *

"Kiera, pick up, pick up the phone! I just left the shop and Laura is still there. What's going on? Is everything okay? I thought you'd be back by now to close up. She said you never returned but that Vonne showed up for a minute then left mad as fuck. Call me back when you get this message. I'm heading to the house now in case you ran into Vonne. Alright, bye."

Lee continued on full steam ahead, solely focused on getting home that he drove past the gallery just as Simon and Ellie were headed inside. He had only one thing on his mind, maybe two, and that was Vonne and Kiera.

* * * * *

Both Rona and Zsasha entered the suite but said nothing. They waited patiently for J'Nae to come in from the balcony as they wanted to respect her privacy and need to gather herself. After a few minutes to herself, she joined Zsasha and Rona in her suite.

"Did you hear what I heard? He said Rick Moss. Rick Moss!"

"I know sweetie, we heard him. Are you okay?"

"Am I okay? Am I okay? Of course I'm not okay. He said Rick Moss...my Rick Moss!"

"We know sweetie."

"This is too much. We shared our deepest feelings with each other in counseling before and after we began dating. We

536

mourned together for a period of time, sharing the stages of grief each of us went through. And now after all this time, having met and grieved together; all the while we were grieving for the same man! A man I cared for deeply and intimately. A man he helped raise from a young boy into manhood. Oh my gosh! What have I done? How did this happen? How is it that we didn't know this by now or at least have figured it out? I know his best friend but that's it. All I know is that he has very little family."

"Well, that may be true, but did you ever meet any of Rick's family? I mean, you didn't attend his funeral because we arrived too late." Rona reminded.

"No, I didn't."

"How about any of his friends?" Zsasha asked.

"Well just the one, Alex. She's a chef, but it was just that one time she cooked for us."

"I don't buy it. How is it that Wesley never mentioned Rick Moss to you before tonight?" Rona questioned.

"After we began working through our grief and connected outside of the grief center, we didn't want to focus on what was lost, just on the future and what was ahead for us."

"And you guys never referred to your lost loved one by name?" Rona asked.

"Well, yes, we did... occasionally, I mean he did. Wes always referred to him as Ed. I guess now I can see it was short for Edrick. And as for me, it was too painful and much to intimate and personal to share those details with him or anyone at the support group, so no, I don't believe I ever referred to him by his name, which as you know, I only knew as Rick. I knew Moss was his stage name sort-of-speak and his last name was really Mosely but that's all I knew. If I had shared his name in grief counseling everyone would have known who I was mourning, and I just wanted to keep that part to myself."

"And what about sharing pictures or family photos, did that ever happen?"

"Let up some Rona, give her a break. No way did she see this coming and stop making her feel like she did something to bring

537

this on herself. I can easily see how this happened. Remember, She and Rick didn't really date that long before he passed, a few months at best. So, if they hadn't met each other's families and close friends, it's reasonable. Could have just been too early for all that. I mean, they didn't exactly have life plans or anything, right J'Nae?"

"J'Nae? J'Nae?"

"I don't want to talk about this anymore. I've gotta find Wes. I just ran out on him, and I owe him an explanation."

J'Nae turned to leave in search of the man she loved, instead she found Reggie standing in the doorway.

"Excuse me, I need to find Wes and explain why I ran out. He must be going crazy with worry right now."

"Well, J'Nae, I found him standing just outside the door a little bit ago. I was coming to check on you ladies and found him standing there, listening. I could hear you all talking so I'm pretty sure he could too. That your Rick and his Edrick were one in the same; that you were both mourning the same person all this time. Yeah, he heard every bit of it or at least enough to understand your dilemma. I'm so sorry sweetheart."

"No no no. He can't find out this way! I need to explain to him. How do I explain this to him? What do I do, Rona? How do I fix this?"

Rona stood there, speechless. It was the first time she could recall not having advice or words of wisdom for anything any of them were going through. But this time she had nothing to say. No one could have seen this coming or anticipated two unlikely creatures like J'Nae and Wes, grieving the death of the same young man. This was unbelievable.

"I've got to find Wesley. I need to at least try to explain to him that I had no idea."

"Go do what you gotta do, girl. I'm here if you need me."

"Thanks, Zsasha. Just pray and if you see him, don't let him leave. Call me right away."

J'Nae rushed off to find her fiancé. Tears were streaming down her face as she skirted from room to room hoping to find him sitting somewhere alone filled with unanswered questions.

"Can you believe this shit Rona? She's only dated Rick for a short period of time, five, six months or so. So how could she have anticipated this outcome? What could she have done to not end up in this situation, hurt and confused to then be abandoned at her own engagement party?"

"I think you're missing the main point of this situation. What is hurting J'Nae the most right now, you don't see it do you?"

"Girlfriend, I know her better than you." Zsasha reiterated. "And I know exactly how she's feeling right now. She's doubting herself. You see, the fact that neither of them became aware of this shared bond or love for Rick speaks to how well they know one another. How could they be 'so much in love' and not have covered this territory? The territory to include those who are important or significant in their lives. Whether Wes called him Ed or Edrick, how could he leave out the most obvious thing about him, that he was a locally known radio host? This situation is feeding her insecurities, I'm certain of it."

"So you do get it. She's probably questioning every decision she's ever made in life."

"We should have been all up in his business when she sprung him on us the way she did. Then maybe this would have come up a lot sooner."

"Well Zsasha, we did what we thought was best at the time. It's pointless to second guess ourselves now besides she really didn't give us a chance for all that. Even if we had uncovered their unknown connection, those two were so far gone it would have been hurtful and devastating any way you look at it." Rona paused for a moment observing her friend. "Is something else going on with you? Is everything alright?"

"Damn it, I'm still getting notifications the alarm is going off at the gallery and Simon isn't answering his phone and Adam's is going straight to voicemail. It looks like I'm gonna have to step out for a bit. Where's J'Nae?"

"Your guess is as good as mine and unfortunately I also have to leave."

"Yeah, you mentioned that you had a flight to catch right after the party."

"Something like that but let's try to find her first so she doesn't feel abandoned."

"Good idea."

Rona and Zsasha found J'Nae standing outside by the main entrance and valet drop-off and pick-up location. She looked worn and heartbroken, totally distraught and obviously lost. The girls took a moment to observe her and her state of mind before approaching.

"Hey sweetie. Most of the guests have left already and we haven't seen Wesley anywhere. Did you find him?"

"No, not exactly. The party planner let me know he left a little bit ago."

"Maybe he went back to the house so you guys can talk in private. This isn't on you J'Nae, remember that."

"I feel like he thinks it is. I mean he just left without saying anything."

"Well sweetie after hearing everything you said, that was quite a lot to take in. I'm sure he needs some time to process everything."

"I do too. I just don't think he's realized that yet."

"Maybe, maybe not." Rona conveyed.

"Well, what are you gonna do? You can't just stay here like this."

"No, I suppose I can't. I'm just gonna head home and hopefully he'll be there waiting for me so we can talk this out. Although I don't know where we go from here."

"He seems like a reasonable man, and I think everything will work itself out. There's no malice here. It was just an unfortunate coincidence, nothing more." Zsasha concluded.

"You want me to drop you off at home?"

"No, that's not necessary, Rona. I've already paid for the limousine so I might as well get some use out of it."

"Okay, well call me when you make it home, so I know that you're safe and if he's there or not."

"I will sweetheart. I love you, both of you."

"We love you too, J'Nae."

"Are you sure you're okay to ride home alone? We can ride with you." Zsasha insisted.

"No, I'm good. I kinda want to be alone for a bit. Y'all understand, right?"

"We do but call us anyway."

"I will, bye."

Rona and Zsasha watched their friend disappear down the road as she was driven away. They were both still shocked and stunned by the way the evening unraveled.

"I wonder what happened to Vonne. Did she text you or anything?"

"No, she didn't. But Wesley said she reached out to him which now that I think about it makes it all the stranger. I'm surprised she even had his number."

"Me too. Maybe Reggie knows something. He was with Wesley tonight, remember. They were together when Wesley said she called and again when they overheard us talking."

"Speak of the devil, let's just ask him."

"Hey, was that J'Nae just leaving?"

"Unfortunately, yes. Wesley left a bit ago so she's hoping to find him at home. Did he say anything more about Vonne and why she never showed up?"

"For starters, Lee called him not Vonne."

"That's weird." Zsasha surmised.

"So no one's actually spoken directly to Vonne, huh?"

"Doesn't sound like it."

"Did he say anything else?" Rona asked. "Is there something you're not telling us?"

"I was going to tell you both after the party but then all this happened."

"What's going on, Reggie.?" Rona asked.

"Apparently, Vonne's at the police station. She's been arrested. Her and her sister got into a fight or something. That's all I know."

"Wow. I wonder what happened."

"I'm sure she's alright Zsasha, you can call Lee for more information."

"I will for sure, but right now I gotta go check on the galley. Adam was supposed to be there checking the security systems but apparently that didn't happen. Maybe I'll just deactivate the alarm until we can have it looked at again, then I'll see what's what with Vonne and check on J'Nae. I'll text and let you know what's what, okay?"

"Alright then, and if I get an update from either one of them, before my flight I'll do the same."

"Cool Rona, see you later. Reggie it was great seeing you again. Take care."

"I will Zsasha, you too."

Zsasha hugged her friend's goodbye and made her way to her car once the valet pulled it up front. She didn't worry about tipping the young man, she just jumped in and thanked him for his service. Once she was inside her vehicle, she noticed a medium size package on the passenger seat with a label attached. In large letters the first line read 'For Zsasha's Eyes Only'. The second line read 'Open at once - Time Sensitive'.

What now, she asked herself as she took a deep breath and thought about it for a minute. She was just about to open it when the valet tapped on her window letting her know she was in the way and needed to move along. She pulled off but only drove about a mile and a half before she pulled off to the side of the road to check the contents. Realizing she should have asked the valet about the mysterious package that somehow found its way inside her securely locked vehicle, her curiosity got the best of her.

Inside the package she found a clear plastic bag containing her small, silver-plated hairbrush that went missing several months ago and another bag with a toothbrush she recognized as one she kept in her private bathroom at the gallery. She thought it had been thrown out accidentally by the staff while cleaning up. Why would anyone take the time to return items like this, none of them were valuable or had any real significance. The more she thought about it the more it all seemed unusual and a bit bizarre like a number of things that happened that day, yet she was still intrigued by what remained in the package and its relevance.

In addition to those items was another clear bag containing something she didn't recognize as her own. It was a small oblong cylinder-shaped bottle about four inches long, but the contents were unclear. Below that item she found a two paged letter from a medical laboratory she'd never heard of or used. Once again, she was distracted by another notification on her phone telling her the alarm was still malfunctioning at the gallery. After archiving the notification, she turned her attention back to the pages she held in her hand. She read through the letter, shocked at what it revealed. She took a deep breath, paused, then put everything back in the package and continued on her way.

The more she thought about the letter, the more urgent her mission became. She needed to talk to Simon as soon as possible. And after the house staff confirmed he never arrived at their estate, she decided to head to the gallery to see if he was there working on the security system. He had to be there, where else could he be and what could've kept him from the engagement party, she wondered. He probably received the same notifications she'd been getting and got held up. Damn, what if he ran into Adam? He still had no idea he was an employee now and was supposed to meet the security people that afternoon. So much had happened in the past few hours, it was all a bit much, too much to process and be on point. Ten minutes later she arrived at the gallery relieved to see Simon's limo and driver parked outside.

Again, the silent alarm went off sending yet another notification to her cellphone. She entered the gallery and didn't notice anything out of place right away but decided to check the offices to be sure. Simon's office was clear, and nothing seemed disturbed however when she entered her own office, right away she saw her private door to *Ahsasz Down Under* was not only unlocked but open. She decided to investigate but not before retrieving the handgun she started keeping in her desk in the

543

event there was an intruder in or around the club waiting to attack her... again. She carefully placed it in her purse.

She made her way down the halls leading to the main check in area and thought she heard something in the distance. She took her time visually checking the rooms in her path as she drew closer to the muffled sounds off in the distance. Who in the fuck could be posted up in my club she wondered? She cautiously continued on her journey with a firm grip on her purse.

She allowed her instincts to direct her to a private room located a short distance from the concierge area that was closed to all members. It was a room her and her husband used during the workday whenever they felt the need for privacy. As she continued on her path, the muffled sounds slowly grew closer confirming she was heading in the right direction.

Ellie could see her reflection in the mirrors that covered the walls where a headboard would normally be. She could also see the shadow of someone coming her way through the door she purposely left ajar. She knew it was Zsasha and she was close enough to hear the noise they were making indicating it was time to turn up the volume on her performance.

Proudly, she flipped Simon on his back and mounted her lover, taking him gently inside of her; her juices flowing heavily as their intensity increased. Up and down, she moved in a slow stride as she became accustomed to his long thick dick. She arched her back allowing him to go a bit deeper than the stroke before, causing her to moan rhythmically with each thrust until she could receive no more. As their pace quickened, she jerked her head back as he grabbed her by the waist, pulling her downward to meet him as he plunged into her wet pussy deeper and deeper, time and time again. Leaning forward, she thrust her hands onto the mirrored headboard to give herself support and balance as she continued to ride her masculine lover.

She could see Zsasha getting closer and closer to where she lay with her lover, Zsasha's husband. Yes, it was all coming together, just as she had planned. She'd made certain of it by leaving no stone unturned and absolutely nothing to chance.

544

At that moment Zsasha was at the door. Still and in utter disbelief. The look on Zsasha's face as she slowly pushed the door open, was a mirror into the depth of her soul, revealing the hurt, pain, betrayal and disbelief now filling up inside of her. But she said nothing. Her mouth hanging open, speechless as she watched Ellie, whom she thought was merely her friend; a young and beautiful person she thought she knew so well; a young lady she became so close too, so quickly; this person calling herself Ellie, whom she now knows was closer to her than she could have ever imagined. But there she was, right in front of her, in a bed she shared with Simon. Ellie, in all her bare-naked glory, fucking her husband; making the same erotic sounds and noises Zsasha was all too familiar with. Sounds she herself heard shrieking from her own mouth. Sounds she thought were hers and hers alone, when making love to her sexually talented and gifted husband. Sounds he never made another woman utter at the level of intensity reserved exclusively for her. Sounds that until now were hers and hers alone. She now shared them with Ellie.

Frozen where she stood, not believing what her eyes were telling her mind was happening. Charging through the door, Zsasha hurled the only thing she could at the two of them, her purse. Her purse hit the mirror that hung just above the custom-made bed, causing the glass to shatter and her gun to fire off simultaneously. No one was hit but Ellie and Simon were both beyond startled.

"Get the fuck off her!" Zsasha screamed. "What the hell are you doing? Oh my God! Oh my God Simon! Stop touching her! Stop touching her! She's my daughter for god's sake! She's my daughter!"

Simon, now separated from Ellie, stood alongside the bed in utter shock and disbelief at what he was hearing. Her daughter? Her daughter? He didn't know what to do with that information at that moment. It didn't make sense. All he could do was just look at his wife's face, distorted in a way he had never seen before. Pain and disgust laid the foundation from which her tears flowed endlessly. Not knowing what to say he said nothing at all. Zsasha tossed the envelope in his direction and just shook her head while they both stood still.

The silence in the room was deafening and only disturbed by Zsasha and the sound of her crying and moaning as she turned her attention to Ellie. She wore nothing more than the look of satisfaction on her face and didn't make any attempt to cover herself. Zsasha just stood there and looked at her, through her for a moment, realizing this was orchestrated by her design. Ellie planned for this to happen; it was anything but a coincidence the look on her face confirmed it.

Grabbing a robe, her robe she kept on the chaise lounge chair for her own personal use, Zsasha threw it at Ellie. She didn't have to tell her to put it on, the look on her face made that clear. She wanted to ask her what the hell was she doing. What was she thinking? But Zsasha did none of that. She said nothing, nothing at all. Instead, she wiped her tears from her face and began to walk up to the young woman, the young woman she now knew to be her daughter; the daughter she gave birth to in college and put up for adoption.

She moved in as close as she could get, wanting to see what was in her eyes and what they might reveal. She could see nothing, no signs of remorse or regret. Pausing momentarily, she took a deep breath before slapping Ellie fiercely across the face; hard enough that it knocked her diamond encrusted hoop earring out of her right earlobe sending it flying across the floor.

Ellie, still silent and unapologetic, didn't flinch. She stood there not at all shocked or surprised and apparently unaffected by Zsasha's actions. As a slightly detectable smile passed across her face, Zsasha's heartbreak verbally revealed itself with just one word.

"Why? Why?", she screamed as she gripped the shoulders of her once abandoned child; shaking her feverishly as if an explanation would fall from her lips. When no words emerged and her facial expression remained the same, Zsasha stepped back, turned and ran from the room, leaving Ellie smirking, fully aware of what she'd done.

Basking in her accomplishment, she felt quite pleased with herself, and it showed. She let the oversized robe drop to the floor while she began gathering up her clothing, traipsing around the room without a care in the world.

"So you had no idea, did you?" Ellie asked.

"What the fuck have you done, you crazy bitch?"

"Watch it, daddy, I mean, step daddy. You shouldn't talk to your stepdaughter that way. After all, we're family......close family, closer than most have ever been."

"Something's wrong with you Ellie." Simon announced. "This is a new kind of crazy even for your generation. What were you thinking? And why? Why would you do this? Why would you hurt her like this?"

"Hurt her... Fuck her! What about me? The way I see it, the bitch had it coming. She tossed me aside like I wasn't shit. Went on with her life and never looked back. So, tell me again why I should give a fuck about hurting her. She drew first blood when she decided to turn her back on me and put me up for adoption, leaving me to be raised by those freaks. I don't give a fuck about her and her temporary feelings. This shit doesn't cut that deep, it can't. That would mean she would have a conscience or at least have a heart and she doesn't have either. She ain't never cared about anything beyond herself. I'm proof of that!"

"You're wrong little girl. You're wrong about a lot of things."

"I doubt that."

"You don't know the circumstances of your conception or your birth. You had no right to do this to her, to us. Yes, I've known. I've always known about the baby she put up for adoption. I know how it's haunted her over the years. You should've come to her straight and asked her why she did what she did. You didn't have to do all this."

"Maybe I wanted to. Maybe I just wanted to hurt her and see her suffer the way I did."

"Well, she's got you beat there, young lady. She was raped, Ellie, drugged and gang raped!"

Ellie looked over at Simon shocked by what he revealed.

547

"You have no idea how broken she was when I found her or how she's been haunted by all of it, for years, many years." Simon continued. "Did you ever stop to think about why she did what she did or what might have been going on with her at the time?"

"She was raped?"

"That's right, drugged and raped by a group of guys at a frat party."

"A group of guys?"

"Yeah, a group of guys at a frat party, but don't act like you're concerned now. You did what you did and hurt the one person I love more than anything else in this world. Now get the fuck out, I mean it Ellie, get the fuck out...now!"

Ellie left without another word or further incidence. The smile that previously resided on her face was now gone as well as the feeling of satisfaction as Simon's words played over and over again in her mind......*drugged.... raped...gang raped. You don't know the circumstances of your conception*. Ellie hadn't thought about that at all. She had been fiercely hell bent on punishing the woman who birthed her and broke her by giving her away.

Ellie didn't quite like how she was feeling at this point. Now, all she wanted to do was escape her own mind and not think about any of this at all. Consequently, Zsasha was feeling exactly the same way at exactly the same moment. Like Ellie, Zsasha just wanted to escape, and she did; without a word to anyone. Zsasha was gone.

* * * * *

Early the next morning Rona hadn't heard from anyone before she and Reggie boarded their flight to a destination she hadn't shared with the girls. She tried not to read too much into it because she knew Zsasha would have called her if Vonne's situation was serious. And J'Nae was just gonna have to go through it with Wesley. That type of drama just has to play out no matter how it came to be. In any event, Rona knew she had to sit this one out, no matter what. Her health is important, and she simply had to put herself first and focus on getting well while time was on her side.

$$* \ * \ * \ * \ *$$

Three days passed and there still wasn't any communication from the girls. J'Nae had reached out to Vonne and Zsasha a few times, however all text messages, phone calls and emails had gone unanswered. Wesley ghosted her as well but at least she knew what the issue was and why he was avoiding her. It wasn't the same for the girls. She didn't become deeply concerned until several more days passed forcing her to reach out to Simon and Lee to find out what was going on with their wives.

Lee was the hardest to track down but was forthcoming about his wife and sister-in-law. He began by reiterating what Reggie had shared with Zsasha and Rona after the party ended but included more information. Based on the preliminary investigation, Vonne had been arrested on an array of charges including attempted murder, 1st degree assault and aggravated assault with a deadly weapon and was being held without bond. Kiera was missing and hadn't been heard from and based on the amount of blood found at the house, there was a possibility she could be presumed dead. That scenario would result in charges being upgraded for Vonne.

On the other hand, Simon was tight-lipped about Zsasha and the details of her sudden disappearance. All he would say is that she left, and he has no idea where she is or when she plans to return. Even Rona was on some cloak and dagger shit. If anyone answered her phone it was Reggie and all he would say is Rona's fine and I'll let her know you called. That wasn't saying a whole lot. It just left J'Nae feeling abandoned and forced to deal with her and Wesley's problems on her own.

Relying on herself to deal with emotional turmoil when a man is involved wasn't really her strong suit. She needed her sista circle for support as much as they seemed to be in need of it themselves. All in all, J'Nae, not knowing what was really going on with her girls left her feeling totally in the dark; isolated, confused, and worried, not knowing what to do next.

Overwhelmed with her situation and theirs as well, J'Nae was left wondering...*Where My Girls At?*

The End

Acknowledgments

I'd like to acknowledge those who have supported me and encouraged me throughout my journey to become a writer.

Corinthia Gray, and Courtney Parks... my **OG**'s - *Original Girlfriends*

Corinthia Gray: I've watched, listened and learned many things from you that I consider invaluable to this day. Thank you for believing in me and helping make this dream come true. Close doesn't describe our bond, *we are sista's*.

Courtney Parks: Your inherent generosity has taught me the significance of paying it forward; a lesson that will be with me until the end of my days. Thank you for showing me what a true friend really looks like. *My OG, BFF and sista 4Life!*

Yvette Revels, *My Main...*Even though you would not help me proofread this book, what you did do was give me something that was and is priceless. Two words: **Insight and Perspective**....*LIFE CHANGING!* And it's all over this book. Thank you.

My son Stephen: The most important person in my life, now and always. I'm blessed to have been your mother, friend and confidant over the years and will continue to do so no matter how old you get or what comes our way. It's been a slippery slope for us at times, but we've always managed to find our footing. Let's continue to do that!

While being my biggest fan, you've consistently encouraged me to complete this project even when life took me away from it. Recently, you shared how impressed you were with a short story I'd written 20 years prior, one I hadn't thought of for a very long time and was surprised you even remembered. At that moment, I was blown away. It was and is one of the best gifts you've ever given me. Realizing you believed in me all along was awesome. ***Olive Juice!***

I must also take a moment to acknowledge the colorful people in my life and those I've come to know along the way, family members, friends, acquaintances, and of course my favorite X. You all played a part in my journey of self-discovery, and each of you added your own touch of flavor to my story. Thanks for making me laugh, cry, and ultimately inspiring me to write this book.

It's been a helluva ride!

Enjoy

About the Author

MiMi Foxx, born and raised in New Jersey, the youngest of seven children was blessed to have the varying perspectives of her older siblings' shape and influence her life as she grew and matured into adulthood.

As an adolescent, she dreamed of becoming a professional gymnast, an ice skater, and then an elementary school teacher, all before the age of 12. Shortly thereafter, MiMi was handed her first set of adult paperbacks novels and soon became an avid reader of fictional horror and suspense thrillers; her favorite authors being John Saul and V.C. Andrews.

After taking on a few entry-level positions in banking and accounting, MiMi, with the influence and support of her 'Favorite X', changed courses and headed to college. It was during her freshman year in an English composition class that MiMi first began writing essays as part of the required assignments. The book of choice, 'The Autobiography of Malcolm X'.

One day to her surprise, she received a standing ovation from her 50+ classmates as well as her instructor, for her deep and introspective interpretation of that week's assignment; 'What was the significance of Malcolm X's journey to Mecca and how it influenced his view of Elijah Muhammed and his teachings.' It was at that time her desire to write was ignited and the flame continued to burn throughout marriage, motherhood and later, life away from family as a single mom. With God's Grace and Mercy, the flame continues to burn today.

Made in the USA
Columbia, SC
20 September 2023

23061849R00338